Stone Angels

Stone Angels

Michael Hartigan

Merrimack Media
Cambridge, Massachusetts

Library of Congress Control Number: 2015947295

ISBN: print: 978-1-939166-79-1
ISBN: ebook: 978-1-939166-80-7

Published by Merrimack Media, Cambridge, Massachusetts
August, 2015

Dedication

For D & Sweet Pea, my very own angel wings.

Chapter 1

We were clearly lost and the dashboard light blinked desperately, telling me I was running on empty. Voiceless, it screamed for help, saturating the car's interior in a red-orange hue, in a last-ditch effort for my attention. What the little light didn't know was that I was already responding to its begging cry for help.

I turned my Ford Explorer from the highway onto the next available exit ramp, prompted by a large blue fluorescent road sign promising twenty-four hour fuel somewhere down the road. I obliged, proud of my attentiveness to my surroundings and the mechanical effectiveness of my aging sport utility vehicle. But as the interstate fell away into the darkness of the rearview mirror, so did any further direction as to where this mysterious gas station was hidden. So disappeared my confidence.

The smooth, state-maintained highway quickly crumbled into a cracked and rocky backcountry road. The asphalt—I was surprised there even was asphalt—rose and split under my fog lights, wreaking havoc on my car's aging shocks. There were no street signs or streetlights along the road. It was darker than the highway was and much narrower, wide enough for one vehicle. Imposing southern pines soared along both sides of the pavement, like sentinels guarding a secret. I tried to see just how tall they were through the moon roof but all that could be seen was a hurried onrush of colorless clouds.

No moon. No stars, either. The treetops peaked somewhere in the infinite darkness above.

Nature was being very difficult. Granted I was attempting to refuel a manmade gas-guzzling nature-killer. I couldn't blame her for refusing to lend a hand. Nevertheless, I could have benefited from some moonlight, a few stars or hell, even a swath of fireflies.

But no such luck. I was on my own.

The three other people in the car were sound asleep and useless. Even if I were to wake them, this was only their second trip through the American South. The first being a week ago when we drove right past this very exit in the opposite direction, southbound. At that time none of them were paying attention, I was sure of that. They were too occupied by anticipation for the Florida sun and our last spring break vacation as college students.

The two girls on our trip, Emily and Lindsey, had terrible senses of direction. And Marcus—or Shoddy as we all called him—was most likely hung-over, if not still drunk, on both the ride down and up the Atlantic coast. All too often he was caught sleeping off the booze and mistakes of the night before.

I felt his pain. Like him, I had a pounding headache. Unlike him, it wasn't only because of rum drinks.

I turned my attention back to the unforgiving darkness stretched out ahead. The station had to be up around a bend. If only I could see farther than the ten yards of pavement illuminated by my headlights. Maybe then I'd notice if there were any bends.

There weren't any. Not even a slight bow since we left the exit ramp. I drove a straight and steady path deeper into the unknown, what seemed like ages away from the relative comfort of the interstate.

I'm usually a very reserved young man. Which to many is odd for a college senior. One would expect craziness, frat boy intensity or at least intermittent jubilation at the upcoming death to homework.

Not me. I kept it all inside, which isn't to say it did not exist. It did.

But long ago I had erected a wall in front of my emotions intended to keep all that in, and everyone else out. For the most part, it worked. Very few people ever got past that wall. I locked away a lot of things back there.

Recently, for various reasons, the wall was weakening. The very real danger of running out of gas on a backcountry road at midnight threatened to add to those recent chinks. Running out of gas was more than just a logistical threat. There would be very real consequences. I'd have to wake up my friends. My mistake and failure would be evident. I'd be vulnerable and scrutinized. The wall would be unguarded.

The headache still lurked behind my eyes. Rubbing my temples didn't help.

Again, I tried to focus back on the road and the task at hand. My mind was being easily distracted. I set my gaze through the windshield and thought only about practical solutions. I'd probably have to leave the car and find the station on foot. Marcus should stay in the car with the girls. I'd have to change into sneakers instead of the flip-flops I had on. I should probably carry some sort of weapon, just in case. Did I still have that heavy metal flashlight in the spare tire well?

I could not help but get nervous after another ten minutes went by with no gas station. The emergence of a soft but urgent *ding ding ding* that began emanating from the dashboard did not help. That little orange light wasn't kidding around anymore.

My practical questions quickly diverged toward paranoia. Did I have my AAA card? Would a tow truck find us? Would a service station be open this late at night this far away from real civilization? What if the tow truck driver was suspect? Would I call 911 or was that too extreme? If not, did I even know what number to call for assistance?

I instinctively pulled my cell phone from the center console and checked the service bars. Full. Thank God. Apparently whatever

Southern municipality we trekked across was in tune enough with the Twenty-first century to have erected a cell tower. That was good, in case the tow truck driver happened to be a serial killer.

I had to chuckle at myself. Nothing had even happened yet and already I thought of the worst possible scenario, something straight out of a low budget horror movie. This sort of thinking spoke to the doubts I held about my own ability to handle a potential crisis situation. Which was actually not that foolish, considering the crises I had dealt with in the past and their horrifying outcomes.

Regardless of my failing confidence, the only choice I had was to continue on the current path and hope the blue highway sign was no liar; hope the fumes we coasted on lasted just a few minutes more. Turning around wasn't feasible. I doubted I had enough fuel to make it back to the interstate. Besides, I had no idea how far away the next exit was or whether or not I'd face the same problem there.

I had to hope the gas station promised me would rise out of the darkness like the Emerald City, ready to fulfill my needs. But I didn't need a brain, a heart or some courage. I needed gas. Gas to help me get home.

Five more minutes went by, the dinging grew more frequent. My body tensed.

Then suddenly the road was smoother. A few yards later it curved.

I must have understood a change in road condition to mean a change in luck. Here was the bend I was looking for.

At the same time the dinging from the dashboard got faster and louder. It was telling me this was it, the last push. We weren't even riding on fumes anymore, just lingering particles. Some people might have stopped then. I usually would have stopped then. But for some reason adrenaline stopped me from stopping. Subconsciously I increased the speed of the Explorer. The dinging hurried and I sped up more, trying to keep up with its urgent pace and maybe beat it to the gas station I was now sure existed. It had to, right up around the bend. I instinctively psyched myself up. My body reacted naturally.

My pulse quickened. My body arched forward in the driver's seat, knuckles white gripped around the steering wheel. I came alive. The hours of driving in virtual silence and darkness slipped away like the blurred pines lining the road.

The words of someone I once loved flashed behind my eyes. "Before this is over, I'm going to lighten you up. I'm going to make you come alive," she said to me. Amen to that. Screw my cracking wall. Screw my sleeping friends in the car. Screw the serial killer tow truck driver. If I were going to break down on a backcountry road, I'd at least get a thrill doing it. If I were going to open myself up to failure, I'd do it speeding around a hairpin turn.

One gradual curve right followed by a wide arc to the left then a twenty-yard uphill straightaway. At the top I sped through another curve left around an especially looming group of dark pines at fifty miles per hour. A quick S bend, my pulse quickened and another wide sweeping turn to the right. Was that perspiration on my forehead? A hard right, sharp left, the speedometer fluttering excitedly. We spit out onto another straightaway and ten yards ahead the road dropped down over the horizon like a cliff.

Without hesitation I took the Explorer over the top, hitting sixty-five miles per hour. As the car breached the hill and came into its descent a sliver of silver moonlight split the clouds above; the high beams from heaven. All at once the full expanse of the road and the decline ahead was visible. The black curtain parted and I saw down below, nestled at the bottom of the hill, a dimly lit gas station. The moonlight mixed with its orange fluorescent bulbs gave it an eerie green, almost emerald glow.

My head, now full of adrenaline, still throbbed. Respite ahead but we were still lost. Maybe clarity was up ahead too.

Chapter 2

I barely took the keys from the ignition before I jumped from the driver's seat. The excitement of finding the station kept my blood pumping fast. The adrenaline kept rising while I popped the tank latch open and removed the gas cap. It only subsided when I reached for my wallet and pulled out my Visa student credit card. My headache had disappeared.

I went to swipe my credit card. There was no place to swipe a credit card.

"Dammit," I said to nobody.

It was then that I became aware of my surroundings.

All around was darkness. In the time it took to descend the hill, the clouds had re-covered the moon and that initial shimmering emerald glow around the station had evaporated. The same southern pines that led the way here now formed a three-sided barricade around the lot's border. Even though the station's existence was our salvation, the trees' effect was more fortress than oasis.

Without the moonlight or my headlights we were bathed solely in the orange fluorescent light from four large street lamps situated at the square lot's corners. Two double-sided gas pumps sat in the middle of the square, just barely illuminated by the perimeter lighting.

The Explorer was parked at one of these gas pumps. Old gas

pumps. The retro, non-digital kind that had rotating numbers and a flip up handle. The orange light accentuated their rusty front panels.

The station wasn't a franchise and there was no canopy or giant neon sign adorned with a Pegasus or tiger. The only identification was a painted wooden sandwich board sign in between the pumps that read, "Welcome to Mo's."

At the rear of the lot was a rectangular clapboard building that housed a one-bay garage and a small store. The garage door was up but no lights were on. Inside I could make out the shadowy outline of a tow truck. The store was three windows long and unlike the garage bay, was lit. A paper OPEN sign hung on the inside of the glass door.

Other than a few trash barrels and a picnic table under the lamp in the back right corner, the station's lot was vacant. Ours was the only vehicle besides the sleeping tow truck. We were the only visible signs of life besides the OPEN sign and lit up store.

It was exactly what I would have expected a gas station to be down a back road in Northern Florida. I should've expected a station like this to be cash only. It fit with the décor.

I double-checked the ancient gas pump before sliding my card back into my wallet. Definitely no place to swipe a credit card but there was a small sticker that said cash only. I missed that the first time around.

Fortunately the lack of credit card payment wasn't much of a problem. We had planned for this to happen at some point. Last Saturday morning, before we pulled out of Providence College's student lot, the four of us each threw fifty bucks into an envelope and stowed it away at the bottom of the center console. It was Emily's idea. She argued—correctly—that at some point on our thirty-two hour drive down to Key West or on the thirty-two hour drive back we'd need cash for gas.

If she weren't still fast asleep in the backseat, I would've kissed her in thanks. Well, probably not. That would have been a very bad idea. But I would've thanked her regardless. I went back to the driver's door and retrieved the envelope full of money from the center console. Two hundred dollars should have felt heavier. I opened it to find one Benjamin Franklin starting back at me. Someone had pilfered our gas stash over the past week.

The memory of last Wednesday night flickered into focus in my mind's theater. We had walked by an ATM on our way down Duval Street. Everyone took out cash, except Shoddy, which was odd since I knew he tapped out his cash the night before at Irish Kevin's bar. That night, when we reached the Lazy Gecko, Shoddy started buying rounds. And he had taken the car by himself that afternoon to find a package store.

Looked like I had prime suspect number one. I reminded myself to address that with him when he woke up. I never did.

I was surprised Shoddy and the two girls were still sound asleep in the Explorer. Lindsey wasn't a very heavy sleeper, I knew from experience. But neither she, Shoddy or Emily had even flinched since we left the highway. I was amazed the sharp turns, racecar antics or the sudden stop at the gas station didn't rouse them.

I checked on them all before walking to the store.

Still sleeping. Emily and Shoddy were out cold in the backseat; Lindsey snoring with her face pressed against the front passenger window. They'd never know how close we were to breaking down. I'd never tell them. I'd just add it to the list of other things, much darker, much more significant things that I wasn't planning on ever telling them. Compared to those, Shoddy's thievery from the gas stash seemed trivial. Perhaps I wouldn't mention it to anyone.

I left my three best friends in dreamland and made my way to the storefront.

Inside was smaller than I expected. To the left, two racks of automotive necessities and snack foods. One drink cooler covered the back wall. Immediately to my right was the checkout counter. A tall promotional display urging customers to change their oil sat on top. A large relic cash register, continuing the retro gas pump theme, waited proudly, to the left of center. A screwdriver and some mechanic's tools were placed next to it.

The register was unmanned and upon further investigation, it appeared nobody else was in the store.

I took a lap around the candy racks and only on the way back around did I notice the small door behind the checkout counter. The oil change display must have blocked my view of it. I briefly debated whether or not someone positioned it deliberately.

When I looked inside the door I saw what was probably used as an office. Right on the wall in plain view of the doorway was a small black safe. There was a folding chair and a metal desk upon which were propped the feet of a young man. He had on a red trucker's hat with the number of some NASCAR driver I didn't know. He wore a blue, oil-smeared mechanic jumpsuit, the zipper pulled down to his bellybutton. Underneath was a similarly oil-smeared white t-shirt. On the jumpsuit was a patch with the name, "Bobbo" stitched on. I had walked into a stereotype and had to suppress laughter.

I knocked on the counter outside the door. Bobbo didn't move. I knocked again. Nothing.

"Hey Bobbo!" I finally yelled, pronouncing it Bo-Bo, like a clown's name.

The man jolted upright, his hat falling over his eyes in the process. He jumped up and immediately zipped up his jumpsuit and brushed it off; as if he could clean the oil stains that way.

"Hey there, sorry to wake you but I just want to fill up out there," I said.

Bobbo recognized the situation immediately. He must have done this before.

He rubbed his eyes and pushed past me, making his way behind the counter. I followed but took the customer's customary place on the other side.

"It's Bob-O," he said with a yawn.

"Huh?"

"My name. It's not Bo-Bo, like a clown. It's Bob then O."

"Oh. My bad. Sorry about that," I feigned apology. "Well I just wanted to fill up. Probably take fifty."

I handed him the one hundred dollar bill from the envelope. His face screwed up in annoyance.

"Not from around here, eh friend?"

"How'd you guess?"

"We don't get many of these around here," he waved the hundred like it was on fire. "Actually we don't get many people in here that I don't know personally. So that tells ya something."

"Yeah, I can see that. But thank God you're open. I coasted in here on fumes from the highway. If you were a few more minutes down the road you would've been coming to get me in that tow truck you got out there."

Bobbo huffed.

"That's if I answered the phone, friend. Pretty deep sleeper, I am."

He punched a few buttons on the relic cash register and started flipping through bills. After a minute it became obvious Bobbo was having trouble making change.

"You wanted fifty, right? I don't have a fifty to give back, friend."

"That's fine, I'll take whatever bills you got."

"That's the problem, I don't have enough in here to make fifty. I gotta go out back and open the safe. Be right back, friend."

"No problem, Bobbo," I said, pronouncing it wrong again. He scowled and made his way into the small office behind the counter.

I moved over a little and watched him dig through the desk. After finding a small black notebook, which I assumed held the safe combination, Bobbo got to finding me some change.

I looked away, not wanting him to think I was a thief. I studied the wall behind the counter. It was covered with local advertisements, lost pet notices and a dispenser for rolls of lottery scratch-off cards. An old plastic cigarette pack holder was hung underneath a novelty singing fish. All were typical backcountry gas station paraphernalia.

All except the frame hung right in the middle of the wall. There were no ads or lost cat papers crowding it, just a halo of off-white cinder block. The black plastic frame outlined its contents, a bright red piece of paper, demanding attention and a tinge of urgency. It must be important. Every regular customer waiting for change would notice it immediately if they just refocused their eyes over Bobbo's shoulder. The paper would have peeked around him, flirting with locals and travelers like myself, daring them to ask the obvious. Since I took an indirect route to the cash register and had an indirect encounter with the slumbering Bobbo, I only just recognized the fiery notice. Without Bobbo, I was free to investigate the paper. It was the only object in proximity that didn't immediately belong with the redneck motif.

I checked on Bobbo still trying to open the safe then glanced back at the frame. In order to read the black letters on the red paper I leaned as far over the counter as I could. I propped myself up and stood on my tiptoes, braced by my hands on the countertop.

Whoever designed the message clearly harbored strong sentiments and certainly wanted every human in search of gasoline to believe in their blazing credo. But he must have had incredibly good eyesight or terribly poor vision because what he had in flare, he lacked in basic color scheme and graphic design.

I dangled precariously over the counter's back edge and squinted to read the text.

In the frame was a list of ten items with the list's title in big bold letters that read: "The Paradoxical Commandments."

I started reading them out loud but softly under my breath.

"One: People are illogical, unreasonable and self-centered. Love them anyway. Two: If you do good, people will accuse you of selfish, ulterior motives. Do good anyway. Three: If you are successful, you will win false friends and true enemies. Succeed anyway. Four: The good you do today will be forgotten tomorrow. Do good anyway.

Five: Honesty and frankness make you vulnerable. Be honest and frank anyway."

I paused at five and read the line over again, this time in my head.

Honesty and frankness make you vulnerable. Be honest and frank anyway.

I read five over once more. I couldn't pull my eyes from that line. I think I hated it. But I totally agreed with it.

Uneasiness and some other uncomfortable emotion began creeping down my brain stem, into the buzzing nest of nerves. I had to move on to number six. I never got the chance.

"Hey friend, what the hell are you doing?"

Startled, my hand slipped and I stumbled backwards off the counter. I caught my balance on a candy rack before I fell, Bit-O-Honeys scattered on the linoleum. As I pondered the fact someone, somewhere still enjoyed Bit-O-Honeys enough for them to continue being manufactured, I looked up to see Bobbo standing behind the counter. He held a wad of bills in one hand and the other was resting on the screwdriver next to the cash register. His fingers started curling around its handle in anticipation of trouble.

"What? Oh shit, no. I'm sorry Bobbo," pronouncing it correctly for the first time. I put my hands up in a gesture of innocence.

"You trying to get into that register, friend? I wouldn't try it."

"No, absolutely not Bobbo. I just want my change and to pump my gas."

"Then why was you climbing over the counter, friend?"

"I wasn't. I was just trying to read your commandments back there."

Bobbo looked confused. His knuckles whitened around the screwdriver.

"What are you talkin' bout."

I pointed to the black frame behind him. He hesitated but I shook my outstretched hand in assurance. He turned quickly and his stressed face calmed. His grip on the tool loosened. He gave me one last look up and down and concluded either I was no threat or that his lumbering frame could easily subdue my inferior one. Or at least he was confident in his ability to stab me with the screwdriver.

Bobbo punched a few keys on the register and the drawer popped open.

"Yeah, that there's Mo's idea of employee training," he offered as he shuffled a few bills.

"Who?" I asked.

"Mo. Mohammed, Ajay Mohammed. He's the owner of this joint, my boss. This is his station," he said and without looking up, pointed to the glass storefront.

There on the window next to the door were white adhesive letters. From inside the store the words were backwards but still easily readable. I read out loud, "Ajay Mohammed—Owner."

"Yup, that's him. Good ole' Mo," Bobbo said, his words laced with sarcasm. He handed me two twenties and a ten dollar bill. "He puts them things up in all his stores around here. Says we should all live by them rules like they're a code or sumthin'. Says if we all did, we'd change the world."

His belly jiggled with a deep, cynical laugh. Bobbo clearly was only a believer as far as it earned him a paycheck.

I put the money back into the white envelope and stuffed it into my back pocket. Then I asked a question just for the sake of conversation. I had to make sure Bobbo wasn't planning on following me outside wielding a screwdriver. I mimicked his cynicism, hoping to keep his mind away from that possibility.

"So this can't be Mo's only gas station. How many stores does he have? Probably need a lot if he wants to change the world with a piece of paper."

"About ten or twelve, I think. Has 'em from here on up through Georgia. Mo's got the dough. He's a little wacko, comes in here once a week always pointing at that damn list and askin' me if I'm livin' by the code. Then goes out back to count his money."

"What do you tell him?"

"I always just say yes, boss. It's easier that way. But I don't think I've ever read the whole list. I figure when you got all the dough like Mo, it must be nice and easy to go around livin' all good and honest and preach to other men. He don't have to worry about two kids, an ex-wife or paying rent."

I was getting more information than I really wanted. It was time to bid Bobbo farewell.

"Well Bobbo, thank you for being open. You saved my ass," I said and turned to exit the store. I took one last look at the framed red paper list before I did.

"No problem, friend," Bobbo said. "Sorry 'bout sleeping on ya. And for not having the change right away."

"No worries," I said. "Have a good night. I'm sure you can head back to sleep now."

I pushed through the door next to Ajay Mohammed's backwards name. As I did, Bobbo yelled out one last sarcasm.

"Hey friend, don't forget to live by the code!"

The glass door closed behind me and I laughed. But it was an uneasy laugh, the kind that jolts your insides for a second like a tiny, unconscious punishment.

I could feel the tremors of another headache. I thought of turning back to Bobbo and buying some Tylenol, or perhaps he knew where I could get something stronger. But I had enough Bobbo for one night. And for some reason, I really did not want to go back into the store. My body was instantly averse to standing in front of that red paper again.

I walked back to the Explorer in a daze, my mind hopscotching around the image of the red list of commandments on the store wall.

A few times it landed on number five. Be honest. Tell the truth regardless of the consequences.

It was a novel concept I never lived by. In twenty-one years of life I had done some bad things. I had hurt some people. Revealing truths would certainly have consequences, life changing ones. Being honest would make me vulnerable. I wasn't comfortable with vulnerable. But was I comfortable with the current state of things? Maybe I was warming to the idea of change.

The rear passenger side door was open. Shoddy was staring unconvincingly at the retro gas pump, a credit card in his hand.

"Hey Auggie," he mumbled when I reached him. He was the only one that ever called me that and he did so infrequently. "You know this thing doesn't take credit cards?"

"Yeah, I already took care of it. Paid inside with Bobbo the attendant," I responded, not looking at him. I was looking back into the car, checking to see if the girls were awake. Shoddy must've noticed the direction of my gaze.

"She's still asleep, don't worry."

"Good," I said, finally looking at his face.

"You alright man? You look like shit, with those bags under your eyes. Like a raccoon coming down off a bender."

Where did he come up with those analogies? It didn't matter. I barely registered this one anyway. The haze of headache surged.

I stared at Lindsey's face pressed up against the glass.

"Hello, Augustine Shaw, wake up bro," Shoddy said and waved his hand in front of my face.

I blinked and looked back into his eyes. We stared at each for a few seconds.

"You ain't been right lately, bro. You've been off all week. I haven't seen you this bad since, well, last Friday night outside Primal Bar," he said.

"What are you talking about?" I got defensive.

"Before we left for Florida, last week, we went out drinking? Something happened that really fucked you up."

I opened my mouth to respond but the words weren't ready. Almost, but not quite.

"Forget it," he said. "I gotta take a piss. Did you see a bathroom inside this shithole?"

"Um, I'm not sure. Go ask Bobbo in there. And don't call him Bo-Bo."

"Bo-Bo, got it. I'll be back. You want anything?"

I just shook my head no. Shoddy shrugged and headed for the store.

After he left the haze descended again.

Taking the handle, fitting it into the gas tank, squeezing the handle. It was all done almost instinctively. I didn't even look at the numbers swirling by on the old pump's face.

I instinctively went back to staring at Lindsey. Her breath had fogged the glass a little near her mouth and there was a tiny wet smudge from drool. She didn't look comfortable. The seatbelt cut into her neck. There was a slight red mark around the strap where it gently compressed her skin. But she must've been sleeping well. With the door behind her open I could hear her muffled snores. They weren't feminine but they weren't Neanderthal either. More like heavy breathing. Her unconscious way of letting me know she was still there.

Lindsey must have felt me staring at her because for a moment she woke up; or at least her eyes snapped open and locked on my own. They were a deep blue: almost unnaturally so, with a hypnotic way of grabbing the attention of the opposite sex. Her lips curled up at the corners in a sweet smile. The way her head was tilted, resting against the window, gave her a coquettish smirk. I had seen it that way before.

The headache I anticipated exploded at that moment. A sharp pang sliced from ear to ear. It was a familiar pain but something I had never become accustomed to.

About a year ago I started getting the headaches. I had migraines as a teenager, but these were different. They came strong and fast; they dissipated just as quickly. I assumed it was some onset of adult migraines. But I never went to a doctor, which in hindsight was probably a bad idea. Over the last week, since the morning we left for Florida, they came with more frequency and force. I never told anyone about them. I stuck with the migraine thing. I handled it as a young teen, wasn't something I had to worry about now. Besides, I was always good at hiding my emotions, especially pain. I hid pain really well.

What I had trouble with was guilt. It was what ultimately was going to get me. Not the headaches or speedy driving, but the mutinous guilt. Guilt over so many things that in so many ways hurt so many people, Lindsey included. It was corrosive. It chipped away the ramparts I erected to hide some things. The guilt was stronger than a sledge, more precise than a jackhammer and more determined than a late-1980s Berlin twenty-something. The pain was just a warning—a warning that the wall would soon come crumbling down.

Yes, the guilt was going to get me. The wall had cracked. I had to get control before a flood spilled through unchecked. You want one thing but you get the opposite, the dichotomy of control. You want to be honest but it makes you vulnerable. It was time to stop seeing that as a bad thing.

Chapter 3

With a snap the gas handle kicked out, breaking my grip and catching the meat of my palm in its ancient metal trappings.

At the same time Lindsey, her face pressed against the inside of the Explorer's passenger window, snapped her eyes shut. She was back in dreamland. Was she actually awake or had I daydreamed it?

I looked down at my right hand, a chunk of which was wedged in the pump handle. It hurt like hell, but I made no immediate attempt to remove it. The world outside the backwoods gas station was in slow motion. The pain in my hand was nothing compared to the searing headache ravaging my brain. And the newfound wound only served to draw my brain—albeit temporarily—away from its own battle.

The synapses fired, sensors started tingling, my fingers numbed. Blood trickled out in a thin, leaky strip over the metal hinge of the pump handle. The blood was rusty looking under the orange fluorescent gas station lamps. The normally healthy scarlet color was off, tarnished and sick looking. It wasn't bright red, like the framed list inside the gas station store behind the counter.

That damned scrap paper. I couldn't shake it. Honesty and frankness make you vulnerable. Be honest and frank anyway.

I watched a blood droplet slip from my hand to the handle to the open air, freefall to the ground and make a tiny splatter in an oily puddle. A rainbow of red-orange hues shimmered in the greasy ripples.

The pain I could deal with. Neither the fresh cut nor the headache hurt as much as the look Lindsey had just given me.

Whether she was awake or not, real or imagined, her look made me realize how poorly I treated her. I regretted taking advantage of her friendship. I felt guilty about making her the rebound after a girl she could never live up to.

I did what I could about that situation. I said my apology. Lindsey accepted it. In an unspoken moment a few hours earlier, we had concluded our affair. But that didn't mean there was nothing left to say.

I still had the headache. The guilt was still hammering away at the wall in my head. I hadn't told her everything. In truth, I hadn't told anyone everything. Not Lindsey, not Emily, not even my best friend Shoddy.

I watched another droplet fall into the grease puddle.

Perhaps it was time to knock down the wall myself. The truth would flood out like blood from an open wound. I would be vulnerable, freefalling, destined to splash down and cause ripples. But I'd be in control. I would have caused it.

A few blood droplets fell in tandem.

It was time for the wall to go. It just needed a little push.

"Hey man, you hit fifty exactly," Shoddy's voice floated into my ears. "How'd you manage that on this old piece of . . . holy shit! Dude, you're bleeding!"

He tossed a plastic bag he was carrying and hurried to me. He grabbed my wrist with one hand and with the other, pried my palm loose from the metal gas handle. The obstruction removed, the handle clicked into resting position. I let my hand fall to my side. Shoddy pulled the handle from the Explorer's gas tank and replaced it back onto the old gas pump.

"What the hell, Shaw?" he said.

I just looked down at my hand, rolled it over palm side up, and examined the gash. The blood glistened orange-red in the fluorescent light. Honesty and frankness: what a novel concept.

I looked up to Shoddy, back at my hand, then back up at Shoddy.

"What the hell?" he asked again. "Are you alright?"

"Yeah," I mumbled.

"Are you sure?"

"Yeah."

His eyes widened with doubt and confusion. Shoddy bent down and picked up the plastic bag from the store that he had dropped. He pulled out a shiny silver can and stretched it in my direction. I didn't take it. After a few seconds he shook it lazily to get my attention.

When I still didn't take it he said, "Fine, more for me."

He cracked the can open. The pop-top clicked and carbonation whistled out. He tipped the thin can in my direction.

"You sure?" he said. "Last chance."

What emerged from my mouth was unfiltered and unrefined, even though I had subconsciously rehearsed it in my mind a hundred times in the last minute. Be honest and frank anyway. There was no more hesitation.

My lips parted and I said matter of factly, "Shoddy, I killed Duncan."

The can in his hand tipped forward from his suddenly limp, outstretched hand and clattered to the ground. It lolled around for a second before settling in the oil puddle amidst my drops of blood.

I didn't move. I waited for his reaction.

"I know," he said.

I don't know what I expected him to say, but it wasn't that.

His eyes caught my own. His arms hung down by his side, limply hanging on to the plastic bag. But he never broke the stare.

"When?" I said softly.

"When what?"

"When did you figure it out?"

"I didn't know for sure until now. But don't forget, last Friday night I was there. Well, for most of it. I was the one who brought you back in the alley behind Primal Bar. Nobody else was there at the time. Then I left you to go to the store for water. A little while later, you stumbled up the street covered in garbage and God knows what else. I guessed blood. I've seen blood before, Auggie and you were smudged in it. When I read the Providence Journal Saturday morning in the car and saw the story about the body they found behind Primal, I made a few educated guesses."

He paused, picking through his vocabulary for the right words.

"The dead kid in that article, beat up behind Primal, the description sounded like Duncan. I'm the only one who knew you were back there. And he's the only one you would ever hurt. To that extent, anyway. Years of rage must be a powerful weapon. It had to be you who finally did it."

He emphasized the last three words. Then he continued.

"You've been off all week, Shaw. I said it to you before. Something wasn't right with you. There was all the Lindsey bullshit but that's been going on for months. I knew there was something else."

"You don't know how right you are," I said. I shuffled my feet a little. I reached up and wiped my hands down over my face from my forehead to my chin. Blood was caking my right hand and I must have smeared some on my cheek. I didn't care.

"Don't worry Auggie, I'm not going to tell anyone," he said quickly, most likely reading my gesture to be fear. It wasn't. It was mostly relief. "I know you don't have it in you to actually murder someone. It must've been an accident. You'll be fine, we just have to get home and figure out the next step."

The moment wasn't over. There were more steps to take than Shoddy could ever imagine.

I looked over at Lindsey still asleep, her head pressed against the window.

I thought of that fucking red paper again. I was in a dark cave and it was a torch, ready to illuminate the monsters that lurked in the shadow. Not a beacon of light but a terrifying tool of truth. Honesty and frankness make you vulnerable. Be honest and frank anyway. Half of the guilt was out there. No reason to stop now. I was finally gaining control. It started here.

"You know, in some sick way I think I knew it was going to come to this," Shoddy said. "The kid pushed you and pushed you and pushed you. I'm not saying he deserved whatever you did to him but there's probably someone, somewhere that would say you were justified. I mean, come on, it was Duncan."

"And Lily," I said.

Shoddy dropped the plastic bag again. Two more cans rolled out and into the same oil puddle.

"What?"

"I killed Lily, too."

He looked like a sunfish pulled from a pond by a teenager. His mouth puffed open and closed, eyes bulging huge. He finally mustered enough energy to stammer out a few words.

"I didn't know that."

Chapter 4

Lily Conroy was born in Hartford, Connecticut. Her parents named her Lily, not Lillian, just Lily. Her mother was a high school English teacher at a prestigious preparatory school and, being a devout lover of all things literature and all things relating to her Irish heritage, she looked to the Emerald Isle's great writers for baby-name inspiration. She found it, ironically, in James Joyce's story *The Dead*. She always loved the layered, complex tale but it was always the supposed innocence and purity of the housemaid Lily that she connected with. Joyce based the nomenclature on medieval art and architecture a time when white lilies symbolized the Virgin Mary and her infinite purity. He only somewhat meant it in that way. Whether Lily's mother fully understood Joyce's intentions was debatable. She mostly liked the sense of superiority that came from explaining the name's roots to her less educated Connecticut housewife friends.

Regardless, Lily loved her name. Turned out when she got to high school and read James Joyce, she found the author dull and stuffy and admitted to me once that she never actually finished one of his works. Not *The Dead*, not *Ulysses*, nothing she was assigned in high school or college. She made me promise to never tell that to her mother. I was an English major. I had read them all cover to cover. It was sort of refreshing that Lily hadn't.

Lily's family had money, the inherited and the earned kind. Her father was some sort of insurance guru; I never understood exactly what and never really cared to. He packed up his young family early on and moved to a suburb called Lyme. I found out from a Trivial Pursuit card that Lyme, Connecticut was where Lyme disease was first discovered. At the time it was useless knowledge but I figured that if it comes from a board game it has to be true. I used the tidbit to start conversation with Lily at dinner once early on in our relationship. She was put off and a bit insulted. Perhaps, I learned, trivia wasn't the best icebreaker.

Her family was one of those families that I had always heard about but never encountered. Their house could have been on the cover of my mother's housekeeping magazines with their crystal chandeliers and enormous spiral staircases leading up to umpteen bathrooms and a labyrinth of bedrooms and hallways. I never went there but Lily described it perfectly, having spent her youth getting lost in the many cupboards and closets on purpose, just to scare her mother or the nanny. Just for the fun of hearing them hustle from room to room, sobbing in frantic search for the young girl. Her best and only memories from her youth were these unplanned hide and seek games she orchestrated without notifying the other participants. She'd leap out at just the right time, as they were dialing the police department to report a missing child. She said the terrified, ashen face of her nanny made her laugh. Her mother's rosy-cheeked relief made her feel warm, wanted and welcome in the drafty house.

Lily had a normal but relatively strict upbringing. Her parents, to their credit, deflated any of the snooty rich-people air of entitlement that I saw in many of the other Connecticut trust-fund babies walking the halls at college. Lily was taught manners, etiquette, polite upper-society lady things that I thought only existed in James Joyce books. The only way you'd ever know it was by watching her walk. She always held her head high, never slouched, her body in perfect symmetry and balance. She was grace and dignity personified. But all her elegance couldn't totally hide that taste for disrupting the status quo, that wild-eyed abandon that made her hide in closets just to scare her caretakers.

After high school, where she was obviously and understandably the popular girl, she escaped south to college in one of the Carolinas or Georgia. She never told me exactly where or the name of her school. Within one year she grew bored of her surroundings and by sophomore year she had transferred back north to Providence College. She always used to say the Deep South wasn't the right place for a Northern Belle.

I could never forget the night when I first met Lily. The memory remained one my most vivid for a long time. When I recalled it to the forefront of my cortex, all five senses kicked into overdrive.

It was early on sophomore year. A seasonably cool breeze carried on it the smell of the vomit that was hurling from a freshman girl leaning into the bushes. I was sitting on the steps in front of McVinney Hall watching the young campus newcomer hug the landscaping. Her friend, standing with her, told me said she took too many diet pills before going out drinking. I didn't really show much interest other than the entertainment value. Her friend soon left her, probably looking to get her night started: a night that would probably end with the friend in a similar position to the girl in the bushes. That aspect was the most entertaining.

Earlier that night I drank in my room alone. All of my friends left campus and went home or stayed in studying. I had no reason to go home and no tests to study for so I poured a few drinks, watched a movie and when the cabin fever set in, took a walk to enjoy the cool autumn night. A slight buzz warmed my body and I stopped at the steps for the view. McVinney Hall was elevated on a minor hill and one could see a large chunk of the college from its front stairway.

I think I remember the vomiting girl so clearly because I saw Lily standing a few yards away right under the street lamp on the walkway: and Lily was something to remember. I never thought that I'd see anything as attractive as she looked that night. She was a true beauty. Not the kind of beautiful that the drunken guys hunt after a few hours of slamming down Buds. But rather the kind of beautiful that should be made into a marble statue. She was the kind of beautiful that made you want to just sit on a bench and stare at every curve in her body. The kind of beautiful that made going to an old stuffy museum worth every second.

At first, all I did was observe. This beautiful creature was out of my league. Plus, she probably saw me sitting next to a vomiting freshman girl. Not the best pick-up scenario in the word. Lily didn't know the freshman girl was not my responsibility; that I didn't want to get involved with that train wreck.

So I sat watching the slim redhead under the humming streetlight with no intention other than to snap a few mental pictures. I had never seen this girl before, which wasn't that strange. It was a big campus but not that big. One would think that after a year I could at least recognize my classmates. No matter, later I'd look through the student directory given to us last year and try to match her face to a name.

After a few minutes, though, watching the redhead under the street lamp became more than just a way to waste away the evening. She intoxicated me. The strange part was that my desire was so much more than sexual. Obviously she was gorgeous, but she was not the kind of beautiful that makes you want to club her and drag her to your cave like most of the Neanderthals around campus.

I must have looked like a dirt bag sitting on the steps watching her chest heave in and out with every breath. Earlier in the evening, before the cool breeze came, it had been warm. She wore a yellowish sundress that hung loosely from her body and blew in the soft wind that now crept across campus. A green ribbon ran from the back of the dress, around and underneath her chest, tying in a bow at the front. It pushed her breasts enough so they bulged slightly, the tops protruding from the spaghetti strap dress.

She tossed her long red hair to the side when she called to her friends further down the path. Lily was very Irish. She was very cute and very Irish. Whisper-pink freckles dotted her pale, cream-colored skin up her bared arms. She had a small nose and soft rolling cheeks, spattered with the same airy pink freckles. Her mouth was small and round when closed, like a cherry. Colored that way too, naturally light red and unadorned with heavy lipstick. When she talked her lips stayed small and full. But then she smiled and they blossomed open, scrunching her little nose ever so slightly and forcing her cheeks to purse inwards, giving her dimples.

No feature entrapped me more than her eyes. Emeralds in a basket of pearls, they sparkled lightly set in her creamy skin. The inimitable green color radiated unaltered by the moonlight, the fluorescent lamp above or any other environmental influence.

That night she was wearing a silver headband that tamed the wild red flaming hair roaring out from her head. It fell softly, without effort onto her shoulders, partly to the front and partly to the back. It blazed under the headband like a campfire under a crescent moon.

She was a piece of art: a single brush stroke away from perfection. I just wanted to look at her, maybe even talk to her at some point. The hopeless romantic in me fantasized in that few minutes about a house on a lake and the long summer nights out on a boat under a starry sky. The fantasies never last as long as you want. Then again the fantasies are never as good as the realities.

I sat on the steps debating whether or not I should walk casually down and introduce myself. Forget the mental pictures and the student directory. I should just break out of my comfort zone and approach her. It was the first time Lily would insight in me the avant-garde. It should have been an easy choice, what with a vomiting girl to my side and an angel in front.

In the time that I spent observing Lily a small crowd had gathered around the sick girl, including the resident assistant and a group of EMTs. The crowd swelled so that people were now stepping over me to see the situation in the bushes. They interrupted my daydreaming and I began to feel uncomfortable and claustrophobic, but still unreasonably interested in the tableau.

I got up, and made my way down the stairs unconsciously in the direction of the redhead under the streetlamp—she was the one reason I was still there. Like a mosquito, I was drawn to the lamplight.

I was like a mosquito smacking a bug zapper when I realized I was within a breath of Lily. She hadn't moved since I first saw her from the steps, but now I was standing on the other side of the very lamppost that illuminated her.

I tilted my head just enough to catch a glimpse of red in my eye and finally I turned my head to look at her.

She paid no attention to the average guy leaning against the lamppost. It didn't bother me, I was just happy for the chance to stand near her. Something inside me, though, kept telling me to say something. *Say hello, you fool.* I got this so much, the constant debate over what to do within my own brain. Now it was a slightly less strenuous debate but they were not all this frivolous.

Just turn around slowly and brush up against her and get her attention. She's beautiful and you want to talk to her so start with that nice guy thing you have going.

My brain was actually making sense, and if it weren't for my heart I would've done it. Something in me told my brain to silence the debate and to just be patient and assess the situation.

Suddenly, without warning the girl in the bushes darted out from the crowd, screaming at the top of her lungs. I glanced up from my cognitive debate just in time to see her bound down the stairs directly towards us, arms flailing uncontrollably. I stepped back away from the lamppost, into a mud puddle, and onto a rock. The girl came crashing into Lily who had not even noticed the frantic girl speeding towards her. The girl's hand, which was clenched in a fist, slammed onto the side of Lily's face sending her careening down towards the puddle and rock I was standing on. Without a thought I jumped down, throwing my body underneath hers and catching her in a trust falls reminiscent of summer camp.

The flailing girl had knocked Lily on the head inadvertently and continued her rampage down into the parking lot. The resident assistant and EMTs bounded after her, yelling and tripping over the orange medical bags they dragged so cumbersomely.

I lifted Lily to her feet and dragged her over to the stairs that I had been sitting on earlier. There being no more vomit or yelling the crowd now dispersed, even though there was an injured girl lying in my arms directly in front of them. I sat down next to her and propped my left arm behind her for support. After years playing hockey, and after taking a few whacks to the helmet, I was wise enough to know it could be a concussion; the vomiting girl had a hefty build and she dealt a powerful blow.

Lily's eyes were open but she had a glazed over look about her that scared me. I was now left alone with her because her friends had followed the yelling girl into the parking lot to deal out some vengeance for their fallen friend. I found out later that they were escorted home by the resident assistant and never even asked about getting help for Lily.

What do I do now? I thought. I don't know where she lives and I can't bring her back to my room. Or could I? Would she be freaked out?

Everything I ever thought about right and wrong entered my mind at that moment. Everything I ever learned about treating other people came into question. I knew Lily would be fine, but I knew I should get her some ice and have her sit somewhere inside. The situation was minimal compared to what went on at that campus daily but it set off a shopping list of cognitive controversies in my brain that affected my very character. I wanted so much to help this girl. I wanted more than anything to carry her off to my room sit her in my chair and put some ice on her head. I wanted her to come back to reality and see me sitting next to her and thank me with a big hug and her undying love.

But I couldn't. Lily didn't even know me. That little voice in me screamed, "red flag, red flag." What if I scared her? What if she screamed like the vomiting girl? I would never forgive myself.

She wasn't hurt badly; I could have yelled after the EMTs or ran and got one of them. They would have helped her. I would have walked away and never met her. I never would have spoken to her. I would have continued admiring her from a safe distance. The series of nighttime events that changed the lives of so many people would never have happened.

But as Lily so often did, she caused me to break from my comfort zone. I didn't call for help. I decided I would be the help.

I knew she wasn't hurt that night because within a few minutes Lily opened her eyes. She did it slowly. The emerald flicker was weak, but it was there. It took her a minute to focus but as soon as she did our eyes locked for a second. When she realized she didn't know me she shot up frantically and moved a foot to my right.

"Wh…what happened? Who are you?" she said.

"You got knocked out by some drunk girl. I caught you before you fell in that puddle and hit that rock," I motioned with my hand to the crime scene.

"Where are my friends?"

"They took off toward the parking lot where the drunk girl was. I think they wanted to bitch her out or something."

She looked suspicious. The emerald flames billowed as they studied me. They went up and down my body searching for any sign of insincerity. I straightened up and stared intently back at her so as not to give the impression I was not telling the truth. As her eyes finished their scan Lily reached up and touched the side of her head where the girl's fist had connected. She flinched. Our eyes locked again and in those few moments any doubts she had about my honesty melted away.

"Thank you, um . . ." She smiled, waiting for me to fill in the blank.

"My name? Oh, I'm Shaw. Augustine Shaw." The hero was gone. I was a bumbling romantic again.

"Thank you, Shawn," she started to say, but I cut her off.

"It's Shaw, S-H-A-W not S-H-A-W-N." I still don't know why I spelled my name but at the time it must've been a good idea. My voice stuttered. "My first name's Augustine. But most people go with just Shaw."

She giggled and smiled widely. "Well Augustine Shaw, S-H-A-W, thank you for catching me." She pronounced the first name without the long I, like Augustan.

"And Augus*teen*," I interrupted again. "Like Bruce Springs*teen*."

Her giggling grew to full-out laughter.

"You don't do this much, then. The whole taking home injured girls while they're passed out. Well that's good, actually. Makes me know you aren't a serial killer."

"Yes, definitely," I said a little too eagerly.

"It probably would've been much worse if you didn't catch me." She winced again, put her hand up to her head.

I tried regaining my composure, which wasn't easy in her presence.

"You should get some ice on that, looks like a nice bump," I said, my body calming slightly.

"Yeah, but we don't have a fridge in our room," she said. "It's probably too late for the dining hall to be open. It's ok, I'll tough it out."

"Where do you live?"

"I live with this girl Meghan over in Aquinas Hall, third floor. How bout you?"

"Oh really? I live in Adams right next door, third floor too. I bet we could look right into each others' rooms."

My brain laughed at my choice of conversation. Of course I never saw into her room but that little comment probably didn't help my chances.

Luckily she giggled again. I was starting to enjoy the fact that she wasn't taking my incompetence too seriously. Hopefully it wasn't just because of the knock on the head. She filled the silence with small talk.

"Yeah, Meghan's not bad. Have you ever noticed how many Meghans are on this campus? Is it some sort of quota, that they need to fill a certain number of ditzy Irish girls named Meghan?"

I didn't know any Meghans but I took her word for it and laughed all the same.

"So where am I right now?" she said and propped herself up on her elbows, drinking in the sudden solitude we enjoyed.

"On the steps outside McVinney."

"Oh, well my hero, do you have ice in your room or are you just going to let me sit here on the cold steps with a throbbing pain in my head?"

It was the first time she called me Hero. In my eyes I was the furthest thing from that. It became her nickname for me, like Mary Jane calling Spiderman "Tiger". Except Spiderman was a hero. I just caught the girl from falling into a puddle. Unfortunately I never lived up to the nickname. I always tried to be her hero. I never actually was. It never stuck except with her, and at times she said it laced with cynicism. But at that moment, she was genuinely grateful.

"So, how bout that ice, Hero?" she repeated when I didn't answer right away.

"Um, yeah sure we have ice."

We walked in silence across the quad to Adams Hall. There were no security guards at the male dormitories so we walked right in and up the stairwell to the third floor, room 203. Adams was a strange hall, the first level was actually the basement due to the sloping landscape and the room numbers were in the teens. The second floor had the one hundreds and the third floor the twos. I never understood it, just another endearing curiosity about the college.

The room was a mess and it embarrassed me to be bringing a girl back. My roommate Ben was a slob and his clothes were tossed to the four corners of the room. Lily didn't seem to mind and made herself at home by immediately sitting down on the edge of what she decided was my bed. Very forward of her I thought, and then dismissed it.

"This is a pretty big room for just the two of you," she started. "It is nice though, lots of space. Hey you can see my window from here." She was glancing out the big window over at Aquinas.

"Yeah I love it. I actually work down in the Residence Life Office for work study so they hooked me up big time."

The initial awkwardness was melting. I was beginning to feel very comfortable around her. The bumbling romantic was still there but he calmed down a bit, releasing the tension in my neck.

She didn't say anything so I kept going.

"I think someone in Residence Life felt badly for the situation my roommate and I had last year so they put two of us in this quad room. Not a bad deal."

"Bad freshman roommate?"

I managed a weak smile. The tension in my neck wasn't totally gone.

"Ha, yea you could say that."

"Really?" she asked, with surprising interest. "Who was he?"

"Oh nobody, he actually switched rooms halfway through the year with one of our friends. At first, we never told Res Life so when they figured it out at the end of the year, I think they figured they'd hook us up with a big room to keep us from complaining about their incompetence."

She must have sensed it was a touchy subject so she dropped it. That was part of what made her the perfect conversationalist. She pierced into you with her vivid green eyes when you spoke. Whether she was actually paying attention or not was beside the point; she gave the appearance of listening intently, like she was starving and your every word nourished her. She knew when to hang words in the air, let the silence draw us closer. And when the conversation slowed, she stared out the window towards her building—not longing to get out of my room but rather, just a little reminder that she wouldn't make this easy for me. I normally wasn't an emotional guy, but this girl drew something from deep inside me never before tapped.

"So how about that ice?"

While she was gazing across the quad I threw the remaining ice cubes we had in our mini-fridge into a plastic bag and wrapped it in a hand towel.

"Here you go, Lily."

"Thanks. Wait, how'd you know my name, I don't think I ever told you?"

I hesitated. She saw me hesitate. I heard her talking to her friends before she was knocked down. I was watching her but I could not tell her that.

"Your friend yelled something about Lily being hit when they were chasing the drunk girl to the parking lot. I just assumed it was you, ya know since you were the one that was hit."

Nice save on my part.

"Oh, right." She seemed content with that response so I took a seat on the bed a few feet from her. We sat for the next few minutes in silence while she held the ice bag to her head. I didn't know what to do. Later in our relationship she confessed to being nervous that night.

As if to cut the growing sexual tension, she let the dripping towel fall to the floor and put the bag of ice on it.

"I should probably be going, my friends must be worried." She said this but she did not get up off the bed. I knew her friends weren't worried and I knew Lily knew they weren't.

She looked at me and nudged closer, putting her hand on my thigh.

"I really am glad you caught me, Shaw," she said in a low voice. Her face drew closer to mine so that she could whisper right into my ear. "I knew your name was Shaw, by the way. I heard some kid say hi to you when you were staring at me earlier."

I froze and before I knew what was happening she kissed my ear lobe, then my neck. Finally her hand slipped behind my head, slid into my hair and she pulled me into a deep, full-body kiss. A warm shiver shot up my spine from the depths of my stomach. When she pulled away my eyes were still closed but I could feel the emerald flames burning into me.

"I do have to go now, though."

I opened my eyes and the fool spoke first. "Do you want to stay?" stumbled over my tongue. I regretted it the second I said it. But again she giggled. I was confused as to whether she pitied me or thought it was cute. But still, she giggled.

"Not this time, hero."

I didn't want her to go but I also had no idea what to say to make her stay. She stood up and pulled the silver headband from her hair and twisted it up in the back holding it there with a clip from her purse. I followed her to the door, gears churning for something witty and urbane to say. But she did it for me.

"Like I said, not this time hero, but hopefully this won't be the only time you'll come to my rescue."

With that she pushed another deep kiss down onto my waiting lips and then strolled out the door. I ran to the window to see her leave Adams and make the quick walk over to Aquinas. The soft autumn breeze blew her sundress and it pressed tightly to her curves. As she opened the front door to her dorm hall she looked up at my window and blew me a kiss. I could tell she was giggling.

Chapter 5

Lily and I never really dated formally. There was never any official arrangement to our relationship; it rose and fell with the emotions of two very busy but very passionate students. There was love, though. I convinced myself of that.

After our initial run-in sophomore year we became close friends. I wasn't initially aware but Lindsey and Emily knew Lily, so she completed our circle of friends.

There was some sexual tension that spring. Lily and I flirted mercilessly, but so did Shoddy and Lily and Shoddy and Lindsey and Shoddy and Emily. We all chalked it up to hormones and the archetypal nature of the season.

I was content with the situation, mainly because I enjoyed being around Lily more than I enjoyed being around anyone at any point in my life up to then.

I decided to remain on campus that summer and work with the maintenance department doing landscaping. Lily was an Orientation Leader and would be on campus for the entire months of June and July giving tours and keeping an eye on incoming freshmen.

The college let student summer workers live in campus apartments, and the jobs paid a small salary. During that summer I cut grass in ninety-degree heat, then I'd go back to my apartment, shower and meet Lily for dinner almost every night. The flirting escalated but for a while I received nothing more than a few bats of her big green eyes and a peck on the cheek every now and again.

One afternoon in July she caught me in between her meetings and asked for the combination to my apartment lock. She said she needed to borrow something.

It wasn't until I got home that evening, sweating and smelling like fresh cut grass, that our relationship truly changed.

As soon as I walked in she stepped out from the kitchen in nothing but one of my long-sleeve collared shirts. She was wearing her fierce red hair pinned up, for the first time I could remember. The shirt hung loosely and only the bottom few buttons were fastened creating a milky V of her skin. The point of the V ended just below her waistline and the shirt's teasing purpose was served.

She bent one of her knees and cocked her body, the shirt folding back on the right side, exposing the majority of one of her perky breasts. The edge of the pink nipple was just visible. Her thin finger was slipped through the eyehole of a half-empty jug of cheap red wine and it hung, swaying down by her thigh. She had two glasses in her other hand and a seductive smile on her face. Her green eyes were hungry. They held the emotion, the desire and the passion.

I dropped the water bottle I was holding and she burst out laughing, apparently at the sudden increase in gravitational pull on my entire body, especially the lower jaw.

She dropped the glasses and jug of wine on the carpet when she leapt at me. The red wine leaked from the jug, staining the carpet and trickling onto the linoleum kitchen tile. I had to react quickly to catch her and was momentarily blinded by the flurry of red hair over my face.

The door slammed automatically, heavily, but we fell gently together onto the kitchen floor. I cradled her head and when she kissed me, she tasted exactly the same as she had the first time she kissed me, in my dorm room so many months before. I never forgot that taste, like the taste of wine after brushing your teeth—minty and fruity all the same.

We made love for the first time. Together, on the kitchen floor we slowly unscrewed the release valve of sexual tension that had been building for months.

She was unhurried and full of passion. And she made sure I was thorough. We rolled over and she was on top of me, her body slick with perspiration and purple streaks of wine. Before pulling my grass-stained t-shirt off she ripped at the few fastened buttons on the shirt she sort of wore, not wasting time to undo them properly. The plastic circles clattered to the linoleum and the motion of Lily's writhing body shook the shirt from her shoulders. It fell behind her back and eventually, but not immediately, she took her arms from my chest to remove it completely.

Her usual energy and vibrancy was there, but channeled into the methodical force pressing her body against mine. Her eyes remained open save the final moments of climax. As her back arched, her hair fell over her face. I pulled my hand from the small of her back and gently draped the crimson bangs behind her ear, brushing her cheek in the process. She smiled and squeaked and opened her eyes. A droplet of wine slid from her moistened hair, down to her cheek. I pulled her face back in toward me and kissed away the droplet.

When we finished we were both soaked through from sweat and the puddle of wine we laid in. The apartment smelled like sex and grapes for the rest of the night. We didn't move from the spot, spending much of that evening staring at each other in a clichéd post-sex haze. Every few minutes I'd run my finger up her inner thigh, over her navel and between her breasts. And each time I did it she kissed my hand when it got to her mouth. We fell asleep there on the floor, naked and at ease in the classic spooning position. When she shivered I reached across my body and pulled a throw blanket from a chair. She instinctively pressed into me tighter. My arm draped over her body, I found her hand and interlocked it with my own. She squeezed my fingers.

For the rest of that summer Lily and I would eat together, sleep together and escape together. We left our respective jobs early one Friday and spent the weekend in Newport. Another morning, I nudged her awake while it was still dark and drove her to Horseneck Beach to see the sun rise. We had sex on the sand in a sleeping bag while dawn's rosy fingers spread across the sky.

Even after Orientation ended and she moved back to Connecticut for the month of August, she would visit me at least once a week. She had concocted some fairytale for her parents about staying with a girlfriend in order to get a jump on thesis research.

I barely saw Shoddy or the other girls that summer. I saw Lily. I saw her eyes, her burning hair and her perfect body and she saw me, whatever it was she saw in me.

I studied her body. I knew the small dimple on her left buttock and the tiny scar on her back where she picked at chicken pox as a child. All over her body had very faint freckle patches one could only notice up very close. She was a masterpiece.

"Shaw, before this is over, I'm going to lighten you up. I'm going to make you come alive," she said to me one night. She stole the line from a song we discovered over the internal radio at a clothing store.

It was one night toward the end of that summer. We were at the Providence Place mall, a four-story, sprawling capitalism Mecca built to revitalize downtown and satiate political backroom dealings.

My dealings that night were meant to be very straightforward and honest. I wanted Lily and I to have a proper date, not just take-out dinner and dorm room sex.

I took Lily to a movie, some Will Ferrell comedy. Before the show we strolled hand-in-hand through some of the stores, happening upon a trendy clothing outlet frequented by the college crowd. As she perused the racks I noticed the song blaring on the store's internal radio. I enjoyed the acoustic tune. The music was good, haunting and didn't seem to fit with the heavy bass or techno twang of the other songs played before it.

I must have been staring because Lily's hand wiped away the musical haze.

"Hey, Shaw, you there?" she said, waving.

I blinked and stared into her green eyes.

"Oh yeah, sorry. I was just listening to the song."

"This song? I actually noticed it too. It's good, isn't it? Not like the crap they had playing before it. I hate coming in here when they're blasting that dance music. I feel like they're going to give me some ecstasy with my jeans."

She held up a pair of jeans she intended on buying and I laughed. We headed for the checkout counter where they had set up an impulse purchase rack selling CDs of the music played in the store.

"Hey, who sings this song?" Lily asked, pointing at the ceiling.

"Um, I don't know," said the girl behind the counter. "The CD is on track three, though."

Lily grabbed a disc and tossed it on her folded jeans.

"The Refreshments. Never heard of 'em. You, Shaw?"

"Nope. But I like them."

"I'll take this too, then."

In the remaining time before the movie we went to the music store and bought out the two Refreshments albums they had along with the lead singer's latest project with his new band, as suggested to us by the music store clerk who said he was a huge fan. Perhaps we were a little hasty, but with Lily I enjoyed acting on impulse.

We also bought a bag of gummy bears to take into the theater.

Once in the theater she settled into her seat and immediately dug into the gummy bears we bought at the music store.

"You know, I like the yellow ones," she said with a handful of candy. She opened her palm and moved the red and green ones away with a slender finger. "I sort of feel bad for the yellow one. Nobody likes yellow. I think because candy makers can never decide on whether it should be lemon or banana. So they give it some horrible mutated flavor. But I sort of like it."

She didn't wait for my response and snatched up a red one, bit the head off and licked the glossy remains. Before I knew what she was doing, she whipped the confection at the screen and to my surprise, it stuck. She burst out into uncontrollable laughter without acknowledging the quiver of shushes zipping our way. She did see the horrified look on my face, which only elicited more laughter.

The movie began and the headless bear stuck high up out of the reach of the usher—a pock-marked teenager who swiped at it with an old straw broom about ten feet too short. Defeated, he huffed up the aisle looking for the culprit.

"They'll never get it down," Lily said, still laughing. "It's like a zit stuck to those perfect million-dollar faces. All the Proactiv in the world couldn't clean that up."

The usher reached our row and soon we were bathed in flashlight.

"Hey, you two," he squeaked. "What's your problem?"

Lily playfully stuck her tongue out in his direction, grabbed my hand and dragged me out the other side of the aisle. Thankfully most of the theater was empty, making for easy escape. As we rushed past the screen she fired a few more headless gummy bears at some overpaid actor; one stuck but most of them just ricocheted into the front row sparking cries of annoyance and a few giddy chuckles.

We ran holding hands all the way out to the parking garage.

"I didn't really want to see that movie anyway," she said in between giggles.

"What was that?" I gasped, catching my breath for the first time. I fumbled with the keys, rushing to get into the car. Mall Security had to be mere steps behind us. Any second, they would pounce.

She spun me around and leaned in her hips to mine, forcing me back against the car door. She threw her arms around my neck and lightly tussled my hair.

"Relax," she said with that perfect mix of sweetness and sarcasm I would ultimately fall in love with. "I think we're safe."

She smiled and leaned in. Right before she kissed me, her lips trembling a mere whisper from my own, she said, "Shaw, before this is over, I'm going to lighten you up. I'm going to make you come alive."

A few weeks later I tried again to have a quiet, sane date night. I thought it was something Lily wanted.

So I splurged on an expensive dinner at a restaurant she suggested. I ordered the filet mignon, medium rare and smothered in a white pepper sauce. Lily ordered a broiled ossobuco over spinach risotto; something I never even knew was an option for the human palette. We shared a twice-baked potato and several bottles of wine. For dessert we skipped the cakes and tarts and went right for espresso martinis, thick with chocolate and liquor.

Towards the end of the meal we both got up to go the bathroom located at the back of the restaurant near the emergency exit. In the tucked away hallway outside the restrooms, instead of entering the ladies room, Lily pushed me against the wall and slipped her tongue in my mouth. She tasted sweet, like the sugary martinis fogging her inhibitions. As always, I fell immediately and totally under her control. And as always, she knew it.

In the instant I closed my eyes to enjoy the moment, she slapped open the emergency fire door, grabbed my wrist and dragged me through, breaking into a full sprint once we hit the night air. She laughed hysterically. I panted and waited for the wailing fire alarm, which never came. When I looked back the fire door had quietly shut and no one was pursuing.

"We have to go back in. We left a huge bill in there," I panted when we got back to the car. "We screwed that waiter."

Lily never stopped laughing. Her eyes teared up from the hysterics.

"You are adorable," she finally said, still giggling.

"What?"

"You, you're cute, all worried about the wait staff at my uncle's restaurant."

Her laughter grew with the revelation spreading across my face.

"Your uncle's restaurant? You didn't tell me . . ."

"Yup, he bought it a few months ago. Our meal was always going to be free. And the waiter is his son, my cousin. Why do you think we got such good seats and service? This place takes reservations months ahead of time."

My jaw must have been on the floor because she reached over a slender finger and stroked up my cheek.

"You should have seen your face when I pulled you out that door," she said. "Priceless isn't a strong enough a description. You looked liked we just killed someone."

She had set up the whole thing for a prank. The strange part was that it excited me. I started laughing with her until she reached across the car and pulled me into a deep kiss.

When our lips broke I said, "Let's go get some drinks."

"That's the best idea you've had all night," she said.

"And this time, let's pay for them."

We joked about the meal all the way to the bar and inside thereafter. We drank watered down beer—a lot of watered down beer.

"Shaw, you don't have to try so hard with me," she said as she finished her second plastic cup.

"What do you mean?"

"I mean I'm not an expensive dinner kind of girl. I love our take out dinners and rented movies. I won't lie though; I do have fun when we go out. But just don't feel like you have to."

"Alright. I just want to keep up with you. Stay on pace, not slip behind and watch you outlast me in this relationship."

"Slow and steady wins the race, Shaw. Didn't you learn anything in kindergarten?"

She winked and kissed the air between us.

"I'm having a lot of fun this summer," I said. "I've never really had this much fun with anybody."

"Somebody had to do it," she said. She reached out and laid a hand on my knee. "I'm glad it's me."

From then on, as much as we engrossed each other, we never defined what we were doing. We didn't call it anything. The word "couple" never arose and we were both happier repressing the urge to identify our relationship. I was afraid the label would scare her off and might create a rift within our group of friends. I assumed she had similar reservations.

There were obviously feelings between us, as carnal as they might have been. But the dinners, the jokes, the nicknames (she still called me Hero) and the conversations spoke to something on a higher plane. I knew everything about her that she let me know and intuited the rest.

We didn't tell anyone else. By August, Shoddy had figured it out. He came to visit me and found Lily's clothes strewn around my apartment. But he kept quiet. He even toasted my success.

Eventually Lindsey and Emily figured it out too. It wasn't hard. They both said it was simple infatuation rather than love. Lindsey admitted to me later, during one of our own squabbles, that she was jealous.

If Lily ever said she loved me, she never said it to me. I was content assuming it. If she wanted to confess it to me, I would gladly and hungrily accept it. But for that summer, I was content with just her.

The outside world was nonexistent to us. Providence was our desert island, our hidden glade, our far, far away.

Lindsey and Emily were right, I was infatuated with Lily—I was infatuated with loving her.

Chapter 6

September arrived and with it, thousands of students. While campus burgeoned, the intensity with Lily diminished.

That fall we saw each other less, which was to be expected with schoolwork and other commitments. As juniors in college, schoolwork mushroomed and on top of that, we suddenly had to recognize the finality of college life. The future must be acknowledged. Within the next year tests had to be taken, graduates schools applied for and resumes polished. Like most, I wanted to postpone the real world. Remaining in my fairytale land with Lily was the top priority.

The fairytale didn't last long. The time Lily and I did spend together was different. Of course we still slept together, but in public she was colder, more distant. We argued a few times over inane things, something we had never done before. I got the feeling she was pushing me away for reasons she refused to reveal. I blamed stress.

"Lily, did I do something wrong?" I asked her one night. We were in my bed, naked and basking in a post-sex tranquility. But something nagged me. I felt a tension in her muscles, which made me have trouble relaxing.

She came to my apartment that night for dinner but instead we argued about where to eat. We debated location in the past but that night Lily got philosophical.

"I want to go to the same pub where you and Shoddy always go to watch football games," she said. "Why do you take Lindsey there and not me?"

"What are you talking about," I said, aggravated.

"Forget it, let's try something different."

"I thought you said you wanted the pub? And correct me if I'm wrong but didn't you say you weren't an expensive dinner kind of girl? Didn't you say your favorite meals with me were of the take out persuasion?"

"Yeah, whatever, not tonight. Let's go somewhere you like to go. Somewhere different that you've never taken me." Her voice elevated.

"So somewhere old and somewhere new? Got it," I said with a little too much sarcasm.

Lily huffed and shook her head. She was all over the map, picking a fight at all four corners.

In the midst of the yelling, I asked her if I pissed her off somehow. She didn't answer then, either. Instead, the argument fizzled out and she pushed me into my bedroom.

The sex was usually good, but that sex was unexpectedly passionate. She was more vigorous. Her hips thrusted harder, she moaned louder and her eyes clenched tighter. She had added energy, like arguing with me untamed her already wild side.

When it ended she pretended to fall asleep. I nudged. "Hey, I know you aren't sleeping." She pulled the blanket close to her chin. "You've been acting weird. What's bothering you?"

She didn't answer. She didn't move.

"Alright, fine, but all I said was I wanted to order in Thai food and you flipped out about a pub and football and God knows what else. Then you called me an idiot and jumped on top of me. Not that I'm complaining, but what the Hell is up with you?"

She rolled over to face me, tears welling in her eyes. Unexpected.
"Shaw, do you love me, like really love me?"
Really unexpected.
She didn't let me answer.
"No, wait don't answer that. I need to tell you something. Something you probably aren't going to like," she whimpered.

Lily propped herself against the headboard, wrapped my white sheets tight around her smooth, bare skin. She took down her wall and finally accepted vulnerability.

She proceeded to tell me a detailed account of duplicity. In the midst of explaining why her trust in men was shot, the levies broke and her jade pools spilled. She cried and I held her while she finished telling me the story.

There was a man she dated at the college down South. He never hit her, but at times she thought he had it in him to. His cruelty was mental, in the form of insults and degrading comments due to, what I gathered to be his own insecurities. She fell into a pattern of loving him and hating him, until it became so blurred that she couldn't tell the difference. They went on for months. She was miserable, she told him so and he exploded. He refused to leave her alone and refused to let her go. He would get drunk and call her to say disgusting insults, so she got a new cell phone. He cornered her in bars and pulled a Jekyll and Hyde, at one moment beg for forgiveness and suddenly snap into a jealous rant. The last time they spoke was a few nights before I had met her, right when Lily moved to Providence. One of her friend's fathers passed away unexpectedly and Lily was consoling her via.

The guy called persistently, leaving voicemails saying he knew Lily was, "fucking her way up the East Coast." He threatened her physically from a thousand miles away. When those threats went unanswered he found other means of assault.

Unless Lily called him back, he promised, he would call her friend's widowed mother and tell her what a whore her daughter was. He left another message saying the girl's father died because he was ashamed his daughter and her friends were sluts. Lily's friend left Providence a few weeks later. Instead of telling the school or the police, Lily changed her phone number again, cut ties with anyone at her former college and tried to forget about the betrayal and heartbreak. Ultimately, she said, she found a refuge in Providence. She found new friends—Lindsey and Emily lived on the same dorm building floor as Lily and her friend. They were there the night this all went down. They comforted Lily even while she tried to console her friend. When the friend left, Lindsey and Emily invited Lily into their world. Finally, Lily said, she found some people she could rely on. I was the one she trusted most.

The cuts the guy left on her heart were deep and still inexplicably fresh. As she lay there telling me the story, I couldn't help but think her nickname for me was more than just because I prevented her from smacking her head on the concrete a year before.

I should have been happy she confided this all in me. I thought I would be ecstatic hearing Lily tell me that she had real feelings for me, that she trusted me.

But instead, as I stared at her naked body, defenseless and fragile, uneasiness melted through my stomach. Was she projecting onto me a man that I doubted I could live up to? In comparison, I was Superman to this guy's Lex Luther. But was I? I couldn't fly.

Maybe I got queasy because instead of having dinner we had wild sex, or maybe it was because I suddenly realized I might never be who Lily expected me to be.

The wall in my head grew brick by brick that night. A mental construction team erected it slowly but with craft and strength.

We never talked about the guy down south again. But our roles switched in the following weeks. I avoided her. I started to feel like I wasn't good enough for her, like she needed a real hero to carry her and erase the scars of her past.

It didn't help that Duncan heard of my relationship with Lily and whether through boredom or pure envy he decided to try and exacerbate my insecurities. He wanted another shot at killing my love life. But a rumor wouldn't work on a close-knit college campus. Everyone already knew everyone else's business.

No, he'd have to try other tactics. A different poison to kill this new flower.

A few times he threw barbs at us if he saw us walking together. Meaningless insults. He convinced a few of his buddies to hit on Lily at a party to incite jealousy. I laughed when she rejected, and then loudly insulted the size of their manhood in front of a large gathering of college girls.

But on Halloween he hit a chink.

He approached me at a costume party. He was wearing a Prohibition-era gangster suit and perspiring profusely.

"Hey, look at Superman over there hittin' on your girl," he slurred and pointed a short, stubby finger across the room at guy in a blue suit and red cape who was leaning over Lily. She wore a skimpy Bo Peep outfit.

It didn't bother me. I ignored Duncan.

"I bet she could handle him," he said.

"I suggest you walk away, Duncan."

"Or what, you gonna ask Superman to save you from me? It'd show your girl what kind of pussy you are."

He stood up on his tiptoes and got uncomfortably close to my face. I tried again to ignore him.

"Hah, you know she's too good for you, right?" he whispered. "Not to mention she's getting it good everywhere else."

My eyebrows raised and gave me away. He peaked my attention and he noticed it.

"Yea, you didn't know? About the hockey team in high school, or that guy she used to fuck for fun down at her redneck college? It's amazing what you learn from banging Lily's drunk friends."

I should have hit him then. Or head butted him; it was the right setting and position.

Instead I pushed him out of my way and left the party. I knew he was full of shit but a queasy feeling reinforced my preexisting inadequacies. Lily didn't come back to my room that night.

After Halloween, Lily and I didn't sleep together for about a month. I adored her but I put her back up on, what I thought, was an almost unattainable pedestal. Duncan's slights to her character and chastity only built her up more in my eyes. She became more angelic. But it still had the effect he was going for: it created a small, nagging tear between Lily and me.

Chapter 7

I wrestled with the idea of not talking to Lily anymore. Duncan would have been the cause of its execution, and that idea enraged me. When I told Shoddy what I was mulling, he punched me square on the shoulder. That's when I knew Duncan had something right: I was being a pussy.

At the end of November the college always threw a formal ball for the junior class to celebrate the distribution of the class rings. They called it Junior Ring Weekend or JRW. Fundraiser money was used to rent out the nicest hotel downtown and provide dinner and dancing for the entire junior class. It was a college prom. It was meant to be a happy memory.

It took me a few weeks to ask Lily to be my date but eventually I realized I was not the only person interested in her. With Shoddy's physical abuse and my own desire for romantic connection, I repressed the inadequacies bubbling underneath.

Lily and I both hinted at the JRW thing on several occasions in the weeks prior to the event. Neither one would come out and ask the other; it was all a juvenile and coy game of politicking. Other parties got involved, lobbying occurred on both sides. I almost expected Shoddy to start erecting lawn signs with, "Shaw/Lily for JRW" splashed in red, white and blue.

Jealousy finally took over and one Friday afternoon, after seeing the same kid from Halloween, the one dressed like Superman, flirting with her during our Seventeenth Century British Literature class. I decided to cut the flip-flopping.

I nudged in front of the other guy leaving class that afternoon.

"Lily, do you want to go to JRW?" I said walking in stride with her.

"Um, of course I do."

"I mean with me, do you want to go with me?"

She giggled and smiled as we exited the building into a dreary, rainy Rhode Island afternoon. She popped up an umbrella.

"That's why I answered 'of course.'"

I grabbed the umbrella and held it high so we could both fit underneath. She brushed her hand over mine and diverted out from under the relative dryness of the umbrella.

"Hey, where you goin?" I yelled after her.

"Class, lower campus," she yelled back. In the few seconds she stood in the rain her hair soaked through.

"Your umbrella," I yelled and started moving toward her. She walked backwards away from me, a huge smile creeping across her face.

"No, you hang on to it. It'll give you a reason to come by my place tonight to return it. I expect you'll stop by around eight, when my roommate is at her night class."

She held her hand up to her lips and then opened it to blow me a kiss. Water sprayed from her upturned palm like a garden sprinkler, the drops shooting up, intermingling and disappearing with the rain. She turned and scurried away, splashing through a few of the larger puddles, I imagined on purpose.

I smiled for the rest of the day.

Lily bought a new dress, a tight, low-cut designer gown in a sort of sea-foam green. Her parents sent her the money. I picked my tuxedo to match. She smiled when I told her of the coordination efforts.

The night of the dance I met her at her dorm hall with a bouquet of large white lilies and small greenish-blue flowers (I don't know what they were called). In the doorway we stared at our achieved elegance, and we both smiled. She plucked one of the lilies from the bouquet and pinned it to my lapel.

"So, before we go can I ask you something?" she said. We were alone in the foyer. She continued without waiting for me to answer. "Why did it take you so long to ask me? After this summer I figured I was at the top of your list."

"My list? Lily, you are my list. I just didn't know if you'd say yes."

"Actually, I didn't know if I'd say yes, either. After that night I told you about my ex down south, I kinda thought maybe this whole thing with you would be over. But you didn't get up and run away, you just sort of drifted away the last few weeks."

The night wasn't starting off as planned. Something was spooking Lily and I had to quash it immediately.

She was right, though. The confidence boost of the past summer with Lily dried up. She suddenly intimidated me and if I deserved her, I didn't see it. But the fact she said yes to my invitation, and the fact that she was now irked I had not asked her earlier, told me that my doubts were airier than a handkerchief in the wind.

"Yeah, I wanted to apologize about that. To be honest, I started thinking you were too good for me, that this whole thing was too good to be true."

"What!" Her green eyes started to fire up. "Where in the Hell did you get that idea?"

"I don't know. I was unsure if you felt the same way I did."

"I slept with you, Shaw. Obviously there is something there. Did someone say something to you?"

"No, no." My eyes shifted to the floor as I said it. To disguise my hesitation I checked the clock above the door. We were running late. "We should really get going."

"Somebody said something. I know you, Shaw, I'm not stupid."

"Fine, let's get going and I'll tell you on the way." We left the dorm and as we walked I told her what Duncan had said on Halloween and how I felt she deserved better than me. I hated telling her, but she deserved the truth.

Initially, Lily was angry. She kept saying I was wrong. She kept trying to reassure me that she was not out of my league. She said some very colorful things about Duncan.

"I'll have to chat with him," she said.

"No, absolutely not," I said as we waited for a cab to bring us to the hotel.

"Why not? He insulted me too, ya know. I think I have the right to smack him."

"Maybe, but just forget it. I'm trying to. The less he's in my life, the better it is."

A white City Cab pulled up. We spent the five-minute ride downtown staring out the windows, not speaking.

A line outside the Biltmore Hotel shook with anticipation. Hundreds of students waited in the cold for them to open the doors to the ballroom. I paid the cabbie and looked over at Lily standing underneath an old gas streetlamp. She looked just like she did that first night I saw her. She looked around trying to recognize people in line and rubbed her bare arms to warm them up. She turned her head and saw me staring at her. I must have been smiling because she gave a coy smile back and diverted her eyes to the sidewalk.

Almost in silent, slow motion I stepped up the curb, removed my tux jacket and wrapped it around her shoulders. Standing behind her, with my hands gripping her arms, I felt the tension between us melt away. She cocked her head back towards mine, magnetically pulling my face over her shoulder. She kissed me with sweet, tender, glossy lips and I surrendered to her completely.

"Hey Antony and Cleopatra, you coming?" Shoddy yelled from the middle of the now-moving line. "Let's go, save it for later!"

The ballroom was decorated with giant snowflakes and icicles, despite it looking like potential rain outside. An elegant, formal dinner was served. Lily and I sat with Shoddy, Lindsey, Emily, and their dates. The food wasn't bad; a thin piece of chicken in a lemon piccatta sauce with capers and potatoes. Shoddy went around the table introducing everyone's Cokes to Captain Morgan. Once dessert was served, a thin slice of frozen chocolate cake, everyone exchanged the dinner table for the dance floor.

Lily and I chatted as freely as when we first met. I felt comfortable again. When we danced, we danced close to both the slow and fast songs; she pecked my cheek a few times. We formed a typical dance circle with a half-dozen classmates. During *Billy Jean,* Shoddy and I made fools of ourselves when we attempted a Michael Jackson impression. The night flowed smoothly, lubricated by liquor and plenty of laughs. Fun came easy and without effort.

Around midnight the crowd dwindled as students left the hotel for various after parties or private time with their dates. Lily had gone to the bathroom with Emily and Shoddy and I stood at the edge of the dance floor making bets on which couples would hook up. A young lady named Kerry from our freshman year Psychology class was sandwiched between two tuxedos, grinding to the bass and sloshing her drink down the cleavage spilling from her yellow strapless dress. That was an easy bet.

On the far side of the dance floor near the DJ, Duncan came into view. He requested a song, gave an awkward thumbs-up gesture and jumped back into a group of scantily clad girls.

One of the girls was wearing a familiar green sea-foam colored dress. She stood out among the others because she wasn't dancing. She was there with a purpose more serious than the rest. And she appeared to be yelling at Duncan.

I pointed it out to Shoddy and we both made our way easily through the waning crowd. As the song faded I could hear Duncan snicker and say, "So you're saying you want to fuck me, then?"

Shoddy reached him first. Lily was in Duncan's face and Shoddy had to wrestle her away.

"Who the fuck do you think you are, asshole? You don't know me. You don't talk about me like that," she yelled.

Lily was drunk. Thanks to Shoddy and me, she had gone on quite a ride with the Captain. She raised her hand like she was going to slap Duncan but I acted first, and in the process of grabbing her hand I knocked into Shoddy who fell into Duncan. Scuffle ensued. Duncan bellowed from underneath a pile of gowns and tuxedos. He was swearing at Lily and me. The words, "loser" and, "whore" came out a few times.

I pulled her away from the melee and back to our now empty table. I tried to calm her down before I spoke to her. She spoke first.

"What the fuck?" she slurred. "What's wrong with you? I was trying to talk to him."

"Yea, I know, and you almost hit him Lily. The real question is, what's wrong with *you?*"

"Me! Nothing, you ass. I was standing up for you."

"Who said I needed anybody to stand up for me? Especially you!" She was taking jabs at my manhood, whether she knew it or not. I was getting angry. "And didn't I tell you to leave him alone? I could've sworn I said that."

"You tell me what to do now? I can take care of myself."

"No, just with Duncan. Stay away from him."

"I can do what I want. I can slap who I want."

"Not him, I don't trust him."

"Wait a minute," she said, and hiccupped. She put her fist to her lips then started again. "Wait a minute, do you not trust him or do you not trust me?"

"You just don't seem to be able to stay away from asshole guys, do you? You're just drawn to them."

I felt bad immediately after saying it but it was too late to retract.

"Excuse me? I am not some whore, Shaw." The emerald pools were back in her eyes. "You are really saying this? After what I told you about that? After what you just told me on the way here?"

It was getting very hot in that ballroom. To buy myself some time, I undid the bow tie and let it hang around my neck.

"Just let me handle things next time, alright?"

"Oh because you were doing a bang-up job at avoiding him."

"Fuck this, I don't need you telling me how to deal with people."

She was crying outright. Her voice went from anger to almost pleading.

"Shaw, I can deal with you letting him call me a slut. But how can you let him just walk all over you for years."

"Drop it, Lily."

"No, talk to me. You just avoid it all the time! Either talk to me or go kick his ass! Enough of this repressing rage, manly bullshit!"

"Don't talk to him, Lily and frankly, I'd like you to just shut up."

"Oh, I'm sorry I wanted to defend my boyfriend!"

It was the first time she ever called me her boyfriend. She got up and ran out the door, grabbing Lindsey who was approaching us with caution.

By the time I absorbed what she said, Lily and Lindsey had left the hotel and jumped in a cab back to campus.

Shoddy was standing at the edge of the dance floor staring at me, his mouth agape. He started towards me but I just turned away.

"Shaw, wait up!" he said.

I could barely hear him; the music had started again. I didn't want to hear it from him. I couldn't stand any of his brotherly advice.

As far as rainstorms go, Providence was the prince of precipitation. I stepped out of the hotel and into a monsoon. Another line of students had queued up at the cabstand and no cabs were in sight.

Screw it, I thought. I'm not waiting for Shoddy to come out and lecture me. I was so angry, mostly with myself for having said such stupid things to Lily that I just wanted to be alone. Braving the risk of pneumonia, I hoofed it the three miles back to campus in the pouring rain wearing stiff dress shoes and a raggedy tux. It was just the latest one of the many decisions I regretted making that night.

By the time I reached campus, the suave, sophisticated, tuxedo-clad gentleman that began the night was slashed down to a mere wet dog. The black tie was in my inner jacket pocket. Of the six buttons on the greenish vest only two were actually buttoned. My white shirt was undone at the neck and the sleeves savagely shot out of the jacket arms. The pants were still intact; save for the half un-tucked shirt covering the left pant leg. My right shoe was not tied and the laces dragged solemnly behind me like wounded soldiers marching home from war. Rain washed over me in loud bursts due to the intense wind that carried it. Everything was drenched.

Noah would've even had trouble that night. We were all together in that ballroom as one happy family of couples. Now I was alone. I was angry and alone. The night hated me. The wind detested me. I disgusted the rain so it tried to cleanse me. As I pushed through the storm onto upper-campus my jacket blew back and my hair dripped onto my nose. I could smell a faint hair-spray aroma from the little droplets. The water was greasy. It clung to my face, slid down my jacket and soaked into the pants like they would a sponge. It was not enough to say I was soaked to the bone. My veins and nerve cells were shivering from the cold dampness.

Then came more wind. I have never been witness to such anger in the atmosphere. Small whirlwinds swirled up the wet leaves to either side of me when I walked past the chapel. In its courtyard the wind was worst. It came from the darkness overhead. In a grand sweeping motion it screamed down from shadow, curled around the steeple and looped back through a large oak tree before cracking back up and around the turret. It slid down the chapel roof, down across the open courtyard and blasted me with all its fury. It entered my throat, scratching all the way to the lungs. It was grainy, coarse, burning. It wasn't air I was breathing. Whatever it was spread through my body and dispersed through my skin into the air before swinging back up to the shadows. All I could notice was its blackness.

My walking had ceased. The wind had blown me back a few steps and knocked the jacket from my shoulders. Water seeped into the fake leather rental shoes in the middle of the flooded courtyard and the trickle from the hair to the face now streamed. My jacket swam in the courtyard pathway between the brick and muddy grass. As I bent over to pick it up the stream of ice water rushed down the back of my pants and along my inner thigh, down to the puddles of my feet. The coldness caused my body to spring upwards. I decided to leave the jacket to be devoured by the mud. I turned my head to the sky to watch for another punch of wind. I didn't like being broadsided. The rain pierced my eyes; even if the wind came again I could never tell.

Instead of turning away or closing my burning eyes, I just stared. I tried to look around the rain bullets. I tried to see through the sheets of glass smashing over me every second. I wanted to look into the rain; I wanted to know why it hated me.

The wind hurled itself around the chapel for another swipe at the broken, soaked victim gazing into the sky. I prepared myself for its second blow but no wind came, only a soft, bubbling voice. I could feel someone watching me.

Maybe it was Lily. Maybe she followed me from the other end of campus, riding the back of the wind.

I spun around to nothing. I spun again, water sloshing in torrents.

Nothing. Nobody. Of course she didn't follow me. She had left first and was dry now.

I looked down to the drowning jacket. The single white lily that had been so neatly pinned to the lapel was gone. On the other side of the courtyard I heard a soft gurgle and watched the flower swirl twice then disappear down a gutter.

A dozen cold stone eyes were studying me. They blinked as the blue light flickered over the faces of stone angels. I stood drenched, defeated and encircled by the stone seraphim sitting silently in judgment.

They watched me drag the tuxedo jacket through the puddles and across the courtyard. Angels, I thought, were supposed to watch over me, guide me. These wore menacing, shadowy visages.

As I passed the last stone angel sitting cat-like at the courtyard exit, questions started popping in my head. I asked myself what had gone wrong; what was wrong with Lily? What was wrong with me?

The last question lingered the longest, probably because I too was lingering in front of the last angel statue.

I bent closer to examine the intricate detail carved in the hair and cheekbones. Water followed the curves and snaked along every tiny etch. Yet, despite the flood, the angel was stoic. It withstood the rain while I was soaked completely through. The angel had its purpose: to unwaveringly light the courtyard. What was mine?

At that moment, staring at an inanimate stone statue under the college torch while heaven's floods crashed over me, I made a decision. I decided to take control. I decided to be steadfast. Lily needed a rock. I decided, for Lily, to be a stone angel.

When I returned to my room that night Lily was passed out in the hallway leaning against the door. I carried her inside and laid her on her back on my bed. Her mascara was streaked down to her chin, the lipstick smudged and her previously styled hair tossed loosely and sopping over her shoulders.

She didn't flinch when I wiped the smeared makeup from her right cheek, erasing the runny Revlon mask and revealing her smooth, milky skin. Why did she even wear makeup, I thought. She's as close to perfect as you can get. The ruined makeup made me furious. The truth was, she didn't need makeup anyway—her natural beauty surpassed anything in a bottle. Now, that true beauty was hidden under layers of mud-flecked and rain-smudged concealer and mascara.

I rubbed it all off, washed it all away. When her soft, lightly freckled nose and cheeks were clean I peeled her dress off. She wore tiny white underwear and no bra. She shuffled slightly and turned her face to me, still asleep, innocently draping her left arm over her exposed breasts. I chuckled, thinking that even in her sleep her attempt at modesty served only to enhance her desirability. I pulled the white sheet up over her shoulders and let it settle, the outline of her body clearly defined in linen.

I shut the light and, realizing the intense heat pouring from the ancient radiator, cracked the window beside the bed.

A rush of moist air ruffled the sheet and Lily, semi-conscious, pulled it up to her chin. She nested deeper into my bed and a smile grew across her naturally rose-petal pink lips

I discarded my wet clothes and tried to dry off. The rain had left me chilled to the bone, icy and ornery. But she melted me.

Before I climbed in bed I watched her breathe, the white sheet rising and falling almost imperceptibly.

At that moment I would have fought windmills just to hear her draw her next breath; I would have launched a thousand ships just to bring her close; I would have strolled through nine hellish circles and pushed the devil aside just to hold her hand.

I climbed in bed next to her and pulled her close, her head resting just beneath my chin. Her cold, naked breasts perked and pressed close to my bare chest. The heart beneath them beat against mine and I fell asleep listening to the torrent outside slosh at the slightly open window.

Chapter 8

Senior year March 13 fell on a Friday – the Friday night before we left for spring break. But the year before—junior year—March 13 fell on a Thursday. The day of the week didn't matter; March 13 became a very unlucky date for me and for those around me.

It was junior year and the Providence College basketball team played its last game of the season. It was the first round of the NCAA tournament—March Madness. They lost. The entire campus buzzed because our logo splashed across a major television network and by the time the clock ticked down to zero and the Friars were heading home, most students were heading out of their dorm rooms and off-campus apartments to commemorate the defeat.

Lily, Shoddy, Lindsey, Emily and I ended up at a party. But we hadn't planned it that way. Originally, plans involved going to the local college bar, Primal, getting drunk on watered down Bud Light and maybe, if Lily prodded enough, watch Shoddy and I do the white-man shuffle on the dance floor. Word was, everyone would be there drinking away the loss and toasting our underachieving ballers.

My professor being a rapid basketball fan let us out of my Shakespeare seminar early that afternoon. I witnessed countless undergrads walking back from the packie, hidden cases of beer in tow. Two guys from my dorm shuffled by, each gripping a strap on a hockey bag, laboring from the apparent weight. Neither of them played hockey. It was a typical Thursday evening.

I had two messages on my cell phone when I got back to my room. One was from Shoddy and one from Lindsey, both describing the same outline for that night's activities. I called Shoddy back to confirm.

After a quick dinner with Shoddy, I went back to shower. I grabbed a cold Bud from my mini-fridge and jumped in the shower. One of the small pleasures in life is a cold beer in a hot shower. Something about the contrasting temperatures or the seemingly unnatural beer-drinking environment makes it an undeniable temptation. Also, a soap tray makes an excellent can holder during rinse and repeats.

I threw on a green long-sleeve button down shirt and jeans, no jacket. It was the middle of March and therefore still brisk, but I knew the crowd inside the bar would elevate the temperature.

Shoddy knocked on my door as I was finishing a bottle of Sam Adams that I had cracked open post-shower. We flopped on the small beat up couch and watched the end of the basketball game. A few minutes into the second half we started playing a drinking game: drink every three-pointer the Friars scored. Five minutes later we hadn't taken a sip. We broadened the rules to include both teams.

When the time clock hit zero, the scoreboard wasn't the only thing buzzed. Shoddy insisted we finish a few more before meeting up with girls. Forty-five minutes, two beers and a shot of cheap tequila later, Shoddy and I were lubricated enough to begin the evening. We met Lindsey, Lily and Emily in front of their apartment building and began the trek to Primal.

We were late and they weren't happy about waiting.

"There's going to be a line now, thanks to you two," Emily said. "We told you to meet us like an hour ago."

She was right. There probably would be a line. But that really didn't bother Shoddy and I, neither of us really enjoyed Primal.

Neither of us liked to dance. I only wanted to go to be close to Lily. Shoddy only wanted to leer at freshmen girls.

"Are you just mad because the basketball team is a thousand miles away and you won't be able to sooth their woes after such a humiliating loss?" Shoddy jibed. One of his favorite pastimes was prodding her to breaking point. It didn't take much.

"Shut up, Marcus," Emily retorted, "that was one time with one basketball player."

"Must have been a lay up," Shoddy said. "Too bad tonight's game wasn't so easy."

"Fuck off," Emily snorted. The other girls laughed and so did I.

Shoddy faked a jumpshot and upon landing, smiled, winked and pointed at Emily.

"I could hit that all day, baby," he said. Even Emily smirked. I'll never understand why, but his crass, insulting and offensive behavior was endearing to those who knew him best. Perhaps it was because his lewd honesty was weirdly refreshing in our secluded college world, where everyone was trying to be somebody else.

The walk to Primal Bar that night took us down the streets with off-campus houses and then a half-mile walk through one of the worst inner-city sections of Providence. That's the nice way of saying to get to Primal, one had to brave the ghetto.

The college had recently, and publicly, deemed that area unsafe for students to walk in at night. It had gone so far as to say that any student who was caught drunk on campus and was found to have gotten that way at Primal, would be severely punished. It was an empty threat, and one the college could really never prove or uphold. But they thought it would deter students from going there, thus keeping them out of the ghetto and safe. The college was wrong. The mere taboo boosted Primal's weekend business and even timid freshmen began braving the trek.

Every Monday, rumors of muggings, theft and even rape spread across campus. A large percentage was more than just rumor. That year, on the first weekend back from Christmas break two freshmen were jumped and had their money taken by three shady characters in hooded sweatshirts. A week later a sophomore girl was reportedly grabbed and dragged into the cemetery that runs along the half-mile route. A waist high stone wall separates the graveyard from the sidewalk and she said the man was holding her down and groping her, all the while she heard groups of her classmates walking by on the other side of the wall. The report was that the groper ran away before anything else happened. Apparently a cop car speeding towards the college campus spooked him.

All of these incidents were reported in small snippets in the local section of the Providence Journal. Only homicides, political scandal or real estate development made their front page. The paper and the city had stopped giving too much ink and credence to these reports. They warned about that area. The police put up fliers every September warning students to walk in groups, never go out alone at night and stay in well-lit areas. They set up a satellite police station on the corner of the campus. What else were they to do?

We had a large group and therefore never had an inkling of danger on our walk to Primal. It was cool and I envied the girls who all had on black jackets. Granted, underneath were strips of cloth they called shirts but still, they had the appearance of being warm.

"See, I told you," gloated Emily.

A long line stretched out the door of Primal and wrapped almost to the side of the building. The bar was located on a corner, with its front door on a main street. To its left was a side street that ran into the center of the low-income housing section. The cemetery that ran along the main road stopped at the corner before Primal and stretched far back into the darkness, with this unlit road as its border. Primal's back lot was directly across from the cemetery along this side street. It was where they received beer deliveries and kept their dumpsters. It was also utilized as a urinal by many a drunk college student.

"Dammit, I hate lines," Shoddy said. We were standing at the corner of the cemetery deciding whether or not to get in line.

"It's cold, I don't want to wait," Lindsey said.

"Well then you'll have to walk back in the cold, so that doesn't make much sense," Emily said. "Let's just get in line. It won't take long."

"Lily, what do you want to do," Lindsey said. Apparently she never thought to ask Shoddy or I our opinion.

"Well, I don't care. Those shots you made us in the apartment are keeping me warm," she said. She smiled. I could tell she was buzzed already. "Shaw, do you want to stay?"

"Me? Well, Emily seems to want to go in so let's just wait in line," I said. Really I just wanted the chance to dance with Lily.

Our relationship was on an upturn since the dousing JRW deluge. It was slow to start. But eventually we bought each other Christmas presents. We spent New Years Eve together in Boston watching the fireworks extravaganza from our hotel window while the annual Boston Pops concert played in unison on the television. The year began anew, fresh with hope.

Lily apologized for antagonizing Duncan the night of JRW. She claimed she didn't remember much on account of the booze. We both knew she was lying but like a bandage it hid the wound long enough for a scab to form. Overall we lacked the same passion that burned during the summer. But I was confident we'd find the fire again. Perhaps a little dancing at Primal would provide a spark.

"Fine, let's get in line," Lindsey said. "If we're gonna wait in the cold it might as well be here."

Emily had a smug grin on her face.

While we were debating, Shoddy had already crossed the street and was offering the bouncer $20 to let us in. He thought because the bouncer lived on the same floor as he did, our group would get special treatment. We crossed over and stood a few feet away at the corner of Primal Bar and waited to see if Shoddy could work some magic.

Profanity began flying from the line. The bouncer was in a predicament. Shoddy was the provider of beer for the underclassmen on his floor, of which the bouncer was one. But the line was cold and each person in it was quickly losing the buzz they had put on prior to their walk. Mob-rule was very persuasive.

Shoddy tried again but the bouncer let a few people from the front of the line in instead of Shoddy. It wasn't going very well.

"C'mon, man, I bought you that keg last week for your rugby party, you owe me," he begged. "The next time you need a . . ." He stopped mid-sentence and turned back to us.

"Hey, forget it let's go, this isn't working."

"What! You had him; he was going to let you in!" Emily pleaded. Shoddy was already walking back to the group and waving his arms to usher us back across the street, away from Primal.

"What are you doing?" I asked. I stretched to see over his shoulder to see if the bouncer had gone inside or if the bar had switched to a less easily persuaded bouncer.

The bouncer was still there. He was beckoning for us to go back, like he was about to let us in. He looked confused.

I yelled back at Shoddy. "What the hell is your . . ."

Then my heart leapt into my throat. At the front of the line, looking at the ground and not a bit confused was Duncan. He had on a tight red sweater and even tighter designer jeans; his hair gelled up in a spiky attempt at fashion. With him was an attractive blonde girl, slender and taller than Duncan with a very familiar face. It was familiar because I had seen it up close and personal. Duncan had brought Rose, my ex-girlfriend, my high school sweetheart, my first love to the one place where she wasn't ever supposed to be.

I froze. It felt like I was standing in drying cement.

That relationship was over, we parted on bad terms. Duncan was a major cause of it. I always thought, though, that Rose and I would never have made it even if Duncan didn't spread rumors about Lindsey and me. Rose stayed home in Boston to go school. She lived at home. I moved south to Rhode Island. Our lives were too different. I was having too much fun and she was having none. It wouldn't have lasted. Duncan's lies just hastened the break-up.

The last time I had seen Rose was a few months before, over Christmas break. We bumped into each other at a coffee shop back home. We chatted over lattes for about an hour. She had forgiven me, told me she was wrong in assuming I cheated on her. She said she didn't want to leave our relationship with bad memories. I agreed. She told me she hated Duncan and she knew he was a liar. She had heard rumors about some of the things he did to me over the years at college and that nobody deserved treatment like that, especially from a former friend. She said he stabbed me in the back.

Now, standing with him a few months later on my home turf, Rose was twisting the knife.

Shoddy noticed me noticing Rose and nervously started pushing the girls across the street.

"Hey, Shaw, let's go, let's head back," he pleaded. He knew I knew. He could see my face growing redder.

The bouncer was still trying to get Shoddy's attention. Duncan looked up and caught my eye. He tried to get the bouncer's attention. Rose seemed oblivious to the entire situation, until she followed the bouncer's yells. She focused on Shoddy, then the group of girls, then on me.

With one cold, callous, slender finger, she tapped Duncan on the shoulder and pointed to me. It was an unnecessary action, he already knew I was there and he was trying to ignore it. She tapped him again and a smirk slowly spread across her faux-tanned face.

The switch was hit. She knew exactly how to flick it. I jumped out of the drying cement and pushed one of the girls out of the way, making my way to the door. The bouncer was still yelling to Shoddy.

Duncan started frantically tugging at the bouncer's shirt, begging to be let into the bar. He was paid no attention.

I was a bull solely focused on the red target. I dropped my head, pointed my horns and charged.

Shoddy the matador got in front of me.

"Hey, forget it, let's go. NOW!" He grabbed me by the shoulders.

I saw right through him, the only thing on my mind was grabbing Duncan and hurting him while Rose watched. I'd wipe the smirk of her face by putting my fist in his.

"Shaw, stop," Shoddy said, his voice rising.

He was going to start yelling any second. I kept charging. He wrapped his arms around my shoulders but I flailed like a fish on a line, trying to get free and jump at Duncan. Shoddy put some force into his restraint. He dug in his heels and pushed back.

Rage I usually tucked away, took over.

"Let me go Shoddy. Don't get in the fuckin' way, let me go."

"Are you nuts? That bouncer will end you. He's not gonna let you in there."

"Duncan's outside, I'll beat him outside. Bouncer can't touch me. Let me the fuck go!"

We were wrestling; I was fighting my best friend. I tried to shrug him off, tried to push him away but he was stronger than me and had me in a very effective bear hug. We were close to the front of the line. Duncan was still there, pressed up against the building, semi-hidden by the bouncer who was now very concerned about the enraged maniac running at his door.

Duncan took out his wallet and was trying to show the bouncer his ID. He waved it around, pleading desperately to be let in, like the last vagabond in the soup kitchen line.

I caught Duncan's eye and took one last lunge against Shoddy. The momentum hurdled us both at the bouncer, the door and the front of the line. The bouncer fell back into the door, which swung inwards, his bulky arm whacked my ex-girlfriend in the chest and she jumped back and slammed into Duncan, sending him reeling into the brick façade of the bar. He stumbled, his arms flailing but he kept his balance. Scantily clad coeds dove to the sidewalk, one after the other.

The domino effect gave Duncan an escape. He quickly grabbed Rose and pulled her into the bar through the accidentally opened door and then slammed it shut.

Shoddy and I were sprawled out on the sidewalk, my elbow lodged in his side and his knee crunched against my ribs. The bouncer was at the bottom of the dog pile. He was clearly not happy.

"Get the fuck off me!" he bellowed. Other people in line were following Duncan's lead and stepping over the bouncer to get into Primal.

"Hey, nobody gets in! Stay in line!" He had lost control because I lost control.

"Dude, get up, now," Shoddy said.

I was being pulled from behind and when I was on my feet I turned to see Lily and Lindsey wiping their hands on their pants. Emily was pulling up Shoddy.

My head was pounding and my ribs were sore. All I could think of was getting in the bar. But the bouncer had other plans. He was on all fours now, catching his breath.

"We're leaving," Shoddy said.

He grabbed me by the arm and dragged me across the street. I tried to resist but I knew he'd throw a punch if I tried to go back.

"Fuck 'em, Shaw. It's not worth it."

He was my best friend again, trying his damn hardest to make me feel better. I wanted to push him away and run back. The rage still bubbled.

"Come on, Hero," Lily said. "That's enough of that."

She came up from behind and brushed her hand across the nape of my neck and ran a finger down my arm.

A sudden shock to my system: a splash of cold water on a bonfire.

Her touch stopped me in mid-stride. I shivered and the rage shook away. The heat that had enveloped me evaporated, the testosterone steaming from my skin. Her one hand, a feathered touch, relaxed me like the hands of a thousand masseuses working my muscles in unison.

Lily turned to smile at me and then hurried up to the other girls who were walking ahead of us. Shoddy still had me by the arm but it was limp and his tight grip unnecessary.

Lindsey yelled back the executive decision the girls had made. We were going to an off-campus house party.

I came out of the trance and wrenched my arm from Shoddy's hand. I looked back at the bar. Shoddy tensed and reached out for me, afraid I'd make a run for it; afraid I still had some fight left in me.

"Nah, no need," I assured him and brushed away his hand. "I'm good. Seriously, I'm fine."

He wasn't convinced.

"You sure you're alright, man? What they did there, that wasn't cool at all. I can't imagine how you must feel."

Jealous was how I felt. Not so much jealous because Rose was out with another guy, but jealous because that guy was Duncan. She had obviously lied to me over Christmas break. She had obviously been talking to Duncan. She had obviously done this just to spite me. I was more jealous because now Rose had the upper hand; she was in control of our lost relationship. Duncan was a pawn and he didn't even know it.

I found out later that year that Rose had heard from Duncan about my blossoming relationship with Lily. She never met Lily but apparently jealousy worked both ways. She had contacted Duncan and made plans to visit Providence, hoping she would bump into me and create a situation exactly like the one that played out. I also discovered she left the bar soon after they went in and drove back to Boston. Duncan tried to make a move on her and Rose wanted nothing to do with him. Guilt emerged inside her during the scuffle and although she never apologized to me, she expressed her regret to a few mutual friends.

I never talked to Rose again. I never needed to. That flower wilted. I now had Lily and what we had was freshly in bloom.

By Lily's hand, Rose was plucked from my past, buried and gone. I left her and our relationship behind at Primal; probably sitting on a torn barstool while Duncan tried to cop a cheap feel.

Lily was walking ahead, waiting for me to follow.

As Shoddy and I stood there staring at the front of Primal, the bouncer regained control of his bar line. He brushed himself off, picked the gravel from his palms and reestablished his air of dominance and authority.

"Back the fuck up," he yelled at three girls who now occupied the front of the line.

Shoddy jokingly punched me in the shoulder.

"Hey, it's a good thing you're a pussy or else that bouncer probably would've ripped you apart," he said.

He put his hand on my shoulder and turned me around, guiding me in the direction of the girls who were now about a block ahead.

"Fuck it," he said, "let's go get drunk. There's plenty of night left."

Chapter 9

I think it was the Basketball Dance Team that hosted the house party. The team didn't budget enough money to make the trip to the national game so the obvious alternative, now that the season had ended, was to throw an all-out bash. Regardless of who hosted, nobody really knew or cared. The beer flowed and the liquor stupefied, the music intoxicated and the people sweated it all out from their pores.

The party that night was especially raucous due to the basketball team's season ending loss. Too many people in too tight a house usually meant trouble. Shoddy and I met some other friends while Lily headed off with Emily, Lindsey and some other girls to get whatever mixed drinks some undergrad was concocting in the back closet. The guys clinked their beers and tipped back a few, enjoying the scenery and exchanging guy comments.

Shoddy and I always enjoyed this kind of party scene. It wasn't just the beer and women but the chance to see college kids in action. The kind of kids that just got wasted every night and hadn't a care in the world except to spend their tuition on trying to score with some freshman girl with pigtails and loose morals. We watched as a classmate of ours slipped his hand into a girl's pocket and pulled her into an unoccupied bedroom. She willingly followed and that was the last anyone saw of them all night. They did nothing unusual: nothing funny but nothing that evil either.

It was getting to be about 1:00am when my head started to ache. I decided I had to get out of the house and into fresh air. I wanted to find Lily, take her home, strip her clothes off and enjoy her and her alone.

To that point the night was definitely not a normal one, mostly because of the fight outside Primal Bar a few hours earlier. But I seemed to be the only one dwelling on it. Everyone else moved on; the brawl was already myth. Lily would take my mind off it.

I left Shoddy in the midst of a drunken debate with some classmates. The topic was vaguely political, slightly literary or incredibly perverted. I couldn't decide exactly which. I knew Shoddy would look for me to support some cockamamie theory he created on the spot. He'd realize I was gone, take a shot of whatever liquid energy was fueling him and plow ahead with another absurd theory he would create in the moment. He didn't need me.

I stepped away from Shoddy and into the swarm. The party was alive, humming as if one entity, always searching for the sweet nectar hidden in the dozen kegs scattered around the house. The individual was indistinguishable. Arms and legs intertwined, the brightly colored clothing flowed like a field of wildflowers in a spring breeze. Voices collected into a steady, loud hum. Every few moments a stray would dart out and skirt the crowd's edges on the way to the stairway or the bathroom.

One of these strays led me around the impenetrable mass to a tucked away hive near the bathroom. I found Lily and the other girls in this back room buzzing around a makeshift bar, sipping from red plastic cups and bantering like college girls do.

"Hey!" they yelled in unison, seeing me from the doorway. "Come over here, we have got to show you something."

I wasn't going to disrespect a group of attractive college girls so I swaggered over there in a drunkenly jovial way only to be greeted by a cloud of alcohol hovering about them.

"My God how much have you been drinking? It stinks over here," I said. "How can you stand talking to each other?"

"We're fine," Lily said.

"I guess since you all have the same rank breath it doesn't matter." They didn't like that too much. Lily cut off my demeaning ramblings.

"So we feel really bad about what happened at Primal," she said. "They suck and don't deserve you anyway."

The group of girls nodded in unison.

"Close your eyes," Lily said. Before I did I could see myself in her glazed eyes. I knew better than to disobey a drunken Lily. I closed my eyes and felt multiple pairs of lips kiss my cheeks simultaneously. Only one set, the smoothest, moved slightly onto my lips and stayed a fraction longer than the others.

"Wow," I said, my eyes still closed. I would have done anything they told me to at that moment.

The drunken giggles began.

"OK, Hero, open your eyes. That's all you get," Lily said. She was standing directly in front of me. My knees buckled, unrelated to the alcohol. The urge to steal Lily away from the party boomed inside me.

"Oh no, wait, I have something for you," Lindsey said. She pushed in front of Lily, fumbling around in her small pink purse. She shuffled aside all the wondrous things college girls tote around with them when they go out. Finally she retrieved something and reached it out to me. I opened my hand and felt her press a small leathery object into my palm. Astonishment hit me, then wonder, then disgust as I realized whose wallet I was holding. I opened my eyes to see Duncan's high school senior picture staring up at me. Apparently when he couldn't find a mirror all he would have to do is open up the wallet and gaze at his ravenous good looks. I commented on that and was rewarded with a series of snide female comments about Duncan's lack of attractive qualities.

"Emily found it in front of Primal as we were leaving ahead of you and Shoddy," Lindsey said.

"Yeah, he didn't stick it all the way into his jeans after he showed the bouncer his ID. I saw it fall out before he went in, when that skank knocked into him. I thought you might want it," Emily said. "Isn't it funny? He's got a card with a naked woman on it from Las Vegas tucked inside one of the folds!"

All the girls but Lily laughed hysterically. She noticed my discomfort.

The wallet got hot in my palm. I couldn't stand it anymore.

"I have to leave," I swallowed as I said it. "And I'm giving this back to that asshole."

"Geez, fine be that way. But still, you can't leave, we aren't ready to go and we can't walk back alone," Emily complained.

"Go with Shoddy."

Laughter roared at that suggestion. I knew it was stupid the second I uttered it. By now Shoddy was either back in his room passed out or stumbling around this house looking for a place to pass out.

"Just stay for a little while, we were just about to go upstairs," Lindsey whined.

I hesitated. I had my fill of that night and the only destination I desired was my bed, full of Lily.

"Come upstairs with us. Just for a few minutes and then we can go, I promise," Lily said and gave me big hug. Even in her intoxication she was playing mediator.

"I know you want to," she whispered closer to my face. "I want you to."

I couldn't say no. After all, she was a goddess to me, the only girl in that entire house that I enjoyed being around. I would do anything for her and as much as I would resist, I actually wanted to go upstairs with them, with her. I finally relented and followed the girls, being pulled along by Lily, who carried a plastic cup full of booze in one hand and had her other hand entwined in mine. Her hand was cooler than the wallet, but still dry, warm and soft unlike the tacky hot leather.

As we left the back room, the cackling girls leading the way across the crowded first floor, I caught sight of Duncan leaning by the front door. I knew it was Duncan because he still had on that goofy tight red designer sweater. Lily tried to pull me faster but I restrained.

"Let it go, Shaw!" she begged.

"No," I said, the temperature rising in my face.

I diverted our path away from the other girls and towards Duncan, who seemingly noticed my presence and turned to face me. He was standing on the landing, about to leave. He was a full step higher than me, but no more intimidating.

"Hey, fuckface," I yelled, needlessly. He scowled. He was alone. "Here you go."

I flicked the wallet at him. It bounced off his chest and fell to the floor, his high school picture slipping loose in the process.

"Next time," I said, "maybe you shouldn't wear your little sister's jeans."

He grimaced, rubbed his hands together, adjusted his tight jeans, pushed up the sleeve on his skinny right bicep and reached out to Lily, leaning on her shoulder. She buckled slightly. Her drink sloshed a bit. I thought I noticed some of it drip onto his shoes and chuckled to myself.

Duncan used her to balance himself and as he bent to pick up his wallet off the linoleum, he flipped me the middle finger. He was a breath away from Lily's body. Chills ran down my spine at the thought of his close proximity to her. I tried to get around her, visions of another brawl—one on one—scrolling behind my eyes. But Lily blocked my route to him.

Instead I watched him slither to his knees to retrieve his property. Even with the party noise I heard a suction noise when he pulled the wallet off the floor, sticky with a semesters-worth of foot traffic and spilt beer. The overturned photo didn't come up so easily. Duncan had to dredge his fingernails through the grime to flip up one corner and slide it into his palm.

Duncan stood upright, using Lily's shoulder to pull himself up. He turned towards her so that they were face to face; the hand holding his wallet was pressed against her cup, the only things preventing their chests from touching. His fingers seemed to be fumbling. I couldn't see Lily's eyes, but I knew the malice in them matched my own.

In this position he half-hugged her, an awkward and sinister embrace. He stumbled and I noticed him cling to her so as not to fall, and in the process a few of his fingers slid into her cup.

A shiver ran up my spine and I didn't know why. Something wasn't right but I couldn't put my finger on it. In an instant the feeling evaporated.

"Gross," she said, and pushed him away. Her drink sloshed again, this time dripping on him so obviously he had to notice.

Duncan stepped back. He wiped off the wallet on his pants and nonchalantly put it in his pocket. In his other pocket he shoved some crumpled trash, which I hadn't noticed in his hand before. His hands free and an eerie grin slithering across his face, Duncan opened his palm and touched it to his lips. He blew a kiss to Lily.

"You have yourself a great night, honey. Stop by my room later on if this loser can't take care of you—I *know* you'll be looking for it."

"With your tiny dick, I'd need a magnifying glass to help me look for it!" Lily yelled back at him.

She took a big gulp from her plastic cup and steadied herself.

"Fuck you!" she screeched.

Time, the noise, the party all seemed to stop in deference to the significance pulsing through the two words. Even Duncan was taken aback, albeit briefly. I had a feeling he was about to retaliate. I tried to launch myself at him but Lily intercepted me.

She yanked my arm and said, "Come on! Forget him. He's not worth it."

She turned from Duncan, whose grin had reappeared. Lily pushed the opposite way with her glazed eyes blazing, and dragged me away with astonishing force.

"What are you doing? He tried to molest you." I said, itching for a chance to return and start a brawl.

"Stop it, Shaw," she said. "Enough fighting for one night. He's leaving anyway. See? He doesn't want to be here with you. You gave him his wallet back. You did something nice. He wouldn't have done that for you. So maybe instead of wanting to kill him you should pity the bastard for being consumed with hatred. He walks around looking for ways to make your life suck instead of ways to make his life better. That's a horrible way to live."

She hiccupped.

We were far enough away from Duncan that going back to fight was no longer an option.

"Ya know, Shaw, my grandmother had a saying," Lily said. She hiccupped every second word. "When I was a little there was this girl who lived next door. She was a few years older than me and she bullied me around every chance she got. She stole my pink Barbie bicycle, broke my favorite dolls, even threw dirt at me."

She swallowed hard as if trying to keep something down inside her.

"I came home one day and my grandmother was there. I screamed 'I hate her!' about the girl next door. You know what she said to me, Shaw? She said Lily, hatred is like drinking a poison and hoping the other person is going to die from it."

More hiccups.

"So you're saying I'm going to die?"

"What? No, Duncan is poisoning himself, Shaw. He hates you for some reason and it consumes him. I don't want you suffering the same fate."

Lily always got philosophical when she was drunk. I didn't think she was that intoxicated but if she was at that level of inebriation, I figured I should be there with her.

"I need a drink," I said.

We diverted again toward a corner where there was a keg and an underclassman mixing up shots from some concoction of unknown liquors. I immediately pumped and chugged a cup of warm beer and grabbed two shots from the underclassman. I gave one to Lily. She hesitated and her body swayed slightly.

"I'm good, Shaw," she said. I saw her eyes drooping. Lily falling asleep did not jive with my desires for how the rest of the evening should play out. I knew she was being coy. She was going to keep drinking with or without me.

"You're going to make me do this alone?" I pleaded.

"Alone? Are you calling me out, Augustine?" she garbled.

She slugged the booze in the plastic cup that hadn't spilled on Duncan. She then ripped the new smaller cup from my hand, tossing the hard liquor shot into her mouth without flinching. She let the shot glass fall to the floor, grabbed the back of my neck and pulled me into a kiss. She hadn't swallowed the shot, letting the liquid slip between our mouths; our tongues skipping and splashing like children in puddles, happy and free. As we kissed she let the alcohol finally slide down her throat. When it did, she pulled back a fraction and opened her eyes. She grabbed my upper lip with both of hers and we stared at each other before she pulled away completely.

She took a long drink from a new plastic cup, kissed me on the cheek and said, "I took my shot, now you take yours." I tried to gather my jaw from the floor and in doing so spilled some of my beer.

We both laughed and I threw back my shot. I tapped the underside of her plastic cup, gesturing for her to finish whatever was left. She did. We each filled up another new cup of warm beer, slugged them down in a half-hearted race, then filled them up and chugged again. The whole party scene became a dream.

I filled up our cups once more and we climbed the creaky winding stairs to the second floor where even more people were packed into one room jumping around and yelling. The other girls were impossible to find in the sea of students. Lily took a few more swigs of her drink and with that same astonishing force, moved me up against a wall.

Lily pressed hard against me and grinded to the music. The two brief run-ins with Duncan that evening melted away with every swirl of her hips.

After the night I was having this was a welcome change. Her reciprocated affection rejuvenated me, and I actually started to enjoy myself. Triumph returned as I gazed into her glassy eyes and saw my own reflection. In that packed room we were alone moving sensually to the baseline. Her red hair was sweaty but it gave it a glossy shimmer. I could feel the moist skin on her back and my body shivered when she slid her hands down my back and into the pockets. Her head now resting on my shoulder brought her lips closer and closer to my cheek. She started kissing my neck and whispering interchangeably but I couldn't understand what she said and I didn't care. To me, it was the most beautiful sound I had ever heard. Her lips moved up my neck and cheek and she started to whisper something more audible.

"I . . . I . . ." she spoke weakly with me straining to hear, "I . . . I lo . . ."

She paused, pulled her head back and looked in my eyes. My heart was tickling the back of my teeth when finally she said, "I . . . *gulp* . . . need water," and stumbled back to the wall. I caught her before she fell.

Chapter 10

Lily clung to me like a scared child to her parent.

I gave her what was left of a water bottle I had; she downed it and stretched out her hand for more. She regressed in age before my eyes, reaching out her delicate little hands, opening and closing them, grasping nothing but air and futility. She required nurturing and protection from this hasty vulnerability.

If I had learned any first aid in my few collegiate years it was the miracle of water. Alcohol dehydrated. Water revitalized.

"I'll be right back," I said to her. "I'm going to go fill up the bottle. Lean against the wall and I'll be right back for you." She nodded and her eyes widened in acknowledgment. I could see the beautiful glimmer in them from behind a pane of alcohol.

It took me a few minutes to get to bathroom. The swarm from downstairs had multiplied and migrated to the second floor.

A guy I went to high school with was in line outside the bathroom door. He wanted to chat about our four years of Catholic all boys Prep school. He started the usual complaints about how we went through puberty without girls.

"But we really did love that place, right bro," he said.

I nodded but I barely heard him. I wasn't paying attention. My mind was focused on the present, on Lily slouching across the room. The situation didn't feel right.

I constantly checked on her, looking back over my shoulder even as the line progressed. I eventually got myself close to the bathroom door.

Then Lily swayed. The plastic cup in her hand swayed with her in unison. She put it to her lips and, after draining it of its contents, let it fall to the ground from her wilted fingers. I noticed a few guys around her that I did not know laughing and prodding at her, Lily too drunk to notice or too oblivious to care. For a split second I thought I saw the same red designer sweater Duncan was wearing earlier that night moving in the midst of the group and then skitter out the doorway down the stairs.

I thought he had left a long time ago.

The bathroom line moved and I checked my status: next in line.

Letting my eyes lose focus on Lily was my first mistake.

As soon as I turned my head back in her direction I saw it happen. It looked like the guy in the black coat next to her had taken a scythe to her legs and sent her tumbling to the ground like a sheared crop. I dropped my beer and the empty water bottle and plowed through the mass of people. My shoulder lowered and my legs churned, driving a wedge into the swarm.

"Hey man, where you going? Aren't you gonna piss?" the kid from high school yelled. The words evaporated into the swarm's buzzing and then lingered as my world turned slow motion.

Lily's body corkscrewed downward and I, halfway across the crowded room, lunged with my hands outstretched, hoping to reach something, anything, in time. How I got to Lily before her head hit the ground, I don't know. The people around her scattered and my hand hit the floor a fraction before her head. My body was sprawled across the floor, laid out at full extension, arms outstretched with skyward palms, my face pressed into the foul, muddy floor. But I had a handful of red hair. Lily had literally crumbled in the blink of my eye; one moment she was leaning, sipping and the next she was falling to the beer soaked hardwood floor without a clue.

In an instant a tall, flowing stalk of wheat was harvested right in front of me. My only reaction was not to let it get dirty. My senses were numb. I tried to speak but nothing came out. I shifted to my knees, propped up her head and stared into her eyes. I couldn't look away from them. It was like staring at an emerald hillside far away in some remote Irish county. Some place that her grandparents raised sheep. Some place where a family sat around a fire and belted out folk songs in perfect tune to dancers. She embodied my fairy tale, my fantasy, and my perfect love story.

Her eyelids drooped; were falling slowly. The green alcohol-stained windows, through which I looked into fantasy, closed their blinds. That hillside song waned and the dancers fell one by one. The slivers of green that were still visible were transfixed on the ceiling.

Two things hit me simultaneously: someone's hand and reality. Lily's clouding perfection wore off as I twisted around to see a group of people looming over us. The kid from high school jabbed my shoulder asking, "what's wrong" repeatedly.

I ignored him. In one single, smooth motion I scooped Lily's whole body and lifted her vertical.

Lindsey appeared from some unseen corner of the room. She propped up Lily's other shoulder.

We carried her through the murmuring crowd of people, frantically searching for the staircase. The other partygoers barely noticed. The ones that did pointed and giggled. One or two looked legitimately concerned but still offered no assistance. The only logical choice was to get her outside, the only place to bring a natural beauty of Lily's caliber. My mind raced away from fantasyland and my legs raced even faster down the stairs, out the back door and into the street.

Emily emerged from the house followed by a few other girls. The other ones screamed at Lindsey and me about how they didn't want to leave. Emily opened her mouth to bellow something but no words emerged. She closed her lips, a vacant stare watching as Lindsey and I dragged our friend across moist crabgrass, over the curbing and into the black street.

"What should I do?" Emily finally yelled.

"Go find Shoddy," I tossed out without looking back at her. "He'll walk you home."

"No, not for me. For Lily. What should we do for her?"

I had no time for her intrusions and just yelled the first thing that came to my mind.

"Pray."

Lindsey stumbled and paused. She shot me a horrified look from over the head of her slouching friend, my fading lover.

"What the hell was that, Shaw?"

"Just walk, Linds," I struggled to talk and keep our balance. I was taking on the majority of Lily's 108-pound frame, as well as the added awkward momentum Lindsey caused.

I looked straight ahead down the road and breathed in to calm my quaking heart.

"Everything will be fine, Linds," I said. "I've done this before."

"Done what, dragged her home blacked out?"

"No, saved Lily. Don't worry, I can do it again."

Chapter 11

I remember a lot of things from that walk, but I remember the darkness the most. It was intolerably dark out. The moon provided some light but no comfort. It really just illuminated the grays and blacks permeating the entire street.

Large weeping tree branches overhung in a dreary canopy. Snarled, twisted limbs intertwined up towards Heaven, reaching like a beggar's fingers searching for alms. The branches that stretched outwards over the road formed a fractured awning that let the slivers of moonlight through in random shards. The broken moonlight crossed and danced on the asphalt as we stepped down and up, down and up on top of it. Thorns wreathed round the trunks and several trees had branches that pierced through one another in a mad, chaotic attempt at order. The chain fence that ran along one side of the street had been engulfed by many of the hideous trees. They grew and enveloped the rusted links, merging nature and metal.

And everything was helplessly fighting off the shadow—it cloaked everything along the street. I saw no color, only various shades of black and gray. The mailbox, the fire hydrant and the street signs all sat silent like tombstones with epitaphs of "stop" or "local mail."

Lily, hanging off Lindsey and me like an old coat, moaned inaudible phrases. We basically pulled her down the street like dogs with an empty sled. The night uttered nothing as we shuffled off the road, up onto the sidewalk in the direction of the main campus.

As we meandered away, the house party seemed far off in time and place. Before we got to the end of the street I looked back at the house, wanting to be sure it truly existed. The blackness of the street hurt my eyes, but the burning sensation they got when they focused on the house was unbearable. A distant, hazy and artificial glow of fluorescent bulbs and burning cigarettes contrasted the house against the pitch-black street. Imagine the Devil's dream house. It probably looks similar to where we just were.

I turned away, disgusted at my peers and myself.

Lindsey and I took a left onto Eaton Street with Lily in tow and caught sight of campus proper. Had we taken a right, walked a half-mile and taken another right, we would have been on the street that led to Primal. We definitely didn't want to go that way. That night, Primal was the beginning not the end.

We crossed Eaton Street and walked next to the varsity soccer field, stopping every few yards so Lindsey could catch her breath and I could make sure Lily was still breathing. I had seen overly drunk people before. I was a junior in college; I had been one of those overly drunk people on numerous occasions. But until that point, I had never seen someone that drunk. She wasn't just drunk she was intoxicated. Her system was poisoned. Lily wasn't right.

Eaton Street was a slightly inclined road and a short stonewall formed a boundary between the fenced in soccer field and the sidewalk. Lindsey leaned against it, resting Lily's hip on her knee.

"Ya know, for a stick figure this girl weighs a ton," she complained.

"Doesn't help that you're wasted," I snapped.

I shouldn't have. It wasn't Lindsey's fault. But she was the only coherent one in our traveling trio and I needed to vent.

"Fine, let's go."

She shifted to push Lily's limp body from off her lap when an acrid smell hit my nostrils. Lindsey's face melted and she started spitting out locker-room profanity.

"Are you kidding me?" She pushed Lily up into my arms and stared at the wet stain on her lap. "She fucking peed on me!"

Lily's eyes were closed and I knew she had no control over her motor functions. Lindsey was lucky it was only urine.

"I'm gonna kill her tomorrow. These are new jeans!"

"Relax, Linds. I doubt she did it on purpose."

I remember wanting to laugh but when I looked at Lily in my arms, with no ability to hold herself up, the humor of the situation disappeared. Lindsey eventually recognized it too. Her snarled lips softened with sympathy. She got up, grabbed a shoulder and we traipsed up Eaton, turned right onto Huxley Avenue and moved towards the beacon that was Lily's ten-story dorm building rising up from the center of campus.

Until September of our junior year, when the school completed construction on a new chapel, Lily's dorm building, McVinney Hall was the highest point in the entire state of Rhode Island. The new chapel's apex, a golden cross, allowed the house of worship to steal that title. That night Lily's dorm building, a utilitarian concrete behemoth full of double bed dorm rooms, underage drinking and parietal-breaking freshmen, would be our lighthouse and our guide, not the chapel.

As we approached the main gate of upper campus I decided to cross the main road, avoid that main entrance and take Lily up one of the less-well lit pathways. Besides the danger of the security guard at the main gate, I wanted to avoid the group of three guys sitting on the wall ten yards away. They all wore hooded sweatshirts, their faces shrouded. The monkish anonymity added to the already palpable aura of danger they radiated. It was easily distinguished even from our distance.

All the orientation seminars and security department notices did nothing to prepare a freshman for the long walk down the dark road past the housing projects and the cemetery, to reach the college bars. Every weekend the hyenas emerged from their dens and stalked the local watering holes, crouching in wait for a wounded adolescent to fall away from the group, ready to be snatched up and devoured. Undergraduates learned very quickly what characteristics separated the generally naïve and thirsty students from the local thugs preying on them. Being juniors, Lindsey and I had run that gauntlet for years. Instinct improved with experience.

"C'mon, let's take her up near DiTraglia Hall and around the chapel, I don't like the look of those kids up there."

"Seriously Shaw, grow up," she said. "They're probably just stoners. If we go that way we have more stairs to climb. And she's getting heavy."

Apparently Lindsey's instinct wasn't as sharp as mine.

"Then let's go that way so security doesn't see us and call it in," I said, keeping the group of thugs in my peripherals.

"Alright fine, I guess it's a good idea," Lindsey said. "You know they'd just love to transport her to the hospital."

Together we heaved Lily off one sidewalk and across the street to the other. Our awkwardly stealth maneuver may have eluded the security guard hut but the group of thugs noticed.

"Hey! Not bad, man, one passed out and one on the way," one of them cackled. "Can someone say threesome?"

"Haha, nah he's probably too wasted for his shit to work. Maybe I'll have to pinch hit for him," hissed the tallest one. A discernable hooked nose protruded from the hood's shadow. They started to cross the street towards us.

"I love drunk girls," the other one said, "And I really love passed out girls."

"She can't say no if she can't talk," the tall one snickered.

"Just ignore these assholes," Lindsey said. She was clearly losing patience with the entire night.

"Linds, if these guys come over here, run over to security," I whispered.

"Oh please, PC guys don't have the balls to fuck with me right now."

"I don't think they're PC guys, Linds, they look like . . ."

A quick siren burst and green lights interrupted my observation. One of the security SUVs pulled up in front of the guys before they could cross the street.

"Show me your IDs, gentlemen," said a portly security guard from the comfort of the car. The guard saw us but decided it was more important to first flex his muscles instead of offer us a ride. I wasn't going to complain; just avoiding serious trouble with authorities would be a positive in a night of negatives. Lindsey and I took the opportunity to pull Lily off the sidewalk, along a pathway with two sets of stone steps, around a corner. By the time the new chapel loomed in front of us, we were out of sight.

Dragging Lily's body through the chapel courtyard was slow going. Lindsey and I were both exhausted. Ooze pulsed in the newly formed blister on my right heel. Luckily, we knew the security guards rarely patrolled this area this time of night. The welcomed feeling of safety slowed our pace and we stopped every few steps to readjust our grip on Lily and catch our breath. I used the relief to indulge in our surroundings. I immediately noticed the intricate detail inlayed into the chapel's edifice and its religious accoutrements. The brick walkway that wrapped around the building converged in a large, circular patio, on which we were standing.

The large reddish oak doors were usually open in the daytime, causing the smells and sounds of an empty place of worship to sneak out onto students passing between classes. The smell that wafted out was flowery, sweet and smoky. The aromatic flavors mixed with a faint, musical sound of tinkling metal and sloshing liquid. Whenever I smelled and heard the chapel during the day I always thought of Alice at the Mad Hatter's tea party. I don't know why, but something about those sounds added to those smells was pleasurably inane. On the off chance I entered the chapel, I half expected (and half hoped) to see the head chaplain sitting around the altar surrounded by animals drinking tea. Maybe I just liked the idea of a world where party hosts spoke in roundabout riddles and wore senselessly large hats; where naïve young people stumbled onto something they could never truly understand, and left better for it.

But that night there was definitely no tea party in the chapel. The doors were shut. The smells were trapped inside. The lights inside were dimmed to almost nothing.

Above the doors on the façade was an upside down triangle, Latin writing etched around the outline. In the middle of the triangle was a single torch and a banner with the word, "veritas" scrawled across. It was the college's symbol, a torch to light the way to knowledge. One small spotlight shined from the ground onto the school emblem. Other bigger spotlights planted at the edges of the patio beamed up to illuminate the golden cross that watched over campus and the state of Rhode Island.

Around the rim of the patio was a low wall of artistic stonework punctuated by six stone pillars. Atop each pillar sat the only other source of light in the courtyard: familiar stone angels, each holding a torch mimicking the one on the school crest, save the 100-watt light bulb that cast an eerie blue glow over each angel's androgynous face.

Whenever I passed that chapel at night, tragedy was on the wind. Those stone angels only herald dread.

Chapter 12

Lily was completely passed out as Lindsey and I pulled her through the chapel courtyard, past the indefatigable stone angels, down a bush-lined pathway and onto the Quad.

"Her room or your room?" Lindsey asked, taking a deep breath. She used to be an athlete, but it was a long walk to be carrying dead weight. I was out of breath too.

"I don't know, I thought her room. I was heading in that direction."

I stared up at the concrete tower breaching up above the rest of campus, save the golden cross. Most of the lights were out. The building didn't look as inviting from closer up. I changed my mind.

"On second thought," I said, "We should probably go to my room. No security guard at my building. There are a few at Lily's."

Lindsey and I both knew the first authority figure to see Lily's state would immediately call an ambulance. That should have tipped me off, but as was usually the case with Lily, my emotions clouded my judgment. I wanted to keep her safe; I wanted to fix her myself. I was her hero, no one else.

We diverged, went across the grass on the Quad and through the side door of my building. No one else was around so we waltzed in undisturbed. The most cumbersome part of the trip was getting her up the stairs. Lily was no help whatsoever and by now Lindsey's strength had given out.

Instead of stairs we chose the rickety elevator that students barely used. We didn't have to wait.

Our motley crew fell into the elevator, and Lindsey hit the button for my floor with her elbow. I leaned back against the metal wall and propped Lily up on my knee. The doors closed and we swayed upwards.

Lily's head bounced around too much. The color, or what was left of color, in her face drained completely. Her light pink freckles dissolved. Her jaw drooped.

Her dinner cascaded out onto the tiled elevator floor and splashed onto Lindsey's ankles.

Odysseus' wax wouldn't have been enough to muffle Lindsey's scream. Lily's full weight collapsed on my knee as Lindsey dropped the piece of Lily she was holding and scampered to the opposite elevator wall.

I had to laugh; there was no other response, what with the dire straights of Lily's health. She might not be conscious, but she still knew how to make me laugh.

Lindsey grunted and huffed at her apparel's misfortune.

Our elevator stopped abruptly, the doors opened and I heaved Lily across the rug to my door. Lindsey refused to help and followed behind.

"What in God's name is that?" she said, as I reached my door.

"Huh?" I pushed Lily against the door and leant my body against her to prevent sliding.

Lindsey pointed at the floor and I followed her finger back to the elevator.

"That black stuff on the floor. Did that come out of her?"

Initially hadn't looked at what Lily vomited in the elevator; I just assumed it was whatever she ate earlier mixed with a lot of booze and stomach fluids. I was wrong. A lumpy puddle of blackish-brown bile pooled on the elevator floor was spread in streaks across the rug where Lily's feet dragged through the puddle and across to my door.

Lindsey didn't realize what was on her shoes and neither did I. I didn't know what kind of bile came out of Lily, but I knew it was not normal.

Lily's head lolled over and her eyes opened. They were limes now, not emeralds. She seemed to be staring straight into me. I wiped some black drool from the corner of her mouth and she smacked her lips. She tried to say something, mumbling only syllables.

"Shaw, that's not normal," Lindsey said. I barely heard her. I was fixed on Lily's face. She was uttering nonsense but the color gradually left her eyes. The limes were graying. I pulled my sleeve over my hand and wiped her entire face, licking the cloth to wet it. I tried to clean her off. With each pass it was like I wiped her with grayscale. She grew more ashen than before. I was doing no good. I was not helping. I was not saving her.

"Call an ambulance," I yelled at Lindsey.

"What?"

"Call an ambulance," I repeated as I lowered Lily to the ground and flung open my door. "Go in and call someone, now!"

"What? No, why? She's fine."

"Lindsey, what did I just say? Call the ambulance, call security, call an RA, I don't care. Just get someone!"

Lindsey wasn't as worried as I was. But Lindsey didn't watch the life drift out of Lily. Lindsey took a few steps toward my door and stopped.

"But she'll get in trouble," she said.

I flipped Lily over onto her side. She lay in the middle of the hallway and I knelt beside her, my hands cradling her still soft hair. But the red had faded and clumped in places were hunks of black bile and floor grime. Her face was smeared with the same sludge and debris from the house party floor, my dorm room floor and the generally disorganized walk. She was a tainted icon, a tarnished statue, perfection smeared.

"You really think getting in trouble matters right now, Lindsey?" I said angrily.

"I'm not going to call security and have them write up my best friend for nothing and get her in trouble. She could lose her scholarship or her student government position or something."

"*We* are going to lose *her*! I can't save her!"

My hands trembled underneath Lily's head. The horror of the situation revealed itself to Lindsey all at once. She leapt over us, Lily on her side across the threshold of my doorway and me, shaking and rocking back and forth on my knees.

Lindsey was in my room calling Security and the EMTs.

"I couldn't save you," I whispered uncontrollably to Lily. "I tried to but I couldn't save you. I tried, Lily, I tried. I can't save you. I just don't know how."

A security guard, the same one from earlier in the SUV, showed up within five minutes escorting an EMT.

They knew as soon as they saw her. I could tell by the way they quickened their pace and stopped chatting airily about some ballgame.

Immediately the first EMT radioed out to the awaiting ambulance. Within a minute a second EMT and a second security guard wheeled a stretcher out of the elevator onto my floor.

"Is that from her?" the second EMT asked as he pushed the stretcher through a puddle of black bile. I nodded. The EMTs nodded to each other.

"Come on, son, stand over here with me," the second, older security guard said. I was still cradling Lily's head and the EMTs obviously needed me out of the way. "She'll be fine, son, come over here."

I looked down into her eyes for the last time. There was a momentary flash of green flame before the lids closed. Something inside me slammed shut as well. I ran my fingers through her hair and gently lowered her head to the floor.

The EMTs were asking questions but I could barely hear them. Lindsey came out from my room and gently pushed me to the side. She willingly took the brunt of the interrogation.

They took Lily down in the elevator. I couldn't fit so I walked down the stairs like a zombie. By the time I got outside the second EMT was slamming the ambulance door shut and ran to hop into the driver's seat. I stood in the doorway alone and watched the boxy white ambulance pull off the grass and into the Quad's roundabout then down the driveway to the campus exit. The ambulance's exhaust smoke lingered and wisped around in the brisk March air, visibly and playfully rising into the night sky like a wild specter searching for its final rest.

Lily died in the hospital that night during the stomach pump. We didn't find out until the next morning when the old security guard called my room. The phone call woke Lindsey up. I had been awake for some time. She and I had both fallen asleep almost immediately after the EMTs screeched away. We lay close together atop my comforter, still in the same soiled clothes we wore the night before.

Doctor's blamed alcohol poisoning; she had way too much. Her blood alcohol content was over 0.20. But there was something else, the distinct possibility of foreign substances in her system. Someone probably put something in one or maybe more of her drinks: a date rape drug or some bad ecstasy or something else. There were no details, other than whatever it was, it was bad and a virgin user like Lily would have almost inevitably had an adverse reaction. They would have to do tests to find out exactly what illicit substance it was that counteracted the incredible amount of booze she drank.

But at the one-year anniversary of Lily's death, none of us on campus had ever heard of any test results, or been told the truth.

As much as I had tried to be like the stoic, stone angels encircling the campus chapel, for Lily I had succeeded in becoming nothing more than an angel of death.

Chapter 13

It rained the morning of Lily's funeral, but only while people filed into the church. The girls cried. I even saw Shoddy wipe something out of his eye during the eulogy, given by Lily's father. Shoddy kept putting his hand on my shoulder asking if I was doing ok. I never responded to him and, overall, I said very little that day. I didn't feel like talking.

By the time we reached the cemetery, the rain cleared and it became a crisp, slightly overcast March day.

I placed twelve white lilies on her grave. Shoddy, Lindsey, Emily and two busloads of students, teachers and faculty had gone to Connecticut for the ceremony.

Lily's parents introduced themselves to me and thanked Lindsey and I for our efforts to help. Lily must have talked about me at home because her mother hugged me and did not let go, like I was family.

We drove back to Providence in a silence.

One month after she died, and every thirteenth day of every month thereafter, I drove to Lyme, Connecticut to Riverside Hill Cemetery. I always went alone. I never spoke. I never cried. Eleven times I stood in front of her, placed a bouquet of white lilies on top of the gravestone and did nothing. My mind was usually empty. My breaths were even. After five, ten or thirty minutes—I never kept track—I would get back in my Explorer and drive back to Providence.

I always listened to the same CD on the ride back, the Refreshments CD Lily and I bought at the mall. But I barely ever heard the music.

For the year after Lily's death a menacing blade of guilt swung over my head, its rope fraying by the day. I hemorrhaged any emotions she had cultivated in me.

My friends bore the brunt of it, mostly Lindsey. What she wanted, what she deserved I could no longer give her. I pretended, but any love I had to give went the way of Lily's last breaths, intermingling with the ambulance muffler's exhaust rising into the cool March night.

Everything went behind the wall in my head, which had been braced and solidified. I learned to feign things like fun, excitement and desire. Internally I was numb: numb from the pain, numb from the guilt. I urged Lily to drink more that night. I made the choice to carry her across campus. I could have called an ambulance right there at the house party. But I was selfish. I wanted to save her. I tried to be in control when all the circumstances were spiraling wildly the other direction.

Was there something in her drink, roofies or something more sinister? Maybe. Probably. But I was the one who challenged her to consume more booze. It was my responsibility to keep watch, to prevent such evils from intruding upon my friends.

I was mostly numb inside from knowing that someday the guilt would overcome me. When it did, there would be a shockwave. There would be consequences.

Chapter 14

I had been told my whole life, in various formats and from various optimists, about true love. From Hallmark to HBO, my parents to rock and roll, my brain was inundated with that age-old idea that a soul mate was lurking out there in the world just waiting to be serendipitously bumped into on a subway.

The problem is, when it happens, how do we know we got it right? Or that we didn't?

We tend to rely on two interdependent things: instinct and feedback. The former comes from us; the latter is frequently in the form of our closest friend. In my young life I found that unless both of those things match up, you could put ten bucks on things not working out. Sometimes we use our own thoughts to justify the opinions of our friend. But sometimes the two come together independent of one another. Thus begging the question, which person is really your soul mate?

When Marcus Shodowski arrived on campus after transferring from a university in New Hampshire, everyone called him by his full last name. He showed up right out of a Nirvana music video. His longish blonde hair fell over his face. He had an extensive collection of old t-shirts that he frequently wore underneath button-downs and not tucked into faded jeans. At 5 foot 11 inches he was slightly taller than I was as a freshman. He wasn't much of a gym guy but he was in good shape—Shoddy liked to workout in his room, following a routine of pushups and sit-ups his older brother created. Despite that he had a genetically round face and a slightly crooked Polish nose.

When he arrived that first year Shoddy was technically a sophomore. But many of his credits wouldn't transfer, basically making him a freshman all over again. Had he stayed up north he would have graduated a year before I did. His move south allowed him to essentially spend an extra year in college and he would be graduating with my class. He started the year living in our freshman-only dorm building, a few rooms away from me and my two freshman year roommates, Ben and Duncan. Shoddy moved into my room about midway through that year when he and Duncan switched places.

I was in my room alone studying one Friday night in October of freshman year when Lindsey showed up and called me a dork. She had with her seven cans of Milwaukee's Best, Twister and her roommate, Emily. I tossed my Intro to Psychology book up into the elevated bed above my desk and dug out the half empty bottle of Bacardi Limon my older cousin gave me as a going-to-college present.

Seven Milwaukee's Best and three shots of rum later I was spinning while two drunken girls reached for left foot green. Not a bad Friday night, considering it started off prepping for a Psych midterm.

I remember yelling, "Right hand red!" just as my mostly-closed dorm room door swung open and crashed off the yellowing concrete wall.

Shoddy stumbled in and spilled onto the couch.

"Dude," he said very close to my face, "I called you earlier to go out."

He had called me earlier. I never answered.

Prior to that call, my experience with Shoddy was limited to Psychology class. In the first two months of school we never spent time together elsewhere, despite our close living proximity. In class, though, Shoddy and I were a tag-team.

Our psychology professor was fond of the pop-quiz method. Shoddy frequently questioned his motives. On one such occasion, when the professor surprised us with a quiz, Shoddy leaned over to me, leaving plenty of space for his words to easily escape privacy. He loudly expressed his theory on the teacher's sadistic love for student failure. A nervous chuckle rustled through the classroom, eliciting a smirk from the teacher. The professor had a student pass out the quizzes but personally delivered one to Shoddy.

"We're going to discuss altruism," our professor said at the outset of class the next day. "It's part of a small section in the next chapter, which we weren't scheduled to start until next week. It's a bit ahead of where we are supposed to be. But since Mr. Shodowski insisted upon questioning my motives, I think we can take a few moments to delve into psychological theory. What do you think?" Even though his gaze rested on the class as a whole, his words snaked directly towards Shoddy.

"Now, Mr. Shodowski," he continued, not waiting for a response. "Yesterday you mumbled under your breath that I enjoyed seeing you all suffer at the hands of my little pop-quiz. I would argue that I actually did it for quite opposite reasons. I administered such a task out of the goodness of my heart and only want the best for all you. In fact, it creates more work for me, so it was a totally selfless act. It was altruism."

Shoddy and I were the only ones who chuckled. I decided to defend him.

"There is no altruism, professor," I said without raising my hand. A girl across the room asked the professor to explain altruism. Again, Shoddy and I were the only two who chuckled.

"Let's say I'm walking by a rushing rapid river one stormy afternoon and I spot someone splashing around and calling for help in the water. I feel like I should do something so I dive in, despite the incredible danger to my own wellbeing and save the drowning person. Some might say that was an altruistic act, a totally unselfish action," he explained.

"Others," he nodded in my direction, "would disagree that anyone can ever be truly altruistic and that all actions have some selfish benefit, whether it be consciously or unconsciously known to the Good Samaritan."

"That's just stupid," the girl said. "Of course people do good deeds without benefit to themselves. You jumped in the river and could have died, what's more selfless than putting your own life at risk to save another?"

I had a psychology class and a philosophy class in high school. I had done my reading. And I was cynical and ready to pick a fight. I raised my hand.

"Shaw?"

"Like I said, there is no altruism. You made the point yourself, professor. You felt like you should do something. Let me ask you, when you emerged from the water in this hypothetical scenario, did you still feel like you needed to do something?"

The professor smiled. He knew where I was going and apparently he enjoyed the freethinking debate.

"No, of course not," he said matter-of-factly.

"And when you said you, 'felt like you should do something,' was that feeling making you uncomfortable?"

"Well, I suppose so."

I aimed my next question at the girl across the room, who was now sighing.

"What about you, if you were in the same position, how would you feel as soon as you saw the person drowning?"

"It would make me sad," she replied curtly.

"So, you wouldn't like that feeling?"

"Obviously not."

Shoddy jumped in. He also knew where I was going.

"Then that proves altruism doesn't exist," he said. "End of story, can we get out early Prof?"

"Maybe you should explain yourself for Ms. Brant, first," the professor said.

"The simple fact that you felt discomfort over what you saw and then you acted to remove that discomfort proves that your action was definitely not totally selfless," Shoddy explained.

"Whether you knew it or not," I said, "you jumped in that river because you had a bad feeling in your gut and you wanted it to go away."

The girl across the room had her mouth wide open. The professor was still smiling.

"Not bad, gentlemen. Cynical beyond anything I've heard in a while, but not a bad argument."

"Yea, cynical is putting it mildly," Ms. Kerry Brant huffed from across the room. "Do you two have any sort of faith in humanity?"

"No, especially not when I'm looking at you. Since you're being all high and mighty and last weekend I saw you leave a house party with three hockey players and one of 'em had his hand up your . . . " Shoddy started to say. I cut him off before he could get himself in trouble.

"What he means is that even though altruism doesn't exist, that doesn't take away from the fact that a good deed was done. So what does motivation matter?"

"Shoddy, go to Hell. Shaw, I'm sure he'll save you a seat down there," she rebutted. "So for you two, the end justifies the means? Yea, that's made a ton of sense in the past."

We weren't given the time to agree with her.

"OK, OK we've treaded the waters of philosophy enough for one day. As much as I'd like to keep you three here I'm almost sure your classmates would not be very happy if we stayed late. And whether or not altruism exists, I would sure like one of them to save me from a river if the need ever arose. So, until next week," he ushered us out.

"Oh and don't forget to read chapter five and review the material on neuropsychology."

I liked Shoddy from that day on, even though for the first two months our discussions were strictly in-class. But when he barged onto my drunken Twister orgy, that boundary was crossed for good.

"Dude, we went out and got shitty tonight. We were so shitty we got shibby," he mumbled. It took him a while to notice the two girls in pajamas entangled on my floor. Lindsey and Emily didn't know what to make of him.

"What the hell are you doing?" he asked.

"Twister, my friend. Drunken Twister."

Shoddy got up off the couch.

"You know what's better than drunken Twister? My nipple!" he squealed, and in one swift motion whipped up one corner of his t-shirt and flicked the aforementioned areola.

Drunk and cackling, still hoisting up one corner of his t-shirt, Shoddy spun on his heel and marched out the door, assumingly to go pass out a few doors down.

The girls never came to my room again to play drunken Twister, but Shoddy and I became close friends anyway. We drank together, ate together, hit on girls together and, if the flirting went well, went home separately. I started calling him Shoddy in sort of a brotherly mocking manner. It was partly a subtle jab at his well-known, sloppy character but it was also homage to the fact that Marcus could down more shots of whiskey than Jack Daniels ever intended.

The boy drank like an Italian ate and the hours of booze, broads and fun were healthily balanced with curiously in-depth conversations about literature, life and even love lost and longed for.

He was always there when I needed him. And on the flip side, I always had to be there when he needed me. He was happiest just driving around in my car talking about Othello or Hamlet or the latest Chaucer work he just finished (we were both English majors and we pledged to write a play or a novel together someday). Dorks?

Yes. Sophisticated? Maybe. Fun? Always. It usually flowed from the car to the lunch table, to the hallway, to the dorm room; basically any type of conversation in any type of atmosphere was all right with us.

We chatted about the girls we had, the girls we wanted and the girls we could never attain but we did it so that anybody around us would understand that we were really just a couple of normal guys: normal in the sense that we were atypical college students. Shoddy and I were two branches on the same tree: the guy that got drunk frequently with his best friends, passing out cold on a frat house floor at 5:00am on a Tuesday morning and the guy who got drunk but carried home his drunker friend, preventing him from being found passed out cold on a frat house floor at 5:00am on a Tuesday morning—or sometimes worse places. All the while, inebriated or not, our highfalutin conversations confused other friends, acquaintances and passers-by. Many of our contemporaries couldn't understand why, in a world full of Britney Spears and Paris Hilton, Shoddy and I would rather discuss Dylan Thomas and Bob Dylan. But that didn't mean we didn't keep a stack of Maxim magazines on our dorm room coffee table or each obsess about the Boston Red Sox. There were a time and a place for everything—Shoddy and I just didn't agree with everyone else on the time or the place.

Some people called us arrogant: many of them our friends. But others were more correct in calling us assholes because we just did not care what they thought. Shoddy would flip off a nun if she demeaned his character, but that's just the way he was.

Complimenting personalities are rare. Two personalities that bring out the absolute best, and the absolute worst, in each other are next to impossible to not only find but to keep meshed together. Shoddy and I weren't that different. But the little differences weighed a lot. They were what drew ire towards Shoddy from most everyone else around us and cause some girls to say to me, "Why do you hang out with that kid? You're a nice guy."

I paid those girls no attention, unless they were naked in front of me. And if they were naked in front of me, they hopefully weren't talking about Shoddy.

He would say what I was thinking. Sometimes it got him in trouble since his restraint on public deviance was much weaker than my own. But others' views about him didn't really amount to more than a splinter in his finger.

A splinter, however, when not taken care of can become an infection.

A few months before our senior year spring break road trip to Florida, I confronted Shoddy about his drinking. He was missing class more than usual, sleeping all day and staying awake all night. By this time he had given himself a crew cut, sick of blowing his own hair out his face. Combined with the unusually short temper he developed, he started looking and sounding like a drill sergeant.

I told him I thought he drank too much. I told him he needed help. He took a swing at me.

A week later he apologized, gave me a manly hug and said he understood why I did what I did but that I needn't worry. He was fine. His grandfather, a World War II Marine hero with whom Shoddy was very close, had died. Apparently the man helped raise him, taught him about being a man. Shoddy didn't tell any of us because he didn't want the sympathy. His grandfather taught him to be strong. The inevitable condolences and hugs from the girls just irked him so he wallowed and mourned alone. I told him I wished he confided in me; that I lost a grandfather and could have helped him through the grief. I regretted not being there for him. He meant the world to me as a friend, as an intellectual, as a brother.

He was strong enough to deal with me no matter what the situation: physically, mentally and emotionally. His loyalty never faltered, he was always faithful.

My time with Shoddy would almost be over when we got back to campus after our spring break Florida trip. We graduated two months thereafter. After four years of companionship, we would both be alone again. In honor of his grandfather, Shoddy joined the military.

He would leave for the Army's Basic Training the day after graduation.

Chapter 15

"Shut the fuck up," said Shoddy.

I had just told him I killed Duncan. Then I told him I killed Lily. The fluorescent orange bulbs hummed on the Mo's gas station lamps around us.

"You're fuckin with me now, Shaw," he continued. "And to be honest, it's not funny. Even with my sick sense of humor."

"I'm not kidding," I said as truthfully as I could.

Shoddy was visibly upset. He kicked the Red Bull cans from the oil puddle then picked up the sopping bag and tossed it underneath the "Mo's" sandwich board sign.

"Seriously man, stop it. I could believe the Duncan thing, as far-fetched as it seemed. I mean, come on, you killing someone? But this is just mean."

He pushed past me and nudged my body away from the Explorer. He started replacing the gas cap on the car. He slammed shut the little gas tank door and started walking around the car to the driver's side.

"If you're done with your stories, I'll drive from here," he yelled from the far side when I couldn't see him anymore.

I wiped my bloody hand on my pants leaving a dark smudge. I followed Shoddy's path around the car to the driver's side.

"No," I said loudly, "you're not driving."

"Like hell I'm not. You're obviously fucked in the head; all that shit you were spouting over there. I'm not getting in a car with a nut job behind the wheel."

"I wasn't kidding, Marcus."

He stopped short of the driver's door and whipped around. He came at me, his nose scrunched up, lifted by anger. His eyes wide under a v-shaped pointed brow and tightly pursed lips. His hand shot up from his side, clenched. I stood my ground. This must be the bad part of commandment number five, the part where I'm vulnerable for being honest.

Shoddy's fist stopped centimeters short of my face. He opened his hand, stretched his fingers a few times and dropped it back by his side. He took a step away.

"You know what, Shaw, I don't believe for a second you did anything to Lily. You loved her. Talking about her like you are right now isn't going to make what happened any better. You can blame yourself but we were all to blame. Don't you dare take that from the rest of us. We all have to live with it. We all should have known better."

My headache began pulsing. Anger I had never felt towards Shoddy percolated inside.

"I gave her those drinks, not you!" I exploded. "I kept pushing the booze down her throat. Just one more, just one more. Not you, Marcus. You were off doing whatever the fuck you were doing."

"You selfish prick. You really want to carry this burden on your own, don't you? Well I'll let you in on something, she was drugged Shaw. By who, it's anybody's guess. Just know that it could've been in any drink she had that night. One you gave her, one I gave her, maybe Lindsey or Em too. We all did it, Shaw. We all killed her."

I wished he had followed through with his punch and knocked me out. It would've been easier to take than to keep reliving Lily's death. The ripple effects it caused would follow me forever. This altercation was just the beginning.

I leaned against the back of the Explorer, suddenly exhausted and overwhelmed by the searing pain in my head.

Shoddy walked over and placed a hand on my shoulder.

"Come on, get in the car," he said. "Try and get some sleep. We have a long drive home to Providence and you aren't gonna make it in this state."

"No, I can drive."

"No, you can't."

"Well you certainly can't. I saw you pop some sleeping pills at McDonalds. And you're probably still hung-over. Plus you dropped your energy drinks."

"I'm fine, Shaw. I slugged two of those things while I was waiting for Bobbo to wake up and come check me out."

His face was as sincere as ever.

"Fine," I relented. "But don't let me sleep too long."

"Sure. And Shaw, whatever you did to Duncan, just forget about it. Seriously, just bury that one deep down. Nobody else knows anything. I don't even know anything. All I know is I was with you all night and I will never say we were behind Primal bar."

He gave a sort of half-nod, half-wink.

I had no response for him. What had happened to Duncan was already buried deep down. Except now a confession had begun. I couldn't stop it now. It was off the rails and everything had to be exposed. There was too much interweaving, too much interdependent cause and effect. Lily died because of Duncan. I killed Duncan because of Lily.

I pushed myself off the back of the Explorer and climbed around to the rear passenger side seat. Shoddy was adjusting the mirrors and changed the setting of the seat. I cringed a little. I always did when someone changed my settings. But I let it go and asked him to turn the radio on low.

"What station?" he asked.

"Station? No, put on the CD that's already in there. You'll like it. Just turn it down low."

The backseat was warm from where Shoddy had been sleeping. Emily was still leaning up against her window, snoring. Lindsey the same in the front passenger seat.

As we pulled out of the gas station and back onto the empty, dark backcountry road leading to the highway, I felt my mind falling into darkness. The seatbelt strap that ran across my shoulder was a comfortable hammock for my head. I shifted to lounge against the window, intending to remain awake for as long as possible. But Shoddy was smooth and steady. By the time we reached the interstate I was comfortable and my eyes felt like mercury.

We merged with the shadows onto the highway. Shoddy stayed three miles over the speed limit and never changed lanes. The wheels hummed a tune on the pavement, something I hadn't notice from the driver's seat. The soothing noise washed over me and mixed with the soft music. The result was a strange, hypnotic, almost monkish drone.

"Oh, hey, Shod, just stay on this highway, keep going north," I said sleepily, a yawn squeezing out with the 'north.'

"Gee, thanks Magellan. I would never have figured out which way to go," he retorted. He turned the radio up slightly.

"Pink Floyd, I love this album," he said.

"Yup, *Animals*," I replied.

Track one ended and moved on to track two.

"Great stuff," he whispered. "But I was always more of a *Dark Side of the Moon* guy."

I barely heard him. In my semi-dream state of exhaustion the lingering, ethereal, psychedelic guitar riffs and Lindsey's snores pulsed in a calming rhythm. Tension oozed from my muscles. Memories began springing up but I tried to guide my mind away from all that and towards sleep. Sleep was inevitable.

Images zoomed through my head, out from behind the wall. Lily and Duncan, Lindsey, Shoddy, Emily. Years of fun and alcohol, sex and studying. All the good and all the bad.

The big picture came into focus.

I had done evil things, illegal things. I had to confess to someone other than my best friend. There would be reality to deal with.

Number five. Live by the code.

I would confess in earnest upon return to Providence. Honesty came with consequences. I could handle them.

Would the people I was to confess to have mercy? Would my friends understand? Shoddy was a guinea pig and that test was inconclusive. Would the others accept the consequences? Would the authorities see it without blinders? Would I ever be able to forgive myself? If forgiveness rose with the sun, then the consequences did not matter.

I pulled at my eyelids, a last attempt to remain awake. I debated starting the confession there in the backseat. A pen rested on a pile of Shoddy's books sitting next to me. I was cheating sleep with each second and could cheat it even more by writing down what I would say later to the police and to my parents and to Lindsey.

I turned away from the pen, its presence magnetic. Instead I stared in a daze out the window.

The highway swirled away underneath and the shadows drifted by. When I was sitting in the front seat, through the windshield the darkness brimmed with detail. Black on top of black. Outlines of anemic trees and cold steel guardrails punctuated the black canvas. But in the backseat, they were washed away. The dark scene through the tinted window was like a much-smudged chalk drawing, with blacks and grays swooping past my retinas at high speed.

I don't remember closing my eyes—the scene was similar in both states—or when sleep actually took me. But I let it take over. My mind succumbed and slipped more and more into darkness. I fell, tumbling and rolling into the grays, blacks and shadows of a dream.

Chapter 16

I floated in dark ether for what seemed eternity, before eternity ended and the dream plopped me on a ground that really wasn't there. In the dream, my body rolled down an embankment away from a train's dining car. I was bloody, battered and bruised. My eyes were closed but I could tell it was sunny outside.

A wheezing voice said, "This train don't carry no gamblers."

A dreamy memory flashed. It reminded my dream-self of the first moments when I stepped into the train car. The tables were covered in cards and chips. It was dusty and smelled like my grandparents attic. The conductor slipped the money I handed him into his coat pocket and simultaneously locked the door behind us and pulled down the shades to all the compartment windows.

A heavy-set man wearing a fedora relaxed quietly at the far end of the train puffing on a cigar. To his left sat a large man, slightly smaller than himself. To his right were two more of these cookie cutter stooges. At his feet yawned two fierce Dobermans attached to chains looking almost benign in their boredom.

While I took in my surroundings the large man in the fedora motioned to the other large men. I was instantly surrounded at the table by a blur of gray and black pinstripe suits. The only primary color in my vicinity was now the bright red baseball cap that sat on loosely on my head. The conductor must have gazed on us with amusement: a wiry, blonde run-down and exhausted young man with a bright red hat sitting at a table with men whose authority system is based on the size of their waistbands. I knew I was out of my league, not to mention engaging in a highly illegal gambling ring that could get me killed at the drop of a hat.

It did not bother me. Of course nothing bothers you when you are broke and desperate, except of course being broke and desperate. Besides, I was the best poker player I had ever seen and my pride balanced out my intense need for cash. This all combined into one great reason to join an illegal game in the back of a broken down train car parked behind a dreary waterfront station.

Why, then, does a man with so much confidence end up lying outside an abandoned train station covered in bruises and mud with an empty wallet? Probably because I thought I could cheat criminals. Probably because I thought I could get away with cheating criminals. I learned that nobody cheats people who cheat for a living.

As I lay there outside the train car, half conscious of the rumbling yells coming from it all I could think of was how my entire life was just tossed into the mud. My wife back at home with my son would never speak to me again if I did not come home with a paycheck. My girlfriend downtown would never sleep with me again if I did not buy her another pearl necklace. Their faces swirled in the blackness of my inner eyelids mocking my impotence and failure.

More yelling came growling out of the train car. I could make out something about payments and chains. Resorting to gambling with criminals was all I could do to fix my life but in all of this I never realized desperation.

Suddenly it all disappeared. The faces stopped swirling and my senses clicked back on as if someone flicked the switch. I could feel a hot, pungent breath weighing down on my face like a smothering pillow. I slowly opened my eyes to see a long black snout bearing ivory daggers dripping with saliva, rumbling under a long, slow growl.

One of the Dobermans stood above me grinning from ear to pointed ear. I was pinned between the cold ground and steaming canine breath. From the corner of my eye I could see that I was thrown from the train car right at a doorway of the abandoned station. The door was hanging off to my side revealing a long, narrow and dark hallway that looked eerily like a coffin.

My eyes flicked back to the dog. It was like staring Death in the face, only Death would not smell that rank. The devilish pointed ears loomed up behind the face like dark watchtowers, always twitching and searching. She just glared at me, waiting for me to flinch so she could dive into my flesh. Her teeth proved that was all she wanted. She cared not for the commands of the large man yelling from the train car. She smiled at me, a horrible mocking grin with upturned jowls and sparkling pearly-whites. She knew I would move sooner or later and if I did not I knew she would eventually lose patience.

My mind raced and stumbled over my very limited options. But her eyes could read me. They were like little black telescopes piercing my soul searching for my next thought or plan. She had me beat, capitalized on my every mistake that I made against man or beast, criminal or gambler. Nothing short of a miracle or a shotgun would save me now. She seemed to be growing in anticipation for I saw a fire burst in her black eyes. Or was it just the reflection of my hat?

That was it, my hat. She was focused on it. I took a chance and pulled my hand slowly out from underneath my aching body. I slid it up my side to my head. She never lost the red flicker in her eyes. I got to my neck never losing eye contact with her. Everything paused for a moment. My hand paused, the saliva stopped dripping, the flame in her eyes stopped flickering.

We gazed, passionately, into each other's eyes.

I snapped my hand to my head and flicked the hat high into the air. The Doberman reacted instantly. Her head flew towards the hat followed by a lunging heavy black body. This was the first glimpse I got of the sinewy muscles coated with a glossy black sheen. She lunged over me and loomed high in the air like one of the four horsemen riding in for judgment.

I was not ready to be judged. I slid my body from underneath her and scrambled to my feet as the dog sliced into the hat in midair. My feet slipped on the dog drool when I began to run through the doorway into the dark hallway.

I expected to be snatched up by the Doberman just like my hat but instead nothing happened. I grew enough courage to glance over my shoulder as I ran. The Doberman still tore at the red hat, shredding it to pieces. I rejoiced and picked up my pace. I glanced back again and the sliver of joy that had welled up inside me quickly shattered at the sight of the second Doberman tearing out from behind her counterpart who still ripped at the red hat.

I ran harder, my lungs exploding in my chest. She bore down on me, closer and closer. I could barely see in front of me down the long dark hallway. The concrete floor rolled away as I fled into shadows, always hearing the constant rapid tapping of dog nails on the hard ground. The same hot breath was burning the back of my legs. All I could do now was run and hope for an exit but ahead of me was only more darkness. I begged my feet to run, to run and not trip. This dog seemed more intent on taking me out. She had a clear plan and I had no more red hats.

When I strained my ears I could hear sinister, mocking laughter from far behind me at the hallway entrance. That same voice growled, "We always win, pal. We aren't gamblers because there isn't a chance in hell that we're going to lose. When they find you, if you can still talk, remember to tell them that this train don't carry no gamblers." His laughter became an echoing cackle. Instead of fading it grew sharper and surrounded me. My feet were not even touching the floor but rather they treaded water. I swam through the shadows, drowning in the hot dog breath and a loud, ear-piercing screech.

Chapter 17

My face slapped against the cold window as I lashed out the hand supporting my head. I swatted at the dream Doberman and punched the air in self-defense. My eyes were still closed because I couldn't look death in the face.

A cool burst of air rustled my hair and dried the drool that stuck me to the window.

"Screw you asshole!" Shoddy yelled out the open window and gave the horn another long beep.

The train, the dogs, the voices vanished. I was awake, resting in an awkward position behind the passenger's seat.

Once Shoddy shut the window and the torrents of icy night air stopped swirling around the backseat, I opened my eyes—no sense in trying to fall back to sleep.

It was still pitch black outside the car. Shoddy was still driving. Emily and Lindsey were still fast asleep.

I sat upright and wiped the saliva off my cheek and then off the window, but managed to only smudge it around the tinted pane.

Shoddy noticed me sit up.

"Sorry, Shaw, a huge trailer truck just cut into the fast lane so I had to beep at him. I didn't mean to swear that loud."

"What? Oh, forget about it," I yawned. The little green glowing numbers on the clock were the only things that changed since before

I fell asleep. I had slept for almost four hours; it was now deep into the wee hours of the morning. The sun would rise relatively soon. A tickle of excitement momentarily bristled the hairs on the back of my neck.

While I meandered into full consciousness, I attempted to understand fragments of leftover dream that loitered around in my head. Something about a red hat and a dog? The images didn't stay long and soon the addictive alter ego my brain had created from the fragments of Rapid Eye Movement, disappeared completely.

A professor once told my class to write down our dreams, claiming they were a snapshot of the soul and would provide inspiration for some very interesting fictional writing. That was an English professor. A psychology professor said dreams are a series of patchy memories firing after environmental cues during waking hours brought them to the front of our mental queue. I liked the English professor's rationalization better.

"I can drive again if you want," I said to Shoddy. "As long as you find me a twenty-four Dunkin Donuts. My head is killing me, I think I need caffeine."

"Shaw, buddy, you just smacked your head off the window. I doubt caffeine is going to help with that. Plus, we're in the South. They don't have Dunks down here."

He was right. A college student's schedule revolved around alcohol to put them to sleep and coffee to wake them up. When one of those goes missing, homeostasis can go awry. If I had to do without Dunks, so be it. I'd find a boost elsewhere.

"Damn," I groaned. "Well, get off at the next exit. We'll find something."

"No problem," he assured me and turned back to singing along with the music. It was a different CD than the one I fell asleep to. It was one of Emily's CD mixes. Her taste was usually quite eclectic. This disc was filled with country music. I wasn't a huge fan and I knew Shoddy wasn't either. I wondered if maybe he was brushing up on his Emily facts, perhaps to beef up his pillow talk.

I let it go. I recognized the song and without realizing it, I started singing under my breath.

"Spent the night in Carolina, got up early out of bed. Bought a Red Bull and a road map and an old Stones cassette. Setting my sights south bound, no reason or rhyme. Threw up a prayer just lookin', just lookin' for a sign."

"You know this song?" Shoddy asked condescendingly.

"Yeah, Lindsey plays it all the time. It's basically about some guy in a cowboy hat driving around thinking about life. Typical country music themes."

"That's wonderful, Shaw. I didn't really need a book report on the song but thanks. I can move on with my life now," he said without attempting to hide his sarcasm.

At least twenty minutes rolled by before we saw a sign for the next exit. The gas station at this exit was much more readily accessible than the last one. We pulled right in to a brightly lit franchise.

I got out to fill the gas tank. This pump had a very easy to find credit card swipe.

"What do you want inside?" Shoddy said.

"I don't know, whatever will keep me awake. Those Red Bulls you had earlier looked like the right idea."

"Got it," he said and ran into the convenience store. The gas pump handle kicked out. Shoddy returned with a coffee and some water, a few candy bars and a six-pack of Red Bull.

We flip-flopped positions again and he jumped into my vacated backseat, cracked a joke about the spittle-covered window and settled into his i-Pod and a Snickers.

It took a minute to readjust the seat settings and mirrors. I checked the passengers once more before pulling back onto the deserted interstate. Emily was drooling on herself, probably took some of the same sleeping pills as Shoddy with much more adverse effects.

Shoddy was reading a book, lost in some random sentence. Lindsey hadn't moved, even when we stopped at the station.

I was somewhat alone with my thoughts.

On an impulse I flicked Emily's CD back to the country music track I woke up to. I wanted to listen to that song again.

I turned the volume up a notch. I didn't sing along this time around. Rather, I paid attention. I took in the lyrics mostly, and the simple, almost regretful guitar backbone. It went down easy and warm, calming my body and weakening my still pounding headache. I let the music fill me up.

I cracked open a Red Bull. After three long slugs I crushed the empty can with my right hand and reached blindly behind me, aiming to drop it on the floor under Shoddy's feet. My hand whacked his knee. He made no sound.

I dropped the can and checked the rearview mirror. The book teetered on his knee, held open by one finger, acting the fulcrum on its spine. His head drooped forward, eyes shut, mouth closed. I prayed his dreams be more magnanimous than my own; that he would not suffer the same broken sleep that I had endured. Perhaps whatever internal spirit controlled and conjured his unconscious, relished in benevolence and would guide him away from nightmare, towards delight. I wished it for him, but Shoddy had his own demons, his own pursuing dogs to evade. Somehow I knew, far away in the shadows of his mind, he too was running from some monster; some vicious beast grinning a wide and sharp grin brimming with cockiness over the certainty of the kill.

In the rearview mirror I watched Shoddy's chest start heaving faster and faster. He twitched and his leg jutted out, smacking the back of Lindsey's seat. His body shook then relaxed. His head tilted to the right and rested against the window. His breathing steadied.

Don't lose your grip, Marcus. Just keep running.

I returned to my own demons. Back out through the windshield the highway blended with the sky into a single, consuming void that I willingly approached one-quarter mile at a time.

Inside the Explorer was quiet except for the country song filling in the background. I was totally alone with the road accompanied by nothing, save the music and the memories.

Chapter 18

Duncan Barker was born on January 1, the first baby of the New Year in the small town of Wilmington, Massachusetts. Duncan's parents lavished him with love and praise, instilling confidence and charisma: until his sister, Sarah was born six years later.

He was the apple of their eye. Sarah was born and he instantly rotted. The girl had physical talent, something Duncan never dreamed of. He was more of a talker, a people person. If the Barker family existed in ancient Rome, Duncan would be in the Senate while his sister was a fierce warrior. The warriors were always more exciting. The warriors got all the attention.

In her youth, Duncan's parents groomed Sarah to be a champion figure skater. She practiced before school and early on weekends. Duncan became an afterthought. He had no particularly outstanding skill for them to nurture.

Duncan got to high school and Sarah was winning competitions. Duncan graduated high school and Olympic coaches scouted Sarah. Duncan left the region for college without fanfare and Sarah enjoyed regional fame. Duncan was swallowed up by deep-rooted jealousy.

I met Duncan late in high school, in the midst of his green-eyed emergence. At our private school filled with well-off suburbanites, Duncan and I were rare, middle-class kids. My father was an electrician, mother worked at a doctor's office. Duncan's father did something with insurance, his mother a homemaker. Nobody was starving but needless to say that the European vacations and yacht club memberships were not as frequent as some of our classmates'. The Haves and Have-nots scorned each other through perfect, whitened, toothy smiles.

Most of the guys I played with on the hockey team were of the same economic bracket. The rich kids rowed, fenced and played baseball. Normally I wouldn't have ever even noticed this disparity, except the Haves were boastful and many enjoyed showing off their family's socioeconomic superiority. The school of course didn't mind because many Haves were also legacy students. Their fathers and uncles, successful alumni, donated generously to the school in various fashions. Therefore, the BMWs and tricked-out Land Rovers filled the student parking lot closest to the main buildings. The Haves couldn't walk too far to class in the morning, or else their name-brand neckties could fray and their Italian leather shoes could scuff. The Haves materialized segregation.

Duncan and I parked with the other Have-nots down a hill in an unpaved lot surrounded by looming oak trees that pelted our cars with acorns in the spring and icicles in the winter.

The disparity was obvious but it wasn't appalling; it wasn't Montague and Capulet. The school dress code did its best to keep us all equal and for the most part it worked. However, it merely said khaki pants, button down shirt and tie not what brand or from what country. Those details were lost on the administration but not on the horde of impressionable and devious teenagers they watched over.

Despite it all, most students I knew never really cared. The Haves were OK guys, just not particularly warm to anyone, especially someone who drove a used sky blue Buick like I did.

Duncan was the one person who cared the most. What irritated him was the fact that he would never fit in with those rich kids. He didn't have a BMW, he didn't even have a sky-blue Buick; he didn't have his own car. He didn't have any name brand ties; he barely knew how to tie a knot in the ones he did own (he kept them perpetually tied and hanging on his bedroom doorknob). His dad wasn't an important alumnus of the school or donating member of the Board of Trustees.

Simply put, Duncan had no identity. He was an average student with no extracurricular activities. He was known as his almost-famous sister's older brother. He wasn't a hockey player, he didn't play any other sports, he wasn't an honor's student, he wasn't part of a club or team or choir or band or group. Duncan was too lazy to be noticed but he wanted desperately to be seen, heard, accepted and loved. This all bothered Duncan.

So Duncan invented an identity. He had a knack for insults, which created a sort of class clown aura around his person. He was quick to mock someone for giving a wrong answer in class, wearing a pink shirt or having an attractive sister—the type of wayward affronts typical of high school boys. It wasn't uncommon to hear his high-pitched voice squeal something at lunch, followed by a cackle that echoed off the high walled cathedral cafeteria ceiling. But with Duncan, it was too late in high school and his sense of humor was too obnoxious for anyone to label him as laugh-out-loud hilarious. Many students, and teachers for that matter, found it strange and irritating. Most people shrugged him off.

Duncan was never really anybody that anybody worried about. He was eventually disregarded as a sad attention seeker. Before I knew his name, I knew him as, "that kid,"—that sort of annoying kid that never knew how to keep his mouth shut. I actually didn't know anyone that knew him as anything else.

I met Duncan in my senior Spanish class, the only class we ever had together. I needed to fulfill a foreign language credit and since the advanced class conflicted with Advanced Placement English, I took the lower level Spanish.

Within the first few weeks we were assigned a group project in class. Three students had to make up a skit, any theme we wanted, incorporate some words chosen by the teacher and act it out in Spanish for the class. Duncan and I were put in the same group, I half-groaned when I noticed "that kid" was in my group. Had he not been so adamant about his idea for the skit, I probably would have continued ignoring him.

"What are the words she wants us to use?" Duncan asked me, in English. He turned his desk around to face mine, his back to the blackboard. The third student in our group pulled a chair up next to us.

I was astounded he didn't know what the words were. The teacher wrote them on the blackboard. I wondered why he didn't just turn and look for himself.

"Well, one of them is 'rock', and 'crack,' which makes sense," I responded, eventually. Then, looking over his shoulder, I read the list of words to him.

"OK, I got a great idea," he said, and proceeded to map out our skit without waiting for approval or input. He wanted to do a drug deal in front of the class, using the word for 'rock' with the word for 'crack' as our drug of choice. I was skeptical, perhaps a little annoyed but I didn't care enough to argue with "that kid" over a three-minute skit. So with help from the third student, I translated the whole scene.

I admitted after we got our grade that the skit was funny, simply because it was not about an airport or a school or a supermarket, like all the others. Duncan sold it. He didn't really know the Spanish words but he pretended like he did, not skipping a beat when he butchered a sentence about what it felt like to be high. I thought our teacher would find it risqué, but being the jovial senorita she was, she laughed along. I don't think she actually knew about the illegal substance connotation for 'crack,' and Duncan assured her, in English, that it was not anything dangerous or taboo.

Before she could critique the content, pronunciation or translation Duncan gave her an explanation, in English. He almost convinced her that we had just acted out a scene worthy of the Bible; she clapped, laughed and gave us an A.

"Wow, with that kid buttering her up, we could've slaughtered a lamb in front of the class and still gotten an A," the third student in our group whispered to me. We returned to our seats to watch yet another skit about an airport.

I knew Duncan was full of shit from that moment on.

I gambled on him and introduced him to my group of hockey friends. They accepted him without question. He was harmless and good for a few laughs.

A few months into our friendship I recognized his charisma for what it was: a desperate plea to fit in. We gave him a chance to fulfill that desire. He filled a role in our group. He never really contributed but he always showed up. We were easy, ambivalent to his lack of discernible talent. He didn't have to prove anything. Most of my friends took him for what he was: a joker. He fit in fine. But that wasn't what he was going for.

Instantly we weren't good enough for Duncan. He wasn't content with a ragtag group of friends. He wanted to be friends with other people; people he felt were more beneficial to his existence. He wanted the Haves. Several times I noticed his green eyes staring lustfully at a kid's Rolex during Spanish class. He started wearing a fake Burberry tie he bought online. He had tried to make friends with a few of the Haves. But he was brushed off, for the same reasons his parents mostly ignored him. He disregarded us as mere stepping-stones or a backup plan. We became a means to an end.

Almost immediately I noticed his resentment of us. I noticed it because I vouched for Duncan. He was my responsibility and I knew him best. He always told me he felt animosity towards his parents for dumping all their affection and attention on their skating prodigy. But I never expected the snide remarks and behind-the-back cut-downs to translate onto people who called him friend.

The jealousy he had towards his sister manifested itself in outright envious desire for acceptance. Not just acceptance by anyone. He wanted acceptance from everyone—especially the socially elite. He wanted what he did not have. The monster was in its infancy.

It got to the point that Duncan became very quiet within our group but outgoing with any outside person we came into contact with. If we went bowling he'd miss his turn chatting it up with the people in the next lane. If we were at a pool hall, Duncan would have the girls around the air hockey table hanging on some fairy tale about his game-winning goal. And for the most part, people instantly liked him. Whether or not the bullshit was flowing, Duncan knew how to tell people what they wanted to hear.

And *that* was Duncan's skill. Few people knew it.

We never really complained or paid him much attention, like everyone else in the school. Besides, when he broke the ice with girls, we only benefited. Duncan wasn't exactly Brad Pitt but none of us were descendents of Cicero, either. So when the more attractive guys in our group were eased into the conversation, Duncan got phased out. He always ended up with one of the less-attractive girls. That was how we always thanked him.

Duncan introduced me to my ex-girlfriend, Rose, the one he would later escort to Primal. He struck up a conversation with a group of girls one night outside an ice cream shop. The rest of us were sitting in our buddy's 1987 Cadillac waiting for Duncan to bring us our food. Instead he brought a group of girls from a private all-girls school loosely affiliated with our own. We talked to them from the car and they ended up following us up to our high school campus.

The school put in a new set of bleachers around the football field and we had yet to check them out. The four girls and four of us spent a few hours messing around in the dark on the new bleachers.

I learned that one of the girls, Lindsey, was the same blind date that I had broken off a few weeks before. I chatted with her on the bleachers for a while before one of my friends interrupted, grabbed her hand and pulled her onto the empty football field.

We played a game of football in the dark. One of my friends found an old ball under the new bleachers. That game ended when one of the girls slipped in some invisible mud.

Duncan escorted the injured girl back to the car and the rest of us retreated to the bleachers. Lindsey disappeared with my friend who interrupted us earlier. I turned my attention to Rose, the girl Duncan made me cover during our little flirtatious Super Bowl. During the game he told me to tackle her and I did, gently. She asked if I'd take her for a walk up to the gymnasium to use the bathroom. We weren't even halfway there before we fell into some bushes and pressed our lips awkwardly against each other.

We were alone when we got back to the car. My other friends had disappeared with girls in similar fashion, behind bleachers and bushes.

The girls' vehicle, along with Duncan and the injured girl were gone. Rose and I spent the time waiting and talking and by the time my friends showed up, I thought I was in love. Thankfully my friend's Cadillac held six people somewhat comfortably and we drove the girls home to various towns on the North Shore of Massachusetts.

Duncan dated the injured girl until we left for college. He made out with a few other girls on a few other occasions. I was certain I'd marry Rose, the girl from the bushes.

Because Duncan and I dated friends, we spent time out together as couples. I grew closer to Duncan. He dropped the overacting charade around me sometimes, I thought, even though he put it on for the girls. Rose saw right through him. She never liked him because she knew he was treating her friend poorly. But she sucked it up and laughed at his jokes when we were at T.G.I. Friday's or Sunny's Bowladrome.

When I started getting college acceptances back and my top two choices both deferred then rejected me outright, Duncan was the first person to call with his condolences. When Providence College accepted me, he called with congratulations.

When he was wait-listed at Providence, I wrote a letter to the Dean expressing how I, an accepted student who accepted his invitation to the school, would deeply appreciate if his best friend could join him at college. I doubt the letter had much impact on their decision to let him in, but nevertheless I never told Duncan I wrote it.

When he got his acceptance letter he drove to my house and appeared genuinely enthusiastic.

"My parents said 'congrats' and then had to take my sister to the rink," he said. "But isn't this great? We can request to live together. I already looked into it. We just have to put each other's names down on that housing sheet."

I remember the queasy feeling that crept up from my stomach. Something inside screamed *bad idea*.

My other friends echoed that instinct; turned out they never really liked Duncan all that much. They never wanted to tell me; they didn't want to hurt anyone's feelings. But since they were scattering to all corners of America for higher education and would probably never see him again, they didn't care what they revealed.

My parents were reluctant to tell me their opinions about Duncan and our housing situation.

Duncan called a few nights later to see if I sent in the housing form yet.

"Duncan, I don't know man. I told Ben I'd room with him," I lied.

Ben Lovelace was a classmate I was friendly with from a few high honors classes. Duncan didn't know him. Duncan wasn't in those classes.

"So what. We could live in a three-man," he said. I didn't have a response.

I stuttered before saying, "Let me call Ben first."

"Sure. I'll just put us down and then you two can do the same."

"Do you think it's a good idea to live together? I mean, lots of people say it's a bad idea to live with friends."

"We'll be fine. We'll meet plenty of new people. I'll make a bunch of new friends and you'll always have Bennie Love," he half-joked and hung up.

"I wouldn't call him that if I were you. He hates that."

"Chill out, Shaw. And tell Bennie Love that too. It's college, baby. College!"

He hung up.

I didn't even put my phone back on the receiver before calling Ben. I tried to convince him it was a bad idea but, after skimming the housing form, we realized that in order to get a bigger freshman dorm room, we had to sign up for a three-man as soon as possible.

"I don't care. I say we go for it," Ben said. "It's got a ton more room than those two person closets. I'll just ignore the kid if he's a tool. Besides, the three-man dorms don't have security guards at the front door. It's easier to sneak stuff in."

Decision made.

Ben was a rough personality, somewhat of a loner but a great guy to hang out with. He was bright, quick-witted and loyal to his friends. He was a champion on the high school debate team, loved politics and reveled in a good argument. That summer Ben began taking out his frustrations on a heavy bag and a speed bag. Sparring lessons became his regular after-school exercise. He already scheduled time at the local gym in North Providence, ten minutes from school.

If Ben could deal with Duncan, I figured I'd be fine. Plus, his abrasiveness might calm Duncan down and intimidate him into being straight with us on a regular basis. Ben would be a nice buffer.

I just had to endure the remainder of the summer and get to that point.

The weekend before we moved to college I made plans to get some dinner with Duncan and his girlfriend. Rose was busy and I didn't mind playing third wheel for a night.

Duncan said he had some things to do with his family and he'd call us when he was ready. I went to Duncan's girlfriend's house to pick her up so we could then go meet Duncan wherever he was.

"I haven't heard from him yet," she said when I walked into her living room. The familiar Instant Message ding chimed repeatedly. She was talking over the Internet to a few people at once. "Let's give him a couple minutes."

"Where was he today?" I asked.

"He was taking his mother out for her birthday. I think they went shopping or something," she said without looking up from the screen.

"I thought that was earlier."

The phone rang a few minutes later. Duncan said he was en route to her house; he'd be a few minutes. His girlfriend hung up the phone and, after glancing briefly at the computer, immediately picked it up again.

She looked at me, ashen.

"That son of a bitch!" she screeched. "This is the last time!"

My confused expression was reaction enough.

"He wasn't with his mother. Look!" She spun the computer screen to me and pointed at a social media post from one of Duncan's townie friends, Jen. The girl claimed to be, "out celebrating with Duncan."

"I'm calling her right now. I'm sick of this," she said.

She waited for an answer but didn't get one.

She dialed the number again and simultaneously sent the girl an online message.

Duncan's girlfriend ranted to me as she typed a response to Jen. I could hear her ramblings but was too apathetic to really hear her argument.

"Do you know this girl, Shaw? Do you know if he's cheating on me with her?"

"I've never met her, sorry."

"Don't lie to me, Shaw."

"I'm not. I don't know any of Duncan's hometown friends. I didn't know he had any."

"Sure. Well, he lied to me last week about being out with this same girl. He said he was studying but she had up a message about hanging out with him. He told me he just ran over to say hi. Clearly neither one of them is very bright. I know he's full of shit most of the time but I always hoped it was never directed at me."

I started feeling uncomfortable; it wasn't my fight. But those character revelations certainly gave me pause.

On the third phone call Jen picked up. She explained that Duncan was with her for most of the day. It was her birthday and they went out to celebrate. She insisted they were just friends, had been since kindergarten. The girl didn't know why Duncan would say he was with his mother; he had nothing to hide from his girlfriend. There was nothing shady going on; there was no reason to lie.

"I don't believe you, bitch," Duncan's girlfriend said and slammed down the phone.

She started crying. I gave her a lame pat on the back and got no reaction.

I left her sobbing and let myself out the front door.

I bumped into Duncan on the front porch of his girlfriend's house.

"You guys ready?" he said cheerfully.

"Ready? I don't think so. I think dinner might be off," I said and laughed. This didn't concern me so I found it somewhat entertaining. Duncan's eyes shifted and his face suddenly went overly solemn.

"What happened? Is everyone alright?" he said, sounding very concerned.

"Yeah man, but you might have to explain why you were with that girl Jen today. Your girlfriend's not too happy about it, just to give you a head's up."

"What do you mean, I wasn't with Jen today?"

I laughed. "OK, sure I'll buy that but I know the crying girl inside will be a little harder to convince."

"No, really, I wasn't with Jen today."

"It's alright Duncan, it's me. I don't care who you were with."

His thick, dome-shaped hair was tussled slightly. The thick black eyebrows that shaded his rodent eyes dipped inwards. He was getting angry and adamant.

"I was with my mom all day. We went to the mall and got some lunch and then I took her around to some stores like she wanted. I even bought her some flowers."

His act was more rehearsed than a high school play, but not as well executed.

"Duncan, seriously, she talked to Jen on the phone. You might want to cut the bullshit, for your relationship's sake."

Duncan took a few steps closer to me on the porch. The one moth-covered light bounced shadows over his face. They danced there, making it seem as if he was looking in opposite directions.

"I was with my mom today," he said sternly. I stared directly into his eyes.

"No. You weren't," I said, clearly irritated. "And that's fine but why are you so bent on lying . . ."

"I said I wasn't with Jen," he interrupted. "End of story."

The awkwardness hung around us like cobwebs. I waved my hand above my head, hoping to brush it away.

"Fine, I'll see you later. I'm guessing dinner is off," I said, and pushed past him to my car. He must have watched me walk to my car because there was a pause before I heard the door slam shut.

I remember driving home that night thinking about how many times in the past I had heard Duncan lie. To that point, he never directed the lies at me. At least, I thought he didn't.

When we stared into each other's eyes on the porch, I knew he was lying straight to my face. His lies did not discriminate. And in the same moment, Duncan realized I figured him out. He had no remorse and, despite the overwhelming evidence to the contrary, he clung to fabrication.

It wasn't even the content of the lie that bothered me. Frankly, I was glad I didn't have to spend dinner with him and his girlfriend. But he lied to me. There was no truth in that story, so what truth was there in any story he had ever told me? As far as I was concerned, if he made one false statement, his entire lexicon was suspect. What was his word, if not reliable?

I discovered an ugly truth. I recognized his affinity for lies then but I did nothing. Ben, Duncan and I already signed and sent our housing papers the day before. We were locked into living together at college. I was trapped.

Chapter 19

Three and a half weeks before Ben, Duncan and I moved to college, my closest high school friends and I embarked on a farewell trip. It was the kind of trip that makes and breaks relationships. When acquaintances become fast friends and friends showed their true colors. It was similar to those family vacations when an uncle insults an aunt and one entire side of the family goes home vowing to change their last name.

I learned a lot about people on that trip, especially the ones I was traveling with. I recognized true loyalty and compared it to opportunistic loyalty. The trip taught me about rage and its ability to hide within a man, deep inside, blanketed by a cheery disposition, an intellectual façade or overzealous sense of honor.

My friend Frank's parents gave him a graduation present: two rooms in Orlando at their time-share resort for a week and a half. We put the group together, minus a few that left early for school due to athletic scholarships and flew to the Sunshine State. Duncan was a last minute addition after one of the other guys backed out. He rounded off our crew at eight, putting four people in each room.

I took vivid memories away from that trip.

The first full night there we went to what the concierge called the Wonderland Parade at Disney World's Magic Kingdom. He told us we'd be able to get on the rollercoasters uninhibited while all the screaming children watched the parade.

After several falls over Splash Mountain we moved on. But on the stroll to another ride we encountered the parade snaking its way through the people-lined streets. I think it was Duncan who noticed the young women dressed like princesses marching in between the oversized electric-light caterpillar and the butterfly shooting sparks from its wings.

Eight pairs of feet screeched to a halt when the fantasy women walked past. I focused on Alice, whose large breasts seemed inappropriate for a children's parade but perfect for the white frock they spilled from. With help from the group, I heckled her, yelling things about magic mushrooms and the walrus in the oyster bed. When I yelled for her to meet us at a bar after the parade, she winked.

Within minutes, five black-clad security guards—definitely not the day shift that walked the park in purple and yellow costumes—surrounded us.

Until my time at college, almost getting banned from Disney World, the happiest place on earth, was the most daring and frightening experience in my young life. Frank didn't help that situation by hitting on Cinderella while she strolled along with Prince Charming. She was digging it. Who could blame her after a long day of smiling at five year olds? The Prince threatened him until Mike, the 6 foot 4 inch college-recruited linebacker, stepped up and told the Prince what he planned on doing with the glass slipper. As she sauntered off, Cinderella yelled out the name of a bar. We took it to be an invitation.

As the parade trailed off so did the security. We waited for the mass of crying children and almost crying parents to vacate the park before we attempted to leave.

By the time we reached the bar, Alice and Cinderella were already sipping cocktails, with some other fairytale characters in tow. They were all college students working summer jobs. We told them we were college students looking to get drunk.

Prince Charming didn't show up that night but each one of us went to Wonderland. Alice was much more attractive than Rose back home and when we went back to the hotel, I found out she was also much better. I told her so the next morning when she was putting her clothes back on.

"That's one of the nicest things anyone's ever said to me," she laughed, and then told me to go see her in the parade again that afternoon. On her way out the door she slipped the characteristic black headband on and blew me a kiss.

"Hey wait," I yelled. "Is your name actually Alice?"

"For you it is," and she shut the door.

Duncan barged into the room soon after my fairytale ended, ignoring the *Do Not Disturb* placard hung on the doorknob.

"They sent me to see if we could come in yet," he said. "They were somewhat pissed about having to squeeze five guys in one room last night."

"Five? Where are the other two?"

"Frank left with Cinderella and Mike took off with Jasmine."

I screwed up my face in confusion but then couldn't help but burst out laughing. Soon the other two guys that shared our room showed up and we all fell into hysterics as the previous night's stories unraveled. The main point of comedy: not one of us knew the ladies' real names.

"So Duncan, what castle did you end up storming?" I asked in the midst of recalling our conquests.

"Fuckin' Mike," he said sharply, in a different tone than the one we were all joking in. His thick brow suddenly furrowed on his round face and the lower edges of his thin lips curled downwards.

Everyone else stopped talking.

"I was about to take down Jasmine," Duncan said. "But fuckin'

Mike jumped in and stole her. I did all the damn work and he got the benefits. Asshole."

There was a tinge of cruelty in his voice I never noticed before.

He saw everyone staring at him, mouths agape due to his jealous outburst. Duncan didn't react, like he was relishing the awkward attention.

In the silence my cell phone chirped. Thanking God for the interruption, I answered to hear a whooping Mike laughing and screaming about a "magic carpet" and various other lame movie references. He was on the bus back to the resort and wanted to know where to meet up.

After a quick discussion we decided to go to one of the parks when Mike got back, just not the one from the night before. We wanted to meet some new princesses.

I told him to meet us at our room.

As we all got ready the rest of our crew arrived at the room, except for Mike who was having trouble navigating the bus routes of Orlando. By the time he returned to his room, showered and changed the rest of us were all in my room waiting.

Mike called down to apologize for holding everyone up. We told him not to worry, to stick with the plan and meet us at the room. Then we'd go hop on a bus.

Someone suggested a few people go wait by the bus stop and call if ours showed up. Three of the guys went to execute the audible while the rest of us stayed in the room waiting for Mike.

I too was running late. Rose called the room phone to chat, postponing my shower. Alice from Wonderland called my cell phone at the same time to invite us all to something she called a, "cast after party" that night in an apartment downtown.

I had just jumped from the shower, dressed and was combing my hair when I heard Duncan's voice elevate above the others'.

"Hey, when he comes down don't answer the door, let him think we left without him," Duncan suggested. He had been mostly silent since his outburst.

I ignored it, continued brushing my teeth until a loud knock at the door. Duncan jumped up and stood in front of it.

"Wait, let him think we left. Just for a sec, it'll be funny," he whispered.

The other guys didn't know what to do; they didn't know how to deal with Duncan. I was the only one who knew him well enough to tell him to shut up and I was in the bathroom with a mouth full of Colgate, barely comprehending the situation. The other guys kept their silence.

Mike knocked louder and yelled in for us. Duncan, his back leaning on the door, put his finger up to his twisted lips.

I came out of the bathroom to see my friends sitting quietly on the edge of the beds and Duncan standing like a pint-sized bouncer at the door. He waved at me before I could ask what was going on and when I heard Mike's growing anger and banging knocks. I got the picture.

"Open the damn door, man, I know you're all in there. You just called me. Stop messing around," Mike yelled. His fuse was short, and lit. "I can hear you in there, someone just flushed the toilet. You guys aren't funny!"

Duncan was snickering uncontrollably; the rest of us remained uncomfortably quiet. It had gone from Duncan's stupid prank to a potentially violent situation. Duncan didn't know Mike like we did. He flew off the handle for no reason, which made him a good teammate and great in a brawl. He didn't know it was Duncan's doing, he lumped us all in together, which meant none of us wanted to open the door. Or maybe Duncan did know Mike as well as we did?

"Uh, Duncan you should open the door," I whispered. "He's pissed."

"Dude, he'll kill all of us," my friend replied. "He's all wound up.

Let's sneak out the back sliding door." He motioned to the small sliding glass door at the back of the room that opened onto a grass pathway around the opposite side of the resort.

The banging got louder and Duncan ignored the rest of us. He was genuinely amused at Mike's anger.

"How's Jasmine doing now, asshole," he uttered under his breath.

He disregarded the obviously bad consequences in exchange for the instant pleasure he contrived from spite. He played on Mike's temper, infuriating him over a nothing issue, guiding his unfounded rage toward everyone instead of just Duncan.

After ten minutes Mike stopped knocking. He called my cell phone, which was on vibrate mode on a pillow, rendering it silent. The knocking stopped and we heard Mike walk away, but in its place we heard rustling along the outside wall of our room. Mike was climbing through the bushes to get to the back pathway and the back sliding door.

"Shit," Duncan said. He ran to the back door, dove on the floor and started slowly pulling the curtain shut, like a soldier camouflaging his bunker.

Mike tried to open the locked sliding door. This only pissed him off more.

"I saw you closing the curtain," he yelled. "I saw you, Shaw. I know you guys are fucking with me, I'm not retarded." He gave the glass a couple kicks. Duncan had gone back to the front door, snickering the whole way.

"Hey, c'mon lets go out the front now and go over to the bus stop. He'll never know," he said.

The other guys were out the door before Duncan even finished divulging his plan. I hesitated.

"Shaw, let's go before he goes back around. He saw you, you're the first one he's gonna go after," Duncan said with a twisted smile. He looked eerily like Jack Nicholson's turn as the Joker, minus the white face paint.

Duncan was right. Personal safety kicked in and the two of us bolted out the door and hurried to the bus stop. The other guys were waiting on a bench, irked because in the twenty-minute interval we had missed three busses.

Duncan triumphantly detailed the scene, estimating that Mike was probably still standing at the back door banging and yelling at nobody like a fool. None of us laughed.

Within ten minutes Mike hulked around the corner. We had missed another bus waiting for him. He made straight for me, his eyes furious and wide open, wound up and landed a solid punch on my left shoulder, followed by a heavy push to the chest and a, "What the fuck is your problem!"

The family of four waiting near us shifted down to the end of the benches.

"Hey, I'm sorry my phone was on vibrate I didn't know you called," I tried to play it off without actually lying.

"No, asshole, I know you guys were in the room that whole time, I saw you." The situation was getting to the point where it could ruin the rest of the vacation. I had to quash this before it became something.

"I apologize. It wasn't on purpose, it was just a misunderstanding."

"Misunderstanding? Fuck you," he said. Then his eyes shot at Duncan, who couldn't help the sneering smirk splashed across his face. "Wait a minute, it was you, ya little fuckin' rat. Sorry Shaw, my bad, now I'm going to kill your little rat friend."

He pushed by me and lunged at Duncan, who darted away behind a trash barrel, the smirk instantly erased and replaced by sudden terror.

"Come here pussy, you better learn not to fuck with me!" Mike boomed. The family left for another bus stop. "Couldn't close the deal with Jasmine, huh? Pissed off that I had to take over? Is that it? Yeah, she told me she wouldn't have touched you with a ten foot pole, which is what I ended up giving her!"

Frank and a couple other guys jumped in and held Mike back. Duncan cowered behind the trashcan. Mike threw his hands up and stopped.

"Ah, whatever, not worth my energy."

He turned around, slapped my back and said, "Sorry bro, but your friend is a douche."

Mike took a seat on the bench. That eerie smirk crawled back across Duncan's face like ants emerging from an anthill. His thin lips twisted and contorted. He muttered something under his breath, inaudible enough that nobody else could hear.

I sort of felt sorry for him—for Duncan, not Mike. I felt guilty for bringing him.

Chapter 20

I was the last of my friends to depart for our first years at college. In the few weeks after the Florida trip the group rarely gathered; too much preparation. Last goodbyes and final good-lucks kept us to our immediate loved-ones.

This included an intermittent communication hiatus with Duncan. He and I talked briefly about logistics but in the days leading up to college, Ben and I had done the majority of planning without Duncan's input. Ben and I talked regularly, much more frequently than we ever did as high school classmates. Whose mini-fridge was biggest, who was bringing the microwave, which video game system was most appropriate—we discussed the kinds of pressing issues ranking at the pinnacle of every first-year college student's to-do list.

I blinked and the residual high-school afterglow evaporated. Moving day blew in like a summer storm, stealthy, chaotic and wet. And I left for Providence.

As with most stressful family events, my father planned to a fault, forgetting every old saying about inevitability, doubting Murphy's Law, ignoring the suggestions laid out clearly on the college website.

So we packed the car the night before. The pyramid of boxes, notebooks, clip-on reading lamps and microwaveable macaroni and cheese that had been looming high above the living room couches, crumbled feebly and neatly, packed away with furious precision into a sport utility vehicle.

Of course I packed the directions and move-in paperwork into a suitcase—a suitcase at the bottom of the packed vehicle. We unpacked then repacked with an exhausting fervor but not as much precision.

We scheduled an early departure. My father diagrammed the strategy with every detail in mind in order to avoid the move-in day bedlam and gridlock enjoyed by parents at colleges nationwide.

We arrived at the Providence College campus right about the same time as eight hundred other freshmen families.

My mother sobbed. My younger brother stared at the girls with dropped jaw and curious eyes. My father did too. He quickly forgot the embarrassment over a poorly planned and obviously mimicked departure strategy.

A Campus Security guard in a white truck guided us to Guzman Hall. The green lights blazing atop his vehicle were a feeble attempt at first-impression intimidation.

We pulled up as close to the main door as possible. In obedience with a makeshift sign jammed into the ground, my parents and I unloaded all my belongings onto the sidewalk grass in front of the dorm building. Apparently Campus Security wouldn't allow any vehicles to idle for too long. It was unload and go, to keep the traffic deluge flowing.

While my parents searched for the parking lot and picked their way back across campus, Ben pulled up with his mother and father. They dumped his material belongings and followed the familiar park and walk procedure.

As Ben and I stood chatting, waiting for our parents or some sort of direction, I was suddenly bombarded from behind by flailing arms and joyous squeals. Lindsey jumped on my back and yelled, "We're here!" She danced around like a cocaine-addled chipmunk.

"Ben, this is my friend Lindsey," I introduced, hardly able to speak because I was laughing so much.

"Excited to be at college?" Ben said sarcastically and stuck out his hand in her direction.

Lindsey shook it vigorously.

"Nice to meet you Ben," she said. "And yes, absolutely am I excited to be here. If you couldn't tell already."

"Never would've guessed!" he said.

"My parents just left. I'm so glad they're gone," Lindsey said. "My mom cried the whole time we were moving in. It was really embarrassing."

"Yeah, I have a feeling my mom's going to do the same thing," Ben said.

While Ben and Lindsey commiserated about their blubbering parents, I scanned the area for someone who looked like they knew what they were doing. A tall, skinny guy wearing a faded white blazer and black tie was walking towards us.

He introduced himself as Timothy, a senior on the Orientation Committee and pledged to help us find our rooms.

"Just leave the big stuff here, nobody will touch it. We'll go find your room and then hold an elevator," Timothy instructed.

"My parents are parking the car, shouldn't we wait for them?" I asked.

"Yeah, mine too, they don't know where they are," Ben added.

"I'll wait here, I'll bring them up to your room. I'm sure I can find it," Lindsey said. "I know your parents, Shaw. And I'll just stand with your stuff, Ben. The first two people I see that ask me what I'm doing with their son's underwear will be, I'm guessing, your mom and dad."

Guzman Hall was a typical dormitory building. A large rectangular box, five floors with one main hallway, twenty rooms lining each side. Timothy took us to room 204, pulled a strip of paper from his clipboard and pointed to the circular keypad right above the door handle.

"Just punch in your room combo, turn the lock and open the

door," he said, insinuating the ease of the process. It took Ben and I five attempts to successfully unlock the door.

When we did, we stepped inside the door and were welcomed by a barren, sterile void. The walls were cinderblock, painted a cream color that really just looked like dirty white. Black and white speckled linoleum floors connected to the same flooring in the hallway. Straight ahead, along the back wall of the room, three horizontal windows looked out onto a small hill that flowed down from the President's House, ending in a brick wall about five feet high. Opposite the windows, immediately to our left, were three closets in a row along the wall abutting the hallway.

There were three student set-ups. They were bunk beds, with no bottom bunk. Instead, a desk and dresser was tucked underneath. On the right side of the room two of these lofted set-ups ran along the wall, end to end. The other, lone set-up was directly across, running parallel with the left wall. We entered the room, eyed the large empty space between the set-ups and started mentally rearranging the furniture. We never ended up moving anything.

Ben spoke first once we got inside the room.

"So, who gets that bed?" he said, pointing to the lone set-up on the left side.

"I don't care, doesn't matter to me," I said.

"Yeah, me either."

"This happens to everyone," Timothy interrupted. "Which is why I always bring quarters when I let guys into their room for the first time. You call it in the air," he said to Ben.

"Heads."

The coin flipped high into the air, rotating like a sideways revolving door. In that instant I thought about Duncan and whether or not we should worry about what bed he wanted. The thought was brief.

"Tails, it's all you kid," Timothy said, handing me the slip of paper with the combination and the quarter.

"What's the quarter for?"

"I'm also your RA. We're having a little, um, unofficial first night gathering in the hallway later on. Your room will need the quarter, make sure to bring it. Nine o'clock, right outside your door."

He left us in the room and I could hear him say, "they're right down there on the right," from the end of the hallway. A few moments later Lindsey, followed by four nervous parents, arrived at our humble abode.

For most of the day we moved in, carrying all the clothes, linens, towels, lamps and computer accessories necessary for a fruitful freshman year. Lindsey made the process much more enjoyable, helping both Ben and I carry the unexpectedly massive amount of stuff we had in our possession.

Ben had an old love seat we set up in the empty space, giving us a sitting area. I brought the television and we set up an impressive array of video game systems and electronic devices between just the two of us.

Underneath my lofted bed I set up my computer on the desk and put my printer on the dresser. With my set up I would have my back to the other two beds, decreasing distractions while I worked. Ben did the same on the opposite side.

Around dinner time the room began to take shape, save for the one set-up closest to the door that had no sheets, no computer, no clothes and no roommate. Duncan still hadn't shown up, despite the school telling us all to show up at noon and ignoring the plans he and I had made to go to dinner with our parents at some place called Federal Hill.

"So, Ben, my family was going to go up to this place Cassarino's at that Federal Hill thing," I said.

"Federal Hill is their North End, Shaw. Their Little Italy," Lindsey informed us.

"Yeah, that place. Your family interested in getting some dinner?"

We figured out how to lock the door after only two attempts and then our families, plus Lindsey, went to eat.

It was the first time Lindsey and I would break bread together at one of the cramped, candlelit Italian restaurants clustered along Atwells Avenue. We frequented that same family-owned eatery countless times over the ensuing four years, ordering chicken parmagiana every time. They made the best in town.

"We have to come back here," Lindsey repeated over and over during the meal. And we did. It was our go-to place.

Eventually, when Lily and I kicked things off, I took her to that same restaurant. Of all the terrible things I did to Lindsey, I'm convinced this was the most painful. Jealousy flickered in Lindsey's eyes when she asked me how the chicken parm tasted without her. I kept the barrage coming when I told her I didn't know, that instead I tried fried calamari and lobster ravioli—Lily's suggestion.

If Lindsey weren't so strong, and if Lily weren't standing right there, Lindsey would've cried. Instead she swallowed hard, shrugged and said, "Chicken parm's better."

Lily, to her credit, understood everything. She knew Lindsey and I were close. She wanted no ruffled feathers. There were plenty of other great Italian spots on Federal Hill. We'd just have to find our own. We ended up trying them all, but never went back to the restaurant I shared only with Lindsey.

After Move-in Day Dinner, when we pulled back to campus, my parents tried to park and come up. I wouldn't let them. I made them drop Lindsey and I off at the front of my dorm. Lindsey said goodbye and walked into the building with Ben, whose parents had dropped him and sped away.

I leaned in the passenger window to kiss my mother.

"I really like her," she said in the most motherly way.

"Who, Lindsey?"

"Yes, Lindsey." She smiled one of those smiles moms get that all at once says, I know you like her and I know you'll screw it up. My mom, and most other moms as far as I could tell, all have that innate ability to sense pheromone fluctuation in their offspring.

"She's just a friend, mom."

"I know, I know. Just be good to her. She's so good to you."

"She is. Sometimes I don't deserve it," I tried to joke.

"Stop it! Don't talk like that."

"I was kidding, mom."

Her eyes went glassy. She sniffed back tears and told me she loved me then pulled down sunglasses that had been sitting atop her hair.

My dad got out of the car, walked around to me and leaned against the hood.

"Nervous?" he asked.

"Nah, not at all. It'll be fun."

"Good, good. It looks like you already have a couple friends. Ben's a good kid, that Lindsey is a sweet girl."

"Yeah, definitely. I'm looking forward to it. Plus Duncan should be here soon, I guess."

He looked in at my mother who was looking at herself in the visor mirror, wiping her hidden eyes with a tissue.

"So, any good fatherly advice for me?" I said, jokingly.

"I didn't know I was supposed to give a speech. How about, don't waste my $30,000."

We both laughed. I knew the financial burden that would be placed on my family and the gratitude couldn't be expressed in words. My father looked at the ground and then back at me. He extended his right hand.

"You know who you are, Shaw. You know what you want. Just be true to that, be true to yourself."

"Thank you, I will," I said, as we shook hands for the first time I could remember; like one man to another. Was he choking back emotion? Or was that me?

He got back in the car.

"Be good," he said. "Remember what I said. Look after yourself."

They both waved and started pulling away.
"Don't worry about me," I yelled.
The car was already turning the corner.

Chapter 21

Ben and Lindsey were sitting on the old love seat chatting when I got back up to the room after saying goodbye to my parents. Ben had left the door open so I didn't have to fumble with the keypad.

I stood in the doorway and examined my new home. Everything was as we left it a few hours before, except a huge pile of clothes now sat on Duncan's bed. The further into the room I got, the more I noticed his set-up. Duncan's computer was assembled, a stereo system on his dresser and a large array of shoes piled under the desk. He had also rearranged the desk perpendicular to the bed, so that if he sat at it, he would be fully underneath, looking out the door.

"When did Duncan get here?" I asked.

"Hey Shaw," Lindsey said. "I don't know."

"Must've come while we were eating," Ben said. "Looks like he doesn't mind the bed we assigned him."

"He'll be fine, it's all the same crap anyway," I said. "I wonder where he went?"

Until the floor meeting at nine o'clock, Lindsey and I decorated, trying desperately to add color to the beige paradise. I hadn't even been there a full day and the blandness blinded.

On my closet door I hung a poster of Eric Clapton. It was a picture of the picker playing his guitar, all in a blue hue. Under the strings of the first fret he had stuck a lit cigarette, the smoke curling up around his face, which had closed eyes and was deep in an emotional riff. Words at the bottom read, "Smokin' Blues."

It took us an hour to hang anything on the cinder block walls. Ben lent us some blue sticky putty that, after some massaging, finally stuck. I hung a horizontal poster. It was a photograph of the backs of naked women, sitting poolside. On each back was painted a different Pink Floyd album cover.

"I love that poster," Ben said.

"It's more like porn," Lindsey replied. "You just want to stare at their asses."

Ben and I both laughed.

"Are you kidding?" I asked her, mid-laugh. "This is a great picture. It's art, Linds."

"Plus, they have great asses," Ben chimed in. We laughed for a while, Lindsey scowling and reprimanding us for being pigs.

"All men are pigs. Some are just cuter than others," I advised her. "Write that down, save it. You'll use it some day."

"That's not true, you guys are alright," she said.

"What are you talking about? We're definitely pigs. Here, think about it this way. You know that warthog from the Lion King? He's an ugly pig. But then there's that pig from Charlotte's Web. He's cute and cuddly and nice and you love him, right?"

"Yes."

"Well, he's still a pig."

"What does that even mean?"

"Same thing with guys. Ben's an ugly warthog," I said. Ben hadn't stopped laughing. "Me, I'm cute and cuddly and nice. But I love these girls' asses. I'm a pig."

Lindsey wasn't a fan of our line of reasoning. The scowl on her face told me so.

"So you're saying that you are allowed to treat women like shit because it's ingrained in your genetic makeup? Sounds more like a justification of being an asshole."

"No, no, no. Not at all. I'm saying that you should just keep this in mind because most people aren't what they make themselves out to be. You gotta be perceptive enough to realize when someone is being real and when they're not. I embrace my piggishness."

"Oink, oink," Ben added.

"See Linds, a pig is a pig is a pig, no matter how cute Disney makes them."

The door swung open violently and slammed against the concrete walls. Duncan strolled in followed by a couple of burly guys I had never seen before.

"Shaw! Benny-boy! Lindsey!" he yelled as he walked in the door. "I'm heeeeeere!"

Lindsey and I both got up and went over to greet him. Ben stayed on the couch but shifted around to welcome our third roommate. The group of us stood around the couch, Lindsey and I on one side, Ben sitting, Duncan and his friends still somewhat in the doorway.

"What's up," I said. "What time did you get here?"

"About six o'clock," Duncan said.

"Where you been for three hours? Did you just dump your shit and leave?"

"Whoa, what's with the twenty questions, Inspector," he said mockingly, looking around the room for reassurance. "I met these guys while I was moving my shit in. They live right above us."

Both of them were taller than me and bulkier. The one to Duncan's left had sandy hair and huge, broad shoulders. He was wearing sweatpants, sandals and a wife beater. The wire-rimmed glasses gave him an air of jock-nerd.

"This is Regan Connelly."

Regan gave everyone a wave but didn't change his vacant facial expression.

"And this one is Tom Goneril," Duncan said, gesturing to the other behemoth standing to his right. "Everyone calls him Flask."

Flask was just as big as Regan, slightly leaner and fitter. He clearly spent plenty of time in the gym. He was wearing a tight leather jacket, jeans and a backwards New York Yankees hat that told me he was probably from Connecticut or New Jersey. It was my experience that ninety percent of Yankee fans said they were from New York. But it was also my experience that ninety percent of people at school who said they were 'from New York' weren't actually from New York. Rather, they were from the ritzy suburbs an hour outside the city but wanted to sound eclectic and mature by asserting their allegiance to the Big Apple.

"They're both from New York City." I was wrong.

"Oh, really? That's cool," I said. "I've only been there once, to Manhattan. Tourist places, you know. Are you near there?"

"Well, actually we're both from Greenwich. Right outside the city."

I wasn't wrong.

"Flask?" Ben asked. "Your mom's maiden name?" he chuckled.

Flask reached into his jacket pocket and pulled out a small gunmetal flask, popped the top and took a swig.

"Always be prepared," he said.

"That explains it. Good advice, though," Ben said.

"Regan, Flask this is Shaw, Ben and Lindsey," Duncan said.

Flask stepped out from behind Duncan and over behind the couch, closer to Lindsey.

"Lindsey, eh? Very nice to meet you."

"Same here."

"I have an idea though, how about we go upstairs to my room."

"What?"

"Let's you and me get out of here and go upstairs. I need to break in my new bunk bed, give it a good initiation," he said.

"Excuse me?" Lindsey scoffed. I could tell she was getting quickly annoyed. Lindsey had no patience for machismo. "I could've sworn you just said you wanted to 'break me in.'"

"No, no. I want to break in the springs in my mattress. I need to test out the durability and I want you to help me."

"Wow, I don't even know how to reply to that."

"Do you know her?" I asked him.

"Who, me? No, why?" he said. He looked genuinely confused.

Nothing annoyed me more than stupidity. And this guy apparently juiced himself up with needles full of it.

"I was just wondering if you knew her because I can't imagine you would say that to any girl, let alone a girl you just met."

"Dude, relax I was just kidding. Is she your girlfriend or something?"

"No, and that doesn't make a difference."

"Actually it does, if I wanna fuck the bitch I can."

"Excuse me?" Lindsey screamed. "Wow, Romeo, you must be great with the ladies. All those sweet nothings must be like honey in a girl's ear. How old are you, you fucking child?"

"Get behind me, Linds," I said, trying to step up to Flask. I hadn't heard Lindsey swear like that in ages.

Flask moved out from behind the couch next to Duncan. Ben stood up next to me.

"Disgusting pig," Lindsey sneered.

"I'm no pig, baby," Flask retorted. "More like a stallion."

"All men are pigs, some are just cuter than others," she said. She put her hand on my shoulder and squeezed. "You aren't one of the cute ones."

Duncan looked increasingly nervous and confused, as if his puppy just bit someone. Lindsey stood next to me fuming, enraged that any guy had the balls to address any girl the way Flask just did. Awkward tension and silence enveloped us for what felt like hours.

"Hey, hey he's just kidding Shaw, he's messing around," Duncan finally said. Nobody moved. "Seriously, relax man. And Linds, c'mon, it's a compliment! You're hot, deal with it."

It struck me as odd that Duncan would defend this guy he had met an hour before instead of the girl who had been his friend for months. At the time, I took it as his effort to keep the peace and prevent an unnecessary brawl.

Whatever his intentions, the intervention worked. Tension dissipated.

"My bad. I apologize, Lindsey—that's your name, right?" Flask said. "I was just teasing, trying to get a rise out of you."

She still fumed.

"Yeah, whatever. But just a word of advice, that line will most definitely not get you laid."

She huffed and flopped into my desk chair, turning her back on the whole scene.

Flask turned to me, stuck his hand out and I shook it.

"No hard feelings. Good to meet you, though," he said. Our hands were still clenched together. We locked eyes and squeezed until our knuckles turned white. I wasn't a small guy but mine looked like a child's hand enveloped by his mammoth paw.

"Overreaction on my part. Blame it on moving day – lots of stress," I said and rolled his fingers against each other in my grip. His knuckles popped. Flask flinched with the sudden pain, surprised by my ability to overcome his strength. My teeth bared a little as my smile widened.

"No worries," I said. Flask let go first.

We both looked over to Duncan. He returned an awkward smile and nodded.

Ben walked around me and over to Duncan and his two friends.

"It's almost nine, we should get out into the hallway," he said, ushering them along. He put his arm around Duncan's shoulder and asked him how he'd been, if he enjoyed his summer and was excited to finally be at college.

Much of that night remains a blur but the next morning I arose in a heap on an extra mattress lying in the middle of our room. Shaky and groggy, I peeked up into my lofted bed to find Lindsey snoring sweetly underneath a jacket; we never fit the beds with sheets or blankets. On Ben's bunk lay a pile of what looked like laundry but after a few seconds rose and fell with my drunken roommate's breathing. Duncan was nowhere to be found.

I sat down to recollect the previous night's happenings. Somewhere between wanting to kill some kid named Flask and stealing someone's mattress I poisoned myself to a degree of total blackout. I put my head in my hands and tried to dig deep for answers.

"Hey drunky," a quiet voice whispered from somewhere near the ceiling.

Lindsey's chin was resting on the edge of the bunk rail. Her hair rustled into a ponytail save a wisp falling over her cheek.

I just grunted.

She flicked me a wide, soft smile, all lips, which made her blue eyes narrow and sparkle. Her cheeks reddened. A vague dimple shimmered on her chin. She was beautiful in a way I'd never imagined her; lustful, curious and all at once content with the way the world was in that moment. The smile told me all this that morning. It was one I had never seen before, reserved only for me; I liked to think. I would see that smile many times over the ensuing four years. It came to be a comfort; my rock and I saw it in many times in the privacy of our own embraces. She smiled like that when she told me she loved me.

"So do you remember anything from last night," she said after a soft chuckle.

"Um, not really," I grunted. "The night's a little hazy. How about you?"

"Well I ended up throwing a pitcher of beer at Duncan's buddy Flask, right?"

I laughed. Memories stumbled into the light.

"Yes, we played Team Quarters in the hallway with my RA and the whole floor."

"That's why he gave you a quarter yesterday during move-in."

"It's coming back to me. Sort of," I said.

Tim the RA thought it would create hall camaraderie if we all broke the rules together on the first night. So he bought a few cases of cheap beer, set up a few glasses on a table in the hallway and made every room bring their quarter and play the classic coin-bouncing game, only team-style.

Duncan deserted us to play with his new bozo friends. Lindsey jumped in with Ben and I and was surprisingly accurate.

"We kicked some ass, I think," I said.

"I couldn't miss," Lindsey said. "I think I made a good impression on my first night at college. What do you think?"

"Half the floor was in love with you before the end of the night."

"Shut up."

"Seriously. I didn't ruin anything for you, did I?"

"What would you have ruined?"

"I don't know, I guess because I'm your friend from home other guys might stay away."

"Please, Shaw. Don't flatter yourself." She laughed.

"Alright, sorry. I just don't want to get in your way."

"Shaw, you're my closest friend here. We'll find the way together."

Silence floated down from her lofted position and enveloped me. I started feeling awkward because even though I looked down at the linoleum floor, I knew Lindsey was still staring at me, her bright azure eyes glistening with the onset of hangover.

"Here's a question: why did you throw a pitcher of beer at that guy?"

Lindsey sensed the tension, whatever kind it was, bristling between us. It may have been carryover from the night before, but I was far from remembering that. We both knew I was still dating my high school sweetheart. I opened the door to new conversation. Lindsey paused and then walked through.

"My fuse is always lit, Shaw. You know that."

"Clearly. But I can't remember why you assaulted him with Milwaukee's Best."

"He called me the c-word, remember? After we beat their team in the final game? It was a close one and everyone from the floor was around us chanting 'Blonde Girl, Blonde Girl!' I hit the last few, we won and Flask, Duncan and their other friend slung some pretty nasty insults at me."

"So you picked up the pitcher in the middle of the table and chucked it at them. You gave Flask a pretty good welt on his forehead too. Now it's starting to come back to me."

"I wanted to throw one at Duncan that night too. He was a royal prick to you. He started acting better than everybody else, like his shit smelled like roses."

Throughout the game Duncan's trash talking denigrated into spewing vile slurs. Friendly at first, he quickly aimed it directly at me. I wouldn't have minded so much had it not been so out of the ordinary for Duncan. But by the end of his rants, which had the entire floor in stitches, my little brother was gay, my mother was easy and I was a charity case let into college because the school had to fill their, 'poor white boy' quota. With almost full sobriety came almost full recollection.

"Yeah, wow I guess he was a jackass," I said. "Did he sleep here last night?"

"I don't think so," Lindsey answered. "I remember you and I arguing about me going back to my dorm. You were pretty adamant about me staying here. You said it wasn't safe to walk alone at night."

Her smile got even coyer. Her cheeks got even redder.

"Well it's not safe. We don't know the campus yet."

"I guess. I appreciate it. I just thought . . . nevermind."

"Thought what?"

"Nothing, forget about it."

"Linds, what?"

"You were really adamant about me staying with you, then you left. By the time you came back with a stolen mattress I was already up here waiting for you. You said something like 'we can't' and then flopped onto the mattress and passed out."

"Oh."

There was that tension again. Awkward? Sexual?

"I'm sorry," I said.

"For what? Don't be sorry for anything," she said with so much feigned enthusiasm and obvious frustration. "I didn't mean to imply anything."

"I think I took the mattress from a closet somewhere," I said to once again change the subject. We were traveling a risky road. "Or maybe someone's room. I honestly don't know."

"You should probably get rid of it before someone misses it."

She shuffled a little out of view up in the bunk, a maneuver resembling someone putting her pants back on. When she climbed down the ladder I noticed she was wearing one of my t-shirts. It had my high school logo emblazoned on the front.

"Come on, let's get this out of here and go find some coffee," she said, playfully pushing my shoulder.

"You should probably not be here if Duncan comes back. I think you ruined his new shirt with flying beer last night."

"Screw him. His new friends are terrible. And you know what Shaw? So is he. He sort of stabbed you in the back last night in front of all those new people. Insulting you like he did just to make himself the center of attention. Just to make himself look cool. That wasn't right at all."

"Whatever," I said as I tried to flip the mattress upright to fit through the door. "I don't really remember that much of it anyway. Maybe he was just drunk."

"We were all drunk, Shaw."

"Maybe. I have to live with the kid, Linds. I can't just go punch him in the face because he called me a few names."

"A few names? You really don't remember."

In fact I did. If one didn't know Duncan and I entered college as friends, they would've pinned us as sworn enemies with the way he verbally assaulted me the night before. I was his punch line; or worse yet, his punching bag. I just hoped it was a one-time deal.

"Let it go. I'll deal with Duncan if I have to."

"Alright, but just keep your eyes and ears open, Shaw. I don't want to see you get hurt."

"I won't get hurt, Linds. I'm a pretty tough kid. Plus, if I ever need anything," I looked directly into her eyes, "I've got you."

Chapter 22

The Providence weather is something of a mystery, for those who've never lived there. Some liken it to Seattle, some to London. Others see similarities with every other New England seaside community.

But in Rhode Island, Mother Nature is more fickle. She is at any time every season, every scenario, everything but reliable. She has good days and bad; hot days and cold; wet days and dry; sometimes all of it at once. And yet she refuses to allow any pattern to emerge so that those poor souls held captive to her mood swings might find comfort in consistency.

In the Rorschach test that is the United States, Mother Nature picked Maine to be snowy because it looks like a mitten. She made Texas hot because it sort of resembles a star. But what is Rhode Island? It is the one, tiny inkblot she had no answer for.

To diagnose her psychosis as manic would be to forget the opposite and just as frequent depression. Thunderstorms in the morning followed by warm, clear breeze at midday. She'd promise snow and give nothing more than a single gray cloud. When all seemed calm, a three-day deluge would wash away any progress.

And so the tiny smudge that is Rhode Island weathers Mother Nature's tantrums like any good, caring family member would, longing for those surprise days when the sun shines and the mood is calm. And when those days do arrive, they pray for some semblance of equilibrium.

So was my introduction to life in Providence. A September fog crept in off the ocean and welcomed the start of classes with an eerie lack of color. The rain popped in for a day or two but by Halloween we were trick-or-treating at the local bars in short sleeves. The next day a snow flurry fell but by week's end the Quad buzzed with active coeds soaking in a late-autumn heat wave.

The hectic and disordered weather mimicked the atmosphere in our dorm room.

As I promised Lindsey, I ignored Duncan's first-night fiasco and attributed it to the alcohol. But it made me aware and soon after I recognized splashes of similar behavior. Like the weather, no immediate pattern emerged but slowly his insults and backstabbing gossip grew more frequent. One night he'd invite me out with his new friends only to make me the butt of every joke. The next day he'd apologize and buy me lunch.

It was as if, like Mother Nature with Rhode Island, he didn't know what to do with me. Should he be warm and kind or frigid and distant? Should he include me or disregard me?

Eventually I gave up. I made up excuses to avoid Duncan. I knew his friends were not my friends.

A high-pressure situation was forming.

Late November proved to be one of Providence's great meteorological conundrums. Students were unsure whether to play Frisbee or make snow angels. Ben and I half expected Skirt Day—the first warm spring day when college girls, who have been itching under wool sweaters for three months, break open their closets and wear their shortest skirts—to happen in the fall.

And then, in severe contrast to what the local Channel 6 weatherman predicted, eight inches of wet, heavy snow dumped over Cape Cod, Newport and Providence for three straight nights. Classes were cancelled on a Friday, the first day of the storm. It was a cruel joke to play on students gearing up for finals, Christmas break so close. Especially since two days prior could have been autumn's version of Skirt Day.

Being from Boston I loved the snow, especially while at school. Snow meant the possibility of no classes and not having to shovel. Snow meant an intriguing case study in hedonism.

Perhaps because with snow came the possibility that tomorrow's day of learning could be buried under several inches of powder, or perhaps because it was just a change of scenery, snowfall at school sent the student body into full fledged party mode—no matter what day of the week or time of day the flakes began to fall.

This particular late November storm was no different. As freshmen it was the first one we'd experienced, so it took some time to catch on to the lightened atmosphere that Friday night.

Ben and I planned on staying inside to catch up on some studying for a take home final due Monday. Regular exams were still more than a week away. But our professor was high-tailing it from campus a bit early. She was on sabbatical during the spring semester and apparently wanted to push her tenure to the limits and escape ahead of schedule.

This, to us, only meant more work spread out over fewer days.

"Damn, you can barely see out our window, Shaw," Ben said from his desk. Our backs faced each other while we simultaneously tapped at keyboards. Neither one of us was working very hard. We were conversing with each other, amongst others, on social media. Our conversation was half verbal and half electronic.

I looked to my right at the dark, horizontal window. Snow was piled on the sill outside blocking half the glass and most of my view of the hill behind our dorm.

"Figures. It has to happen mostly over the weekend so we don't get more days off," I responded. "If this was Monday we'd be off all week! There's no way Physical Plant is coherent enough to clean this place up."

"Or sober enough," Ben laughed. He stopped typing. Voices in the hallway grew louder and closer and soon a piercing laugh cut through our heavy wooden door just as someone punched the keypad buttons and swung it open.

Duncan entered dripping wet in his new winter jacket and thick boots. Ben and I both watched him stride to his computer, sloshing muck and slush across the floor, click a few times and head back out. He said nothing to us and didn't even so much as acknowledge our existence. The only recognition he gave was as he shut the door and took one last look over his shoulder, directly at me, and then shoved off.

"Doesn't he have work to do too?" Ben asked.

"Beats me, he's not in any of my classes."

"Well I know he's in mine. And we definitely have a huge paper due next week that I'm positive he hasn't started yet."

"Is that the one you've been working on since Halloween?"

"Yeah, it's half our final grade. We can turn it in next week whenever we want, then the rest of the classes are pretty much a joke."

"Ah I see, so get it done and relax until Christmas."

"That's the plan, my friend. That's the plan."

We sat in silence for about half an hour, flipping between online chatting and take-home exam essay questions. Our hall was quiet. Outside the snow fell silently.

But outside was far from peaceful. Snow always caused a ruckus and something began to percolate soon after Duncan came and went.

A few times I got up to stretch and stared longingly out at the snow, which illuminated the entire night by reflecting the orange streets lamps along the campus walkways.

It was on one of these frequent breaks that I noticed a group of guys, red cups in hand, climb to the top of the hill behind our building. They lugged what appeared to be lunch trays from the cafeteria.

"Hey Ben, you gotta see this. These guys are going to kill themselves."

He joined me by the window, after first stopping by our mini fridge and grabbing two cans of Pabst Blue Ribbon. I didn't even hesitate to crack the beer. We pushed up the window an inch and, with the rush of brisk, icy air came the slurring laughs of the group peaked behind our dorm.

"They know there's a ten foot wall at the end of the hill, right?" I said.

"Are you asking me if they know there is a ten foot wall or are you asking me if they know they are going to fly off a ledge with a ten foot drop onto frozen dirt?"

"Either way I don't think they care."

"Now you're getting it," he said, and slugged the rest of his Ribbon, cracked another one and took a long drink.

"Do you think those trays will work?"

Right on cue three of the guys dropped their red cups, bolted for the incline, lunch trays in hand, and launched down the snowy hill, careening headfirst on rickety plastic. One of them was thrown off immediately and the tray skipped away behind a set of bushes. But the other two dueled en route to the cliff, slamming into each other with surprisingly accurate control over their makeshift sleds.

Our question about their knowledge of the wall was quickly answered when one of them noticed it for the first time just a few feet before falling. He rolled off his tray and tumbled to a stop at the edge of the wall, eating a mouthful of snow along the way.

His combatant wasn't so skillful, or lucky. He tried to turn the tray but caught a slick spot that only increased his velocity and shot him from the ledge like a slingshot. The tray shattered upon impact with the ground, ten feet below. But when the kid hit, with a very noticeable thud, he kept skidding right across the frozen ground, over the snow covered walkway that ran behind the building and slapped smack into the dorm wall, directly below my window.

Every window along the backside of the building erupted in laughter. It seemed like everyone decided to stay in but couldn't help but feast on the impromptu entertainment. The laughs from the building were drowned out only slightly by the laughs from the remaining guys at the top of the hill.

In the next ten minutes they put on a show worthy of any Warren Miller film, if Warren Miller was hammered and using stolen kitchen items. Some of them lost their nerve at the last second and bailed right before the drop. A few were too drunk, too stupid or too macho and careened over the ledge, screeching like schoolchildren.

The perceived fun was apparently too much for Ben to handle. He caught cabin fever in the few minutes we stood there, finishing off the Ribbons from the mini-fridge. I could see a rosy color flush his cheeks, which could have been from the beer or the brisk wind slicing in the barely open window.

"That's it, I'm going out," he said.

"Huh?"

"I'm going out there; I need to get out of here. Enough work for one night!"

"You're going to go sledding on a lunch tray? Are you alright? At least one of those kids has got to have broken a bone, and who knows how many of 'em got concussions."

"Sledding on a lunch tray? Who said anything about that?"

Ben opened his closet door and pulled out a pair of old skis, boots and poles from behind his bathrobe and winter coat. The smile on his face boasted pride and one-upmanship.

I laughed. I wasn't going to stop him, nor did I want to really. This would be just as funny, if not exponentially more hilarious, than the cafeteria tray luge team.

The initial crowd of a few drunken guys had ballooned into a somewhat large and rowdy gathering atop the hill. More household items had been McGuyvered into sleds—trash can lids, recycle bins, even a stop sign still attached to its pole someone had ripped from a street corner (this ingenious idea did not fare so well, seeing as how its rider was slung from it and subsequently smacked by the metal pole, almost impaling himself).

Duncan and a few of his friends were clearly visible under one of the orange street lamps for part of the exhibition but disappeared just before Ben arrived on scene.

Whether out of showmanship or sheer stupidity Ben put the boots and skis on before climbing the hill. But the duck walk up the slope brought more cheers and even a chant from the spectators.

He stood at the summit to catch his breath, pulled some ski goggles over his glassy eyes and wrapped the pole straps around his wrists. He clicked the poles together above his head and without hesitation, pushed off down the hill.

My first impression was a marionette—arms flailing, legs jutting out at odd angles and strange, jerking movements. But Ben got himself under control just in time for the skis to straighten out and pick up speed.

He hurtled toward the wall, snow spraying in wide arcs. He threw his arms out for balance and for an instant was vertically spread eagle.

The left ski tip snagged on the top of the wall, pulling his left leg to one side. The bindings clicked loose and Ben was catapulted out of the skis, equipment flailing, over the ledge and slapped onto the frozen ground below.

Silence clung to the snowflakes. I stopped laughing and gazed down with my jaw on the sill.

Ben was lying face down in a pile of dirty snow. One pole was propped neatly against the wall of the dormitory building while the other lay next to Ben, the strap still tightly around his wrist. Both skis teetered at the top of the wall, gazing down at Ben with contempt and pity, quivering ever so slightly as if shaking their heads in a, 'we told you not to do that,' scolding.

The once raucous crowd was frozen still and silent. The crowd, from the bottom of the hill to the top, held their collective breath. Nobody moved.

Except Ben.

Without getting up, he raised his right hand, flipped the middle finger in what was probably the direction of the top of the hill, and yelled an ungodly painful, but victorious, whooping sound. The crowd exploded into a, "BEN, BEN, BEN," chant. Their drunken, late night, snow-covered revelry was renewed.

The foolish things we did for fame and acceptance.

I shook my head in awe and horror, shut the window and went back to my computer. With the echoing noise outside, inside the room became eerily lonely.

The familiar ding of an incoming message on my cell phone interrupted my musings.

The number was blocked but I checked it anyway.

Fuck you, pussy!

That's nice, I thought, must be one of my high school friends being drunk on a Friday. The noise outside was rising and falling with each lunch tray that rose and fell down the hill. Maybe I should go out and hang with Ben?

Go home, loser!

That was strange. My friends typically just said hello with insults. They didn't carry on entire text conversations with them.

Who is this, I wrote. No response. I decided to go outside after all.

No sooner had I reached for a heavier pair of socks than my printer on top of my dresser kicked on and started warming up to print. I didn't remember printing anything. I figured I hit the print key on my essay when I closed it out a few seconds before.

Then it started printing. The sheet that spit out was not part of my unfinished take home paper.

I read the sheet twice before the rage filled every inch of my body. The paper in my hand shook from the violent trembling that began as soon as my brain comprehended the big, thick black words on the paper.

GO HOME, LOSER!
YOU HAVE NO FRIENDS. EVERYONE HERE HATES YOU.

The printer kicked on again. Another sheet spit out.

GO HOME TO YOUR WHORE MOTHER AND
YOUR POOR LOSER OF A FATHER!

I hadn't even finished reading the second sheet before the third started printing.

TRUTH IS, YOU'D BE BETTER OFF DEAD. KILL YOURSELF.

Sweat was beading in my palms and my fingers curled around the papers, crumpling them into a ball and squeezing it tighter and tighter in my fist.

I don't know how long I stood riveted next to the dresser but when I heard rustling in the hallway and saw Duncan slowly crack the door and peer in at me, I snapped.

I flew over the chair, the couch and the pile of laundry, flung the door fully open and grabbed Duncan by the collar. His body made a weak-slapping noise as I smudged him against the open door.

A mix of pizza and Coolwater Cologne hit my nose like red to a bull. I lifted him almost off his feet.

I barely noticed his group of friends standing, smirking, ready to burst into laughter.

I had him pinned against the door, a good chunk of his collar clenched in my fist.

He must have seen the anger in my eyes because the fear was clearly visible in his.

I knew Duncan was behind the printer prank. I didn't password-protect my computer and it would have been easy, even for him, to go onto my computer and put my printer on the campus network. He must have texted me to make sure I was in the room before hitting print from somewhere else.

I knew that he was aware it would really bother me. It pricked at something deeper than any usual insult—the obvious invasion of privacy, the lewd remarks, the subtle threats were all bad, but nothing compared to the fact that he was supposed to be my friend. Or he used to be my friend. The knife he had been plunging in my back the past few months was being twisted.

Throughout November, Duncan and I were virtually oblivious to each other. For the first few moths at college Duncan did nothing but belittle me in front of others. He became the bully and I the nerd, ridiculed for the amusement of all and the ego-driven satisfaction of one. When we were alone he acted like nothing was different. I finally stopped talking to him altogether, in public and private. Eventually he reciprocated into an awkward silence. We spoke only when necessary, to give a phone message or ask for a volume change on the television or computer (Duncan went and bought expensive headphones to eliminate the need for this latter conversation). Tension lingered. Ben felt it. Duncan and I never spent time in the room alone (he would always leave if it were just the two of us, usually without a goodbye).

With my hand around his collar, I was about to break the silence. And possibly his nose.

"What the fuck did I ever do to you?" I said softly, so his friends could only make out whispers. I leaned in closer to Duncan's face and repeated it. "What the *fuck* did I ever do to you?"

He said nothing. So I did.

"Tell me the truth you little rat. Tell me, what did I ever do to deserve this?"

My other hand was still crushing the crumpled piece of paper.

I raised my clenched fist, intending to shove the paper ball into Duncan's mouth.

His friends must've taken it to be an act of aggression because I suddenly felt numerous hands grabbing me and pulling at me in multiple directions. I didn't even struggle. I never broke gaze with Duncan.

I was on the verge of being pummeled when Ben came striding down the hallway, Shoddy and a few other guys in tow. The hands that held me loosened and as Ben arrived, Duncan and friends skipped down the hall the opposite way.

"What the hell was that all about?" Ben asked.

I didn't answer him and just walked back into the room and flopped on the couch. I tossed the balled up paper to the trash basket next to my desk, and missed. I didn't care to go pick it up off the floor.

Ben walked into the room, dripping wet with a purple mark on his cheek. He limped slightly.

Shoddy was carrying his skis—Ben was using the poles to help move around the furniture. But despite his obvious physical maladies, he was grinning from ear to ear and didn't stop talking for two hours.

While Ben regaled his alpine skills, Shoddy, who was sitting at my computer desk, found the crumpled paper by the barrel. He opened it up and was reading it just as I saw him doing so. Like a bad child caught red-handed, he dropped it in the trash and avoided eye contact with me for the rest of the night.

Duncan did not come back to the room until the following Monday. He never answered my question. He never told me the truth.

Chapter 23

By the end of our first college semester Ben and I hit a series of weekends where workload overtook party time and the inability to decompress socially and alcoholically caused unsaid tension. But Ben and I understood each other. It was Duncan who was the outsider, at least within our four walls.

Luckily, the school set aside the week before finals as study period for underclassmen. Classes ended and the real recognition and recall began. That first freshman semester I endured two intense final exams that certainly warranted real studying, plus the final paper that, by study period, was close to being finished. Had I not been sidetracked the week prior by a certain printer incident, the paper would be finished, polished and sitting on a professor's desk awaiting early review.

So began our first final exam season in earnest, laced with stress and doubt. Ben took off that weekend and headed for home. Home allotted him a comfort and a quiet unattainable in our parochial cinderblock dormitory among a hundred freshmen cramming frantically to remember their notes or drinking wildly to forget some sudden academic amnesia.

Ben logged out of his computer, packed up his books and took the train north to Massachusetts. I drove him to the train station that night and decided on the way back to campus that I'd stay in and finish that final essay while the info was fresh. Granted, the bars would be packed on the Friday of study period because no student had a test the next day.

There would be plenty of nights out if I got that paper done. It was freshman year—I was still idealistic about academia.

The room was dark and empty when I walked in. The three computers glowed from under our lofted beds, which in the dark room made them look like they were hovering. I promised myself I would get right to the work. Three episodes of Seinfeld reruns and two old cans of Pabst Blue Ribbon later I got off the couch and started writing.

My eyes and my fingers typed until 1:30am. I hit the print button, threw on a staple and shoved the completed essay into my bag.

It was too late to go out. It was too late for anything good to be on TV. I killed our stock of old beer. There was nothing left to do but go to bed. With the fire blazing behind my eyes and lines of Times New Roman, twelve-point font racing through my brain, sleep was not just the only option, but also the best.

After a half hour of cleaning up and shuffling around I was out cold, high above the cool tile floor in my warm lofted bed with only the soft glow of three monitors humming in the blackness.

Then white. Everything was instantly not dark, even though my eyes were still closed. The crash of the dorm room door on the yellowing concrete walls brought me all the way back from the comfort of dreamland.

I didn't move as lucidity washed over my body and mind and whoever waltzed clumsily around the room. Through a cracked eyelid I saw the green alarm clock lights flick over to 3:37am.

Dammit, I thought, that bastard woke me up. He was probably out getting hammered.

I had no desire to interact with Duncan at 3:37am so I rustled a bit, got more comfortable and tried to force myself back to sleep.

He moved around for a few minutes before, to my surprise yet extreme pleasure, he threw the door shut and snapped the lights off.

I sighed. I can get some sleep.

But Duncan didn't climb his ladder into his lofted bunk. And because of that, my brain refused to shut down. Every sound of his movement placed him at a specific location in the room—his closet to change, the fridge for some water, his desk to check his IM, the middle of the room to climb up to bed, past his ladder to Ben's corner, under Ben's lofted bed to Ben's desk, directly across from my bed.

I opened my eyes fully but still didn't move. I could see Ben's computer screen perfectly, especially with the lights off. Duncan was leaning over Ben's chair, not sitting in it, but seemingly looking for something on the desktop. I was curious. Duncan normally only cared about Ben when he needed help getting something from a high shelf in his closet.

But this was something different—something more sinister. Duncan crept around the desk, making sure not to move anything out of place. As if testing for an alarm system, and being satisfied with the result, he jumped into the chair and logged on to Ben's computer.

It was hard to see exactly what he was doing since his head blocked a large portion of the monitor but, from my high vantage point, I made out with certainty a long Word document, followed by an email website, followed by a message window that said *Email Sent*.

Duncan had emailed what looked like an essay paper from Ben's computer. To who, I did not know. But with treachery in the air, I had a pretty good idea what I just witnessed. I felt guilty watching, enraged at what I assumed he had done and relieved that it didn't involve me. I wondered if that was how Watergate went down. Our own scandal unfolded right before my eyes.

Duncan closed everything out and logged off Ben's computer. He quickly went to his own desk underneath his own bed and jumped on his own computer.

From my bed the view wasn't nearly as good as it was to Ben's desk. Since Duncan was now diagonally behind me, I would have to shift my whole body to get a full view of the screen.

I debated myself. Should I try and see what he was doing? Did I owe it to Ben to get as much info as possible? Or did it not involve me so therefore I should try to go back to sleep? Whatever I chose, I was positive that I did not want Duncan to know I was awake. His reaction to that revelation would be either terror or rage, both of which I wanted to avoid at 4:00am.

I shifted a little so I could at least see the back of Duncan's head. The debate was answered for me. Duncan had put on his huge, expensive earphones. They were the kind that musicians wear in the studio—the kind that covered the whole ear. Duncan wouldn't hear me move around. He wouldn't hear me if I jumped out of my bed and started jazzercising in front of the couch.

I moved a little more so I could see the computer screen. Duncan was checking his email, one of which was new. I couldn't read it, or whom it was from, but it had an attachment. He went right for it, downloading the long text document, saving it to a folder and then deleting the email.

This evidence supported my suspicions.

I had to tell Ben when he got back. He could check his computer and see what document was recently opened. For some strange reason, maybe Duncan's late night cat burglary, I guessed the document was a final paper for a class that Ben and Duncan had together.

What else could I do, I thought as I shifted back to my original position and tried to fall back to sleep. Should I confront him? No. Let Ben do it. But what if Duncan deleted everything or Ben didn't believe me?

Fury started building. Everything from the past few months bubbled up. The printer incident, the first night on campus, the countless times that Duncan had put me down in front of people to make himself look good. Every insult he slung my way combined with every lie I knew he told me and every lie I just assumed he uttered on a regular basis.

I felt guilty. I brought Ben into this ugly living situation with this ugly sham of a friendship I had with Duncan. Since we got to Providence Duncan slung bile at me in front of potential new friends, girls, administration and teachers. Did it make him feel better about himself? It lifted him in the eyes of people I didn't care about—if they thought that Duncan calling my mother a whore made him a better person than me, I wanted nothing to do with them anyway.

It didn't bother me, at first. But the repression boiled over that night lying in bed, knowing he had probably just stolen a paper from our roommate—knowing that he would probably get away with it.

That was it. I had to say something. My temper won out and I wasn't even involved.

I sat straight up, fully prepared to come to blows over an assumption and a few months of him being a terrible friend.

I was punched in the gut before I even got a full glimpse of the situation and I shot back down immediately. What I saw was the full intrusion—from Watergate to a Bill Clinton-esque scandal in one fell swoop.

All at once I realized why Duncan had no problem invading Ben's computer: he had no idea anyone else was in the room. Which was why he had no problem watching hardcore pornography.

Duncan wore his big headphones; totally muffling any moans, cries or bedspring creaks.

Lying there, apparently invisible to the other person in the room, I prayed for continued silence. But then the nightmare was reality and I heard a strange noise—the noise skin makes when skin is rubbing up against it at a quick pace. I winced.

He was oblivious to the world, masturbating with me ten feet away. I didn't know what to do.

Vomit was one option. I could feel hot bile creeping into my throat.

I coughed as loud as I could, partly to disturb the sour taste and partly to signal my presence in the room. Nothing. He couldn't hear me. I coughed louder, kicked my feet against the baseboard, shook the bunk until it slapped against the concrete wall.

"Hey," I said. "Heyo, hey!" It wasn't loud enough. All Duncan could hear was the climactic scene from one of Silicone Valley's cinematic masterpieces.

I tried to think what I could throw at him. My pillow, but I didn't want that anywhere near him. My alarm clock, but as much as I would have enjoyed seeing him in pain I decided this situation did not merit blatant assault.

Genius washed over me. I pulled off my socks and balled them up.

I laid on my back, the socks held gingerly in my right hand. The blue light from Duncan's screen sent shadows gyrating on the white ceiling above me. I was involuntarily included in this perverted voyeurism and I hated him for it.

Thoughts of trench warfare materialized. That was what we were engaged in—hostile encounters leading to a spark that would blow the powder keg sky high. He sent shots across my bow as soon as we arrived. I tried to negotiate—my attempts were met with nothing but contempt. I had to return the volley.

My right arm tensed. I rocked up once, twice, the third time far enough to see over the bunk railing to take aim. As my back came down to the mattress my right arm cocked, fired and launched the sock grenade. I watched it arch towards Duncan, scraping the ceiling and fracturing the smut shadows thrusting around the room. The sock grenade was out of sight. I didn't hear it land but I knew I was accurate. I waited for the reaction, the impending embarrassment and enormous awkwardness.

As I expected Duncan's chair scraped on the tile and I heard the noise of his headphones being dropped on the keyboard. Female moans, muffled and overacted, spread around the room. He had those things turned way up.

The orgasmic cries somehow made the anger in me fade away. Instead, I was overcome with the absolute absurdity and comedic value of the situation. Hilarity boomed deep in my stomach and in seconds I was in full out silent laughter, grinning at the possible jokes I could make at Duncan's expense. Soon, I thought, he would realize where the sock grenade came from, I would jump down laughing and we would joke about it and then never speak of it again. We had a hatchet to bury and as perverse as this situation was, it may be the best hole to bury it in. I laughed at my slew of unintentional puns.

Feeling a bit more relieved, I started to sit up. But before I even peered over the railing Duncan was moving towards my bed.

What the fuck? I thought. I laid still.

He was directly underneath me, the moans still echoing off the concrete walls. Duncan was stealing my tissues. He shuffled back to his desk with the entire box and it was then that I noticed his underwear around his ankles. My sock grenade lay, ineffective, on the tile next to his desk chair. During his duck walk across no man's land, Duncan unknowingly kicked it under the couch.

He still had no idea he wasn't alone.

The situation was getting funnier by the minute. Especially since it had only been one or two minutes since Duncan sat down at his desk to start the festivities.

I realized, though, that we had almost reached the point where, if I did not say anything, the situation flipped from Duncan being horny, disgusting and hilariously oblivious, to me being some sort of sick voyeur. For comedy's sake, I had to keep it from crossing that line.

But I was saved from even having to do that.

"Dunk! Hey Fuckface, open up!" shouted someone from outside the door. Flask's voice vibrated the walls, along with his fist pounding on the door. "Open the door, Dunk. You gotta hear this. Hey!"

"Son of a bitch," Duncan whispered to himself.

I remained motionless, lying on my back high aloft.

Duncan threw away some tissues in his trashcan, minimized the porn window on his computer and went to the door.

Flask burst through with the click of the lock and hallway light snuck in. Duncan shielded his eyes, pretending to have been asleep.

"What the hell, Dunk? You disappeared earlier," Flask said. He flicked the lights on himself and instantly the dark room was bathed in yellow fluorescent glow. He rushed to the couch, all hyped up for a reason he was about to recount to Duncan in truly embellished fashion. "Were you sleeping? Already?"

"Yes. What do you want?" Duncan said.

"That shit you gave me was awesome, kid. It totally worked. I had that blonde from the soccer team back to my room in about five minutes."

Duncan acted intrigued but was trying to block Flask's view of his computer.

As Flask started to recount his female conquest a low moan suddenly crept out from the big black headphones on Duncan's keyboard.

Flask stopped mid-sentence and stared at Duncan who was leaning against the desk, trying to pretend nothing was unordinary.

Realization dawned on Flask's face and he instantly looked uncomfortable.

From my perch, I watched a string of emotions unfurl: awkwardness, discomfort, anxiety, pure horror and ultimately, unfathomable embarrassment. The entire scene, from porn to present, mixed all the drama of *Romeo and Juliet*, all the tragedy of *Othello* and all the comedy of *Animal House*. From Duncan's stupidity to Flask's obvious use of some sort of foreign female-getting substance to Duncan's lame attempts to hide his scandalous activity, I was in the midst of pure irony; pure hilarity; pure retribution.

Flask stood up from the couch, seemingly to wrap up his tale and get the hell out of the room. His voice started to waver as he clearly rushed along, skipping the more elaborate details.

"Yeah, so she sort of came to when we got back to the room man and then, ya know I gave her another drink and took her pants off. So that shit was the shit, I've been trying to . . ." Coming to the climax of his story Flask had gotten animated and in doing so his line of vision landed on me up in bed. My eyes were closed but the lump of a human being under blankets was unmistakable.

"Awe shit, man, I'm sorry I didn't know Shaw was sleeping," Flask said. He looked a little more relieved, like what he thought Duncan was doing couldn't be right if I was in the room.

Duncan's expression went from anxiousness to anything but relief.

"What?" he said, almost in a whisper as if his voice was snatched away by an invisible hand. "Shaw's not here."

Flask's smile, ear to ear, matched my own. That was the point of climax. The entire dorm room was set to explode in laughter.

"Yeah, man, he's right there," and he pointed up to me. At which point I sat up, rubbing my eyes.

"Hey Dunk," I said, "Could you toss me my socks? After you wash your hands."

Flask and I exploded in laughter. Flask guffawed like an idiot. My laughs were more directed, heavier and vicious. They were different; they were laced with anger. Every vitriolic chuckle burst out of me like I had bitten a cyanide capsule and spewed the mocking poison across the room at Duncan. His face screwed up in pain, tears forthcoming. I felt the sickness of it all seeping backwards into my own throat; I'd be poisoned too. But as is the purpose of a cyanide capsule, I had no other choice. I needed to regain control, even if the guilt killed me. It was a last ditch effort for the social upper hand. It was a long, slow suicide of the soul that hastened with each sneer at Duncan's exposure. Duncan's face flickered and burned from pain to embarrassment to rage.

The fact that his big, tough guy friend figured out the situation made it ever more satisfying.

"Hey Shaw, were you up there for the whole thing?" Flask snorted between laughs.

"Yeah, all minute and half of it!"

"Fuck you!" Duncan screamed, loud enough for people in the hallway to peer in through the open door. "Fuck you," he yelled directly at me, eyes boring holes into mine. He pushed Flask, who wasn't even phased by the small hand on his broad chest and ran out of the room like a ten-year-old boy who was just scolded by his mother. I couldn't see his face but I imagined tears streaming down.

Flask, still chuckling, repeated, "priceless," to himself and walked out after Duncan.

I hopped down from the bunk, laughing so excessively a sour taste crept into my mouth. I ran down to the bathroom with a sudden urge to vomit, either from laughing so hard or because of what just occurred a few feet away.

Duncan was nowhere to be found.

Duncan disappeared for the rest of the weekend. Either he knew when I was in the room and came and went when I was gone, or he just avoided the room altogether. No matter, the story spread around our hall like herpes on the men's hockey team. Flask was at fault, mostly. I recounted it to my friends and a few others but by Sunday night *Dunk* had a few new nicknames.

Chapter 24

Shoddy defined irony as, "God's little practical jokes."

Shoddy was also the least religious person I had ever encountered. The Catholic Church, Protestantism, Judaism and Islam were simply variations of the same fantastic story used to manipulate mortals into giving of themselves and their wallets.

He was an indefatigable cynic.

Seeing the RA out at a bar getting hammered the night after breaking up a dorm party; the director of the Student Program Board forgetting an extension cord for the outdoor Spring concert; the local Irish tavern running out of Guinness on St. Patrick's Day. These were the little "practical jokes" Shoddy enjoyed. I called them fate, karma, bad luck, good luck. He said it was the truth—the little slipups that showed you who someone really was, and someone, somewhere (perhaps a higher being) was watching and laughing.

If Shoddy believed in anything, it was this credo. He loved exposing people: his passive-aggressive revenge. A large percentage of his acquaintances held Shoddy in very low esteem. Enemies outnumbered friends but Shoddy never cared. He was still usually the life of a party, mostly due to his charismatic ability to spark or fuel a conversation (for better or worse).

In a crowd, Shoddy was an instigator. But he also played the agent, manager and referee all in one. He could set up the prizefight, draw in the spectators, square off the opponents, and then sit back and watch the chaos, controlled at intervals by his own skilled conversational manipulation. He almost always walked away the winner, usually without ever throwing a punch himself.

Shoddy liked to test common sense versus book smarts and it became a hobby. To his credit, he overflowed with both; which is really what pissed off his detractors. They never understood that he was examining human behavior; prying and poking around the little intricacies that make us individuals; attempting to rip away those facades we all erect to keep out unwanted advances on our real vulnerabilities. Maybe he thought he was doing God's work, in his own twisted sense of the deity. Maybe he just got a kick out of making smart people stumble over themselves.

I understood all that about Shoddy. Most everyone else did not.

Shoddy's favorite instance occurred when someone, usually a classmate in the middle of a highfalutin rant about some chapter in some novel, made reference to "irony" or something being "ironic" when, in Shoddy's opinion, it was merely sarcasm, facetiousness or pure coincidence. Whatever it was, whether he was right or wrong, Shoddy made his disagreement known. He was neither just nor kind.

However, this same person that relished in the ignorance of America's young adults and called out anyone that he thought was using less than his required amount of intelligence, was the same person who was going to risk his life so those people had the right to be that way. He insulted them and then insisted on their right be insulted (one of Shoddy's favorite arguments for liberty was its comedic value).

"Hey, if God's playing a little practical joke, who is it on?" he would say. "You, because you don't know what irony means? Or me, because I finally get to see how stupid you are."

But he never pushed it too far, which was something he would need to control in the spittle-spewing hierarchy of the United States military. For all their bravery, valor and honor, soldiers were not famous for their Shakespeare recitations and flawless diction. Shoddy was well aware and to a degree, it excited him. He was to be a wolf in a land plentiful with sheep. But he must take heed the shepherd.

I always imagined him as Hamlet being ripped from Denmark and dropped into Othello's world. With his melancholic, observant intellect came Shoddy's knack for recognizing someone's triggers, anticipating the breaking point and removing himself from an interaction before the explosion.

Shoddy saw life as a great experiment and those around him were his unwitting and sometimes unwilling participants. All he had to do was manipulate the variables. But what it was he hypothesized or sought to discover never really became clear to me. The strange relationship we shared was possible because to me, he dropped the tests. I don't know how I did it, but I passed them way back when we met. Or perhaps it was because, as he put it one night in a drunken emotional rant, he knew I was thinking the same way he was. I just had the tact or respect to not vocalize it to the world.

Despite the cynicism and the disparaging remarks to stupid people, Shoddy exhibited one character trait that outweighed everything else, both in quantity and value: loyalty. Very few people knew it, and I was certainly the only one not blood related to him who was a benefactor. Shoddy was simultaneously the cockiest asshole on campus and the personification of *semper fidelis*.

He may have been blind to all these little circles of irony: his hatred of religion while constantly using non-secular language, his criticism but staunch defense of ignorance and his bad reputation yet undying loyalty. Somehow, though, I always thought he simply relished in their genius.

When Ben and I returned to our dorm room the final weekend after the masturbation incident, we found Duncan's belongings strewn down the hallway and Shoddy moved comfortably into his spot. We both started to believe that maybe Shoddy was a genius.

"Hello gentlemen," Shoddy said, standing up from his desk chair with a can of Pabst in his left hand. "My name is Marcus Shodowski, I'll be your new roommate," he laughed.

"What the hell happened here?" Ben asked.

Shoddy answered him by slugging down an oversized gulp of beer, crushing the can and tossing it into the barrel.

"Follow me," he said, and strolled out into the hallway. He took a left and headed towards his original dorm room, pointing to the boxes of junk and some bedding strewn about the hallway. He arrived at his old door, punched in the combo and kicked the door open.

In the far corner was Duncan, trying desperately to pull a sheet over the top bunk mattress of his new bed. He looked up and scowled.

Shoddy reached deep into his cargo shorts' pocket and produced another Pabst can. He cracked it open, took a small swig and pointed at Duncan with an accusatory, outstretched arm as if to yell, "he did it!"

It took Ben a moment but upon realization, he grinned. "Hey neighbor," he said, "congrats on the new home."

"Sorry," I added, "We forgot a housewarming gift."

All we got in return were squinted eyes and low, growled, "fuck you."

"Let's let him finish his interior decorating," Shoddy suggested as he pulled the door closed and started back to our room. "He's going to have a hell of a time with Flask. That kid is a mess."

Shoddy reached into our fridge and pulled out two more beers. He kicked his one box of possessions out of the middle of the room and under his desk and handed us the Pabst.

"So roomies, a toast," he said, raising his can to eye level. "To new beginnings, fresh start, another chance—a rebirth, if you will."

He tapped his can to ours and took a drink. Ben and I followed suit, still somewhat confused as to how this situation came to fruition.

"One question," Ben said after downing half his can. "How'd you pull this one off?"

"Ha, how? That was nothing. I mentioned it to Flask this morning, that Duncan and I should switch rooms. Basically I told him I was going to do it whether or not he helped me. You know how Flask sucks at that little weasel's teat, so he immediately jumped in to help me move Duncan's crap. Trying to brown nose for some odd reason. But anyway, we figured it'd be easier to just get in and move the stuff rather than get the RAs involved. Fuck paperwork. Who cares if I can't get my phone messages in your room? So I broke into your room—I watched Shaw punch in your combo a few weeks back and remembered it. We pulled all of Duncan's shit out, moved me in and here we are."

"Duncan didn't know?" I asked.

"Oh he knew, when he came home and half his stuff was in the hallway. Flask told him what we did, said it was his idea so that Duncan didn't have to live with you anymore." Shoddy tipped his can in my direction.

"Surprisingly, Duncan was pretty pleased with the situation. He said a few things to me about his shit being dirty from the hallway floor but he was just flexing his muscle in front of his new roommate."

"OK, follow up question," Ben asked. "Why did you do all this?"

Shoddy had flopped back into his desk chair. He reclined onto the back legs, propping his feet onto his computer keyboard that lay among the strewn papers on his desk.

"I mean, don't get me wrong, I love not having Duncan in here. I'm just curious as to why?" Ben reiterated.

Shoddy took a drink and stuck out the same accusatory finger, this time in my direction.

"Because one of you was going to kill that little fucker, and my money was on Shaw. And for the record, I don't want Shaw to go to jail unless it's for something worthwhile. Snapping that little bastard's neck is definitely not worthwhile."

"Well, thanks I guess," Ben said.

I, for some reason, was speechless. I hadn't known Shoddy for six months and he was pulling tricks to protect me. No other friend I ever had would have even thought to switch rooms, let alone actually done it.

"Yeah. Thank you," I said. Shoddy stared at me and tipped his beer in my direction again. He understood my sincerity. And he appreciated it. That moment was the start of a mutual loyalty; an unspoken agreement that I would put my faith in him and he in me; that from then on, there was no pithy argument, senseless squabble or slutty freshman girl that a cold beer together could not fix.

"Anytime bro," he said. "Plus I really couldn't stand living with Flask anymore. I saw or heard that kid do some pretty fucked up stuff, especially to girls. I'm no Boy Scout but that kid has issues."

Shoddy really did hate Flask, but I knew he only mentioned that to give our two rooms a more us versus them feel. He painted them the bad guys. The three of us were now a team.

"Oh, I almost forgot. I have something to celebrate the occasion. My older brother is an Army specialist—Task Force Odin."

He reached under his desk and pulled out a paper bag, from which he extracted a golden bottle with a raven on the label.

"He sent me this at the start of the year, as a college move in gift. I never had anybody to drink it with."

Ben and I sat down. It seemed like the right thing to do. The bottle was clearly important to Shoddy, as we determined from the change in his voice as he uttered 'my brother.'

"What is it?" I asked.

"Mead. Honey wine. Like they used to drink in the old days. Knights, Vikings, you know, all those great warrior types. What better way to celebrate our recent victory?"

He cracked it open and poured a glittering golden liquid into three dusty glasses.

He again raised his to eye level. Ben and I followed suit. This was becoming a ritual.

"Love, loyalty and life—to you my friends," he said, and we all gulped down some mead.

Our three faces reacted the same. First a one-eyed squint at the strength, a half pucker at the bitter start and finally, a mellowed calm from the sweet, honey finish as the warm liquid trickled through the body.

We poured three more glasses without talking and raised them to the gods. I reclined and relaxed and when Shoddy broke the silence to tell us about his brother's task force, it set off a discussion that lasted until three in the morning. We talked about war, about mythology and Norse gods and about some crazy girl that wouldn't stop calling Ben and how Shoddy should handle the next psychotic late night phone ring.

Duncan's name wasn't mentioned.

Chapter 25

As Shoddy had suggested, second semester was a new beginning.

Duncan had moved out, Shoddy had moved in. Ben and I were taking a few classes together and I had taken on a second major—psychology. Combined with my English major, I thought I'd be able to finally start figuring out what I wanted to do with my life. I quickly realized the two subjects had a lot in common. In English, I studied language. In psychology, I studied the people who use it. I would come to see both disciplines in action very shortly thereafter and continue evermore.

When we had all left for winter break, the mead-colored sun and situation shifts left my room a little more content. It was believed that Duncan was now an afterthought.

Despite the new knowledge and new potential, the semester began unexpectedly.

Prior to returning in early January, our first ever college grades arrived home in the mail. I was proud that my academic achieving carried over from high school. Ben, however, was not as consistent. He received an incomplete on his grades and was put on academic probation.

"Can you believe this?" Ben screamed as he burst into our room the first day back. "I can't even start classes until I figure this out."

I was confused until he explained to me that the Dean of

Academics and Student Affairs, Dean Midland, had called his house over winter break and said Ben was part of a plagiarism incident and that he would be investigated for his role.

"He wouldn't tell me the other person involved, though."

Shoddy came rumbling in a few minutes later, a huge smile on his face. He chucked his duffle bag up onto his bed and flopped onto the couch, ignoring the obviously intense conversation Ben and I were having.

"Dude," he said to us both, "I was just talking to that kid Terry down the hall and he said Duncan is on academic probation for copying someone's work. Isn't that hilarious!"

Ben's eyes shot at Shoddy. If I could've read his mind, I'm sure the mental image would have resembled a death scene from a Tarrantino movie.

"Well," I said, "at least that answers your question."

"I'm going to kill that son of a bitch," Ben growled and made for the door.

"Whoa big boy," Shoddy said. "He's not there. I already checked. Hasn't come back yet."

Since we had a couple days before classes started up again, I grabbed some beers from the mini-fridge that I re-stocked and turned on the X-Box. We spent a few hours virtually killing Nazis, which helped calm Ben.

By noon I had received a phone call from Dean Midland's receptionist, Mary, telling me to be to his office in an hour.

"What the hell does he want to see me for?"

"Did you steal my shit, too?" Ben said, only half joking.

"How do you think I passed Brit Lit?" I laughed as I grabbed my shampoo and headed out for the bathroom.

Ben and Shoddy weren't in the room when I returned. I had some time to collect my thoughts before trekking across campus to the administration building.

Campus was quiet and gray. Even the golden cross atop the chapel was tarnished by the bleak winter day. I took the main concrete pathway across the Quad—the only pathway they shoveled and salted. The grass and radiating walkways remained covered in frozen gray slush, the aborted remnants of a holiday blizzard. By the end of the walkway, water had seeped into my shoes. I sloshed to the left towards the administration building, the oldest building on campus and frequently the front cover photo of its promotional materials.

The main gates of the college, sleek iron-wrought and spiked, admitted visitors to a long driveway that curled past the science laboratories and the friary, ending at a dead end circle in front of the administration building's beautiful, gothic archway. In the summer, spring and fall the grass in the circle was clipped to a perfect crew cut and the flag pole shined; flowers bountiful unlike anywhere else on campus garnished the landscape and the jagged spires and ambiguous cement façade were spray washed to reveal an unnatural cement color. In the winter the plows focused on the driveway and the circle. Maintenance workers were seen hanging from the stained-glass windows, using brooms to brush away snow from the façade's statues and more unique structural quirks. To the outside world, this was the college's front door. To everyone behind the walls, it was rarely seen. Nobody ever really came that way.

I didn't. I snuck in a side door and stomped the slush from my shoes as I walked down the hallway towards the rotunda. Before checking the brass faculty directory, I looked up and examined the high colored and castle-like windows. On brighter days the sun splashed through them and glistened the spectrum around the stone circle immediately inside the building's front door. To prospective students it was like walking into a carnival, vibrant fun splayed out in front of them. All they had to do was sign on the dotted line. To their parents it looked like a medieval church foyer, the light of God shining down on their son or daughter.

I chuckled because that day the dreary winter sun wasn't having the same effect. I saw no sign of clowns or the Lord. I checked the directory and headed for Dean Midland's office on the third floor.

I had never seen Dean Lucius Midland before. He was one of those administration people who you always hear about but who never makes an appearance outside his office. He dealt in discipline. And by all accounts, he was good at it.

His reputation preceded him; he was conservative in his politics but liberally dealt out punishment. A few students talked of him as they would the grim reaper; a curious inevitability for any student caught breaking the rules. Most said the scariest moment was when he let his thick Louisiana accent wrap around your name for the first time, like a swamp snake slowly coiling around its prey.

I wasn't afraid, though. I had done nothing wrong.

When I reached his office and entered the waiting area, the cute girl behind the desk quieted the horror stories.

Mary the receptionist was a brunette graduate student, thin and buxom with a slightly oversized nose. It actually added to her attractiveness, balancing out her other oversized body parts. She wore black-rimmed glasses and her hair in a ponytail and didn't say a word when I walked into the foyer outside the Dean's office. She simply pointed a well-manicured finger at a long wooden bench against the wall and went back to whatever studying she was doing before I came in.

The massive oak double doors to Dean Midland's office were closed. They looked ancient and heavy, resembling the rest of the architecture in the old castle-like administration building. This outer room's décor matched the school's outdated perspective that handcuffed it to religious philosophies. If the administration building was the campus citadel, Dean Midland's office was where the inquisition took place. If the Dean was dressed in full knight regalia, I wouldn't have been surprised. The entire place gave off an air of sophisticated incredulity and intellectual castigation. Mary didn't even have a computer on her desk. The only modern touch besides the industrial plastic no smoking sign hung above her head, was Mary. Even her beauty couldn't bring the place out of the Dark Ages.

"Dean Midland will see you now, Mr. Shaw," Mary said sweetly. I must have been the only appointment that afternoon because I never told her my name. She glided over to the double doors, swung them open with ease and shut them behind me with the same grace and poise, like Audrey Hepburn studying for her MBA.

At once a rush of musk and tobacco filled my nostrils. The Dean obviously broke at least one rule himself.

The room matched the doors and if I hadn't been lucid, I'd have thought I traveled back to a medieval scholar's library. Dusty bookshelves reached from floor to ceiling and were filled with equally dusty books. Dark oak furniture filled the room, centered on an oversized desk behind which sat a vulture of a man.

He wasn't wearing full knight regalia. Rather, he wore a dark green sweater vest over a pinstripe shirt and dark necktie pulled painfully tight at the collar. A gray tweed jacket was thrown loosely on a sitting chair in the corner. His bald head sloped down into a hooked nose similar to Mary's, although definitely without the same effect.

He did not peer up from the manila file he was paging through on his desk but simply adjusted his wire-rimmed spectacles, pointed to a chair and said, "Please sit down, Mr. Shaw."

His Southern accent looped around my name, elongating the pronunciation and suffocating it, as if he were trying to snuff out my very identity.

I sat for a few minutes before he acknowledged I obeyed his order. He was engrossed with reading my file, doing his background research. It was a tactic to scare me into talking. At first, I fell into the trap and my leg started twitching nervously. But once I understood his game, the drama and romance of the building, the room's ancient preamble, the man and his mythological reputation, all vanished.

I walked in ready for a normal conversation. But this was actually an interrogation. The Dean should have thought of a better approach, one where I wasn't treated like a truant. The assumed antagonism was common between students and administration. Nevertheless, it still annoyed me. His stalling made me less apt to cooperate.

"Mr. Shaw, thank you for coming in," he said finally. His small black eyes behind the glasses inspected me intently. "I would like to talk to you about your roommates, Benjamin and Duncan."

The news of Duncan and Shoddy switching rooms clearly hadn't made it to the administration. We wanted it that way.

"You know them, I presume?" he continued. It was an absurd question but he said it with purpose, slow and methodical.

"Yes, sir," I said, not masking my annoyance.

"Good. Now please tell me if you ever saw them studying together?"

"Actually I never saw either of them study. Ben always went to the library to study and I have no idea if or where Duncan read his books."

The Dean wasn't pleased with my sarcasm.

"Do your roommates ever use each others' computers? For games or internet chat or anything?"

He was being very direct. He wanted answers. He wanted a rat. I was no rat.

"They both have their own computers. I don't think they need to share," I said. Then I got bold. "Sharing went out with Kindergarten, sir."

"Mr. Shaw, I assume your behavior means you know why you are here and have spoken to at least one of your roommates. I would also like to assure you that if you are trying to protect someone from punishment, you are going about it the wrong way. And should you be found guilty of obstruction, punishment will not avoid you."

He was strong-arming me. In reality, I had no evidence besides what I saw the night Duncan was on Ben's computer. And although it was more probable than not, what I had was far from conclusive evidence. Also, I had no reason to be difficult. But the Dean was pompous and as I kept repeating in my head, no matter how much I disliked Duncan, I was no rat. I didn't want that on my conscience. The Dean could squeeze me all he wanted.

"I'm sorry sir, but I really don't have any evidence or anything for you," I said calmly. "I do know that Ben and Duncan are involved in some academic incident. I have spoken to one of them. There was nothing of benefit to your *investigation* said to me."

"I see," he said. He stared at me for a few seconds, calculating the impact of his initial tactic. He knew his mistake.

The Dean leaned back and picked off his glasses. He pulled an embroidered handkerchief from his pocket and proceeded to clean them. His fingers had the identifying stains of a chain smoker. He let the silence linger and right at the cusp of awkwardness, he spoke—his accent warmer and slightly less intrusive.

"Augustine, I think we got off on the wrong foot, as they say. Let me tell you a little bit about myself."

He finished cleaning his glasses and returned them to perch on his nose. He continued.

"I serve a purpose here on campus. Most students don't know what that purpose is save the rumors and stories pervading every dorm room and drinking establishment. That is by design. Because of my business I need to seek an advantage. The Midland myths only enhance my ability to accomplish my mission."

"What exactly is your mission, sir?" I said.

"To find the truth, Mr. Shaw," he slowed his speech even more. The accent was becoming hypnotic. "Everyday I sit in this chair and listen to people spin stories and lies out of malice or desperation. All of them do it, even the innocent ones. But I know hidden somewhere behind the words is what actually happened the night they got caught with a fake ID or broke a window in the dining hall. That's why I'm successful at my job. I can see the lies fueling the fire. And

I know only the truth can extinguish it. What emerges from the resulting ashes, well, that depends on the arson. It really is a dreadfully tedious occupation."

He was bringing our encounter back to my original expectation. He threw out a conversation topic. I bit.

"Then why do you do it?" I asked. I caught him off guard. He had not expected me to approach him so directly.

"You aren't scared or nervous right now, are you Augustine?"

"No, sir. I didn't light any fires."

A smile cracked slightly under his bird nose. He adjusted his glasses and it was gone.

"I understand that, Augustine. I'm just looking for some guidance. As I said, I'm looking for the truth. I learned at a very young age the importance of telling the truth and ever since then, I've hunted it without mercy. Honesty at all costs. The only home for liars, Mr. Shaw, is a fiery circle far beneath the ground. What do you think of that?"

"Well, sir, I must admit I've lied in the past. I'm not sure any human can go through life without spinning a few yarns, dropping a white lie here and there."

"Agreed. I myself have fallen off the wagon once or twice. But I came clean under my accord. You're an observant boy. You must've noticed I have a slight nicotine addiction."

"I guessed as much."

"You also know smoking isn't allowed indoors anywhere on campus. However, by expressing my habit years ago, the school has decided to grant me certain liberties. I enjoy a stigma of concealment and should I be seen running outside every hour to puff greedily like some starved animal, my effectiveness could be rendered moot."

"Sounds like a fancy way of saying you got around the system."

"By telling the truth, Mr. Shaw. Like I said, I learned at an early age that keeping the truth from anyone can be just as detrimental as outright lying."

"Uh huh," I said skeptically. The Dean could tell I was beginning to think him hypocritical. He closed my file and flopped it onto a pile of folders sitting at the corner of his desk.

"I've been around on this earth a lot longer than you have, son. I've traveled many different roads. The one that I started out on, the one that prepared me to do what I do here, started way back in Louisiana," his heavy Southern drawl lingering just a bit too long on the last word's second syllable.

He continued. "In Baton Rouge, I grew up the youngest of three boys. My daddy was a strict disciplinarian. He resembled very much the man you hear about in the Midland myths, the legend of the man you now sit in front of. Only difference, my daddy found his vice at the bottom of a bottle whereas mine is at the end of a cigarette. My family was poor. Our clothes were tattered. Our home was dilapidated. Even with the peach trees my father grew, food was a luxury. My brothers and I never wanted more. We never knew what else existed in America. All we knew was a family stuck together. It was us against them, whoever 'them' was. At least until I became one of 'them.'"

As his memories came to light, so did the thickness of his accent. Each word was emphasized, heavy and curled. The Dean leaned further back in his chair and the black pebbles behind the glasses shifted to the ceiling and away from me.

"I was young when we used to play around the peach trees," Midland said. "My older brothers would hide up on the branches out of my reach and I'd scramble around looking for ways to catch them. We weren't allowed to eat any fruit. That was for sellin' only. Our daddy was strict with that rule.

"One afternoon my brothers ran into the orchard to take their usual peach tree perches. I remember being frustrated more than usual but because the harvest was so poor that year, I could easily see my brothers' hiding spots. There was one bushel of peaches on the front porch, ready for my daddy to take to the farmers market.

Instead, I stole it and ran into the orchard. When I reached my brothers, I began hurling the peaches in their direction. I hit my oldest brother square on the face three times. They laughed and applauded my creativity but vowed revenge. When I ran out they jumped down, peach mush smeared their faces and juice soaked their shirts. I took off, retreated, having been the victim of their tomfoolery multiple times before.

"I hid from them far in the woods behind our house for about an hour. When I thought it was safe to emerge, I made my way home. About a hundred feet from the back door I ran into my daddy dragging my oldest brother across the yard by the ear. My brother was still covered in peach remnants.

"'Did you steal the peaches, Lucius?' my father heaved at me. He reeked of whiskey.

"'I know your brothers stole them peaches. You need a beatin' too?' he said. My young brain registered only self-preservation. I watched my brother's heart break when I said, 'no daddy. I was out in the woods all day.'

"My daddy beat my brother worse than ever that evening. My brother screamed with each belt lash but it was my daddy that yelled loudest, mostly about telling the truth and how those peaches were going to bring in enough money to feed the whole family. Ever since then I've hated peaches.

"But as I'm sure you can infer, I've always told the truth, Augustine. Basically, my brother was whooped by my own hand. If that's the price of withholding the truth, I'm not willing to pay it. I have a bit of an obsession. I'm persistent. Most people don't leave here without revealing something. It's why I get paid for what I do. There is never a reason to hide the truth."

I didn't move. The Dean certainly changed his tactic. A tinge of sympathy crept up my gut. Before I could fully digest his story, Dean Midland leaned forward in his chair. He reassumed the hunched posture he had when I first entered his office. His black pebble eyes gazed directly into my own. Even his Southern drawl lost the tobacco-sweet, nostalgic edge. It was still genuinely Southern, but was once again serpentine, coiling with purpose at the limit of each phrase.

"Please, Mr. Shaw," he said, "Now that I told you a story, would you please indulge me with one of your own?"

I was still perplexed, like being caught up in a web of words. Midland continued.

"We are merely trying to sort out a situation that has caused significant confusion among some faculty members. Your friends Benjamin and Duncan are accused of committing a very serious crime. I would appreciate any assistance. You said before that you heard nothing of benefit to us. But I will ask you directly: did you ever see anything suspicious? Did you ever see a roommate copy the work of another?"

I came back to the reality of the moment. I stayed silent, watched the second hand on the grandfather clock tick around the face once and tried to gather my thoughts.

"Mr. Shaw, please answer the question," Dean Midland said. Was the annoyance shifting to his side of the desk? "Did you ever see one of your roommates copy the work of the other?"

"I'm sorry sir, but I don't have an answer for you."

He got agitated and more animated. He took his wire-rimmed spectacles off and set them gently on the table. With his elbows on his desktop, he clapped his hands in front of him and touched his fingertips to his lips.

"Look, Augustine, I know these boys are your friends but . . ."

"Actually sir, that's not true at all."

". . . but please look at it from my point of view," he interrupted. "I am trying to understand why two young men who share a small dormitory have each produced the same version of a very important document. I need to know the truth."

I still wasn't going to rat anyone out but it was getting to a point where I had to say something. My best choice was to help Ben.

"Ben is a smart kid," I finally said. "Ben has always been a smart kid. I went to high school with him. Actually, he won some sort of writing award our senior year."

"What about your friend Duncan? Has he always been a *smart kid*, as you say?"

The Dean caught on quickly. I was no rat but I had no problem giving him directions.

"Well sir, I'm not sure. I've never read any of his past papers. I'm sure if you looked at his previous work yourself you'd be able to tell me if Duncan has always been a smart kid."

Realization and relief washed over the Dean's face. He stuck his glasses back on his face.

"I see," he said. He stood up with surprising quickness and agility. He gestured for me to do the same and strolled out from behind his large oak desk.

"Mr. Shaw, thank you for coming in here today," he said and extended his hand. I gripped his yellowing fingers and shook. "I appreciate you taking the time."

"I don't think I gave you much help though, sir."

He gave a slight wink. It was like a hand closing around the black pebble.

"No, no you were right not to tattle on your friends. But again, thank you. After our discussion I am back on the road to truth. I have a clear map that should lead me to it, as was the goal from the start, right? If you ever need anything just give my receptionist Mary a call."

"Thank you, sir. Have a nice afternoon."

He led me to the big double oak doors and just before he pulled them open he said, "Best of luck with the semester, Mr. Shaw. And please don't start any fires." He gave me another half-wink.

Just outside Ben and Duncan sat on the same bench I had sat on thirty minutes earlier. Neither one looked up but Duncan's posture screamed timid and terrified. He heard the Midland myths from several friends. Ben, on the other hand, was blatantly furious. They sat on opposite ends of the bench.

"Mary," the Dean yelled from inside his office, "Could you call young Duncan's professor and get copies of all his essays from last semester? Have them sent over immediately. In the meantime send Duncan in here."

Dean Midland's drawl squeezed the life out of the name. There was no escape there.

Duncan and Ben both looked up and saw me exiting. All our eyes met. My only reaction was a shoulder shrug and confused look. It had an opposite effect on each. Ben's angry exterior seemed calmed by my inclusion in the incident. Duncan's face instantly screwed up with rage, mingled alongside the terror.

Duncan started to get up, staring in my direction. I stopped at the other end of the bench. But before anything materialized the young receptionist cut between us and grabbed him.

"Right this way, the Dean is waiting for you," she said.

Duncan looked back over his shoulder.

"You better not have fucked me," he said bitterly.

"Excuse me, young man!" Mary squeaked. "That is no way to talk in the Dean's office!"

"And no way to talk in front of a lady," the Dean hissed from the doorway.

His reprimand continued as he closed the large doors and the three disappeared into his office.

Ben and I were alone for a few minutes. He asked me what the hell was going on.

"Don't worry about it," I said. "They know you're a smart kid and as soon as they get Duncan's old papers, they'll know he's not."

"Be honest with me, did you know he was stealing my shit?"

"I'm not going to rat anybody out, Ben. You know me. But

anything I might have had a hunch on, I wasn't going to say until I was sure."

"What the hell, Shaw. If you knew you should've told me. I could've stopped it then."

"Come on, Ben. You would have killed him. Really, he would at least be in traction right now and you'd be the one in trouble."

Ben knew I was right. He looked back at the floor.

A student with a thick manila folder burst into the outer receptionist area huffing and out of breath. He looked around for direction.

"I have some files for Dean Midland from Professor Gilmore."

The large wooden doors opened a crack and Mary slid out.

"I'll take those, thank you," she said. Before she went back into the Dean's office she looked back at Ben and smiled an encouraging smile.

I told Ben I'd wait for him back in the room and we'd go grab some lunch.

The Dean must have decided Duncan's guilt before I was even back to our room because Ben arrived about thirty minutes after me. Ben was given an A for the class and the express apologies of the Dean and his staff.

But he wasn't happy.

"They didn't expel him," Ben said immediately when he came into the room. "That little weasel copied my work, verbatim, and they let him stay here."

I was as shocked as Ben. The school had a very clear zero-tolerance policy on plagiarism. I definitely didn't expect Dean Midland to loosen his grip on Duncan.

Ben didn't even wait for me to inquire.

"Obviously he fails the class and he's going to get incompletes for every one of his other classes until they can investigate whether or not he cheated in them too."

"So it's like he was never here last semester."

"Exactly. So the Dean said something like well since he was never here, we won't throw him out. He'll start all over again this semester and if there is any inkling of treachery, he's gone for good. Plus he's gotta do some kind of community service thing."

"Well, that's sort of harsh. Especially for Duncan, he hates helping people." I thought the minor joke would make Ben laugh. It didn't. I couldn't blame him. Inside I was furious at the Dean for not tossing Duncan to the curb and ridding him from my life for good. Maybe I should have come right out and said I saw him stealing Ben's work. Maybe the clear evidence would have sounded the death knell.

"What the fuck?" Ben grunted. "I hate that little prick!"

"Forget about it. You got your grade. He got his. He's out of our room and out of our lives. It's over," I said. I knew it probably wasn't.

Ben relented, grabbed his coat and said, "Yeah, let's just go get a beer."

"It's lunchtime," I said.

"Like I said, let's go get a beer."

Chapter 26

The antics from freshman year faded fast. But in the ensuing three years, Duncan and I played cat and mouse: a dangerous, gossip-fueled game of tag.

After the cheating incident, Duncan blamed his academic woes on me. He refused to accept responsibility for blatantly stealing his roommate's work. How he thought he'd get away with it all, I never understood. But from that incident forward, the rift I had seen cutting between us ripped open and flooded with bitter resentment. Friendship terminated, rivalry blossomed.

Unfortunately, as a former friend he knew exactly how to hit each of my nerves. Initially, it worked. He prompted me several times to lose my temper in front of others. What friends I didn't lose to those outbursts were caught up in the series of lies and rumors Duncan spread around our dormitory. The lies were rarely about my family, my friends or me.

Rather, Duncan spread rumors about other people and attributed their accuracy to me. Suddenly it wasn't Duncan telling people that Jim in room 306 used Nair on his chest or that Gordie from the rugby team got an STD from sleeping with his roommate's sister. No, it was Augustine Shaw spreading the juicy tidbits. No matter that Shaw didn't know Jim from 306 or that Shaw never saw a rugby match. Duncan played to the right people, weak people, who believed an earnest face and serious tone of voice. Most people never really cared what was true and what was false; they just cared who said it. The source was the crux of their reaction.

I talked my way out of several jock beatings. The adamant ones who ignored my innocence plea frequently backed off when Shoddy and Ben appeared at my side. When backup was scarce, I endured some unwarranted pain. Jim in room 306 pushed me through the screen door in the common area. Gordie the rugby player went so far as to kick in our dorm room door, splintering it at the hinge. Thankfully no one was there because Gordie was unnaturally strong.

Eventually, most people got wise to Duncan's mischief. He simply overplayed his hand. Even Flask started asking him how he knew I was the root of the rumor mill, especially since Duncan and I never talked to each other.

By the time we left freshman year for summer break, I lost any opportunity to form lasting friendships with anyone other than Shoddy and Ben. Nobody thought I was an undying gossip anymore but nobody cared to be my friend either.

Duncan, on the other hand, readily assumed the jester's role. In our private high school, surrounded by academic-obsessed overachievers, everyone saw him as a pathetic joker. But in college he found his gang of fools. He was their clown king, spreading malice for entertainment value.

For the next three years he embraced the persona. He took swipes at others in any way he could that didn't involve physical interaction. But I was always his pet project. Augustine Shaw was always the default punch line.

Sophomore year I received a series of prank phone calls. Some I fell for. I was directed to not attend a class because the professor was ill. He wasn't. Others were much more obviously organized by Duncan. These questioned Lindsey's virtue and called Lily every insult from whore to wench.

Junior year he took it to the next level, introducing technology to the game. He had a friend working in the Residence Life Office steal my dorm room lock combination. One Friday night he and his friends set up shop in my building's hallway, cell phone video cameras at the ready. Duncan, wearing a backwards New York Yankees cap, ran down the hallway jumping and smashing a dozen drop ceiling tiles. He then pulled the fire extinguisher from its holder and sprayed it, immediately causing the fire alarm to blare. His accomplices then taped him approaching my door and type in the combination. He waited until some of the other doors in the hallway opened and people emerged. With the fire extinguisher's contents emptied and floating about, the other emerging people saw only a Duncan's backside enter my dorm room and slam the door.

I saw the tape during my disciplinary hearing. I admitted it was convincing evidence but Duncan missed one important fact: I hated the New York Yankees. I was a diehard Red Sox fan. Plus, countless people saw me out at the bar that night.

No one ever got in trouble but the broken ceiling tiles and fire extinguisher carried a hefty maintenance fine for our dorm building. Again Duncan succeeded in creating me a long list of enemies.

We carried on an immature animosity for four years. We traded blows. I wasn't completely innocent but I consistently lagged in creativity and hostility level. I tried to forget him but he never let me.

My college timeline was dotted with incidents of Duncan's subterfuge. They were a pox on an already plagued four years.

He was there the night Lily died. If he wasn't she would still be alive. I was sure of that. I couldn't prove anything, but the nagging suspicion over his involvement crept through me like a disease that never cured.

Did he use roofies? Was it something worse? What was he hoping to get from it? Why her? Why? Of course, deep down I knew why.

More recently, in my weakest moments—usually laying next to Lindsey trying to recapture some of the love or at least the lust I shared once with Lily—I admitted to myself that I shared the blame equally with Duncan.

That was only part of it. I hated him most because despite my torrid attempts to separate him and her, to eliminate one and elevate the other, to walk in the light and leave the darkness behind—Duncan and Lily became inextricably linked. Their stories were interwoven with me being the focal point; two long ribbons, one the darkest black the other pure white, spun in unhappy ceremony around me, the maypole. Their lives wrapped around my own until they were all I could see, all I could sense. I was caught, tied too tight to feel the outside world and forced to watch my tripping, laughing cohorts stumble through their collegiate celebrations, unable to participate, unable to enjoy.

Most times when I thought about Lily, some form of Duncan appeared. In fact, a pleasant memory of her was always followed by an unsettling one of him. If my mind daydreamed about a dinner Lily and I once had, suddenly Duncan would be the waiter serving the meal. His face lingered in the shadows around the golden visage of Lily emblazoned on my memory. The glow slightly tarnished. He somehow managed to hold down her spirit like an ethereal chain: the weight of him preventing her from ascension. She was an angel and he clipped her wings. Hers was a tilted halo. And I hated him for it above anything else.

Chapter 27

Senior year.

The night before we left for our last spring break.

My friends and I celebrated the onset of our one, last breather before graduation by doing what we did best: getting drunk. Lindsey, Shoddy, Emily and I slammed some tequila shots in a dorm room—it may or may not have been one of ours—and went to Primal.

We were leaving the next day for Key West. Because I would start the drive in the driver's seat, I planned to drink moderately. Emphasis on *planned*.

Primal was surprisingly crowded. I had assumed the majority of campus would leave as soon as possible for home or some tropical destination. The school said they locked the doors promptly at 6:00pm the Friday before break. Everyone knew they were full of it and their keys and electronic ID cards would remain useable throughout the weeklong vacation.

Pondering the existence of such a large crowd, I waded through Primal, my head already in a fog and getting foggier with each step deeper into the music and alcohol haze. I barely noticed when I bumped into Ben.

"Hey, what's up Shaw?" he yelled, straining his voice over the loud music.

I hadn't seen Ben much since we moved out of our original dorm room. We did our best to stay in touch but it grew increasingly difficult, and increasingly tiresome, to do so once he moved off campus into a one-bedroom apartment, claiming he wanted to spend his senior year in peace.

"How's it going," I yelled, attempting to get my voice higher than the speakers. We gave each other the typical college guy hand shake/half-hug. "I thought you were going to Cancun with like, half of campus?"

"Yea, I am," Ben said. "But we don't leave until tomorrow morning."

"So are all these people going too?" I said, sweeping my hand out over the pulsing mass.

"Most of them. Some travel company came to campus a few months ago and sold everyone the same package deal to Mexico. All the flights leave tomorrow. I have the first flight out bright and early."

"That explains why this place is so packed."

"Everyone's getting a head start on Spring Break," he said.

He raised his plastic cup and waited for me to copy. I tapped the rim of my cup to his and moved my lips in the motion of "cheers" but didn't say anything and didn't follow up with a sip.

"Not drinking?" Ben asked.

"Saving it for Florida," I replied, again reaching for a vocal volume my throat wasn't prepared to reach. "We're leaving tomorrow morning. Early. I've got the first leg of driving, so . . ."

"Oh that's right, I forgot you were driving to the Sunshine State. Quite a hike. At least you have Shoddy, though."

"Yeah, Lindsey and Emily too. Going as far away from this place as you can go, at least on this side of America."

"Key West? Jesus, are you really driving all the way down there?"

"Every god damn mile until we hit the end of Route 1. Lindsey claims it will actually save us money in the long run, if we split gas money and all that."

"That's all well and good, but does she realize how far it is? You literally can't drive any farther away. The road just ends there."

"I'm sure she knows that," I said without hiding my sarcasm.

Ben shrugged.

"Well then I just have one more question for you."

"Oh yeah? What's that?" I said, smiling because I knew what he was about to say.

"Are you out of your fucking mind?"

I had to laugh because the tequila presently worming its way through my head was doing a good job of putting me out of my fucking mind.

"Not yet," I said, "but ask me that again after twenty-four hours in a confined space with those three."

Ben's nod was laced in agreement, and sympathy.

"If I were you," he said, "I'd be doing anything but staying sober tonight."

A line of underclassmen pushed between us. We both shuffled backwards and were temporarily separated. We were drinking and chatting in a high-traffic footpath.

As I shuffled back towards Ben, I knocked into someone's elbow. I knew I probably sloshed their drink but that was part of the package in Primal, a nightly casualty of partaking in a crowded bar.

"So how's living alone," I started to say but was cut off by the same elbow I previously nudged, digging into my lower back. I ignored it. Some drunken asshole was trying to get me going.

I tried to restart my conversation with Ben but another vein of traffic slid between us.

I shuffled backwards again, this time half-deliberately hitting that same kid's elbow, just a little reminder. People passed by and pressed me up against the boney joint and it responded in force. The elbow pressure retreated, thankfully. With the amount of tequila in me, it wouldn't have taken much to loosen the constraints I placed upon myself that night. Then pain shot up my side from two short jabs into my right kidney. Constraints unlocked.

I swiveled my head as much as the crowd of people allowed, my angry eyes searching for the kid with the bony arms who was about to get cracked. They landed on Duncan.

The music pumped louder and the strobe lights came on. Duncan and I stood face to face (or his face to my chin) on the edge of the dance floor. He was waiting for me to confront him.

The crowd behind me swallowed up Ben. Shoddy and the girls were dancing. Duncan's friends leaning up against the wall ten feet away weren't paying attention. Duncan and I were alone in a sea of people, not one person noticing the tension crackling in the minute space between us.

Duncan and I stared at each other for a few seconds. In that short time, every memory I had that included him boiled up behind my eyes.

The gap between us started closing even though I couldn't consciously feel my feet move forward. If looks could kill, the night and both our lives would've ended there.

Duncan spoke first.

"Happy anniversary." His voice pierced the music-saturated room and went straight into my ears. It was pure rage, woven around a center of hate.

I knew what he was talking about. I also knew what I wanted to say but all I could muster in return was a grunt. I was grinding my teeth so hard I think the people around us started dancing to the noise.

"Maybe you didn't hear me," Duncan repeated. "Happy anniversary. A toast is in order. Cheers."

He took a drink from his beer bottle; barely moving his arm up due to the lack of space afforded us in the crowd. He just sort of tilted his shoulder at an awkward angle and let the warm domestic lager slide into his mouth's corner.

The increasingly bacchanalian throng danced and groped around us. An orgiastic beat pulsed with the crowd, a harmony of music, swirling hips and dripping sweat. To my left, two pretty things sandwiched an underage boy. Three sets of eyes closed, three heads lolled and three crotches swayed together. He placed one hand on the hip in front, one reached over his shoulder to grip the nape behind. A flurry of female hands meticulously picked their way around him. The hedonism reserved for spring break awoke prematurely and was running wild around Primal Bar.

Duncan and I were oblivious. Two stones trampled on by a herd of satyrs. Revelers bounced and slammed into us from every angle but we did not respond. Neither one of us lifted a finger, indifferent to their intemperance.

I thought of how I wanted to rub the smug look off Duncan's face with my knuckles. All of my responsibility, pleasure, contentment and anticipation had diffused, replaced by an expanding fury that saturated my already tequila-lubricated self. I felt like an over-filled balloon.

Duncan was the pin.

"What did you give Lily for your anniversary? Flowers would seem appropriate. Lay them right there on her headstone. I hope you sent my regards."

Since I was too confined to raise my hands, I lunged headfirst. I kept my eyes open because I wanted to see the blood spatter from his nose and spray over the crowd. Call it some sick sacrifice to the god of wine we all worshipped.

But while my forehead was en route to Duncan's face, the sea around us parted to let another vein of foot traffic scuttle past. Duncan shuffled sideways and instead of lambasting his arrogant mug, the top of my head hit something soft, with give. I was nose deep in the cleavage cleft of one of the passing revelers. Even from that angle, I recognized her from a few of my classes. She may have registered my identity, maybe not. But it didn't matter either way because she squealed and jumped backwards, spilling her lime green drink down my back.

The icy, sticky liquid did little to cool my boiling rage.

By the time Ben got to me the vein of foot traffic had closed, Duncan disappeared and the large-breasted sophomore girl from my classes went off to get a new drink. The celebration resumed around us, barely pausing to register the minor disturbance.

"What the Hell was that?" Ben asked as he dragged me to the bar.

"Nothing," I said. "Get me a red bull and vodka, will ya?"

"I thought you weren't drinking tonight?"

"Shut the fuck up and get me a drink."

"Whoa. Fine. Looks like he pissed you off as much as you aggravated him."

"Who, Duncan?"

"I saw you too staring at each other, then you head butted that hot chick in the tits. She bumped into him and his beer went everywhere. It was very funny from my vantage point."

"How were they?" Shoddy's voice begged from behind me. He had seen my head falling into a low-cut V-neck tank top overflowing with breasts. "They looked soft. Were they soft? Did you motorboat?"

I pushed him but said nothing, using my mouth instead to chug the Red Bull and vodka handed to me by the bartender. Before he could walk away, I ordered three shots of Jagermeister and swore off sobriety for the evening. Neither Ben nor Shoddy complained and the shots disappeared instantly, replaced by three more at the insistence of one of my companions.

Ben and Shoddy helped me loosen up and forget the Duncan encounter. The poison made me forget about the dredged-up past. I drank just enough over the ensuing hour to be content in my own head and erect a thin veil in front of the anger that still lurked in there.

At one point I told the bartender to bring us a round of house special shots. He mixed peach schnapps, Jagermeister and cranberry juice, plopped them on the bar.

"What are these?" Ben asked.

"It's called a 'redheaded slut' shot," replied the bartender.

"Sounds terrible," Ben said.

"It is," replied the bartender.

"Lily woulda thought that name was hilarious," I blurted. "And appropriate. Let's drink to her."

Shoddy and Ben hesitated and screwed up their faces. They weren't comfortable with where this was going.

"Hey, fuck you both," I said. "It's been a year since she died. This was her favorite drink. Plus I paid for them, so take the shot."

They both shrugged, their reluctance apparently gone. We raised the three shot glasses, clinked them together and said, "cheers."

I tried to stop drinking after that shot. Maybe it was the burgeoning specter of Lily or the ever-present nagging of the responsibility I just couldn't kill with alcohol. Or maybe I had just had enough. No matter what it was, I wanted to stop drinking. That doesn't mean I did. The rate slowed, though, and I mixed in several glasses of water to stem the tide. Nevertheless my inhibitions dissolved with each, "cheers."

Eventually Ben faded into the crowd. Lindsey and Emily appeared and tried to get me to dance. I politely declined and they stole Shoddy while I remained at the bar, watching my three friends shimmy and grind to the pulsing beat. I drank and allowed the alcohol to take the wheel and fill my sails. It navigated my mind past my friends—those gyrating a few feet away and those six feet under. I half reminisced and half surveyed.

The party pulsed and flowed around me as it had all evening. Everyone was especially drunk and, of course, especially horny. Most of them couldn't tell you the name of the bar they were at. Most of them couldn't even tell you the color of the strobe lights. None of them cared.

In the midst of the organized confusion, and my drunken stupor, those flashes of colored light on the beer soaked floor held my attention. To an inebriated brain, they were much more interesting than the people grinding over it. I watched the lights washing over everyone, dousing the sweaty dancers like a spicy marinade over raw meat. The glistening bodies writhed and swayed almost in unison to the *thumpa thumpa thumpa* of a heavy baseline. It was transfixing, like a lava lamp made of Red Bull and vodka.

Lindsey, tripping in her drunkenness, caught my eye and beckoned for me to join her on the dance floor. I smiled at her and she sent back a seductive grin. I was right about everyone being horny.

She was sweating in that sexy, female way. The liquid pheromones melted down her neck and trickled over the exposed tops of her breasts. It resulted in an enticing sheen cast over her lightly tanned skin. It was the tempting kind of sweat, the kind that perspires just before and just after passionate sex. She took her eyes off me, closed them and pushed away from whoever's hips she had been grinding with. Her body slithered in unison with the bass line, her exposed midriff rolling over her hips. The colored lights illuminated parts of her body then hid them in shadow. I was entranced, drunk and on the verge of reclaiming positive feelings.

Then light violently snapped on and off and on again. Lindsey was there then she was gone, then there again. I thought it was the strobe light until a sound like snapping celery echoed in my ears and all at once pain drowned out all else. Light dimmed, the colors blurred and the back of my head screamed. I stumbled forward and caught myself on a pole in the center of the room, gathered my senses and whirled around to see a small, bony fist hurling towards me.

I stepped to my left and Duncan's clenched hand collided with the pole. He screeched and turned his black eyes to me. I lowered my head enough to meet them with my own hazel eyes. Immediately he looked away, gazing back over his shoulder at the two imposing oafs framing him. Duncan's round body heaved with short, excited breaths while Flask and Regan stood motionless, like granite, but in their faces you could read greed, like pigs waiting for their farmer to empty the slop bucket.

I spoke first, this time.

"You missed," I said, even though the first shot he gave me was still ringing around my ears.

"Fuck you," cried Duncan. "We end this now. I'm going to kick your ass like I should have done a long time ago."

I don't know why it caught me off guard, but for some reason I didn't expect him to be so blunt.

"You want me to fight you here in the middle of the bar, with these two goons standing guard?" I knew the answer so I straightened up.

Duncan squealed something I couldn't make out. When Duncan got excited his voice elevated a few octaves and cracked like a pre-pubescent nerd, straining for an adult tone. The adrenaline coursing through his body wouldn't allow him to be anything but shrill. Flask bent down and whispered something in his ear.

"Outside," Duncan said. "These idiots will stay here. You and I go outside."

"I'm done with you," I said, knowing how painful a rejection would be to Duncan's ego. I started walking in the direction of the bar but the lingering alcohol in my system forced me to keep talking. I added, "You're not worth my time. But your little sister might be. Tell her I said congrats on that figure skating title. Or maybe I'll give her a call and tell her myself."

The pain in my head that had started subsiding pulled a sharp U-turn when three bodies lunged and landed on me—two heavy, controlled and overbearing, one frantic and furious. I could do nothing but throw my arms behind my head, flailing, and try to make contact with some flesh and bone.

I was doubled over, with one large oaf pinning my shoulders almost to my knees and the other oaf helping him. The scuffle cascaded to the people around us and Duncan got partially caught in the chaos. He had enough appendages free to get in some choice shots to my cheek and head.

The crowd tumbled but seemed to barely notice our fight. The pressure of Flask and Regan forced me down to one knee, my face pushed closer to the rancid floor. Rotten alcohol vapors and dirty feet wafted into my nostrils and I choked back vomit. My throat burned from it.

I tried to push off and stand but my shoe slipped and slid out from underneath me. I sprawled to the floor, face-first, the two lumbering fools falling with me. Duncan got his footing and stomped like a pro wrestler.

Feet were everywhere. A few slammed into my face, kidneys and groin as I struggled to stand up. Most, but not all were Duncan's. People were palpitating and swinging like they got caught in the tide. Duncan's friends stood up and were swept back away from me by the crowd, while Duncan and I were isolated once more.

I pushed up to one knee and caught a kick to the shin, sending my spinning back to the floor. I pushed up again to one knee and anticipated Duncan's move, deflecting his shoe away with my forearm and jumped to my feet.

There was no hesitation and my fist caught his cheek dead on. He wheeled back in surprise. He obviously thought his goons would protect him, or that I wouldn't even fight back. I did tell him I was done with him. But I was lying. I wasn't done with him yet. Not until everyone knew him like I knew him, exposed and fragile, pitiful and manipulative, jealous and fake. Physical violence was the path to the truth; anger and emotion just the means of transportation.

Duncan was on the ground and I stood above him. I reached down and yanked him to his feet. There may have been fear in him but all I knew was what was in my own body—all the frustration, malice, and emotions I had never dealt with surging into my heart and from my heart into my fist. My whole body thrust into a punch that sent him stumbling towards the door of the Primal Bar.

Then the bouncers were on us. Reaching in with their vice-like hands, they snatched me up and tossed me easily through the door and onto the sidewalk. Only then did the rest of the club react. The only thing more enticing to drunken kids than more alcohol was a brawl.

Most of the club spilled out onto the sidewalk and into the street, surrounding Duncan and me. Flask and Regan were at the perimeter of the makeshift human ring. I was at the center of a large semi-circle of shadowy faces. Everything around me darkened except the two large and one small body skulking towards me.

I wasn't going to wait to be pummeled. I grabbed Duncan and dragged him towards me, he tried to wrestle away but my left hand clenched his shirt while my right hand beat his face like it was pizza dough. My arm extended, made contact and retracted.

For a split second it stayed motionless and then extended, made contact and retracted. I wasn't the only one punching, as other fists collided with my stomach, my kidneys, even my thighs. Flask and Regan paid me in body shots but I didn't stop hitting Duncan. Extend, contact, and retract. Extend, contact, and retract. Extend, contact, and retract. Every extension was towards Duncan's nose, every contact with the nose, and every retraction away from the nose.

Pink liquid sprayed from his nostril and spattered my own face, then liquid began oozing from it, colored a reddish-amber in the streets lights.

My heart stopped. It was the color of Lily's hair. Suddenly it wasn't Duncan anymore. All I could see was Lily and I yelled. I was suddenly terrified and ashamed.

I let go of Duncan and fell back, knocking Regan and Flask to the ground. I caught myself on a mailbox on the sidewalk edge.

No more fighting. She would not have wanted this. His blood wouldn't bring her back.

It must have been only a few seconds before Flask and Regan were on me again. The furious whacks knocked me back and the vision of Lily vanished, white bursts pulsing behind my eyes instead. I was on my back like an upended turtle. They dragged me away from the mailbox. A fist hit the side of my head. A foot smashed the back of my left knee. Another flurry of punches peppered my torso and what felt like someone's knee hammered into my shoulder.

Then it all stopped. I waited for more but none came.

I slid open my eyes and saw the outline of two smudgy figures looming over me. I lunged.

Before I could land a punch, one of them spun me around and clutched me in a tight bear hug. The other slapped my cheek, not violently though.

"Shaw," Shoddy said, "calm down. It's me. And Benny. We're here." He squeezed my shoulder and nudged me away from the crowd.

My body slumped in Ben's arms as the adrenaline leaked away. They dragged me a few feet down the sidewalk, and I heard the crowd groan in disappointment as their entertainment was taken away.

We took a hard right around the corner to the side of Primal. Lindsey and Emily leaned against the bar's dirty brick exterior but instantly jumped when we appeared. They were on me, doting and pawing and wiping what I assume was blood from various spots on my face and shirt. I didn't have the energy to shoo them away.

The brawl's immediate aftermath came and went in a blur. I sat on the sidewalk along the dark side of Primal, which was directly across from a cemetery. I stared into the darkness of the gravesite, trying to regain my focus by looking past the endless headstones. The girls continued to flit and swoon over my bruised face (which was now raising). Their perfume, ignited by elevated body heat, poofed and clouded my senses even more. I choked and coughed at the sweet and sweaty stench sauntering into my nostrils. It stuck somewhere behind my teeth.

After some amount of time, it could have been a minute or an hour, I coughed and the pain crashed in my chest. The external bruises pulsing said nothing about whatever internal damage was done by Duncan and his clan.

Shoddy saw me wince.

"Alright, time to go," he said to the others. "We better get you girls out of here."

He responded to Lindsey's outcries with disinterest and a flick of his hand.

"Ben, can you walk Emily and Lindsey home?" Shoddy said. "You know how this neighborhood is."

"You sure?" Ben replied. "You two going to be alright?"

"Yes, we're fine," Shoddy said.

"No problem then," said Ben. "We shouldn't be sitting around out here anyway."

Ben quickly started ushering the girls up the sidewalk towards the main street.

"What about you two?" Lindsey yelled back. "I want to stay with Augustine!"

Shoddy turned his back so as not to see Ben manhandling a screaming Lindsey up to the main road, turn right and continue towards campus. Lindsey struggled and screamed until out of earshot. Emily followed silently. She had a horrified look on her face through the entire ordeal. It was the first and only time I ever saw her legitimately scared.

"Now that they're gone, I have to go take care of something. Will you be good for two seconds alone?" Shoddy asked.

He didn't wait for an answer before leaving me sitting on the sidewalk, my back propped against the side of the bar. He turned the corner and went back to Primal's front door.

He told me later that his goal was to calm the crowd still left on the

237

sidewalk: those too drunk to know the fight ended or too sober to not care about the drinks Duncan and I had made them spill. Shoddy knew he had to make good on my behalf. After a few false apologies, some invites to non-existent parties and too many promised rounds that would obviously never be fulfilled, the swarm started to disperse with the help of the Primal bouncers. Most buzzed back into the bar and rejoined the revelry as if nothing happened. Shoddy escaped before the mob sacrificed him for his wallet and his blood.

By the time Shoddy returned, my eyes were open fully and the bruise on my face purpling.

"Everyone is gone," he said. "And I didn't see that little weasel or his idiot goons."

"Probably good for them," I muffled and then coughed. I immediately clenched my side.

Shoddy stood over me, a smirk slithered across his face and a thousand different praises scrambled through his mind. He had every right to hate Duncan as much as I did. Duncan had caused problems for the both of us. Shoddy may have been thinking about Lily. He may have been remembering all the trouble Duncan caused me, his best friend. Or maybe he was thinking about the rumors Duncan spread about Shoddy and unwilling young women. Duncan tarnished his reputation, even though none of what he ever said was true. Not many people ever believed the stories but the damage was done. For years Shoddy and I discussed the day one of us would get a chance at revenge.

"Come on Rocky, let's get out of sight for a while," Shoddy said.

"I need a minute," I replied. "My chest and side are killing me."

Shoddy lifted me effortlessly to my feet and propped my arm around his shoulder.

"That's fine. Let's just go back here and get our bearings," he said, a touch of compassion and fatherly pride in his voice. He dragged me further down the side of the bar, away from the main road. We followed Primal's outer wall and then turned a sharp right into an alley behind the bar. He leaned me against the back wall of Primal.

"Do you want to sit down?" he asked.

"No, I'm good. I just need to collect my thoughts."

The history that defined Duncan and I throbbed in my head, or it may have been the bruises. Either way, the pulsing in my veins just would not dissipate. I thought my heart would explode. I remembered every insult and every backstabbing maneuver Duncan made. All of the lies he told to my friends and to my face surged back. I thought about Lily and her easy, thin smile. My body shivered and Shoddy put a hand on my shoulder.

"You look like you're gonna kill someone. Or like you just saw a ghost. I'm not sure which. Maybe both?"

His voice was like a breeze through a tree. I heard him speak but I just shivered and ignored it. My devil and my angel climbed in from my shoulders to my ears and were waging an epic war on the battlefields of my conscience.

"Fight's over, Shaw. You won. Duncan got a beating and you're the one who gave it to him."

I didn't want to hear it.

"Leave me alone," I said.

"What?" Shoddy gasped, his breath short like I had physically slapped him.

"Give me a couple minutes," I pleaded. "Alone."

"They must have hit you harder than I thought," Shoddy said. "If you think I'm leaving you alone in a sketchy alley, you must be out of your mind"

"I'm fine," I shouted.

Shoddy's face screwed up, confused and concerned. I didn't look at him.

"Please," I said, and made up a lie just to get him away. "I need some water or ice or something. I can't walk back to campus like this."

His face softened. He bought it.

"Alright, fine. But if Lindsey ever finds out I left you alone she'll beat me worse than you beat Duncan. I'll take a walk up to 7-11 and get you a bottle of water and something cold. Just sit here, I'll be back in a few."

I nodded my approval but instead my whole body swayed. Shoddy put his hand on my shoulder to keep me standing upright.

"Or maybe I'll stay here," he said, his hand steadying me.

"I'm fine," I said. "Water would be fantastic right now."

"Suit yourself. I'll be right back. Don't do anything stupid while I'm gone. Any more stupid things, I should say."

It was a poor attempt to get a laugh out of me. Internally I chuckled, though I didn't have the energy to vocalize it.

Shoddy walked away slowly. He looked over his shoulder persistently as he moved out from our alley behind the bar, turned up the dark street, took a right onto the main road and walked past the corner cemetery and up toward the convenience store and campus—the same route Ben had ushered the girls.

I was alone, rubbing my sore knuckles against my sore head.

The darkness was heavy, pulling down on me like a drenched wool coat. I slouched against the dirty back wall of Primal, slid down until the small of my back wedged where the building met the pavement. I let myself crumble onto a broken wooden palette, just another discarded piece of garbage waiting for the pickup. I roused something that then splashed through a puddle a few feet away, scurried beneath a torn Dunkin Donuts bag and vacated the alley.

Then I was completely alone in the darkness and the filth. Emotions rushed over me. That sour, sick taste crept up my throat and I longed for that scurrying creature to return to distract my body and mind.

I thought of Lily. I thought of the one year that had passed since she died. I could barely remember any of it. One whole year; more than two college semesters, three months of summer internships, vacations, nights out, nights in, other girls, innumerable beers, Lindsey, Shoddy and I couldn't think of a single worthwhile memory to cling to. They all felt hollow, lifeless, like dead goldfish floating upside down in a glass bowl.

Sitting on the cold alley ground, I searched the files for anything significant that occurred in my life since Lily died.

Nothing. Empty. Black as the night closing in on me.

Then the files updated, the search got to something recent. Suddenly I was replaying a few minutes before, the mental video of my fist hitting a face. I thought of Duncan's nose breaking earlier in front of the Primal crowd, and it rolled over and over again, his nose cracking repeatedly like a broken record on loop.

I started recalling the entire fight. There were the two massive bodies bearing down, accompanied by a jolt of pain in my head and my kidneys and chest.

The video skipped into full rewind, shooting past this evening, back to all the jabs, the snide remarks and the cruel jokes that dotted our years of knowing each other—years that began with friendship. Everything that Duncan said, did or insinuated played quickly in reverse, all the way back to high school. Then the tape ran out, spun off its reel and with it, my equilibrium that had thus far been maintained by a steady dosage of repression. My throat burned and a haze blurred my vision, nausea took over.

I was crouched on all fours staring across the alley at an old metal dumpster and a pile of dented trashcans. I vomited on the splintered wooden palette. The sour sick dripped through the slats. When there was nothing solid left, liquid acid scorched its way out, purging my throat and tongue of the digested bits of that afternoon's lunch.

After vomiting, the haze and the nausea cleared, but in its place the truth crept in.

Suddenly I was alone, broken, and sad. Only one bare yellowing light bulb buzzed above me, hanging over Primal's back door.

What was I doing? A year filled with best friends, girls, possibly love and I fixated on a dead girl. A year filled with potential, opportunity and memorable events and I only recalled fights with Duncan. Fighting at Primal? Puking in an alley? Proud because I broke the nose of some ignoble jerk? I needed change.

I was consumed by her life and his, not my own. I wanted to stop being that way. It had to end.

Chapter 28

The old Westerns followed some pretty standard archetypal patterns when it came to endings. Two cowboys would meet under a hazy high noon sun, dry and dust-covered in their raggedy hats and spurred boots. If he wasn't John Wayne he was Clint Eastwood. If he wasn't Clint Eastwood he was about to die.

A tumbleweed or two would always dance past, lightly kissing the dirt as it skipped across the line of fire oblivious to the tangible, dense air that smelled like impending death, if impending death had a smell. The two archenemies would stare each other down; perhaps the camera would close up on the rigid, determined eyes set deep into a cracked, parched and morally vacant face. Until one flinched. Then, with a leathery snap and a metallic crackle one would fall, slowly and lifelessly and explode the dusty ground, disappearing for the last time in a hazy cloud of dirt and desperation. The other, the winner, rode off into the sunset, a hero to the beleaguered townspeople and an icon to the satisfied audience.

But that's Hollywood—old Hollywood, and it may not even exist anymore.

Behind Primal, on a cold, damp, morally vacant March night, it definitely did not exist. There was a less-than-epic showdown. There was no sun, just moon. There were no hats or boots, just collared shirts and jeans smeared with mud and dried blood. It was not scheduled. It was not witnessed. There were no citizens besieged by the bad guy. There was no audience salivating for good to triumph over evil. There was no prize or pride to be won. Honor was suffocated by the stench. Dignity buzzed with the flies in the dumpster.

The midnight moon broke from behind the clouds and lit up the alley behind Primal like it was midday. It consumed the single bulb above the doorway and in an instant, revealed the sunken mass of a human, hunched over on the grimy pavement in a pool of his own sick and self-pity.

My eyes adjusted to the moonlight, enough to fully take in my surroundings. I recognized my reflection broken into a dozen shards in the puddle between my knees. My eyes were set deep and, even in the liquid mirror, seemed dry, tired and fragile. A few crumpled sections from a week-old Providence Journal skidded across the wet asphalt alley, pushed along by the steady March breeze that also carried the incoherent smell of rotting garbage. I thought, perhaps that is what impending death smelled like—a myriad of disregarded junk that, at one time, meant something to somebody.

A rat sprinted from a corner, skirted the edge of light where the shadows began and disappeared behind the dumpster.

Whether it was the rat, my reflection or the moonlight illumination that distracted me, I never heard the footsteps and wheezy, heavy breathing behind me until I felt the pain they accompanied.

Duncan's bony fist cracked into the back of my head, just above the base of my neck, and sent my already kneeling body sprawling forward. My broken puddle face kissed my broken fleshy face as I crashed headfirst into whatever fluids had concocted on the alley ground in front of me. I never had time to put my hands out to brace the impact.

"I'll keell you, beetch," Duncan wheezed. His breathing was intermittent; I assumed the broken nose contributed to that. It also made him sound like he had the flu and was every now and then playing a slide whistle.

"Geet up and fight!"

Still on all fours, I peered over my shoulder and saw blood coagulating under his swollen nose—a wad of toilet paper protruding from one nostril. Instantly, he swung his foot like a Brazilian soccer player into my ribs. My entire body hiccupped and I collapsed onto my back.

Duncan wasted no time taking advantage of the upside-down tortoise position. He took a short stride forward and drove his foot into my right kidney. The dull thuds pushed all the air from my lungs and up through my mouth in the form of a long, low, "fuuuuuuck."

My eyes closed. I didn't want to reopen them. If I could have relaxed all my muscles, forgotten the world and drifted into sleep, I would have right there on the soiled pavement behind Primal.

Instead I was drawn back to reality by another foot-jab to the side. This one was more startling than painful.

I opened my eyes wide and stared them directly at Duncan. It jolted him and he fell instinctively into a half retreat.

That was easy, I thought. All I had to do was look at the kid. I didn't want to fight him and apparently I didn't have to. I just had to pretend like I would. But I wouldn't fight him.

"Hey Dunk, have you ever seen any of the Rocky movies?" I asked him, keeping my voice as steady and nonchalant as possible.

"What?" he replied and got antsier. His eyes searched mine for meaning. "What are you talking about?"

"Have you ever seen any of the Rocky movies?"

"Fuck you, man. I know what you're doing and your buddy isn't going to come save you so stop stalling."

"I'm just asking you a simple question."

"Yes, of course I've seen Rocky. What the fuck does it have to do with anything, besides that I'm going to beat you like that Russian guy did?"

"The Russian guy lost, dumbass. But that's not the point," I said. "Do you remember what Mick said to Rocky after Rocky got his nose shattered? Something like, you broke your nose but it's an improvement."

He sprung, leg cocked back ready to shoot another kick, this time aimed at my head.

Instinctively I rolled in his direction, reached out and grabbed his foot in mid-stride, twisted it to the left like a steering wheel and with the help of a slippery ground, sent him spinning.

Duncan did an involuntary triple Lutz about three inches off the muddy asphalt. I chuckled at the similarity he finally had with his younger athlete of a sister. Pain stung my ribs as I did and I fell onto my back. I made a mental note to refrain from laughing.

Rather than move we both lay motionless with the streaks of moonlight and dirty light bulb dancing over the whole tired, morbid scene. A passerby would have mistaken us for bags of garbage strewn about the alley or homeless men taking refuge by the dumpster.

I rolled my head to look at Duncan, still lying motionless, seemingly collecting himself. I looked past him, out the gaping alley entrance, across the side street and into the darkness of the cemetery. Here and there, the moon illuminated some of the gravestones, which all looked like they were in prison because of the wrought iron fence that encircled the entire cemetery.

Taller than the rest, one headstone rose above the iron fence. There was a carved stone angel perched atop a heavy granite slab. The moon shone on the angel's face, a face that gazed down on me from afar—but not too far. Even from across the street, lying on my back in a shadowy alley, I could make out deeply carved and worn crevices. This stone angel was unlike those I walked past outside the college campus chapel. The chapel angels were new, emotional and passionate but unabashed standing watch outside a house of God. Pain and mourning lined this stone angel, cutting deep under its eyes that were set far under rock locks of unkempt hair. Its mouth was closed and the corners of its lips bent slightly downward. One of the wings was chipped; hewn by vandals, I assumed, or simply weathered away by years of solitary vigil. This angel was not sad. Rather, disappointed or maybe just apathetic.

My stomach churned and it felt like a combination of too much booze and too much guilt.

A boney elbow darted into my shoulder, brought me back to the now.

Duncan clamored to his feet, his hands slipping on the ground. He steadied himself on the dumpster, leaning most of his weight against the flimsy green metal.

"So are you going to geet up and fight meee or just lie there and take it like one of your girlfriends," he squeaked, air struggling to get out of his deformed nostrils.

He didn't wait for an answer, but swung his left leg at me just as I slid my body upright into a sitting position. He missed my entire body and let out a small yip of pain at the hyperextension.

I dragged myself to my feet and once standing, assessed the situation. Duncan was in pain.

On the ground was a broken wooden palette. He had fallen through it and now was clutching his abdomen, wincing with every movement.

The churning in my stomach called again. Duncan looked like a mongrel dog, small and mangy and wretchedly in pain.

I surprised myself by saying, "Duncan, this is ridiculous. Let's call it a night. You go your way, I go mine."

"Fuck you," was his response.

"I don't want to fight you," I said. "I mean, I do, believe me I do. But this fight to the death thing is a bit extreme, don't you think?"

I couldn't help but throw in an insult. "Plus you'll get your nice new Wal-Mart sweater all dirty."

He spat at me but it just hung from his tongue, then his lower lip and chin, stretching almost all the way to the ground.

"You always were funny, Shaw. But you never knew when to shut your mouth."

The dumpster barely shifted when he pushed off of it and threw his body at me, headfirst like a bull to the matador. And like that matador I shifted easily to the side, swished, unscathed, 180-degrees around to catch a glimpse of Duncan throw his hands out to stop from slamming into the back wall of Primal.

He stopped himself from falling to the ground again, but said with wheezy malice in his voice, "I've beeen wanting to shut you up for a long time."

"Jesus, Duncan, why are you still so angry?" I asked. "Can't be about the cheating thing. I told you I had nothing to do with you getting in trouble. You fuckin' cheated, man. Own up to it. Own up to something in your life for once. Be a real man."

"I'll own up to tagging your leettle girlfriend. I was the only real man she ever had!"

I knew he was trying to get under my skin, and yet it was a feeble attempt.

"Oh please," I said, "Lily would never have touched you."

Duncan looked confused, then instantly smug then immediately satisfied. His grin curled up like the cartoon version of the Grinch.

"I was talking about Leendsey," he said low and with a newfound confidence backing up the wheezing. "But while we're on Lily, just like half the hockey team by the way, why don't we talk about her."

"That's a bad idea, Dunk. For your own sake leave that one alone."

He straightened up, wincing and clutching his kidney but never losing the coiled sneer.

"Why should I do that? She was such a preety thing. Such a shame she had to go out like that."

"I'm serious, asshole, leave it alone."

Having found the right button, he continued to push, like a rat at the end of the maze, one final obstacle before the cheese.

"One year since that happened, huh? What'd they say, alcohol poisoning? Weird. She was Irish. I figured she could handle whatever I, er, anybody gave her."

He was almost cackling with malicious delight. The swaying bare bulb above his head highlighted a changed face. It was no longer the warped, sneaky sneer but rather a toothy, knowing hyena grin.

There was no more moonlight, as it had since been covered over by darkening, purple clouds. But darker clouds formed inside me.

"My only reegret is that I never got up to her that night to take advantage of my handiwork," Duncan whispered, almost to himself but to me as well. He was all the while still grinning.

"What?" I said. "What did you say?"

He cocked his head and arched his eyebrows as if to say, I might be joking and I might not, but you'll never know.

The storm clouds inside me began to thunder.

"You put something in Lily's drink last year, didn't you?" I said. "Didn't you?"

The past twelve months, the trips to her grave where I stood alone thinking about everything but saying or doing nothing, all cycled through my brain. I was suddenly convinced of something I had suspected for so long. I was all at once furious and calm. I was steady, poised like a taut bow fitted with a deadly arrow.

Duncan said nothing but he must have realized that I was regaining control of our little mental chess match. My voice was steady, my eyes focused and my mind clear and no longer on the verge of vertigo. I was in the eye of my inner storm and chaos swirled around outside.

"I saw you at the party last year," I said. "I saw you near the booze."

Duncan's grin faded into a grimace, his plucked eyebrows pointed in at the ridge of his weasel-like nose. His fists got whiter under the mounting clench. But a slight quiver in his lip gave away the wave of fear brushing down his spine.

"You've always been a selfish prick," Duncan said. He tried to add weight to his voice to mask the nervousness. "You never liked me, really. You never stuck up for me. You never supported a bro before a ho."

What was Duncan trying to pull here?

"You know how much I hate you," Duncan continued. "And you know why."

"Really though, I don't," I said. "I really never understood that part. Tell me."

Duncan ignored my request. Instead, his eyes went a little glassy and he said, "You're smart, have friends, always get the girl. You should be pretty proud of yourself."

"So this is all based on jealousy?" I asked.

Duncan actually laughed. "If you think that, you're not as smart as I thought."

"Then I'm not getting where you're coming from," I said.

"Of course not," said Duncan. "And that's part of your problem. You don't get who you are or, well, who you should have been. Instead of enjoying all you have, taking full advantage, you mope around feeling sorry for yourself and blaming others for situations you created and did nothing to solve. You don't appreciate any of this." He swung his arm into the night air, vaguely in the direction of the college campus.

"You lied to me, Shaw," Duncan continued. "When we got to college, I thought you'd grow out of it, jump feet first into the fire with me. You said you would. You lied."

Duncan shifted his weight. I was dumbfounded that he was opening up to me.

This was the longest conversation we had ever had.

"You didn't want to change. You didn't want to drink, meet girls, rule the school like we envisioned. Shaw just wanted to be the same old Shaw. Well I didn't need the same old Shaw. I learned quickly that same old Shaw would be an anchor around my neck."

I knew for fact that Duncan learned at a young age—mostly from his father's and mother's neglect & sister's meteoric rise to family importance—that he was nobody's top priority. As such, he learned to self-motivate, devalue others and disregard the sort of empathy or understanding most of us get from a strong family core. Even though his father worked two jobs to pay his tuition, car insurance and cell phone bill, Duncan never felt like he needed anyone else, no matter how much those other people were supporting him—financially, emotionally or otherwise. To Duncan, others were just garnishes on his plate, serving a minor purpose only to be discarded when the real meal began. People were just, as he liked to say, "means to an end, Shaw, means to an end."

Duncan crafted and practiced his powers of persuasion. He wasn't athletic, book smart, good looking or compassionate. So if he couldn't climb the ladder of success the conventional way, he'd talk his way onto the elevator. He blamed me for hitting the emergency stop button. Duncan truly believed I accused him during the plagiarism incident, even though I never pointed the finger directly his way. But he didn't know that and in his mind, I was and always would be a rat. Maybe in a roundabout way, I was. Duncan would never forgive or forget that whole debacle, but our frayed roots ran much deeper. I was suddenly realizing that Duncan never could forgive the fact that I wasn't like him and that I did not want to be like him. Maybe I misled him or betrayed our friendship. Or maybe Duncan was just seriously screwed in the head.

"I'm nobody's means to an end," I said.

"Correct. You're just nobody," Duncan replied. His eyes were burning now. "You're friends are nobody. That dead bitch is nobody, just dissolving into dust six feet under some rock up in Connecticut."

I should have broken his neck for that comment but before I could act, Duncan swung something out from behind his back and crashed it into the side of my head.

"She was a slut anyway," he yelled, and slapped the piece of wood off my skull again. "You didn't deserve her."

I bellowed in pain while Duncan continued, his voice ranting and raving now, spittle flying from the corners of his thin lips.

"You asked if I was jealous?" he screamed as he smacked me in the neck again with the wood. "Naw, I can't get girls like Lily or Lindsey. I don't have the patience for their bullshit. But why should you be happy if I'm not? Fuck you, Shaw. You deserve everything you got. She's dead now move on. I wish I had a stable of girls waiting for me like you do. You just fell in love with the one that couldn't handle her booze. Then you got upset when you gave her too much to drink. Maybe you should've been watching her cup a little closer. You never know the type of shady people lurking around those house parties."

"It was you," I blurted, and spat blood on the alley ground.

Duncan let his face contort into a malicious smile.

He said, "Just added a little too much poison to the apple."

I was disoriented and dazed and doubled over, but what he had said was as good as an admission of guilt. I straightened up in time to see Duncan lunge at me, arm raised and in a full sprint. He lanced the long shard of wood towards my face. I sidestepped and parried. We rotated to face each other, my back to the dumpster.

"Tell me the truth," I yelled. "You killed her, didn't you?"

"*You* killed her," he wheezed, running out of breath. "My special drink wasn't her last of the night, Shaw. Don't you remember? The booze you poured down her throat trying to get her loose enough to drop her panties? I might've brought her to the cliff but you pushed her over."

Rage crashed over me. He lunged again and I sidestepped once more, but this time I gripped his collar and shoved him with full force back behind me. His feet slipped, he hurtled, airborne.

A metallic boom echoed around the alley when Duncan crashed head first into the dumpster. His body immediately went limp, his grip around the wood piece loosened and it clattered on the pavement. He collapsed awkwardly sideways, landing with a dull wooden creak on the already broken wooden palette. The metal dumpster rippled, a low thrum fading into the silent night air.

I reeled back against the brick wall of Primal bar, clutching at my skull, ripping at my hair trying to tear out the pounding pain. My vision blurred and I stumbled trying to keep myself upright.

Duncan wasn't moving.

I hunched over again, put my hands on my knees and vomited only liquid. In between heaves I opened my eyes to try to focus on something to stop the spinning. What I saw was Duncan's motionless body and instantaneously the sour bile came out again.

He was face down in a crumpled heap. His wallet was on the ground next to him. It must have flown from his pocket as he flew through the air. Broken wood stuck out from underneath him. There was dark liquid spreading out from under his body, possibly from a puddle or possibly something more fatal.

From my perspective, the gory tableau was spinning. I grabbed my head in my hands and stared at the ground.

My eyes settled on Duncan's wallet and after a minute or two my bearings returned. I was able to stand up, swaying only slightly.

Without thinking, I took a few steps towards Duncan's still body. I reached down, grabbed his wallet and strolled to the edge of the alley. Before I could stop myself, I hurled the wallet like a Roman spear out of the alley, clear across the dark street, over the iron fence, and into the cemetery. It slapped against the face of the stone angel and dropped into the shadows at its feet.

I didn't turn back to look at Duncan, to check on him or even to spit on him. He was knocked out cold, or worse, in the mud and yellow light of the Primal alley, demoralized and broken for one last time. And I had consciously been the cause of it. That meant, for me, it was over. In that moment, I planned to never speak to him again, never think of him again and never plot vengeance upon him again.

The stone angel stared in my direction and a tinge of common decency slipped back into my conscience. Maybe I should get Duncan's wallet for him, I thought.

The angel's gaze watched me cross the street from the alley to the cemetery, its eyes like those of a great portrait, following me with every step through the darkness. I knew it was still watching when I yanked myself up and over the iron fence and picked my way around tombstones.

The shadows were thick around the low-lying stones and at the base of the angel's plinth. I barely noticed when I stepped on Duncan's wallet, pressing it into the soggy ground. I could have picked it up but my body wouldn't bend over. Instead, the most primitive corners of my brain took over the controls and I ground my heel into the leather wallet, submerging it in moist dirt.

I looked up into the angel's eyes and the churning feeling in my stomach bubbled stronger than ever. A sour taste squatted in my throat. Pain rolled and roared in my brain, then emanated down my neck, across my shoulders and throughout the rest of me.

Then a shrill noise pierced the moment. It was a cackling laugh, maniacal even. And it was close by, but not too close. It evoked imminent danger, the reason desperate animals choose to fight or fly.

I forgot the angel. I forgot the wallet. I turned around to look back into the alley behind Primal.

Duncan was still alone and motionless, face down on the filthy ground.

A lanky figure slid from the shadows around the mouth of the alley. He was tall and made up of all sharp angles. Two smaller, but just as jagged figures emerged at his side. They moved effortlessly into the alley towards Duncan.

The tall one laughed again and I winced in darkness across the street. I took a few steps away from the stone angel, silently moving closer to the iron fence.

"Look who we have here," said the tall one, his voice as shrill and maniacal as his laugh.

I want to say I crouched involuntarily at the sound of his voice, further hiding myself behind gravestones, iron bars and thick veils of shadow.

The tall one took another step into the alley and said, "This must be my lucky day."

Chapter 29

The smell of stale urine and old pizza wafted from the dumpster and carried on a breeze across the street. The stench must have been exponentially more putrid to Duncan and he jolted awake with a start.

Duncan Barker came to and immediately grabbed his head with both hands, as if it were pulsing from pain. His eyes remained shut while he slowly, agonizingly slid his body from prone to sitting. He looked as if he was trying to regain motor control or clear fog from his mind. He was on his ass propped up with his back against the dumpster.

Across the street I was cloaked in shadow, unmoved from my vantage point behind the iron fence, not far from the stone angel, waiting to see how the depressing scene would play out. I was close enough to hear everything said and see all the minute details, facial expressions and gestures. But I was far enough away that none of the people involved knew I was there. It was now my turn to be motionless. I watched.

Liquid oozed down Duncan's face to his lips. He reached up to wipe it away and flinched as he dragged his flayed knuckles across his cheek. He seemed dazed and confused. He tugged at his shirt, which was covered in grime and blood. It was when he noticed the grime and blood stains that he yelled.

"Shaw. Son of a bitch!" he bellowed. He was stewing in his hatred. He knew I had beaten him, badly. Physically and mentally he was on the losing end of this battle. I not only probably broke his nose in the initial brawl inside Primal, but one on one in the alley Duncan fared even worse. He'd probably catch a heaping helping of shit from guys back on campus for his poor pugilism.

Then he did something that caught me off guard. Duncan went quiet. He cocked his head up towards the black sky. His body seemed to relax and the tension in his muscles evaporated.

"I am sorry," he said out loud. He emphasized the second word.

"I am sorry," Duncan said again to the darkness. Or to what he thought was just the darkness.

"Is that an apology?" the shadows hissed back at him.

Duncan jolted upright. Three figures materialized from the blackness at the end of the alley. They walked abreast, the two shorter ones making bookends of the tall, lean centerpiece. As the light above Primal's back door illuminated the men, I began to get a sense of the danger Duncan was in.

Each of the three wore loose jeans and walked with his hands in the pockets. They all wore dark sweatshirts with the hoods pulled low down over their heads. Their faces, though, were covered in shadow. The only visible skin snuck from their hoods to form three thin, viperous mouths encircled in unkempt goatees. Other than the height differential the only difference in the three thugs was an invisible and palpable excess of cruelty crawling over the tall one.

It was his voice that had split the shadows. He repeated himself.

"Is that an apology?" the tall one said. His voice was laced with cynicism and sadism. The three thugs stopped a few feet from Duncan, who remained frozen, propped against the metal dumpster. He was beaten and fog probably still clouded his brain, but there was no doubt that Duncan sensed danger too.

He gathered himself and sat up straight, making himself as big as possible, like a peacock preparing to battle for a mate. As he did he coughed and hacked, spitting out a glob of blood.

"Apology?" Duncan's voice cracked and wavered slightly when he said the word. The three monsters noticed. Duncan took a deep breath before continuing in his tough voice. "I have nothing to apologize for. So go fuck yourself."

"Big words from a little man, eh Jester?" the one on the left said.

"Big words, Jester, big words," parroted the one on the right.

When he heard the name Jester, Duncan seemed to relax a little.

"Jester," he said, "I didn't recognize you, man. Haven't seen you since you sold me that stuff last year."

Jester didn't say anything and the momentary ease vanished from Duncan's body, replaced by fear. He began speaking quickly.

"It's me, Dunk. I bought that good shit, for the girls. You said pop it in the drinks and well man, it worked. Fuckin' shit was all the rage. Did the trick."

Flattery got him nowhere.

The tall one they called Jester finally said, "As I previously asked, do you have an apology waiting for *us*. Right now you're just a little rat hanging out in our alley. Trespassing."

He let that last word linger in the air like smoke from a fine cigar.

He took a step toward the beaten and broken college kid slouched on the ground. Duncan slid backwards until he couldn't anymore, resulting in a resounding clang against the metal dumpster. Jester barked a loud hyena laugh, baring his teeth.

Duncan's formerly green eyes suddenly blazed yellow with terror. His muscles tensed further. Even from the shadows across the street, I saw sweat dripping down his cheekbones and thought I heard his teeth grinding.

Jester approached until he was directly above Duncan's legs. He took his hands, two meaty paws, from his pockets and held them out to his sides. It would have been a benevolent gesture, had he not been so cruel.

"How about that apology, rat?"

Duncan shivered uncontrollably. He knew the stories of the neighborhood. He knew leaving that alley in one piece would take a miracle.

"I'm sorry," he whispered weakly, more because fear sapped his body of energy rather than out of disrespect.

"Sorry little man, you'll have to speak up," Jester said. He leaned over and brought his head down to Duncan's level.

The shadow on his face ebbed slightly, revealing a hooked nose, pockmarked and scarred right across the bridge.

Some spittle collected at the corners of Jester's mouth, which bared his corn-kernel teeth in the same hyena smile. He thoroughly enjoyed Duncan squirming and shaking like cornered vermin.

"So you were saying?"

"I'm sorry," said Duncan, barely louder than before. Jester was so close, the apology drifted from mouth to mouth. Under the hood, locked away again in blackness, Jester studied the boy. He seemed to make a decision then.

After a moment, Jester straightened upright and as he did, snatched up Duncan from under the shoulder. The boy was in no state to fight back. He just hung from the tall thug like dirty laundry. Jester pushed him against the dumpster, forcing him to stand on his own before stepping back between the other two thugs, reforming the hooded wall. Duncan faltered but then caught himself and leaned on the dumpster.

"How about he shows us his apology in material form?" the thug on the left said. The thug on the right nodded and said, "or he just pays us the cash he owes us."

"Come on boys, we aren't animals. We can forgive that debt for now. It was such a long time ago," Jester said, almost congenially. Then his voice went back to snarl. "But a little compensation for our hospitality would be appropriate, I think. Don't you?"

Duncan was swaying. The head rush from being ripped upright

after being knocked unconscious (by me), partnered with leg-numbing terror put Duncan in an inescapable haze. So much so that he didn't notice when Jester's two bookends left his side to go and bookend Duncan. One grabbed a piece of the broken wooden pallet wedged under the dumpster.

Jester swooped swiftly down upon Duncan. I wondered if he was even real? He moved like a ghost.

He got face to face with Duncan again, who was swaying so much it looked as if he were on a boat adrift.

"How about your wallet? I think that's fair compensation," Jester said with less cynicism in his voice. It was replaced with pure malice. "Right now, little man. Give us your wallet."

Before Duncan could comprehend, a thug slammed a fist into his kidney. He doubled over in pain just as another jab like an electric shock jolted his groin.

Jester propped Duncan's chin up with one wiry finger.

"Your wallet. Now," he demanded.

Another kidney shot before Duncan could react.

I was frozen in place, unsure of my feelings about the grisly tableau. My brain said go help but my feet just didn't budge. It all happened so fast, but it felt like the world was blurred and in slow motion.

Duncan was helpless. He coughed and spat blood redder than before. The fists came from nowhere, from the shadows of shadowy figures looming over him, each one precise and calculated, exacting maximum pain. They demanded his wallet, robbed him of any remaining dignity.

I don't know if he knew he was doing it, but Duncan reached into his right pocket for his leather wallet. He pulled out nothing but the inside liner. His senses came back to him in part. His wallet was gone. He shoved his hand into his left pocket, then to his back pockets. Empty. Nothing. He had no wallet, no money on him. He had no sacrifice to give these demons.

Cold, hard clarity slapped him on the cheek followed immediately by Jester's cold, hard open-palm.

Duncan shook his head; sweat spewing from his drenched hair.

"I don't have anything," he said with as much confidence as he could muster. "I lost my wallet."

Jester looked offended, like a boy picked last for kickball on the playground. At least his mouth did, the only visible part not hidden by the shadowy hood. The spittle on the corners of his lips fell away as they turned downward into a frown.

"That's disappointing," he said and turned his back on Duncan.

"Well, *I'm sorry*, but I have no money," Duncan said. He put a little extra sarcasm on the *I'm sorry*, either out of last-ditch bravado or sheer stupidity.

"That's not what he's disappointed about," the thug to his right said.

"I'm disappointed because I never pegged you for a liar, little man," Jester said, his back still to Duncan. "I guessed you'd just give us your wallet and we'd be on our way. Why won't you just give us your wallet?"

"I don't have it!" Duncan screamed, terrified. "It's gone, look!" And he pulled out the liners inside all his pockets.

"Come on little rat, tell me the *truth*," Jester said. He put extra emphasis on the last word. As he did, the two thugs collapsed onto Duncan. He slid down the dumpster, falling to one knee as a knee smashed into his shoulder. Two fists cracked against his already bruised face. A pair of huge paws pinned his shoulders against the dumpster. Another pair jackhammered his torso, working wildly and sporadically across his body with no intention or direction other than to do damage.

Warm, fresh blood ran down Duncan's face and he struggled to lift the lid on one swollen eye. Through it, he was watching Jester hopping madly above him. Then Duncan's head cocked to the side, putting his gaze in the direction of the cemetery, in the direction of me.

I looked at him from the blackness and knew he probably couldn't see me, but that he could probably see the stone angel a few feet behind me. I wondered if Duncan knew what it was, or if he thought it was a real person, maybe his sister or Lily. I hoped he saw it for what it was—an angel.

Jester stooped to pick up a piece of broken wood. He tapped one end on the ground like a homerun hitter stepping into the batters box. He swung it with purpose, directly at Duncan's head.

The alley was silent save one final wooden thwap and then the celery-snapping of Duncan's various bones. Duncan never took his gaze off of the stone angel. He blinked once, twice and then the lids stayed down.

Like hyenas they tore at the carcass, ripping open pockets and tearing away clothes. One even took off the boy's sneakers.

When the body was picked clean they scurried from the alley, lightly laden and disappointed with their meager spoils.

"I guess he really didn't have any money," one said.

"What kind of kid goes out without his wallet?" the other snarled.

They scrambled out of the alley and crossed the street at an angle, moving closer to where I crouched in the cemetery. I held my breath and my heart was pumping wildly. They got to the iron fence and turned up the street.

Jester grunted, "I guess the little rat was telling the truth."

He took a quick look at the broken pallet piece he still gripped and then hurled it over the iron fence into the cemetery. The plank clanged off a low headstone before coming to rest at an angle against the base of the stone angel, blood still dripping from the splinters.

When I knew they were gone, melted back into the shadows, I finally took a breath. I dropped from a crouch to all fours and vomited, not thinking about Duncan's leather wallet I buried beneath the stone angel.

Chapter 30

Shoddy was surprised to see me emerge from under the hazy streetlamp at the corner of the 7-Eleven. He thought I had snuck back to campus and was home in bed with Lindsey. But the drying blood on my face and neck, the grime and vomit and mud covering my clothes and the general look of a disheveled hobo not only startled him but elicited a slightly embarrassed crimson in his face.

Instead of responding to me forthwith in the alley behind Primal, Shoddy had been flirting with a bunch of girls outside the convenience store. His pride, which was largely based on loyalty, was bruised. But like a true comrade Shoddy pushed the young girls out of his way and ran over to me on first sight. He had a bottle of water, a Slurpee drink and some sort of meat and cheese snack stick thing, which smelled like the alley I just left and almost re-induced vomiting.

I snatched away the water, ignoring the mish mash of apology and questions scrolling from his tongue.

I splashed my hands and face with the spring water, which was warm. I grabbed the Slurpee and held the icy cup to my throbbing skull. The cup was mostly empty.

"I'm so sorry bro," Shoddy pleaded. He repeated it a few more times, his voice wavering. He was nervous and worried I was angry.

Shoddy always devolved into superfluous apology when he was nervous. I wanted no apology.

"That was the gymnast girl I've been trying to get with, you know? Anybody else I'd tell to go screw. But I figured you could wait while I . . ."

"Forget it, Shoddy."

"But . . ."

"I said forget it, Shoddy. You don't have to say you're sorry. Just forget it."

He nodded acknowledgment and put his hand on my shoulder. We both turned toward the sidewalk.

We walked back to campus in silence, away from Primal, away from the cemetery, away from the 7-11, past the house from the Dance Team party, past the chapel, past Lily's old dormitory.

Shoddy followed me home and only pressed the issue at my door.

"What happened, Shaw?" he said.

I didn't answer but fumbled with the doorknob.

"You look terrible, like you just climbed out of a dumpster. Tell me what happened."

His voice had a tinge of compassion I'd never heard before.

I opened the door and walked inside the pitch-black room, not intending to answer Shoddy. Out of fidelity or curiosity, he persisted. He ditched the compassion and substituted strength.

"Shaw, what the Hell happened?"

I turned to face him, took my hand off the heavy door. It began to shut in an almost comical, slow dramatic sweeping motion. I was barely visible to Shoddy, tucked away behind a closing door and unrelenting darkness.

"Nothing," I said before the door clicked shut. He may not have even heard me. "Nothing," I repeated, probably to myself. "Nothing happened, it's over."

My sleep may have begun as soon as the door shut. There was just nothing in my mind, or my heart. My body plummeted onto my bed. I didn't dream that night.

Chapter 31

I stumbled into a wakened state the next morning; my memories of the previous night overlaid with pain. Pain so palpable in my neck and shoulders, I could hear my muscles throbbing. When I opened my eyes, the throbbing became pounding.

It was Saturday morning, March 14, and we were supposed to leave bright and early. The plan had been to get out of Rhode Island and drive twenty-four hours straight to Orlando. We would then spend Sunday at Disney World and Monday morning take the final eight hour jaunt down through Florida, past Miami and across the series of bridges that link the Florida Keys to mainland America. We'd be in Key West until the following Friday, March 20, when we would turn around and do the entire trip in reverse.

But the night before, Friday the 13th, I went out to Primal and let the night get a little out of control. Way out of control. Lying in my bed the morning after, I didn't realize how far out of my control it was. I was more concerned that I messed up our departure schedule. And dealing with the intense, pounding pain that surged across my upper body.

Duncan got me good, I thought. *My head is ringing like a church bell.*

The pounding turned to banging. I sat up and rubbed my shoulders as another wave crashed over me.

This time it was accompanied by what sounded like, "Hey, Shaw!"

I was hearing voices.

"Shaw, get up. We're late!"

Reality slapped me fully awake and the pounding in my head became the pounding at my door and drew me out of bed. The clock told me I had overslept and missed our designated departure time for Florida.

"Come on, Shaw. What are you doing in there?"

That would be Lindsey, or Emily. I couldn't tell from in my bedroom.

As I made my way to let them in I realized I was still wearing the clothes I wore the previous night. They were caked in mud and what looked like dried blood. I disregarded it but quickly changed and pushed the dirty clothes all the way to the bottom of my hamper.

I opened my apartment door.

"You suck," Lindsey greeted me with a tray of Dunkin Donuts coffee in one hand and a roller suitcase in the other. "We were supposed to leave forty-five minutes ago. Now we might . . ."

"Good morning, Lindsey," I cut her off. The pounding reemerged, this time not from her knocking at the door. "Just go pack my car. My keys are over there."

I waved half-heartedly in the direction of the kitchen.

"Way ahead of you, jackass. Shoddy used the keypad on the driver's door. We're all packed and ready to go. Now you need to be, too."

"Yeah, yeah. I just need to find a bag or something and toss some shorts in it and I'll be ready."

She shoved the roller suitcase into my hands.

"There, you're almost done. I knew you didn't have one, so use this one. I half filled it with clothes you left in my room."

She blushed a little when she said it. I felt a little guilty when she did. The little hammers were tapping away on that mental wall.

"OK," I said and took a coffee from her tray. I gave her a discreet peck on the cheek. "Give me five minutes and I'll be right down."

She started to go.

"And Lindsey," I called after her, "thank you."

She blushed again.

Thirty minutes later we were pulling out of the campus lot, turning left on Huxley Avenue, left on Eaton Street and away from Providence College. I had to stop at the gas station at the end of the road to fill up.

"Anybody want anything?" Emily said, walking towards the 7-11 across the street from the gas station.

"Grab me a bottle of water," Lindsey said.

"Yeah, me too," said Shoddy. "Actually, you better get Shaw one too."

I was leaning nonchalantly against the Explorer, pumping overpriced unleaded when I saw the pretty girl in the next car over flip open a Providence Journal newspaper. I'd need something to do when I wasn't driving.

"Hey Em!" She was just about to cross the street but turned around at my voice. "Grab me today's ProJo. I'll do the crossword later on."

Emily nodded and skipped across to the store.

Ten minutes and twenty gallons later we were repacked and set off down Douglas Avenue towards the onramp for Route 95 South; basically the only road we would drive for the next day and a half.

I looked out the window and still had trouble recalling all of the previous night's events. Most of it was hazy. I knew I had walked along that same street, Douglas Avenue, last night, bumping into Shoddy and stumbling home with a headache. But the prior happenings were slow to materialize.

Regardless, the night was over, the sun had risen, I had a fresh coffee to kill the headache and we were on our way to less stress and more sun. Stopped at a light, I took the folded ProJo on my lap, creased it a bit more and wedged it between the driver seat and middle console. We were coming up on the cemetery and the local bar called Primal. I thought I remembered being there the night before.

Emily and Lindsey chatted airily about the beach.

"I heard the sunsets are beautiful," Emily said.

"I heard the bars are beautiful," Shoddy butted in. "And the ass isn't bad either."

Lindsey balked. Shoddy was chuckling, most likely because he was saying things he knew would piss her off.

"Well there's a big gay community in Key West, Marcus. I'm sure you'll find plenty of friends," Lindsey retorted. "But be careful, they may not be the kind you're looking for."

"You know what Linds, I don't say this often, but you're right. I should be careful down there. I do have a sweet ass, I probably shouldn't bend over too . . . whoa! Shit look at that!"

Three heads swiveled to look out the driver side windows as we crawled past Primal Bar. Two Providence Police cruisers, blue lights whirling, were parked on the side street that separated the bar and the cemetery. One car was perpendicular to the street, its nose hidden behind the bar, protruding into the hidden back alley that housed the bar's dumpster. Yellow tape bearing the warning, "Police Line: Do Not Cross," hung loosely from the side of the building. A few passers-by lingered long enough to get reprimanded by an officer on the corner.

"What happened?" Lindsey asked.

"Something serious," Emily said.

"Yeah, Shaw, do you know what happened?" Shoddy asked, a tinge of sarcasm in his voice.

The memories hit me like a punch to the gut. All at once I remembered what I did.

I barely noticed the light ahead turned yellow and I needed to turn left through it onto the highway. I sped up, made a less than 90-degree turn and escaped from Douglas Avenue, away from the

Primal crime scene. I met eyes with Shoddy in the rearview mirror. I kept my expression vacant. His expression begged for explanation.

The police cars faded in the distance and conversation about them disappeared as Emily and Lindsey lapsed right back into conversation about Shoddy's chauvinism. He gave me one last glance in the rearview mirror and that was it. He jumped right back into it with the girls. The conversation took everyone away from the mystery on Douglas Avenue. Soon Providence was a faded memory.

The first leg of our ride south flowed smoothly after that. We avoided traffic around the major cities. The chatter was light and excited.

Not until we passed through Washington, D.C. did I relinquish driving duty to Lindsey. By then everyone had settled into his or her iPods and e-books. I moved to the backseat, driver's side next to Shoddy and wedged out the Providence Journal. A long crease ran down the middle but the photo and headline above the fold were clearly legible.

A nighttime photo of Primal Bar, police cruiser, ambulance and fire engine surrounding it, glared up at me underneath the words: STUDENT KILLED OUTSIDE LOCAL COLLEGE BAR. The subtitle read, *Unidentified student said to be victim of foul play.*

That punch in the gut from before returned with force. All the joy drained instantly as the thought of Florida, the sun and the beach melted into oblivion. I looked up, blinked and from the corner saw Shoddy staring at the words blazing off the paper. We locked eyes again, his mouth agape but silent. I couldn't keep my face vacant. He read the terror spreading over me. I know because it scared him. He was no fool. We were both thinking the same thing. I blinked again before looking back to the paper, wishing my eyes were playing tricks.

I ignored Shoddy, who was clearly forming an elaborate image in his mind. I scanned the story, barely registering it with my brain. Sentences jumped out:

Owners of the establishment confirmed the young man had entered the bar with Providence College students. Police believe the young man was also a student at the college . . . at the time of this newspaper's publication, no identification had been made on the body . . . according to police, the body was found behind the bar near the dumpster early this morning by the bar owner . . . death resulted from blunt trauma to the head . . . the young man is said to have reportedly been engaged in a physical confrontation earlier in the evening, but police would not comment on the ongoing investigation.

The words hurt to look at, each punctuation delivering shockwaves. I breathed heavier and slouched in the seat trying to hide from Shoddy and the oblivious girls in the front. All the strength sapped from my body and had I not been sitting in a car, I surely would have collapsed.

Shoddy's hand steadied my shoulder. I looked at him again, his expression changed. My face was blank as he pulled the paper from my lap and folded it back up, dropping it on the floor of the Explorer. He kicked it under the front seat.

"Take a nap," Shoddy said with sympathy in his voice. I closed my eyes but didn't sleep.

"Shaw, sleep it off. Take a nap," he repeated.

I knew we couldn't prevent the girls from finding out about the story. I expected them to receive cell phone calls from their friends back on campus within the hour. But the calls never came. Campus was deserted; everyone had left for Spring Break. The news would surely travel but at a snails pace compared to if it had happened when classes were in session.

Not wanting to watch Shoddy work out the previous night's events, I pretended to sleep. Maybe I slept and dreamed but what followed felt real.

The hot sweats and cold chills spiking through my body; the red and blue fireworks exploding in my head; the helicopter view of a chalk outlined body bathed in blood and spotlight and then the spotlight turning on me; it wasn't a bad dream, it was a bad hallucination.

I watched myself jump behind the wheel of an old car and try to outrun the spotlight. I jammed down on the pedal, trying to shove my right foot straight through the floorboard. Then I was in my own head, looking in the rearview mirror. Nothing was there. No one was chasing me anymore but I picked up speed anyway. Faster and faster the car sped.

The speedometer melted off the dashboard. The car hurtled forward. I wasn't even pressing the gas anymore but the speed increased. The windshield strained against the pressure, shattered and tore away disappearing into blackness. The bumper and doors followed immediately.

I was pressed back into the seat, the steering wheel wrenched from my grip and that, too, sailed away. And still the car flew on.

As it broke the sound barrier I heard mumbled streams of a young man's voice slip by. The rearview mirror, which was affixed to nothing since the windshield was gone, snapped away and fell into my lap. A beautiful redhead girl was standing in the mirror. Did I know her? I turned around to look at her behind the car. She wasn't there.

I looked back to the front, through where the windshield used to be. There she was. She was ten yards away. Nine yards. Eight yards.

I slammed on the break pedal. The car didn't flinch. She was five yards away. Four yards. The redhead girl didn't move. Three yards.

I screamed and jumped up and down on the break pedal. My screams were instantly swept away in the swirling tornado winds, as useless as the break pedal. Two yards.

I yelled louder, my lungs about to pop. I flailed and stomped the pedal, even tried to punch it. The redhead girl didn't move. The car didn't slow. One yard.

As the car barreled down on her, she smiled. I screamed so violently my teeth vibrated and the whole car shook.

I blinked and she was there, inches from annihilation. I blinked again and the redhead girl was gone. I blinked once more and it was all gone, replaced by the back of Lindsey's head and Shoddy shaking my shoulders.

"Shaw, wake up," he said with concern in his voice. He slapped my cheek and then wiped my sweat on the seat between us.

"You're soaked dude. What the hell."

I was bathed in my own perspiration. I was breathing heavy. The skin over my knuckles was stretched like a drum. Bits of my palms were underneath my fingernails.

Three sets of eyes turned to stare at me. Lindsey even asked if she should pull over.

I waved them off.

"I'm fine," I forced out meekly. "Bad dream."

"No shit," Shoddy said.

"What the hell did you drink last night?" Emily asked rhetorically, before turning back around and diving back into her magazine. Shoddy went back to reading a book. Lindsey gave me an awkward look through the rearview mirror and then put both eyes back on the road.

I had to concentrate on slowing my breathing. With every breath the explosions in my chest diminished. I put down the window and felt a rush of cool highway breeze dry out my sweaty air. My body cooled too as I waited for my turn to drive again.

For the rest of the ride down I looked up into the rearview mirror frequently. Each time I did, Lindsey was watching me. From the angle she was sitting, and the angle I was slouching, only one of her eyes was visible; one clear, deep blue eye keeping watch. It seemed like it was always on me.

I didn't sleep again on the ride to Florida, whether I was driving or not. But somewhere at a rest stop in one of the Carolinas I saw Shoddy discreetly throw away the Providence Journal.

I decided then that drinking heavily for the following week would be a sort of queer requiem for all the ghosts I left in Providence.

Chapter 32

Despite the late start we arrived in Florida early. It only took twenty-one hours to reach Orlando instead of our expected twenty-four. Even though we were all exhausted we wanted to make the most out of our short time there. We checked into two rooms at the All Star Movies resort and were directed to the *101 Dalmatians* section.

"We should go right over to Magic Kingdom and go on a few roller coasters," Emily suggested. "Then go over to Disney Studios for their rollercoaster and the Tower of Terror. Then tonight we can hit up Epcot for the fireworks show. We have these hopper passes that let us go to any park we want."

It sounded like a lot to me.

"I'd rather take a nap," I said.

"Me too," Lindsey agreed. She was at the helm for a large chunk of driving.

"Come on! We're here, we have to do stuff!" Emily pleaded.

"Easy for you to say. You drove for two hours up in Virginia," I said. "Lindsey, Shoddy and I each drove like ten hours today."

"The trip only took twenty-one, Shaw," Emily corrected.

"Whatever, you know what I mean," I said. "What do you wanna do Shoddy?"

"I'm fine with whatever but I just slugged two Red Bulls. I'm not going to nap right now."

"Why don't you guys go to Magic Kingdom and Shaw and I will meet you at EPCOT in a couple hours. We can drink around the world," Lindsey said.

Emily and Shoddy were suspicious.

"You two are going to nap?" he said.

"That's the plan," I said, knowing what he was suggesting.

"Sure," Emily said.

Lindsey either knew what they were hinting at or feigned understanding pretty well. Emily and Shoddy looked back and forth between Lindsey and I. They smiled at each other and nodded.

"Alright, meet us at the pub in England in two hours," Emily said. "You've been here before, right Shaw? You can navigate the bus route?"

"Yeah, I'm good Em. We'll see you in a couple hours. Say hi to Cinderella for us."

"Have fun in Wonderland," she replied.

Emily sent a smirk my way and dragged Shoddy down the path, disappearing around a corner next to a massive replica of a cartoon Dalmatian.

Our rooms were on the second floor right next to each other. There was even a door inside that opened into the adjoining rooms.

Initially, Lindsey and I separated with our luggage into our respective rooms. I was changing my shorts when the adjoining door swung open.

"Hey, I have no pants on!" I yelled, startled.

"And? That's never stopped me before," Lindsey said. She walked slowly into the room and sat down on my bed right on top of the shorts I was about to put on. I wasn't sure if she was seducing me or deliberately putting me in a vulnerable position of weakness.

"So do you really want to take a nap?" I asked. "Or was that all a very poor ploy to get rid of them?"

She was looking at the floor and didn't answer right away.

"Linds?"

"What are we doing here, Shaw?"

"Here? We're stopping for the night so we don't drive off the road into an alligator swamp."

"No, stupid. You and me. What are we doing here?"

Leave it to a twenty-one year old Psychology major to bring up a deeply emotional and complex relationship conversation at the start of Spring Break.

When I didn't answer she looked up at me, her lip quivering like a teenager in the final moments of virginity.

Followed by the crying.

"I can't do this anymore, Shaw," she said through a sweeping curtain of tears. "I need more from you than just drunken hookups."

"We aren't always drunk!"

Wrong response, Shaw.

"You asshole. After everything we've been through you can't give me a straight answer."

"What do you want from me, Linds? What do you want me to do, define our relationship? Go out and announce it to the world? Want me to climb to the top of the Tower of Terror and yell it out?"

"Don't patronize me. You owe me more than that," she sniffed back tears. I reached over to wipe them from her face and she brushed my hand away. "This is never going to work because of her."

"Who?"

"You know who. The girl you were in love with, before, you know . . ." she trailed off, probably remembering the worst night of both our lives.

"Come on Lindsey, don't do this now," I pleaded.

"Why not, Shaw? What difference does it make? Shoddy and Emily already know, they aren't blind. And don't think it hasn't been awkward with the four of us. Maybe you don't feel it but I sure do. Shoddy looks at me like the enemy now. Emily thinks the same way about you. She thinks I'm a fool for falling for you. Like all I am is some kind of replacement girl."

She wasn't crying anymore. Her eyes were still seeping. Those beautiful blue pools were overflowing and spilling down over her high cheekbones. But it wasn't crying. She was in complete control, speaking with purpose and clarity.

"So you need to tell me, Shaw. Am I going to risk my friendship with them and continue what we've started? Or am I going to lose my best friend, am I going to lose you, because you can't move on with your life?"

"I want to make it work, Linds, really I do. There are just a lot of things going on that you wouldn't understand."

"Try me."

I hesitated. I looked around the room, trying to buy time I knew wasn't for sale.

"Does this have anything to do with what happened at Primal the night before we left?"

She caught me off guard but damn she knew me well. I don't know what nonverbal communication I exhibited the past twenty-four hours, but she read it loud and clear. My mouth was closed but I pressed my lips tighter together in defiance.

"Fine, don't talk to me. Just like you, Shaw. Things get complicated and tough and you just run and hide."

If she only knew how wrong she was.

"I bet you'd tell Lily. How bout we jump in the car and drive up to Connecticut, swing by and see her?"

It was a low blow and she knew it. She immediately regretted it and hurried an apology.

"I'm sorry. I didn't mean that. You shouldn't have anyone telling you what to do about all that."

"No," I said in almost a whisper. I looked down at my feet. "It's alright Lindsey."

It was true that the loss of Lily—Lindsey's good friend—changed everything.

"I'm over all that," I said and looked up into her glistening, wet blue eyes. I said it hoping to elicit a specific reaction from her. Lindsey knew me better than anyone. The flip side being I knew her in the same way. I got what I was looking for.

"No. No I understand, Shaw. Too soon is too soon. I can only pretend to know how hard it was for you."

"What do you want me to do about all this, Linds?"

"I should be asking you that. Look, I meant what I said. I can't keep going on and on like this. But for now, let's just get through this trip, through this week and then we'll sit down and talk."

That was easier than I anticipated.

"Are you sure?"

"I'm sure. But you have to promise me you won't flake out again."

"I promise."

She tugged at my arm, pulling me, still not wearing pants, down onto the edge of the bed. With me sitting, she stood up and took a few steps to close and lock the interconnecting door.

"You have both of your room keys, right?" she asked as she unbuttoned her tight pink polo shirt.

"Yes. I never gave Shoddy his key."

"Good," she was standing above me. "We don't want any surprise interruptions."

She pulled her shirt off and tussled her own long blonde hair. There was something else in her big blue eyes. No longer watery desperation but hunger. She pushed my chest so that I fell back onto the bed, my legs still hanging over the edge. She crawled on top and knelt straddling my torso. She took my right hand and placed it on her back, right at her bra clasp.

We were late making it to the pub in England that afternoon. Emily and Shoddy must have anticipated our tardiness because a half hour after our scheduled time they too had not yet showed up. When we finally met up they were giggling and pointing at us a little too obviously. We dove right into a few pints before moving on to margaritas in Mexico and some sudsy brew in Germany. We spent the night watching fireworks and eating overpriced concession treats and when we got back to the Dalmatian hotel Shoddy and I went to our room, Emily and Lindsey to theirs. The interconnecting doors between our rooms stayed shut.

Chapter 33

The next morning, Monday, we took off for Key West earlier than planned. The ride was quiet and the scenery of southern Florida was less than impressive, until we reached the three-hour stretch over the ocean through the Florida Keys. They all voted that I should drive, citing that I was the best driver in the group. I knew it was because the two-lane highway spanning miles of open water was quite intimidating. I relished the opportunity I was given to focus on the road without interruption.

The girls nervously gazed out at the blue span of water, little white boats dotting the horizon. Barely anything was said, which was fine with me. I was too busy reliving the previous afternoon's delight with Lindsey. I didn't feel one hundred percent comfortable with what we did, considering the conversation she attempted to have prior to. Did I take advantage of her weakness, again? We were both so hungry for the carnal connection. I justified it that way. If we didn't unscrew the sexual valves, the tension in the group would've been unbearable.

As it was, the group had yet to find our collective frame of mind and establish the unspoken ground-rules of our vacation dynamic. The initial excitement about vacation wore off a few miles outside Providence, followed by hours and hours of schizophrenic emotional waves ranging from happiness and anticipation to jealousy, pettiness and extreme boredom. Perhaps Florida was the cure, the day before just an appetizer.

Our arrival at The Southernmost Hotel and Resort that afternoon did alter the mood of our group considerably. As soon as we stepped out of the Explorer into the mildly humid Conch Republic air, simpatico clicked in. We instantly became a calm, cohesive unit with common goals: to get as much alcohol, food and sexual stimulation as four people could get in a tropical paradise in four days.

We checked in at the lobby without issue, stored our bags and immediately walked across the street to the tiki bar on the beach.

After a few margaritas we asked the bartender for advice on where best to begin our journey to inebriation. He suggested a personal favorite, Irish Kevin's, a tropical Irish pub, if that makes any sense.

We tipped him generously and walked the two miles down Duval Street, the island's main drag. Between the quaint cafes and bars sat art galleries featuring local artists' renditions of island life. And snuck in between the art studios were one-man stands selling hand-rolled cigars. We saw the Key West Lighthouse, the original Jimmy Buffet's Margaritaville bar and my personal tensions floated away with the live tropical music wafting out of each open door we passed.

I forgot about the long drive. I forgot about the almost-feud with Lindsey. I forgot about the troubles and chaos of the past year. At one point I even reached out and grabbed Lindsey's hand. We were walking in front of Emily and Shoddy. She shot an anxious glare my way; worried our friends would notice the public display of affection. I smirked my best "I don't care" smirk and squeezed. She squeezed back.

"Awe isn't that adorable," a man's voice said from behind us. I turned to tell Shoddy to shut up but instead saw something unexpected. Shoddy and Emily were there but the comment hadn't come from either of them. It had come from a tall woman, taller than Shoddy or me, standing at the opening of a bar. She was dressed in a sparkling red sequin ball gown. Her cherry-red hair was swept up in an old-school beehive do and her makeup was too caked on to be classy. Then she spoke again.

"You two are just precious," she said in the deepest voice possible. She must have read the obvious confusion on my face.

"Why don't you guys come in for a drink? It's OK, you can bring the girls too, everybody's welcome," she said and pointed one long, red-polished finger at a sign in the bar's window.

Four brightly colored and flamboyantly dressed people adorned the ad with the words, "The Queens of Key West" emblazoned over their heads. There was the red-haired woman in the center wearing the same red dress and a pink feather boa. Surrounding her were Barbara Streisand, Cher and a woman with short-cropped black hair I didn't recognize.

Lindsey started laughing, as did Shoddy and Emily. It took me a second longer but eventually realization slapped me in the face. I couldn't help but laugh along. The woman, or man, in the red dress chuckled heartily.

"You must be the smart one in the group," she said looking right at me. "How about you come in and buy me a martini and I'll explain the whole thing to you?"

Shoddy, Lindsey and Emily burst out in hysterics. Passers-by stopped and whispered, some pointing at the drag queen. Again, I couldn't help but laugh.

"No thank you Ma'am," I said.

"Ma'am? Oh come on, honey. I know I look better than a ma'am," she said with a charming mix of sass and humor. "But that's alright. I can see you're already taken by this lovely blonde biscuit."

I was still holding Lindsey's hand. She was grinning widely.

"Just remember, nothing beats a red-head. You stop by on your way home and I'll prove it," she said and blew me a kiss.

Before I could stop myself I said, "Oh, I know."

Lindsey immediately let go of my hand. Lily was a redhead.

"So," Shoddy said when we were once again on our way, "looks like Shaw has a new admirer."

"Apparently he's a fan of redheads," Lindsey chimed in. I reached out and grabbed for her hand. She pulled it away. On the second try she reluctantly took it but held it limply.

"It must be weird living a lie like that," Emily said. "Those guys go around everyday lying about who they are. They can't choose who they want to be—gay or straight, man or woman, Sonny or Cher." She laughed at her own joke.

I thought about what she said and squeezed Lindsey's hand.

"I think they're the most honest people down here," I said. I felt the eyes of disagreement burning into the back of my neck. "Well, think about it. They're the only people with enough balls, literally, to show the world who they really are. To go around and not be ashamed of what they've done or what they want. I bet ninety-nine percent of the tourists and travelers down here have more skeletons in their closets than those drag queens do."

"That's because they've been out of the closet for a long time, Shaw," Shoddy said, snickering.

"That's just what I think," I said. "The world would be a better place if everyone were that open and honest with each other."

Lindsey finally squeezed my hand back. I felt good because what I said was actually honest. I wasn't just saying it to get a girl to sleep with me, although, it probably would end up having that bonus side effect.

"Alright, thanks Plato," Shoddy said. "Enough philosophizing. We're here. Irish Kevin's."

Sure enough we had arrived in front of a raucous building, huge floor to ceiling windows opened to the street and a large leprechaun holding a pint of beer hanging above the main door.

Even on a Monday night the bar was crazy. On the wall was a large chalkboard with a list of specialty shots for the week. We started at the top with something called an Itchy Crab. It was a bright red shot that tasted like cinnamon schnapps.

The place employed generous bartenders who guided us through lemon drops, redheaded sluts (to which I did not make any extraneous comments), mind erasers and many other potent shooters with funny tropical names. Two full rotations through that list and Emily, Shoddy, Lindsey and I were clearly in Spring Break mode. The eponymous shot for the evening was the Hazy Summer's Night, which we hit—for the third time—right around midnight.

I was the first awake the next morning. I stumbled around Shoddy's bed. He was face down and wearing his jeans, one sock and no shirt. How we got back to the hotel was a little blurry. I did remember that on the walk home we crossed to the other side of Duval Street when we neared the drag queen's bar. The rest was blacked out. Did I hook up with Lindsey? Shoddy passed out on the bed next to me suggested no, but it wasn't concrete evidence.

I felt better than I anticipated. Either my tolerance was at a pinnacle or the hangover had yet to surge ahead. I went to the bathroom for a cup of water, splashed some on my face and brushed my teeth. I slipped on my boat shoes, hung a Boston Red Sox jersey loosely on my shoulders and didn't even bother changing my shorts from the night before.

The air conditioner under the window rattled on, circulating a frigid, fake breeze.

I wanted fresh air so I headed outside. A not-yet humid tropical wind caressed my cheeks as soon as I closed the hotel door behind me. In a way, it was much more refreshing than the industrial-strength artificial air swirling inside the room. I walked across to the tiki bar at the beach and found a little table in the sand.

The ocean was rough. Large piles of seaweed and debris lined the water's edge. There must have been bad weather last night. Resort workers were clambering to clean and rake the sand.

"Rough night last night?"

I looked up to see a man of about fifty blocking the sun. He was wearing a flowered Hawaiian shirt and nametag that said Charlie.

"You have no idea."

"Oh, I'm sure I do."

His dark natural tan meant he had been a local for a while.

"You're probably right. Well then, what's the cure, Charlie?"

"The cure? The cure is an extra large margarita, with rocks and salt. But since the bar isn't open yet, I'd suggest that hammock over there by the water. And coffee. Want some coffee?"

"Absolutely, yes."

"Make it two, please," said Lindsey from behind Charlie the waiter.

"Right away young lady," he said and shuffled off across the sand to the tiki hut. But not before giving Lindsey a second look.

She was showered and fresh, clad in her skimpiest black bikini visible just barely underneath a sheer cover-all. She wore big dark bug-eye, celebrity-like sunglasses propped up in her hair and was carrying a pink beach bag.

"Can I sit?" she asked as she sat. "Quite a night, huh?"

I just nodded.

Charlie stopped by with two black coffees, piping hot, a tiny pitcher of milk and a few packets of sugar.

"Just wave if you want some nice, greasy food to sop up the alcohol," he said before shuffling away again back toward the tiki hut.

"Hey don't take this the wrong way, but did we have sex last night?" I mumbled.

Thankfully she laughed.

"No. We made out in the hallway near your room and I think we probably would've but Emily started yelling from our room. She was puking everywhere and freaking out."

"Ah, OK. It's coming back to me slowly."

She laughed again.

"So is Shoddy all banged up?" Lindsey asked. She used one delicate finger to tip the milk into her coffee. Some dripped onto her hand and she licked it away.

"Banged up is an understatement. I think he might be dead," I replied. She laughed.

"Looks like we're the only ones who can hold our booze," she said.

"Always were the only ones. Even back in high school."

She laughed again. I don't know if it was her laughter, the sun or the fact I was ninety percent still drunk, but I couldn't help thinking about our long history.

"Do you remember how we met, Linds?"

"Do I remember? Yes, actually, clear as this beautiful day."

"So you remember that night at my high school?"

"Actually, Shaw we met earlier that night at the ice cream place down the road."

She was right. Lindsey and I met our senior year of high school. She went to the sister school to my all-boys Catholic prep school. We had similar traits and upbringing. We were supposed to be fixed up on a date by a couple we both knew. They said we'd be good for each other. We never had that first date.

One random night at an ice cream parlor two groups of horny high school students, sexually repressed by their respective religious, educational and parental authorities, flirted outside. We all drove back to my high school. I ended up kissing Rose, one of Lindsey's high school friends, in the bushes alongside the gymnasium. Lindsey made out with the goalie from my hockey team.

Even though I dated Rose for more than a year, Lindsey and I became close friends. We connected on every level. We liked the same music, the same movies, laughed at the same jokes and had no idea what we wanted out of life. Lindsey felt like she wore the pants in our relationship. I let her have that because I grew accustomed to having her around, whenever I needed her or wanted her. From her I learned loyalty was a rare and precious commodity among friends.

When one found it, like a vein of gold in the Yukon, one defended it with any method available.

When college decision time rolled around later that year, we got together with a few other friends who had similar choices. In that group was Duncan, an outsider I befriended. Lindsey never liked Duncan. She never trusted him. But the three of us decided to go to Providence College. Duncan and I were going to room with a kid I knew from high school. His name was Ben. Lindsey did like Ben.

Within the first month of arriving at college, my relationship with Rose crumbled. As all high school friends do, our group tried to stay in touch as much as possible. We relied heavily on online chatting and grapevine gossip. But because Lindsey and I were away together, the obvious rumors swirled through our group of friends and soon Rose confronted me with some damning, albeit untrue, evidence. She claimed a firsthand source witnessed my infidelity with Lindsey. I was a horrible person. I was to tackle college on my own, without Rose's supposed love at my side. Duncan comforted me. He was dating one of Rose and Lindsey's other friends but they too had broken up only weeks before. We commiserated.

Immediately Lindsey blamed Duncan for speaking out of school. She accused him of spreading rumors that she and I were cheating. Of course Duncan denied it, but in retrospect Duncan denied everything.

"You look sad," Lindsey said, interrupting my memory. She was stirring her coffee and staring at me.

"Me? No."

"Yeah, you do. Your smile just went away, like you thought of something terrible."

"It did? I was just thinking about how Duncan spread those rumors about us."

"I knew it!" she said a little too loud. The few other customers that had wandered in cast us an annoyed stare. It was too early and most people in Key West had too much to drink the night before.

"That little rat was the one who started those rumors. Wait, you knew?"

"Well, yeah. He admitted a few days after Rose and I broke up. I thought I told you?"

"No, you never told me. I wish you did. What did he say?"

"He told me the breakup was for my own good. He said, 'Rose was holding you back, Shaw. Now you and I can really enjoy college.'"

"But he admitted he spread the rumors that you and I were hooking up?"

"Yeah, he even sent Emails directly to Rose. I guess that was why she was so pissed off."

"That'd explain it. It's too bad because she and I were good friends. But if she was that quick to judge, I guess I chose the right side."

She smiled and reached over to touch my hand.

When she pulled her hand back she said, "so did Duncan ever apologize or try to fix what he did?"

"Not exactly. Actually, he admitted he did it for selfish reasons. Since he just broke up with his high school sweetheart he wanted me to be single too. Like Rose's feelings never really mattered to him. Weird thing was, he had this crazy look in his eyes when he told me but was really calm. Like cool and calculating, ya know? Like the demeanor the villains in movies always have. It was almost like he was bragging to me about how he manipulated the whole situation just for the fun of it. It's the one thing I'll always remember about him. The obvious malice."

"That's great, but did he apologize?"

"Never."

She sat in front of me noticeably trying to repress a new anger caused by a long forgotten situation. The soft hand she had just touched me with clenched.

"Figures. It's probably better you never told me. I would've killed that little weasel. Maybe I still might. Yup, I'm gonna kill him!"

She raised her voice again. I flinched.

"Don't say that," I said, looking down at the table.

"Say what? That I'm going to kill Duncan? Come on Shaw, since when did you care about him. You hate Duncan more than anyone."

"Regardless, it's not good to talk about people like that. Duncan was a human being."

"Was?"

"Is. Whatever. You know what I mean."

"I'm not sure I do," she said. She squinted her big blue eyes as if trying to see into my brain. Finally one corner of her lips rose in frustration and pursed to take a sip of coffee.

"Anyway," Lindsey continued, "I still don't know why you never gave him a good beating. I know you scuffled with him a few times, but you should have taken him out behind some building and kicked his ass. Actually, I was always surprised a lot of people didn't do that."

Obviously Lindsey hadn't read the past weekend's Providence Journal.

"He could use a good beating," she repeated.

She looked back out at the ocean. The sky was blue but the water was stormy.

We sat without talking for a few minutes. In the silence my brain switched off Duncan and back to Lindsey. Her temper had gotten better over the years but she still had a fire inside rarely seen in the fairer sex. It was part of what turned me on to her. She was sweet and sour all at once.

After four years of college the only people still close to me were the balanced ones. They were the people who were simultaneously perfect and imperfect. Emily was a smart, compassionate, callous bitch. Shoddy was a loyal drunk. Lindsey was a short-tempered angel. The strictly good and solely bad were gone. I was amongst the undecided.

Four years of college had rolled by. People came and went. Friends were gained and lost. And after all the scars and lies, role-reversals and regrets, Lindsey and I were sitting like adults at a beachside café at the bottom of America; as far away from Providence one could get on East Coast.

For all intents and purposes Lindsey and I were a couple, even though I wouldn't define it and we tried to hide it. But because of our strong friendship, we were at a point in our relationship that most couples only reach after years of marriage, or years of counseling. We knew each other's little quirks and stupid intricacies that only best friends or lovers appreciate.

I knew she was a quarter Native American on her mother's side. I knew she had a secret love of the Bee Gees and had an unnatural crush on Barry Gibb. I knew depending on her level of drunkenness, she would tell any guy about the small butterfly tattoo she had in a very private place; and I knew from experience it didn't really exist. I knew that when she slept she snored—but not a rumbling thunder snore. It was something more innocent, like a pigeon coo in stereo. I knew the last thing she deserved was me messing with her heart. I knew she was too good for me.

On the flip side, she knew about my sloppy but determined guitar playing. She knew I rarely showed emotion but she knew that deep down it was there, somewhere hidden behind a wall. She knew the last two times I cried were at the movie theater during the Lion King and the day the doctor found a BB size lump on my right testicle that turned out to be nothing. She knew I dreamed of being a professional writer but lacked a proper Muse. She knew what and who that Muse should look and act like and she knew it probably wasn't her.

"I always knew you had a crush on me," I said, bringing her gaze from the ocean back to me.

"Really?" she chuckled. "How sure were you that I liked you in that way?"

"I was pretty sure. I noticed it freshman year, after all the rumors started."

"If you were so sure, why didn't you ever act on it? I was pretty hot freshman year."

She was.

"I don't really know why. How come you never acted on it?"

She looked down at her coffee mug and stroked the handle.

"Because I didn't want to prove the rumors. I'm a better friend than that. I didn't want Rose and whoever started the rumors to be right."

She paused and drank the last dregs of coffee.

"Then Lily came along," she continued, "and my chance was gone."

Again, she was right. Not until Lily was gone did Lindsey and I take our relationship past friendship. I think I needed her then, more than she ever needed me. Since Lily had gone, Lindsey was stronger than me. Lindsey was always stronger.

"Sorry about that comment yesterday," I said. "The one about redheads."

She fluffed her hand at me.

"Stop it, don't worry. I shouldn't have been angry. You were just kidding around."

"Yeah. But sorry anyway."

I thought I saw a little sadness creep across *her* face.

Another warm breeze, a little more humid than before, blew in from the ocean and tossed Lindsey's hair up into her eyes. I reached across the table, over our two empty mugs and pulled the strands out of her face and back behind her ear.

She looked surprised I had that much caring in me. She touched my hand, held it to her face.

I pulled my hand back quickly as pang split my temples. I flinched and my eyes squinted.

Suddenly melancholy washed over me like the waves slipping over the debris on the beach. The lingering good feelings from the previous night were gone. I tried to look back up at Lindsey, who was staring out at the ocean, but all I saw were the broken promises. All I felt were the negative emotions. And all of it was totally my fault. I put us in this predicament. Yes, I promised her that when we returned home we'd have a talk about our future together. But I knew I'd avoid it like the black plague. And when it came down to it, when she finally forced me to choose between a future with her or my past with Lily, Lindsey could not win. Deep down, I think she knew it too.

I almost wanted Lindsey to jumpstart the argument we were having in the hotel, like it would wash away the remorse I felt about dragging her heart around for so long. I almost wanted her to yell at me about how poorly I treated her after all she had done for me, especially in the past year. I almost wanted her to retract the "I love yous" and tell me I was a bad person.

But she didn't.

She looked back at me, straight into my eyes. I could tell by the look on her face that the sadness had returned to my own. We just sat staring at each for a few minutes. Charlie stopped by and silently refilled the coffee mugs then disappeared. Then Lindsey and I turned our gaze out to the open ocean and watched the waves crash onto the sand.

Chapter 34

That night we continued the Key West tradition we had established the night before. We started drinking at the tiki bar, followed by a stop at the Green Parrot, Sloppy Joe's and then back to Irish Kevin's.

After our morning conversation, it seemed Lindsey and I regressed back to just friends. No handholding. But that night when alcohol took over, we let our carnal desires out of the cage. We slipped into her hotel room and snapped the deadbolt before Shoddy and Emily could climb up the stairs. The sex was brief but powerful and we fell asleep immediately afterwards, still naked and covered in sweat.

The next morning I woke up before Lindsey and stepped out without her waking. I went to the concierge for advice on a breakfast place and was given directions to Pepe's, the oldest running restaurant on the island. It was a local favorite and was celebrating its Centennial anniversary this year.

Destination in hand, I decided the others should join me. By the time I got back to Lindsey's room she was already showering.

Emily still hadn't returned from my room so I snapped the deadbolt again and snuck into the bathroom. Lindsey stuck her head from the shower and stopped me short.

"Hey, not now," she said, anticipating my intentions. "Emily is going to come in any minute."

"So? I dead-bolted the door. We have plenty of time."

"No, not now," she said and closed the curtain. She put a vibe of annoyance in her words. Real or feigned I couldn't tell.

Turned out she was right. Ten minutes later Emily and Shoddy showed up ready for breakfast.

Pepe's was a small shack of a restaurant next to another old art studio on the far side of the island, a long walk from our hotel. But I was assured it was worth it—try the pancakes, they're the best around. Pepe didn't disappoint. The food was hearty and delicious and served to cure our lingering hangovers.

After breakfast we stopped into the abutting art studio. A chalk drawing of the Key West Lighthouse at sunset had grabbed Emily's attention.

While the girls were browsing, Shoddy and I went to the rear of the studio. An old man with a grizzled beard and dark tan sat sketching on an easel. He had the general Ernest Hemingway air about him, as did most of the Key West locals in homage to their island's most famous former inhabitant.

"Good morning, boys," he said without looking up from his easel. "Enjoying the day?"

"Absolutely," Shoddy said. "We're fat and happy."

"Ah, so you ate at Pepe's, then?"

"Yup, just finished," I said. "Had to see what all the fuss was about."

The old man just laughed and kept sketching.

"They aren't really a hundred years old, you know," he said.

"What?" Shoddy looked hurt.

"That place was built in 1971. I know because I helped him build it. He's been saying it's his hundredth anniversary for the past ten years. Sucks in the tourists."

"Wow," I said, my pride a little wounded and my sense of adventure a little snuffed out. "Well it worked on us."

"I'm starting to think Pepe actually believes it," the old man continued. "You lie about something everyday for as long as he does, you start believing the lie. I bet you hook up ole' Pepe to one of them lie detector machines and ask him how old his place is, he'd say one hundred. And the machine would agree."

Shoddy gave me a look that said he wanted to get away from the crazy old artist. I was intrigued by him and by his story. I guessed if we had a case of beer and a few lounge chairs, he'd sit around for days telling more stories. But my friends were ready for the long walk back and a blessed day lounging on the beach.

"Well you have a nice day, sir," I said. "And regardless of how old the place is, Pepe makes some mean pancakes."

He finally looked up from his easel, the years of life brimming in his eyes. His face cracked with a smile.

"That he does, son. That he does."

Wednesday was full of familiar, relaxing hammock naps and ocean dips. We ate fresh seafood and drank frozen cocktails. When we weren't lounging by the sea we were laying out by the pool. Vacations in the tropics were meant to be spent the way we spent ours.

We became students of a devout and hedonistic lifestyle.

The only exception was Lindsey. I concluded she regretted having sex with me while drunk. She carried herself the same but I knew her better than the others. I knew something was amiss. And in turn, something was off with me. I had trouble looking her in the eye. On the off chance I did, waves of sadness washed over me like the waves washed over the debris on the beach. A storm was building over the sea and it was washing ashore bits and pieces of guilt and the tattered remains of my shipwrecked love life.

Wednesday night was a replica of Tuesday except we ended up at a bar called the Lazy Gecko. They billed themselves as the "Southernmost Red Sox Nation." So of course, us all being card-carrying members of that widespread sports cult, we had to stop in. The dive was painted lime green and adorned with Boston Red Sox memorabilia, photos and televisions showing classic highlights and early Spring Training coverage.

Just like any good Red Sox fans in a tropical paradise, extreme drunkenness found us all again. Lindsey and I loosened up around each other with each sip and by midnight we were sneaking to the back of the bar to make out. An hour later we had ditched Emily and Shoddy and half-skipped back to the hotel. The sex was wild, fueled by underlying frustration and a tinge of anger. We were just hitting our stride when we heard our two friends rustling in the hallway.

"Dammit, not again," Emily yelled. Lindsey and I continued without a hiccup in motion.

"Forget it, just sleep in Shaw's bed again," Shoddy said. "They both need it. Let 'em go."

He dragged her away but the annoyance in his tone was obvious.

Shoddy showed it the next morning when he banged on our room door.

"Hey lovebirds, get the fuck up! We're gonna be late for our boat!"

Lindsey and I shot up, still naked, and grabbed the alarm clock radio. The red numbers blared up, hurting our bloodshot eyes. We overslept.

The day before we had scheduled a snorkeling trip out on one of the reefs. They offered free beer and the price was good. The catch was you had to be there before nine o'clock in the morning. This was tough when you were engaged in a drunken and passionate love affair until sunrise. But it was Thursday, our last day in Key West and we decided to do something more than just waste away hours lounging in the sun.

As I expected, Lindsey acted in the same distant, regretful way as she had the morning before. Despite her nagging me to hurry up and brush my teeth, we made it to the boat in time.

The majority of pedestrians roamed Key West that morning like zombies, looking as bleary-eyed as we did. When the boat crew went over safety rules and gear advice, only one older woman was enthusiastic or awake enough to demonstrate the proper technique for the rest of us. An hour went by before we arrived at a seawall that the captain claimed had the best reef diving around.

Suddenly we all sobered up and the situation became very real. I had never snorkeled before, nor was I a fan of open-ocean. Lindsey and Emily shared my sentiments. Shoddy's family took frequent trips to the Caribbean when he was a child so this was to be a nostalgic adventure for him. His smile made it impossible for any of us to back out.

Up on the deck we stood at the rear of the line queued up to jump into the water. I put on the buoyancy vest, flippers and mask and waddled toward what I envisioned a pirate-style plank.

Shoddy went first, leaping from the boat's edge like a kid into a swimming pool. Emily was next, hesitant but determined not to look timid around Shoddy. Lindsey and I moved up to the edge. One of the crewmembers, a petite girl who couldn't have been older than eighteen, treaded water about eight feet below with a floatation device lolling loosely with the rolling waves. The water around her was a deep azure blue but still clear as polished glass. It crashed forcefully against the boat and tossed the girl around but she quickly regained composure and yelled up for Lindsey to jump.

Lindsey looked back at me and gave an unconvincing smile.

"Go ahead," I said in my best reassuring tone. "This is nothing compared to some of the things we've done."

Her fake smile grew a little more confident and she pulled her mask down over her blue eyes. She jumped, splashing to the left of the girl, disappeared for a few seconds and then popped back up, mask and snorkel intact. She spit out some seawater. A dribble of drool slid down her chin. But she looked up at me and smiled, gave a quick wave and kicked off in the direction of the other snorkelers.

My turn. I was the last passenger to go. The crewmember in the water beckoned me to jump. I waddled to the edge, my big black flippers sticking out over the water. I was hesitating.

"Ya know, we saw an eighteen foot hammerhead out here last

week," someone said from behind me. I turned to see another crewmember, a guy about my age with long surfer hair and sunglasses. He was grinning.

"Come on man, really?" I said. "I'm about to jump."

He just laughed and made a hand gesture like an usher at a movie theater.

I looked back down at the girl in the water. She had red hair, slicked back but shiny. Not red like the drag queen but a natural red, like Lily used to have. My courage suddenly perked up.

I thought of when Lily told me she was going to make me come alive, and then I grabbed my mask with both hands and jumped.

My feet hit the water with such force that it pulled my hands off the mask, which in turn popped up off my face. Water rushed up my nose and down the snorkel tube, following the natural path into my mouth and down my throat. I tried to cough but was punished by more saltiness in my nostrils. The ocean was filling me up, like a glass under a faucet. I panicked. My eyes were clenched shut like fists but my arms were flailing, reaching wildly above me in slow motion, grabbing for the mask or the boat or the girl or anything other than the salt water. Nothing. I kicked but the flippers were like cement shoes. My legs were drained of energy and propelled my body only inches upwards. I reached out again above my head, tried to punch through to the sky. I hit something solid and metallic. There was a booming echo under the ocean.

I opened my eyes but the crystal blue water wasn't as crystal clear from an underneath vantage point. I closed them almost immediately. The salt was like a stinging poison. But in that instant I saw a hazy bottom half of a human, kicking under the water. It looked like Lindsey's black bathing suit bottom.

I thought of her and tried relaxing my muscles.

What if I didn't come back up? I thought. What if I swallowed the ocean? What if I let it swallow me? What if I let it grab me and drag me away from everything?

Then I was being pawed and pulled at, sideways under the water. That was it; I was being dragged away. But then I went upwards rapidly.

Right as my head broke the surface I wondered if my surrender to the ocean was justified.

Then a rush of air, the same salty taste but less dense and liquid. It pushed up my nostrils and back out my mouth, with it came a mix of ocean and sick. I started choking.

"Kick your feet!" someone screamed. It was a command, though, not an urgent cry. The crash of the waves on the metallic boat combined with the wind made it difficult to hear. "Kick your feet now!"

I reacted instinctively. I imitated the scissor motion the crew demonstrated on the ride out. All the while coughing up the sea.

"Hey, open your eyes man. You OK? Open your eyes and say something."

I obeyed. The sun glare blinded me but my eyes adjusted and I saw the guy from the boat deck treading water next to me. He shoved a red plastic torpedo under my right armpit.

He used one hand to pull the soaked hair from his face then back to the water to stay afloat. He grabbed one end of the red torpedo and began towing me to a ladder hanging from the back of the boat. I was slowly getting my bearings back and kicked a few times to ease his burden. We swam past the young girl whose horrified look told me she wasn't the one who pulled me to the surface.

"You OK, man?" the surfer guy said when we were back on the boat. He had brought me a towel and glass of fresh water. We were sitting on the front of the boat with our legs hanging off the side.

"Yeah, I think so. I don't know what happened. I'm sorry, though. I feel like an asshole."

"Not your fault, bro. You slipped underneath the boat. Pretty dangerous thing. Celia should've told you to jump further."

"Celia?"

"The girl in the water. I don't even think she saw you go under. The waves are massive out there today."

"But you saw me and jumped in. Thank you. Um, sorry but I didn't get your name."

"No worries, man. That's what I'm here for. And my name's Zak."

He extended a hand and I took it.

"So you going to head back in?" he asked.

"No, I think I'm good for today. I can look up eighteen foot hammerheads on the internet if I really want to see one."

"I was just joking. We've never seen anything like that out here. We get a few barracuda every now and then, but that's it."

Another crewmember delivered us two foamy, ice-cold beers. I drank mine in two gulps, still trying to quench the salty thirst permeating my entire body.

Zak left me to help call in the other snorkelers. I sat on the edge of the boat and tried to pick out my friends from the school of floating fish voyeurs.

I picked out Lindsey, still about twenty yards from the boat. Her body was parallel with the ocean surface but her backside protruded out. That's how I recognized her. That was how I recognized her under the water, right before I gave in to Poseidon.

Did I really almost die? Did I really surrender that readily to death? I had no fight. It was like I welcomed it.

The entire boat trip back to Key West I sat in a corner alone. Zak recounted the story to Emily, Lindsey and Shoddy. They tried to talk to me at one point but I waved them away. I was lost in my own head, ashamed at myself in many ways. I could not resign myself to the fact that I almost died or especially that split second I may have wanted it.

Obviously something was wrong inside me. I was depressed and sad. From what? There were some things that might justify it. Like every time I looked at Lindsey something gnawed at my insides. I hated how I treated her. But it was more than that. It was deeper and much more sinister.

By the time we docked I had burrowed through my feelings and concluded something had to be done. My near-suicide experience opened my eyes to my current melancholy. It was evidently dangerous.

But I'd wait until we got back to Providence. No need to start bringing up my past indiscretions and ruin our last few days of vacation.

We went back to the hotel after the snorkeling excursion and spent some time sleeping by the pool. I tried to clear my mind and sleep. I succeeded in merely lying on my back, staring up into a cloudless blue sky for over an hour.

Finally we all retreated to our respective rooms to clean up and get ready for dinner. It was our last night in Key West so we had made reservations at a swanky restaurant called Hot Tin Roof. It was located on the opposite end of the island overlooking the marina. Shoddy and I met the girls in the parking lot. He and I were dressed in white shorts and matching Hawaiian shirts. We had planned this outfit for weeks as a joke. Emily and Lindsey hated Hawaiian shirts so to spend an evening at an expensive restaurant with us clad in that style would be the perfect ending to our vacation.

They laughed when they saw us, obvious tourists with obvious obnoxious taste. We clashed with their classy, done-up demeanor. Emily wore a flowing skirt and white blouse with her chestnut hair pinned back. She looked quite attractive. Shoddy told her so. Shoddy never said anything nice about Emily. She gave him a strange look but then blushed when he repeated the compliment.

Lindsey wore a white sundress with barely visible flowers stitched over the bodice. It was tight to her body, accentuating all the curves. I mimicked Shoddy's compliment in Lindsey's direction.

"Thanks. But try to be a little more original next time," she joked.

At dinner we began drinking gin and tonics with the calamari appetizer. Two bottles of wine disappeared during dinner. We all tried the local lobster, which turned out to be sweeter than the New England lobsters we were used to. One more bottle of wine with dessert, and then a glass of twenty-year-old tawny port to finish the evening.

By the time we stumbled down the stairs at Hot Tin Roof, giggles were starting and inebriation was certain. We walked over to the famous Captain Tony's Saloon for a few beers and then finished off the night at our old standby, Irish Kevin's. We attempted the shot board race one more time. Our success was much more muted due to the gallons of liquor we had already drunk. Nevertheless, we clinked glass after glass, reminisced about days gone by and further discussed my apparent ocean cowardice and lack of snorkeling ability. Alcohol cured all ills. My mind, foggy with booze, was the clearest it had been all day.

Emily and Shoddy were the first to leave. I went to the bathroom and upon returning was notified by Lindsey that they just stepped out. They never returned.

Around three o'clock in the morning Lindsey and I found ourselves stumbling hand in hand down Duval Street singing Jimmy Buffett songs at the top of our lungs. We still carried our beers from the bar and took a swig every few seconds to quench our parched vocal chords.

When we reached the hotel Lindsey didn't stop. I turned to go up the stairs to our room but she didn't let go of my hand.

"Not yet, Aquaman. You're coming with me," she said, a sensual smile spreading across her face.

She broke into a trot across the street to the beach, dragging me behind. When we reached the sand she kicked her shoes off and stepped with drunken politeness over the chain blocking the beach entrance.

The moon was out in full, sending a broad ivory beam over the ocean, across the sand and right to the palm tree Lindsey settled under. She grabbed my shirt and pushed me against the trunk of the palm tree. She pressed a kiss hard onto my lips, forcing me down to my behind as she did so. She knelt in the sand between my legs.

"You know I hate Hawaiian shirts, Shaw," she said.

"Yeah, so what are you going to do about it?"

She reached under one of the buttons and pulled. The button popped off. She reached farther down and tore a few more buttons off with one rip. Her lips started at my neck and moved down my chest, leaving soft kisses in their wake. When she reached my waist she slid her body fully onto the sand. She was lying down, her lips exploring the skin under my waistband and she unfastened the fly and buttons with expert quickness. She pulled my underwear to my knees and a chill ran up my spine, either from the cool sand on my bare bottom or the warm lips on moving along my inner thigh.

What seemed like a heavenly eternity later, Lindsey knelt back on her knees and reached up under her sundress. She shimmied off her panties and threw them over her shoulder, a devil-may-care look blazing in her eyes.

I was still leaning against the palm tree. She climbed on top and reached her arms around my neck and around the trunk of the tree, pulling us closer than ever before. She closed her eyes and threw her head back, letting out a soft squeal. I reached up under her dress and grabbed her bare behind.

In our slow, rhythmic thrusting one of her shoulder straps fell loosely. Her dress slid down exposing one perfect breast to the moonlight. I bent over and kissed it. My five o'clock shadow must have tickled because Lindsey giggled and pulled me harder.

The experience grew steadily wilder and soon Lindsey was underneath me in the sand, her legs wrapped up around my waist. Then her legs tensed, squeezing me tight, and her pretty pink painted toes pointed up at the moon.

When we finished we stayed spooning in the sand under the palm tree. When I tried to move she stopped me.

"Wait. Not yet. I want to remember this, stay like this for as long as we can," she said. "You know I'll always love you, Augustine."

I said nothing back. I think we both knew it would be the last time we would make love. We had thrusted and kissed and pawed at each other like we knew it would never happen again. It was years of emotions erupting in one final act of physical desire.

Lindsey fell asleep in the same position. When she did I stood up and pulled my clothes back on as best I could; my shirt was torn to shreds. I pulled Lindsey's dress strap back over her shoulder, covering her chest. I made a lame attempt to find her underwear, unsuccessfully.

Finally I knelt down beside her and slid my arms into the sand underneath her body. I lifted her up, cradling her sleeping head on my shoulder. I carried her back across the street to her hotel room. I had a hunch Emily and Shoddy were together in my room.

I laid Lindsey in the bed and brushed the sand from her dress. After kicking off my clothes I climbed in beside her and fell asleep, drunk and satisfied and knowing that I'd probably never feel that way again.

Chapter 35

Friday morning actually began at noon when Lindsey and I awoke to our room phone buzzing loudly. The front desk was calling to remind us that checkout time was at 11:00am and we had to get moving or else they'd charge us for an extra day. Chaos ensued. There was no morning afterglow or wake up kiss.

Lindsey jumped out of bed and right into the shower. I didn't even try to join her. I learned my lesson about that.

After twenty minutes of hectic packing and a few yells from her to me, we were in the lobby throwing around credit cards and apologies. Emily and Shoddy met us at the car, awkwardness brimming between them.

Lindsey and I both noticed it immediately. Shoddy was still drunk, slouching, his eyes glassy and drooped. Emily didn't look much soberer, but stood upright at least. They stood a safe distance apart and never looked each other or Lindsey or me in the eyes. They had slept together, that was obvious, and by the look of things, it was especially raucous and regretted. I chuckled to myself. Alcohol certainly worked miracles.

Shoddy suggested food. We all greatly obliged and partook in one final breakfast/lunch at a quaint little place called the Banana Café. Greasy eggs, hash and sweet crepes splashed into our alcohol-flooded stomachs.

We were on the road out of Key West by two o'clock, subdued and quiet, exhausted and awkward. Lindsey asked to take the first leg. She said she was wide-awake. I obliged, taking the front passenger seat and letting Emily and Shoddy retreat to opposite corners of the backseat.

Lindsey and I weren't much closer. She had gone cold again. I could feel the tension. I sat inches from her and yet we were farther apart than we'd ever been.

One of my headaches started bubbling in my temples. It could've been part of the hangover.

When Emily and Shoddy appeared to be asleep, ugly silence remained.

"Hey, about last night," I said softly, just trying to kill the quiet. "That was amazing."

"I don't want to talk about it, Shaw. Not now."

"Yeah, I know, we will when we get back. But I just wanted to say it was amazing, and what you said to me afterwards . . ."

"Stop right there. I was drunk. Forget it, Shaw." Tears started welling up in her eyes.

"I'm sorry."

"Just stop, Shaw. I told myself I wasn't going to do that with you anymore. Not until we talked. And every night since I made that promise, I got drunk and broke my word."

The headache started in earnest. I closed my eyes and fireworks exploded in the darkness. Both hands were on my temples, rubbing in a circular motion.

"Um, alright. I don't know what to say," I said, opening my eyes but still rubbing. "Felt like you enjoyed it at the time."

"Of course I enjoyed it, Shaw. That's the problem."

"Now I'm really just confused. I really don't know what to say."

"Say nothing, Shaw. You're much better at that."

I caught a glimpse of Emily's eyes open in the backseat. She wasn't asleep. They snapped shut when I turned my head her way.

The easy pressure from my fingers on my temples eased the pain a little. I stopped rubbing. I let some silence build before making my next comment.

"For what its worth, Linds, I'm sorry."

When I said the words, I wasn't sure if I even meant them. It just felt like that right phrase at the time. In retrospect, I absolutely did.

She didn't respond immediately. Her lips straightened and flattened, as they always did when Lindsey was thinking hard on something. Her dimples caved in. We drove up the highway without talking. After ten minutes Lindsey relaxed, her mouth opened and drew in a long, relieved breath. Her dimples evaporated. She arrived at a conclusion.

"Thank you," she whispered, so soft our friends in the back couldn't have heard. "I'm sorry, too Shaw. I'm sorry I couldn't be her."

My only response was nonverbal. I nodded, looked out the window at the rush of traffic and then back at Lindsey in the car, into our little world. She took her eyes off the road for a second to meet mine. Everything she had to say had been said.

The remainder of the first leg was uneventful. I pretended to sleep until Emily woke up and started reminiscing about the beautiful beaches and bouncing bars in Key West. Shoddy joined in shortly thereafter and Lindsey and I were saved.

About six hours from Key West, we saw signs for Cape Canaveral and Lindsey pulled off the highway reckoning if there was a space shuttle nearby, there had to be a restaurant for dinner. We easily found a McDonalds.

Four burgers later we piled back into the Explorer, soda refills in hand. Lindsey and I switched places and I took over driving. During dinner I had noticed Lindsey's eyelids dropping at the same rate as the sun in the sky. She had had enough.

It was just about nine o'clock when I pulled back onto Interstate

95, due north. Within minutes the heavy fast food sandwiches took their toll and my three fellow travelers slipped quietly into dreamland.

Before she fell asleep, Lindsey asked me if I was alright. I simply nodded and gave her a thumbs-up sign without letting go of the steering wheel. She yawned and I was left with just an increasingly dark road and an increasingly painful headache.

Chapter 36

I had spent almost four years tossing blame at Duncan Barker and only grief bounced back. There were intermittent stretches of joy caused by Lily, Lindsey and Shoddy, and up until now I blamed Duncan for taking those away from me too. But not anymore. I carried that burden. I assumed that guilt.

But what struck me as odd, perhaps a bit cold, was that the guilt I felt over what I did to Duncan was nothing compared to the gnawing uneasiness that slithered around deep inside me on that dark, empty northbound highway. The uneasiness was connected to a thought I was repressing all week in Key West. After all, the guilt alone was hammering away at all my emotional defenses. What else could I handle?

What bothered me most about Duncan's death, the origin of the uneasiness, was that if Duncan was gone, whom was I supposed to hate?

The easy answer was myself. That's where the gurgling in my stomach came from. The majority of my recent history was saturated with grudge-filled animosity of, at this point, convoluted and immature origins. Having an enemy was comforting. He was always there—in person or in name—to blame, to take out aggression on, to act as a heavy bag for releasing tension.

Now he was not. And the only logical replacement was in control of a Ford Explorer filled with three sleeping confidants, a few hours from home, a confession and a whole heap of unknown consequences.

I think I always knew it would come to this. That eventually Duncan would be gone (although I never planned for it to be by my hand) and that I'd eventually have to go it alone. What I never counted on was how hard it would be to forgive myself.

The week in Key West was over. We were well into our long drive home to Providence and I was well into my long self-imposed inquisition.

I checked on the passengers: sleeping. How many hours I had been driving, I did not know. Since Shoddy fell asleep with his book on his lap, I was alone with nothing but the music and memories.

When I turned back, the shadows from the open highway that had bombarded me through the windshield so relentlessly for so long suddenly were not so imposing.

The darkness that had blanketed our journey since its inception—the darkness that weighed upon the night, permeated the steel shell of my Explorer and filled my brain, my heart and my soul—was lifting.

We careened towards the horizon, the tops of the large roadside pine trees just starting to silhouette against the sky. The pitch-blackness draped over us steadily lightened into a misty gray-blue.

A striptease started to play out before me. Daylight, something I had not seen for what seemed to be ages, slowly, seductively peeled off layers of the night, exposing itself bit by bit with a determined purpose.

I was all at once aroused by the temptation but terrified of what the day would bring. The darkness was my companion for so long, its impending death haunted my already fragile state of emotion. The night hid me, let me alone and isolated me from the world. I was able to wallow in guilt and regret while my friends slept nearby, blissfully unaware of the emotional strain caused by being trapped in my own mind.

Guilt hammered around in my brain and the gurgling erupted in my stomach.

I needed to stop. Driving was no longer an option. Something said pull over, get in back and close your eyes, block out the sun and prolong the darkness.

A foggy blue sign flashed by emblazoned with the unmistakable gas station symbol. We hadn't filled up since Mo's station, since I saw that fucking red paper with his commandments, since I confessed a couple things to Shoddy.

I turned the car onto the exit ramp and slapped Shoddy's knee with a hard knuckle flick. He bolted upright in mid-snore, eyes still closed, hands grasping for whoever woke him up.

"What the hell, man," he groaned and rubbed his eyes with the two hands that had kept his book from clattering to the cabin floor. No longer braced, the book slid off his lap and thudded closed on the car mat. "Damn, where are we? Last thing I remember is slipping the dress off some chick and . . ."

"That was a dream," I cut him off. "It happens when you're overtired and over-horny."

He chuckled as I turned the car from the exit ramp onto a two lane local road.

"Keep your eyes open for a gas station," I said. "Hopefully it's not as far from the highway as the last one."

"There it is," Shoddy replied and pointed out the passenger window. "Over there on the right. Looks like another local pump."

From the road the station was an orange, shimmering replica of Bobbo's garage from hours before. Shoddy and I groaned in unison as the hand-painted sandwich board sign came into focus between two gas pumps.

"Not again," he said. "This place looks just like the other one you stopped at a while back. You know, the one where you acted like a jackass."

What he really meant was don't start revealing any more secrets. I just nodded and knew he was staring at the back of my head.

"Bobbo did say his owner owned a bunch of stations up and down the highway. This must be another one of Mo's."

"Who?"

"Oh, Mo. The guy that owns the place. His name was on the door."

"Sure, whatever. I just hope Mo hired a less narcoleptic attendee for this station. If I go in there to pay and the guy's asleep, I'm jackin' the place."

"Wait a minute," I replied as I pulled the Explorer up to the first pump. "Wow. Look at these, Shoddy. Brand new pumps!"

He pressed his face to the back window and gazed in amazement at the series of glistening blue, modern gasoline pumps waiting for the next thirsty traveler to swipe his credit card in their technologically savvy faceplate.

"Is this a mirage?" he said, opened his door and slid out.

I followed suit and met him at the side of the Explorer.

"Mo must be upgrading," Shoddy said. "Must be doing pretty good for himself to afford these expensive new things."

"Good for him," I said. "Good Karma pays off, I guess."

"What are you talking about?"

Shoddy shifted his confused eyes from the new pumps to my face. I shook him off.

"Nothing, nothing. Never mind."

"Driving's making you loopy, Shaw."

I slid my credit card in and instantly saw the numbers flash on the digital reader. Ready to pump.

I replied as I slid my card back into my wallet. Shoddy inserted the pump handle and clicked it to the automatic setting. "Could you take over driving from here? I don't think I can do it anymore."

"Yeah, sure bro—*yawn*—I'm sick of sleeping anyway."

"Thank you. I could use a breather."

"No problem. But first I gotta piss. You want something to eat or anything from inside?"

"Nah, I'm good. I have to piss too. I'll take a walk with you."

As we approached the storefront I noticed the little white letters to the left of the door. I was right. Mo owned this one, but it was a simplified version—no garage, no tow truck but the same storefront windows and a similar inner setup.

But as Shoddy and I got closer the brand new gas pumps faded away and our hopes of a different Mo experience dwindled. The lights inside the store appeared dimmed or perhaps even shut off. An orange OPEN sign hung in the window but there was clearly nobody behind the counter: apparently another employee of Bobbo standards.

Shoddy reached out for the door handle but I stopped him.

"Check it out," I pointed to a sheet of bright red paper hanging on the glass door to the right of the OPEN sign.

Scribbled in black marker was the message, "No public restrooms inside—use nature when nature calls."

"Dammit!" Shoddy yelled. "Mo fucks us again!"

"Calm down."

"No, I will not. What kind of entrepreneur is this guy? New pumps and no bathrooms?"

I had stopped listening to Shoddy, who continued his rant against the spectral gas station owner. Something about the red paper gave me pause. It was familiar on a multitude of levels. I inched closer to the door and the faint inside light made the paper slightly translucent. Computer printed black text was barely visible on the paper's flip side. It looked like a list.

Something jerked on my shirtsleeve.

"Come on man, let's find somewhere else," Shoddy said. He had a firm grip of my shirt and was already tugging my entire body in his direction. I flipped my head back to try and read the reverse side of the red paper. Was it what I thought it was?

Shoddy tugged again and turned the corner of the store—paper out of sight. He was still griping.

"What kind of state is this? Don't these people shit and piss at night or is it strictly a day job down here? What state are we in, anyway? Maybe if we wait a few minutes for the sun to come up the store will wake up and let us in to go the bathroom."

He was groggy and grumpy and thankfully had forgotten or forgiven our little altercation at the first Mo's gas station. He released my sleeve.

"I'm gonna go over there and piss behind that hut," he said.

I looked around and saw a small, tattered shed that would afford him some privacy. There weren't many other options except past the shed the ground rose a bit into an embankment. Over the embankment looked to be a small clearing that skirted the edge of some looming, dense pine trees. With the sky slowly but steadily lightening with each passing moment, the cover of darkness may not have been enough to just go drop trough out in the open. The embankment would have to do.

"OK, I'll head over there on the other side of that embankment," I said.

Shoddy shrugged and disappeared behind the collapsing shed.

I walked away from him and hesitated for a moment at the grassy hump before scrambling up. At the top I immediately slipped on the slick grass and landed hard on my ass.

"Dammit."

I gathered my composure, what little of it was left, and willed myself upright. I was brushing blades of grass from my pants when I noticed some shadows moving around inside the gray Explorer windows far away across the parking lot. Someone was awake. The cabin light flicked on and I slouched a little behind the embankment, suddenly embarrassed by what I was there to do.

Just as suddenly, a small red Honda pulled in from the main road and parked opposite the Explorer. The driver had a clear view of the shed, the embankment and the college kids about to urinate.

"Dammit," I repeated again, louder.

I moved towards the trees. The patch of foliage was less thick than it looked from back in the parking lot. I easily maneuvered past the frontline of shrubbery and picked my way into the woods, turning back a couple times, the Explorer less visible with each look.

But that wasn't good enough for me. I wanted it totally hidden from sight. I was being driven less and less by my bladder—although I still really had to pee—and more by a sudden desire to completely ditch the car, everything and everyone that came with it. I wasn't just walking away from prying eyes. With every step, with every crushed leaf and snapped twig, I escaped further from all the prying minds unknowingly waiting to hear the truth, the confession I promised myself I would reveal.

I turned one last time and then didn't look back again. I walked for at least five more minutes, focusing intently on picking a path through the thinning trees.

Where did I think I was going? I did not know. I knew I'd have to go back sometime. I couldn't escape it forever. But no matter how hard one part of me tried to steer back, my feet—my cold feet—kept moving away. I wasn't ready to go back.

Directly ahead, between the last two thick, black tree trunks, a sliver of gunmetal gray shimmered in the increasing dawn.

I brushed past a few branches, sap sticking to my fingers, and stumbled into a small copse of saplings running downward to a clearing.

A thrush of birds broke away from the last sapling I brushed by. I followed their silhouettes upward.

With the sky overhead cleared of the monstrous pines, I could see that the night was waning but it wasn't going away without a fight. It was not as light as I had thought and a lavender darkness nestled comfortably over the clearing and the sliver of gunmetal that lay before me, shrouded in mist.

I was entranced by my surroundings, staring blankly into the mist. Daylight increased timidly and dawn's striptease gyrated with every layer of night that fell off. As another article slipped away the mist lifted, dissipating along with the purple darkness, leaving behind a blue-gray haze and revealing the gunmetal sliver—a narrow, slender lake that materialized in front of me. It was about the size of a football field, flanked on all sides by thick gatherings of tall pines, which loomed like sentinels protecting some forbidden treasure.

Dawn ramped up her exotic dance, slipping off a stocking, letting an auburn glow permeate the air. I could see the lake clearly now. No movement. The surrounding trees still stood pat, black as pitch.

I felt a tickle in my gut and was reminded of why I entered the woods in the first place. I did still have to pee.

I looked down, my mind torn between mental surrealism and physical necessity, and started fumbling with the button and fly of my pants.

A flick and a splash broke the silence. I snapped my head to the lake, caught a jagged shadow spin across the water through the ripples and took a step backward. My right foot caught on a rock. Balance was a lost cause and because my hand was still on my pant waist, I went down without a brace, falling backward onto the slightly inclined embankment. My pants, however, had dropped to my ankles leaving me sitting on wet undergrowth in boxer shorts.

The rising auburn glow and the waning darkness exposed me—the exact thing I first came into this forest to escape from.

I sat in my own foolishness, embarrassed because of it and then angered because I was embarrassed. My pants were half off, I was in the middle of a forest and I was totally alone. It was one of those moments where your only choice is to take stock of your life, have an epiphany or something like that.

I adjusted my eyes to the growing reddish light and I saw a

frog stroking her way elegantly across the lake away from me. She must have leapt from the shore, got caught in a spear of light and cast a shadow. I forgot about being angry with myself for being embarrassed and watched her swim away, feeling almost voyeuristic in the half-light, half darkness of the near dawn.

Even when I could no longer make out the little frog body, the ripples still moved toward the other end of the lake. I watched them, following them one hundred yards to the far bank. My eyes moved up from the water, over the dark bank and onto the far away trees.

From behind them a fiery ball was just starting to blaze, the auburn of the air was giving way to a bright pink. The fireball grew hotter and bigger, scorching the black pines that stood like prison bars. Almost immediately they were rendered thin black sticks, then dust and ash as the shards of red burst through them. Intense flame shot into the clearing, roared around the lake, setting the entire forest aflame. The fireball grew. The fire grew. It was an inferno, then, everything completely ablaze, crackling and spreading at breakneck speed around the lake, up the trees with flames licking the sky.

As the sun peaked over the treetops one hundred yards away the white heat shot straight across the lake, turning the water into a burning mirror, reflecting the firestorm that had engulfed the trees, the frog, the sky and soon would overtake me.

I dared not get up—I couldn't even if I wanted to. All I could do was sit upright, still exposed, and gawk. I took great deep breaths but it was as if the cherry-red flood surging towards me was consuming all the air.

Then, with a silent but deafening explosion, a soundless sonic boom, the sun broke from behind the far trees, screamed upwards as a hungry, purging, blazing crescent scythed across the clearing, swallowing everything and smashing into my chest. I felt myself yell, slammed my eyes shut, threw my elbows up futilely and was sent reeling onto my back. The hot light pierced painfully right through my eyelids.

The scarlet blaze washed over me. I put my hands behind me and arched my back upwards, craned my neck and opened my eyes. I was staring directly upward at a blood-streaked sky—darkness was gone, crimson waves rippled through the wispy clouds and that thrush of birds darted past.

The pain behind my eyes vanished, evaporated even while I gazed at the sky for a millennium.

It was beautiful. The wild, untamed red streaks that flowed effortlessly across the heavens—they comforted me, warmed me. Even though my pants were around my ankles, I was no longer exposed. Emotions I hadn't felt in at least a year crept into my throat and burned with a sweet, acidic flare.

I don't know how long I sat there gazing into dawn's masterpiece. But I did until Shoddy found me. It must have been quite a sight—me, lying at the edge of a secret lake, my pants around my ankles, bathed in scarlet morning light.

"Hey, Shaw!" Shoddy yelled as he slapped away branches from the small copse of trees. He emerged but I didn't even flinch.

"Jesus Christ. What the hell? How bad did you have to go?"

He helped me up and then when I didn't pull my gaze from the sky, he hesitantly aided in pulling up my pants.

I fumbled hypnotically with the zipper and button.

"Hello," he said, waving his hand in front of my face.

I barely heard him. My mind, a place that was so recently a cold, crumbling barrier struggling to conceptualize and reconcile the notions of truth and forgiveness, nestled itself into a warm, comforting and perhaps a bit quixotic blanket. The wall was gone. There was no more hammer. All of it vanished, dissolved by the potency and power of a magnificent scarlet sky.

And then I was moving. At first I thought the painted red clouds had found some velocity. But then my feet stumbled on a root and I knew it was my body picking its way up the bank, away from the silver lake.

"Auggie. Hey, Shaw," Shoddy tried again. "Did you get attacked by zombies or something? What's up with you?"

His voice was just noise. When I didn't answer this time, he resorted to navigating us silently through the trees to their edge where the embankment, the dilapidated shed, the parking lot and the Explorer waited.

A blur shot past my sight line; then again, backwards.

Shoddy waved his hand past my face a few more times.

I did not want to stop looking at the sky. We broke through the tree line; I kept my gaze directed upwards. Wisps of dark red morning poked through the treetops.

"I'm driving, bro. I don't even want to know what happened down there. All I know is, you've had a long night. So now I'm driving."

He snapped his fingers violently an inch from my face.

"Wake up, bro. I need you to come to and climb over this embankment," he said. "It's time to go."

With one final gulp, I took in the scarlet locks that swept across the sky and finally turned my gaze downwards to Shoddy.

I studied him. He had a look made up of equal parts concern, confusion and relief, like I had just come out of a coma. He tried to grin. It came across his face as more of a crayon scribble.

"Thank you," I said to him, so quiet I wasn't sure if I actually said it.

"What?"

"Thank you."

"You're welcome. I guess."

"No really. Thank you."

"What the hell is this, some sort of Good Will Hunting moment? I swear to God, if you hug me and start telling me it's not my fault, I'm going to hit you."

The concern and confusion drained from his face, refueled by sarcasm and testosterone. There he was. His defense mechanisms kicked in right on time. Back to normal Shoddy, exactly where I needed him. No more worrying about me, there would be no time for that in Providence.

"Come on," he said and nudged me toward the embankment. "Get up over that thing you weirdo and let's get the fuck home."

I smiled and nodded. He nodded and smirked back.

We clambered over the top and skidded down to the parking lot like kids at a playground.

I remembered seeing someone moving around in the Explorer. One of the girls would be awake: all the better.

But when we reached the Explorer, the car bathed in the sun's reddish glow, the two girls were still fast asleep inside. The only difference was that Lindsey had moved to the backseat—my seat.

"Hey look at that," Shoddy said. "I thought I saw one of them awake when I was pissing. I thought she was just trying to get a glimpse of the goods."

"She would've needed the Hubble telescope to see anything from there," I retorted, taking a big step back toward reality.

"Oh ho! There he is. I was wondering if you were still in there." He playfully tapped a finger on my forehead. "Jump in the front seat. Let's get going. But be quiet. I don't want to wake up the girls. Those two are horrible first thing in the morning."

I knew Emily and Lindsey would probably wake up soon after we got back on the road. They would see the dirt on my clothes and make fun of me for rolling around on the ground or whatever they assumed happened to me.

But I was glad they would. I knew I wasn't dirty; I was purged and fresh. Their forthcoming girlish jokes would be refreshing, a clean distraction from the hours of solitude that swathed the past night.

Shoddy jumped in the driver's seat and before I joined him on the passenger side, I glanced back over the embankment. I knew that just beyond the now illuminated pines, a lakeside habitat was awakening to a gorgeous, red-maned morning. Then I checked on Mo's storefront: still no activity inside. The only movement was a crumpled piece of trash dancing around the pavement, urged along by a soft morning breeze.

"Shoddy, hold on one second," I said. I pushed back from the Explorer and ran over to the storefront. The crumpled trash bounced across my toes. I snatched it up, unfolded it and nodded at the confirmation of my suspicion. I hurried back to the car and hopped in before Shoddy could ask what I was doing.

Shoddy adjusted the seat and mirrors and I nestled into the copilot's chair.

I stared down at the red piece of paper, wrinkled and torn and covered in mystery stains. But clearly legible was the black printing. Number five as bold and bright as the North Star.

Five: Honesty and frankness make you vulnerable. Be honest and frank anyway.

"What was that about?" Shoddy whispered. He hadn't started the car yet. He reached across the center console and tapped the paper on my lap with the car keys. "Picking up other peoples' trash now, Augustine?"

"You could say that."

"Since when did you care?"

"Since right now."

He tilted his head and tried reading the list.

"What is that, some sort of cult credo? God, these people down here are whacked," he said. Without waiting for an answer he popped the keys in the ignition and turned them as silently as possible.

"They're not as crazy as you might think," I said as we pulled out of the parking lot, Mo's latest fueling station engulfed by the sunlight, a haloed glare in the rearview mirror.

Shoddy just shrugged with his two hands on the wheel. He had already lost interest.

I reached into the center console and removed a small leather-bound journal. A black pen was tucked inside. I opened the journal to the pen's page. It was blank. I refolded the red paper and switched it places with the pen then slid the pen easily under the journal cover's leather strap.

I shifted the book onto my lap and relaxed back into the leather seats, keeping one hand on the journal. I closed my eyes. Sleep was coming hard and fast.

In the penultimate moments of consciousness, sporadic visions flashed. My parents stood in front of my home. Lily popped in and out of shadow; Shoddy and Emily in my dorm; Lindsey was in my bed. In my visions the people all smiled, even the crippled body of Duncan with a trickle of crimson blood under his nose.

They were giving me their blessing, their permission to inform their earthly alter egos of all the sins I committed against them. I could write my confession. The sleep I was about to enjoy was their gift, my reward. When I awoke I would write. I anticipated filling the entire journal. It wouldn't take me long.

When we arrived in Providence, I would first give the confession to Shoddy to read. Much of it would be redundant to him; would simply confirm his suspicions that were borderline fact already. But he was the brightest grammatical mind I knew and could be my editor. If I were to go to jail I'd at least go without any spelling errors.

Then the clean copy would go to Lindsey and Emily. When they looked at me in disbelief, as I was sure they would, I'd verbally tell them everything about Lily. Then before the tears got too heavy, I'd recount the night behind Primal, about how I beat Duncan and then watched the life leave his body.

I hoped they would understand. After all, part of it was self-defense. He had lunged at me with a wooden stake. Ironically, he harbored the intention to kill, not me.

I hoped they would forgive me for hiding the truth for so long. I hoped they would forgive me for not feeling bad about it for so long.

I'd have to talk to Lindsey alone. I needed to thank her and to apologize. If she hated me, I'd understand. If she still loved me, a sentiment I did not deserve, perhaps I could love her back. Inside me was newfound potential. But I wouldn't tell her that. She would be free of me soon, free of everything I came with, free to move away and to move on. There was no need to re-muddy those muddy waters, especially since I'd probably be going up the river.

That would depend on what the cops did. I decided I would go alone to the police station at the edge of campus and hand them the confession. I hoped they, too, would have mercy—but not as much as I hoped my friends would.

There was one person who needed to hear my confession first before we even reached Rhode Island. She was the last stop before Providence. I had to kneel at her feet, on top of the soil and the dozen white lily bouquets, dried but never removed, and read aloud the confession I was to pen.

"Hey Shoddy," I said, with sleep tugging gently on my eyelids. "Do me a favor. Wake me up in an hour."

"Are you sure?" he asked. "You look pretty tired, man. Maybe I should let you sleep the rest of the way home."

"No, definitely not. Wake me up in an hour. I have some writing to do and I want to get it done before we reach Connecticut."

"Why?"

"Because when we reach Connecticut I want you to let me drive. We have to make a quick detour. One more stop. I know the quickest way there."

"Oh. Alright."

He looked slightly dejected but then his face contorted as he began contemplating the reasons why I wanted to diverge from our course. He adjusted the volume of the radio and put on a new song, all the while fitting the pieces together.

The music rocked me in its arms and carried me to the brink of sleep. My head was clear and the memories were erased. I knew when I fell asleep, I wouldn't dream and I was grateful for it.

I felt the wheels underneath me chewing up the highway. With each mile the Explorer came closer to Providence, I came closer to the truth. We all did. We would be there soon.

"You want to go to the cemetery. You want to go see Lily, don't you?" Shoddy said, suddenly, his concern rising with the inflection in his voice.

"Yes," I said calmly. My eyes were closed but I knew he was staring at me and not the road. I just smiled. "I need to tell her something."

Chapter 37

I never wanted to change my life until I was down on my knees praying for it to stay the same.

Funny how things turn out that way. You want one thing and some uncontrollable cataclysm shakes the opposites into power. You want to be friends with someone but you end up at his throat. You want to love someone and you end up the end of her. You try daily to gain control only to finally understand the implausibility of that pursuit.

For the majority of my young life, I traveled a common road. I was raised right, but the good values instilled in me chipped like those of any teenager. I took solace in compatriots who influenced sin, who played on the group mentality of indulgence. Lest I seem a rebel, these transgressions were of the most minor, youthful offense. Had I not just mentioned them, no one, not even those I shared them with, would even remember.

But of those typical, youthful trysts, one person went unchecked; he became a catalyst I could not rein under control. What I could control was my ability to not follow his lead, and from that spawned antagonism, competition, jealousy and fury.

As I grew accustomed to that relationship and its enmity, I lost a grip on how it influenced those I cared for. I committed sins on behalf of this rivalry. I destroyed lives.

I learned the pain of love and the pain of loss. Because of the loss, things I used to love I began to hate. Everything reminded me of that which I no longer had. I could not understand the kindness my friends showed; I did not appreciate or accept it. And still I did not see the need for change. My actions were for the sole purpose of maintaining the life I thought I controlled.

Ultimately the forces that be, be they God or guilt, grew strong enough to spark epiphany. I wrestled with the decision to pen my indiscretions and their ramifications. A confession is easy to think about: much harder to bring into existence. I even practiced on my most trusted friend.

I was trying to save my life but in order for that to happen, my life had to change. A confession is the vehicle to bring me there.

I accept the consequences, moral and legal, associated with what I have outlined here. The entire document will be hand delivered to proper law enforcement authorities, lest you think I'm just practicing self-pity, introspection and self-indulgence for the ego of it.

All of these words are not for me. I primarily want to confess to those I hurt. I look forward to their justice and punishment far less than that of any court.

Notice I have not offered apology. Very rarely have I said, "I'm sorry," and meant it. I've said a sincere "I love you" more often. And then, I am not sorry for much of what I did. At a time past, I was. The guilt was overwhelming but it has since been washed away.

Two deaths stain my hands, caused just as much by what I didn't do as what I did do. I will pay for them with my old life; change it for the better. In what tangible way, I am not sure yet. Perhaps I'll find God and become religious, or take on a new career path, or re-educate myself in a new field. That is the next step and I am eager to set afoot. That is, if I don't end up in prison.

If all of this sounds depressing, too heavy-weighted for a young collegiate who should otherwise be out chugging vats of skunked beer, then I've succeeded. Why? Because this is a confession. My confession. Confessions aren't fun.

My name is Augustine Shaw and I'm a killer.